# THE PRICE OF MERCY

DYING FOR LOVE

BOOK TWO

## MISTI WILDS

**The Price of Mercy**

# Dedication

*To all the girls whose Happily Ever Afters are unconventional... but no less perfect.*

# Author's Note

**You cannot read this book on its own.**
I mean, *you can*, but you'll be thrown in the middle of the story without any context. If you have not read book one *Begging for Mercy*, please close this book and come back once you're caught up.

Now, onto the fun stuff:

**This is a dark romance.**

There are mature themes within this book, including red flag main characters who have poor coping mechanisms, bad judgement, and morally gray ideologies. The fictional world this book takes place in is not much better.
**Please check content warnings on my website prior to reading.**

# CHAPTER 1

## MERCY

*Don't go easy on me.*

Those simple words latch onto my bones, pulling me down, down, down, until I'm lying on the floor and staring into Sam's summer eyes—shimmering like a dark green lake bathed in sunlight, inviting me to dive into their warm waters. If Sam owned such a lake, he might ask it to swallow me whole, drag me down to the darkest depths, and shroud me from the rest of the world. Safe. Hidden. *His.*

I can see the desire swirling in his eyes, the regret and guilt glinting off the surface not strong enough to hide it. He thinks that what happened tonight—the assault, the murder, the sudden distance between us—is his fault. But we can't control what other people do or say, so I don't blame him. Not like Kane does. Not like Sam blames himself.

In the end, despite any alleged wrongdoings or things Sam may have overlooked about tonight, I already forgive him. What I want more than anything is for him to forgive himself. Judging by how hard he's holding his breath, I have to assume that self-forgiveness is a long time coming. I wouldn't be surprised if he never forgives himself. He stares at me like I can give him the world—but I can't give him peace of mind. That has to come from within. So if I have to wait to voice my forgiveness until he can accept his own, then so be it. I'll wait as long as it takes. For his sake.

A breath falls past my lips, and I tear my gaze away from Sam. I need to get up. We need to keep moving. The clock is ticking, and the longer we sit here, the more we're tempting fate to fuck us over. It's only a matter of time before the neighbors show up—or the police. Taking another tiny breath, I peel myself off the cold floor and fight the numbing tingle in my limbs.

Kane kneels, helping me sit up without asking for permission, his gaze soft as it sweeps across my face. "Take all the time you need," he murmurs, brushing his hand over my hair and kissing my forehead. "We aren't in a rush."

The dead body bleeding out on the hardwood suggests otherwise.

I've seen death before—or I thought I had. But yellowed bodies and embalmed corpses don't bleed. They aren't still warm to the touch. They weren't alive mere moments ago, gripping your ankle so tightly that it bruises.

I stare at an angry red mark wrapped around my ankle, its four distinct lines proof of how tight of a grip the bastard had on me. Kane's gaze follows mine, and he clenches his jaw without saying anything. Maybe it's better if we don't talk about what happened—if we let it fade away into obscurity, where it can't hurt us... or haunt me.

But the longer we stay here, the more the memory will imprint. The rock of the table, the raucous noise from the crowd, the heat of strangers' hands on my body... Bile rises to the back of my throat, and I force myself to swallow.

I need to leave.

I need to leave *immediately.*

"We can't stay here." There's blood on Kane's cheek, and I attempt to wipe it off. It sticks to his skin, refusing to come clean, much like the stains on his soul that I can't see. He killed a man in cold blood and hasn't shown an ounce of remorse. Is that who he is? Have I been deluding myself into thinking that there's more to the man than sex and violence?

The slow curve of Kane's lips makes my foolish heart flutter. He envelops my hand in his and turns his head to kiss my fingers, his icy gaze melting at the slightest touch between us. "Taking care of me, Siren?" A chuckle rumbles through his chest, and butterflies erupt in mine. We aren't usually this close to each other without tension brewing between us, but now, in this cursed room, things feel... different. Softer. Reminiscent of the way he texts me, like there's more to the man than what's on the surface.

That's what I choose to hold onto—the hope that

Kane is more than what the world thinks; that his persona as The Reaper is just that: nothing more than a mask hiding the real man underneath.

"I don't know what I'm doing," I answer honestly, searching his eyes for the truth. Tonight showed me something important about who he is and what he values. If only I could just... put the pieces together. Figuring him out is like holding a puzzle box without the knowledge to unlock it. I have to play with the pieces, twisting them this way or bending them that way until the pattern falls into place. I cup his stubbled cheek, and his eyes glitter like diamonds. "I'm still trying to figure you out."

His smile widens as he presses the tip of his finger to the bow of my lips. "Want a hint?"

My heartbeat drums louder in my ears. A hint? What exactly is he offering? "Does it come with strings?"

"Everything comes with strings, Siren." He plays with a loose strand of my hair as he speaks. "You have to decide if those strings are worth the risk... or the reward."

We stare at each other for a moment longer as his words sink in. "I'd like a reward," I murmur, grabbing his hand to keep it from wandering any further. "Please."

"A hint," Kane clarifies, squeezing my hand. Time stands still as he eliminates what little distance remains between us and brushes his lips across my cheek. "I enjoyed saving you tonight, Mercy. The blood on your skin is..." He takes a shuddering breath as his eyes skate down my body. "Turning me on." Tugging my hand, he holds it against his growing erection and puffs out a breath as he cups my fingers around him. "But I like being needed more than I like being feared, and tonight, you needed me." His dick twitches beneath my palm. "That's the hottest fucking thing you've done for me yet, Siren, and I have Sam to thank for it. So..." Meeting my eyes, he draws a shallow breath. "Keep needing me, Mercy."

I'm stunned into silence as we hold each other's gaze. I don't know what I expected him to say, but that... wasn't it. "You're twisted," I murmur, pulling my hand free from his grasp. A heated shiver rolls down my spine. Everything about what he said is fucked up, and yet... I'm grateful for the honesty.

He shrugs. "You asked."

Sam's voice cuts across the room. "If you're done with... whatever that was," he sighs, rubbing his forehead, "*please* move. The cops will be here soon, and I don't want you here—" His gaze pierces my heart— "when they do."

Right. The cops. *The body.* Icy panic tears through my veins. How the hell are we going to talk our way out of this one? I don't know how I'll handle an interrogation about my best friend slash boyfriend and our murder-happy acquaintance. I have trouble wrapping my brain around my relationships with either of them, and trying to explain what we are to each other will tie more knots instead of unraveling them.

"Better get moving," Kane says, taking a step back. "Or you'll have to bail me out of jail next." Grinning at me, he winks like the idea of him sitting behind bars is funny.

I'm pretty sure that Zane would implode if Kane were arrested. Speaking of—"Where's Zane?"

A switch flips, and Kane's easy demeanor transforms. Tension ripples through his muscled frame as he clenches his jaw. A vein in his neck pulses angrily. "Home," he grunts, frowning. "He's at home."

Ooookay. I clearly hit a nerve.

Sam scoffs, looking just as tense as Kane all of a sudden. But rather than explain, he pulls his cell phone from his pocket and glares at the screen. "I can handle the police. Just—" He takes a tiny breath, winces, and averts his gaze from mine. "Don't leave without me." Standing, he walks to the back patio and leaves the door open while he places a phone call, positioning himself so that he has a direct line of sight to me and Kane. I can't hear everything Sam says on the call, but I can see the way he shifts his weight from foot to foot, either impatient to leave or nervous about leaving me alone with a known killer.

Or, more than likely, he's anxious about news of tonight's murder getting back to his father, which is... regrettably, unavoidable.

"He's calling his dad," I guess aloud. Or rather, his father's hired men. Little good can come from getting Samuel Wright's money involved, but if I had to guess, Sam is desperate to fix things. Contacting his father is a sacrifice towards that goal.

Although the father-son pair look alike, they couldn't be any more different if they tried. Samuel is cold and calculated, always angling to come out on top of any situation, whereas *my* Sam is warm and inviting. Or at least, he used to be.

The version of Sam watching me through the open doorway looks more like his father than I've ever seen before.

Kane grunts. "We don't need *daddy* to come save us." Rolling his eyes, he chuffs. "You're both forgetting that I'm a goddamn professional." He takes off his leather jacket and drapes it over my bare shoulders. Warmth seeps into my skin as Kane zips up the front, rethinks it, and unzips the top few inches to reveal my cleavage. He flicks his gaze back up to my face. "We'll handle the body ourselves."

"We will?" I don't feel nearly as confident in our skills with hiding a body, let alone getting away with murder. My mind blanks and reverts back to what I *can* do: clean. "I'll, um, get a mop." Before Kane can stop me, I turn on my heel and walk away, determined to do *something*. Keeping myself busy, contributing in any way I can, both are good things right now.

Standing idle means that the voices in my head start to speak.

*You should be sad that someone died.*

*No! Fuck that! He deserved worse. Cut off his dick and shove it down his throat.*

*It's not his fault that Kane's crazy enough to shoot him.*

But he shouldn't have assaulted me.

Period.

If he is—*was*—villainous enough to assault a women

who clearly didn't want it, then fuck him. He deserved to get shot.

He deserved to die.

I tune out the voices as Sam's phone call ends. From a distance, I watch as he and Kane spring into immediate action, discussing their next steps for the briefest second before working in perfect tandem to lift the corpse and carry it out the front door.

Both men hardly bat an eye at the gore. Or the death. Kane, I might expect that from, but Sam?

The boy whose cheeks dimple when he smiles—the one who holds me through the night to keep my nightmares at bay—the man I've grown to love more than a friend. It's like I'm watching a stranger as he lifts the dead body into the back of his pickup truck and wipes his bloodied hands on his jeans.

Since when is Sam more comfortable with death than the daughter of a mortician?

While they strap a tarp over the truck bed to hide the body, I turn away from the window to find a mop. There's a dirty bucket and a discolored mop stashed in the back of the hall closet, and I dump out the dead spiders and dust bunnies to fill it with dish soap and water. I stare at the suds as they appear and move on autopilot as soon as the bucket is full. Carry it into the living room. Set it down beside the puddle of blood—no, beside the fresh trail of drops leading out the front door —and dunk the mop into the steaming water. I don't have a way to wring out the mop head, so I splash way too much water over the edge and smear bubbles in a wide arc. Bubbles and blood. Blood and bubbles. A metallic scent in the air. On my tongue. Covering the floor. The water turns red, the bubbles bright pink. Dunk and repeat.

Nothing gets clean. All I'm doing is spreading the evidence around like paint.

As I stare at the bloody mess, made worse by my poor attempt at cleaning, Kane appears from the doorway. He doesn't try to stop me from cleaning; rather, he slinks over to me and sweeps my hair off my shoulders, bunching it in his hands and quickly rebraiding it with the finesse of an artist, his dextrous fingers combing through the knots, separating the strands, and tying my red ribbon into a bow at the end. Licking the pad of his thumb to wipe specks of blood off my cheek, he hums happily.

I can't imagine what has him so chipper.

"I like seeing you like this," he murmurs, answering my question on his own. He tugs at the bottom of his jacket, a small smile curving on his lips. "You look good in my leather."

*Ah*, so it's a man thing.

Sam appears a moment later, his expression stormy as he spots us. "You're making her clean?"

"I'm not making her do anything." Kane tosses a glare at Sam for a split second. "But he's right, sweetheart, you really don't need to do that." Gently prying the mop from my hands, he lets it clatter to the floor before scooping me into his arms, damn near purring as I cling to his neck. I catch him grinning as he shoulders past Sam to step outside.

"But we're leaving evidence," I protest weakly.

The blood. Our fingerprints. My dress and shoes and phone, lost somewhere upstairs. Bullet casings. Witnesses. I tally up a list of potential problems based upon the crime docs my sister used to watch when she still lived with us. There are too many of them for us to come out of this unscathed. The police are going to identify us as soon as they step onto the crime scene and do the slightest bit of sniffing around for suspects.

Everyone at the party knows who we are.

The Dead Girl and her Murderous Men.

It almost has a nice ring to it.

Kane sets me down beside his motorcycle. "Don't worry about that." His expression softens as he attempts to smooth out the dimple between my eyebrows with his thumb. "Don't worry about anything, Mercy."

I've spent my entire life worrying about something, whether it be my mother's health, my brother's mean streak, or my own spiraling depression. Telling me *not to worry* is like telling the wind not to blow or the sun not to shine. It's an impossibility. Drawing a breath, I consider telling Kane this but ultimately decide against it. He might try to prove me wrong. "Okay."

That pleases him. "Yeah?" His face lights up instantly, and he backs me up against his bike, easily caging me between his arms. Lowering his head, he brushes his lips against mine.

"I'll take care of you, Mercy."

My heartbeat picks up as he kisses me soft and slow, like he's savoring the idea of it: me needing him.

His breath is warm on my lips. "Won't you let me?"

Gravel crunches nearby, and I open my eyes just in time to witness Sam's fury. Jaw clenched, emerald eyes flashing, he grabs Kane's shoulder and wrenches him away from me. "Get your hands off her!"

Kane can't keep a smug smile off his face. "She likes my hands," he quips, "among other things."

That pisses Sam off. He clenches his fists. "Don't you touch her."

"She likes that, too."

Sam growls. "Fuck!" His head snaps to me, like he's waiting for me to deny it, but I can't. Everything Kane is saying is true.

"I like both of you," I admit softly, biting my lip. My cheeks warm. This isn't exactly news, but both men light up like they're hearing my confession for the first time. "I like it when you both touch me."

The glimmer of hope in Sam's eyes extinguishes once he realizes what I'm saying; I like *both* of them, not just him. Cursing under his breath, Sam clenches his eyes shut. "Jesus Christ, Mercy." Groaning, he rubs the back of his eyelids. "I can't believe this is happening."

I can't believe that he's *hard*. Sam's dick punches the zipper of his jeans, aching to break free. Kane notices it, too, unable to stop himself from laughing. "Fuck, Wright, I didn't take you for a cuck. If you wanted me to touch your girl for you, all you had to do was ask."

"That's not—" Sam runs a hand through his hair, his

gaze pinging between the two of us. "It's not—*fuck.* It's not like that."

"It sure looks like that."

Ignoring Kane, Sam closes the distance between us in a heartbeat. He presses my body against the motorcycle and tangles his fingers in my hair while his other hand grabs my hip. Panting, he covers my body, pressing his bare chest to mine and digging his erection into my stomach. "Mercy," he groans, our noses bumping. "Fuck, you look good." He says it like he hates to admit it, the words burning like acid in his throat.

Then he kisses me, and it's nothing like the gentle sweep of Kane's lips. Hot and heavy and desperate, pouring his desire into my body like gasoline, his grip tight, the heat of his body burning. I didn't anticipate wanting anyone's touch after the events of the evening, but as Sam licks into my mouth and moans, I realize that *this* fire can burn through the fear and the pain and the *what ifs.* With Sam—or Kane—or both, I don't have to worry about what could have happened.

What matters is what's real, and right now, Sam feels *very* real.

I whimper from the heat and desperation of his touch. This isn't like him. He normally waits—forever, if he has to—for permission. Maybe he's taking a page from Kane's book. Maybe he's realizing that he doesn't have to be so careful.

All at once, he backs off, tearing his body from mine and turning his face away. Chest heaving, dick hard, face flushed, he shudders. "Shit. I'm sorry. *Fuck.*" It's like he shoves all of his pent-up desire into a box and slams the lid shut. He goes from slipping his tongue into my mouth one second to repenting for it the next. "I'm so sorry, Mercy." The fire in his eyes is doused by a wave of guilt. "You shouldn't let me touch you like that. I'm—"

Kane claps the top of Sam's shoulder as he breezes past. "Yeah, yeah, we've heard it all before. You're sorry. You fucked up. You owe her. Which, to be clear, *you do.*" He bares his teeth as he sweeps me under his arm and pulls me into his side. "I might have to tie you up, Pretty Boy, if you can't keep your hands to yourself. Or all of that..." Kane lifts the hand off my shoulder to wave vaguely at Sam. "Messy shit you've got going on. Your aura is *yellow*, dude."

Since when does Kane read auras?

Rather than explain, he grabs the helmet off the back of his bike and fits it on my head, taking extra care with the chin strap. "Let's get you home."

I blink up at him. "What about the body?"

"Sam and I will take care of it."

A wrinkle of annoyance flares inside my chest. So, what, he wants me to sit around at home while he and Sam do all the dirty work? I purse my lips and grab Kane's chin. "You are *not* leaving me at home like some —" I search for the right word. "Child. You don't have to baby me, Kane; I'm fine."

The edge of his lips twitches as he fights a smile. "I'm not babying you. I'm being nice."

"You've been through a lot tonight," Sam interjects, clearly agreeing with Kane. They both want me to sit alone in my bedroom and wait for them to finish the job. "Let me—" He sighs. "Let *us* handle this part."

I glance between the two of them. I'm outnumbered and outvoted, but I refuse to back down. "This *fucker*—" I throw my hand out towards the body hidden in the bed of Sam's pickup. "—tries to rape me, and you want me to go home?" The echo of guilt in my head about the man's death quiets, squashed by the anger boiling in my blood. "Screw that. If you're getting rid of the body, I deserve to watch him burn."

If they make me go home, if they lock me in my bedroom, I know that I won't sleep. I'll replay tonight over and over in my head, running through all the possible scenarios, the outcomes, the *what-ifs*. That man's face—pretending to be Reaper—will haunt me. He didn't get away with hurting me, and I'm grateful for that. But it's not over until he's erased from existence.

The gears turn in my head as I come up with a plan. I don't know what the boys discussed, but I don't care. I'm a Morningstar—handling the deceased is what we do.

# CHAPTER 2

# KANE

MORNINGSTAR MORTUARY IS FUCKING PERFECT. Exposed red brick both inside and out, with original hardwood floors that date back decades and old glass windows that warp incoming light. At night, the building looks as haunted as the surrounding landscape, and I fucking *love* it. The recent updates to the driveway, doors, and inner workings feel out-of-place but up to code, a necessary evil for running a business in today's world. The lobby has been remodeled for modern times, but the back hallways and rooms preserve the morgue's original charm.

As Mercy leads us through the front door and humors me with a brief tour of the building, she lights up like the North Star. Every room has a story, and she sifts through them all to tell her favorites. What began as mild curiosity about her family and their business experience quickly turns into something deeper. The stories are fine and all, but Mercy is exceptional. Everything she says makes me fall in love with this place—and the woman within it.

She may as well be guiding me home. I never want to leave.

While she brushes her fingertips over an old velvet couch and speaks fondly of a man who couldn't bear to leave his wife's side—for three days!—while the Morningstars prepared her body in the next room, I watch the subtle intricacies of Mercy's face in the lowlight, committing them to memory. To Sam's credit, he doesn't interrupt, keeping his hands in his pockets as he nods along to Mercy's story. I guess he's heard this one before, or maybe he was here with her when it happened. He could have met the mourning man and listened as he sang songs of love for his dearly departed.

As we enter the next room, an ornate stained glass window casts soft blue light across the floor. An image of a riverbank, complete with a crescent moon hanging in the sky overhead, decorates the center of the far wall. Here, Mercy tells a story about a woman whose sister drowned in a nearby river after the current carried her away. Heavy rainstorms had filled a lake past capacity, so the city authorized more water to be released from the dam than usual, thus picking up the current, cooling the waters, and subsequently resulting in her sister's untimely death. But the strangest thing about the tale is that her sister was smiling as she drifted away, letting nature carry her into the next life.

Mercy tells at least half a dozen of such stories in a hushed whisper, likely aiming to be respectful of the dead and their loved ones, but there's no need for caution. The warmth in her eyes says it all. This place—these stories—are as much a part of her as the bricks are to the walls.

Taking her hand, I lace our fingers together. For one of the first times in my life, I don't have anything to say. Nothing to contribute to the conversation. But I *feel* it—the gentle tug on my heart—and I want to share this moment with her.

She stumbles with her story, pulled out of a monologue by our joined hands. Blinking, she looks down at our interlocked fingers, like she's surprised. We held hands the other day when I led her from the fine arts building to the cemetery, so it's not like this is new.

But somehow... it feels different.

I don't pull her closer like I have in the past. Instead, with a gentle nod, I encourage her to keep going. "I'm listening, Siren."

The blush on her cheeks makes holding back so fucking worth it.

Sam, the fucker, slides up to Mercy's other side and takes the opposite hand, copying me as he laces their fingers together. Our eyes meet over Mercy's head, and I glare. He doesn't deserve to touch her after what happened tonight. As far as I'm concerned, everything is his damn fault for taking her to the party in the first place.

The spell between Mercy and me breaks, and she laughs awkwardly. "Um, we should—it's getting—I mean—"

I hate to cut the tour short, but *fine*. We're technically on the clock. If Zane were here, he'd be throwing a fucking tantrum about the delay. Keeping my eye on Sam, I address Mercy without looking at her. "Prep the room for us. We'll bring the body around back. Can you prop the door open?"

"Sure," she breathes, tugging her hands free. When neither me or Sam let go, a tiny laugh fizzles past her lips. "Guys, c'mon, this is ridiculous."

"Is it?" My eyebrow lifts. "Let go, Sam."

The guard dog shows his teeth. "You let go."

"Both of you, let go!" Mercy jostles both of us. "Stop playing tug of war with me."

I lick a stripe across my top row of teeth. "He hasn't earned you, Mercy." If I have any say in how things unravel between them, he'll have to watch as I split his girl open with my cock. My girl. Our girl. Fuck, this is getting complicated. Regardless, I want to watch Sam crumble into a pitiable pile of dust while Mercy writhes beneath me. Is that so fucking bad?

My lips twitch into a frown. Zane won't like that. He's already possessive of me. When I fuck Mercy—because I will—he'll be right there with us. Watching, grinding his molars the entire time, unable to see the beauty past his own jealousy.

But that's the thing. There's nothing for him to be jealous of.

Running my fingers through my hair, I sigh and let go of Mercy's hand. I need to talk with Zane before I get too carried away with Mercy, or he'll never forgive me.

Jealous bastard. *Greedy* bastard. He's had me all to himself for years. *Now* he decides to throw a fuss about who I sleep with? When he's the only one who's seen the parts of me that matter most? What's more intimate—a quick fuck against a gate with some stranger or spooning the most important person in your life during a thunderstorm?

Knowing him, he wants all of it. The quickies in the dark corners of the graveyard and the long nights wrapped in each other's arms.

Fucking hell, man. This is why I don't date. It's messy.

Mercy seems taken aback when I let her go, and I absolutely hate the way her tiny little smile rattles in the wind, falling flat in a heartbeat. She drags in a lungful of air and carefully pries her hand free from Sam's grasp, too.

At the very least, *his* faltering confidence brings me a spoonful of satisfaction. Not a lot, but enough to keep me from being completely down in the dumps about pumping the brakes with Mercy.

Sam's not getting any, either.

While Mercy steps away to check the crematorium and do whatever the fuck else morticians do before receiving a body, I grab Sam by the base of the neck and haul his ass out the front door. He slams into the back of his truck and growls at me.

Like I give a damn about his feelings. "Listen up, Samson fucking Wright—"

Spinning around, he aims a punch at my jaw. I barely

dodge in time, feeling the *whoosh* of air from the power behind it. Shit. That was close. My heart pumps harder, and I adjust my stance for a fight.

"You're a dick!" Sam throws the words at me and squares his shoulders, resetting his posture as he lifts both fists like a boxer. I know he's an athlete, but I didn't realize they taught martial arts as an elective at the college. He continues to surprise me. "Where'd you learn to fight?"

The question throws him off for a half second. "What?"

"Your stance." I widen mine and nod towards his feet. "It's pretty." He's been taught good form, but he doesn't have much experience or he wouldn't leave his side open like that. He's forgetting to tuck his elbows in. An idea pops into my head, and I have to bite the inside of my cheek to keep from grinning. "Wanna make this interesting?" It's a stupid idea, and it goes against my attempt at restraint with Mercy, but fuck it.

Zane isn't here. What he doesn't know won't kill him.

Exasperated, Sam huffs. "Is all you do play games?"

"No." How stupid would that be? I just like to have a little fun sometimes. "Are you in or not?" Excitement zings up my spine. He'll take the bait for the right incentive. "The first man to hit the other, no blocks, gets to kiss Mercy while the other watches." I lick my lips. "Tonight. While we burn the body."

Yes, yes, yes! She'll be trapped in the morgue with us all night. It's the perfect chance to stoke Sam's fury and make him do something stupid. Then I can kill the bastard, and Mercy might not hate me for it if I have just cause.

I tap the edge of Sam's knuckles with my own while he stands there, glaring, and not taking this seriously enough. I'm being genuine. Yeah, I want Sam to suffer for what happened to Mercy earlier, but I'll throw the man a bone for a little entertainment. "Second base," I offer, trying to sweeten the deal. Or is it third base? I always get those fucking things confused. "Whatever, I want to eat her out." It's not fair that Zane fingered her and Sam already got a taste of that sweet pussy. When is it my fucking turn?

*Tonight*, I tell myself, quickly getting lost in the idea. Tonight is my fucking night. I've earned it. I saved Mercy's life. Her virginity. Her dignity. A whole truck load of things. That was me—I'm the one who pulled her out of the fire.

And Sam's the fucking one who lit the match.

I strike without thinking as my anger boils over. Sam dodges, sidestepping the hit, and tries to jab me in the ribs. I skid out of the way and look back at him to find that his demeanor has completely changed.

I'm suddenly standing in front of a different man.

Eyes narrowed, breaths even, completely in control of his body and emotions.

I guess I gave him the right incentive.

"What, you don't like that?" I can't keep the grin off my face as I try to rile him up. "I bet she'd moan so sweetly for me. Did you hook a finger inside of her last time, or will I get to be the first to hit her G-spot?"

Zane already had that honor, I'm sure, but Sam doesn't have to know that.

A muscle in Sam's jaw tics. "You're fucking sick."

"Yeah, yeah, that's all you ever say. Come up with something new."

"She isn't a piece of meat. You can't just—" Sam's face twists, and I know I've struck a nerve. "—chew her up and spit her back out."

I might have done that a time or two with other partners in the past, but Mercy is different. I can feel it. That's the real reason why Sam feels threatened by me—it's not because I'm going to fuck her and walk away. It's because I might stay a while. Enjoy her body. Enjoy her *company*. Just the two of us without an audience, my sweet Siren singing only for me to hear. All the while, she'll fall hopelessly, madly in love with me—

Zane's face pops into my head as a memory surfaces, a bouquet of red roses clutched in his hands as he briefs me on one of our targets. Jasmine, her name was. The memory's hazy, the details blurry, but I remember how he refused to smile that entire night. This wasn't that long ago—maybe a year or two at most—and still, the signs were there. Frowning all the time. An increased number of migraines. Trouble sleeping. Each passing month made him more irritable than the last. He spent a few of our early years pretending to be invested in our kills, but the cracks in his facade were hard to miss. Even though he hasn't vocally complained about handing me bouquets or feeding me romantic things to say for each of our targets, the signs were there. Have I been ignoring them? For how long? Why?

And what makes this time any different than the rest?

I know the answer lies with Mercy. She changed the game without even realizing she stepped onto the board. When I stopped Zane from killing her that night in the graveyard, our reality shifted. The board tilted in her favor. The systems Zane put in place to keep a safe distance from our targets stopped working. The original rules don't make sense in a different landscape with new players—hell, with *teams*. Us versus them. Only...

At some point, I decided to bring Mercy over to our side. I like her. A lot. And *that* is what's driving Zane over the edge.

Fuck.

I completely miss Sam's right hook. His knuckles hit bone, and I crash to the gravel below, out of breath and out of luck. The bastard hits harder than I anticipated. My face throbs as the ache spreads from my eye socket to my cheek, and I can't keep from grinning as nostalgia hits.

When Zane and I were kids, we used to get into fights with the other foster children. I'd stand up for him when they called him names for being too quiet or too smart, but he was the one who got revenge in the middle of the night, scheming in silence until they were tucked into their beds, completely defenseless as he shoved socks in their mouths and poured glue in their eyes.

Zane's always been a mean fucking bastard. Revenge is his thing.

I'm halfway up off the ground when the truth slams into me like a freight train, nearly knocking me over. I can't believe I didn't see it before. It's so fucking obvious. Sam's fist must have knocked something loose in my brain—the missing puzzle piece that I couldn't find. Wouldn't even consider as a possibility. Because Zane wouldn't hurt me.

Much like how Sam wouldn't hurt Mercy.

But what Zane and Sam have in common is a compulsion to keep their loved ones safe. They aren't cut from the same cloth, by any means. I doubt Sam would do something as nefarious as kill Mercy's lover to ensure she stays with him rather than run off into the sunset with someone like me—although, the thought might cross his mind.

Zane wouldn't dare kill Mercy while I'm still interested in her. That's grounds for a big fucking problem between us.

But even if killing her is a no-go, hurting her isn't off the table. The gears turn in my head as I stand up. Zane has never been one for flashy violence. Hurting her overtly isn't his style. Especially not while I'm watching her so closely. But ensuring that she loses that virgin sparkle I find so alluring—*that* sounds like Zane. If he wants to keep my interest, he needs to dull her shine so that I come crawling back into his bed.

So he thinks.

The fucking *idiot.*

Sam looks like he wants to hit me again, so I shake my head and laugh. "Don't push it, Wright. You got in a solid hit. She's yours for tonight." What I don't say is that despite how much I want Mercy's sweet virgin pussy on my lips, I won't be able to get Zane out of my head until I confront the bastard, and Mercy deserves better than half-assed oral.

My mind quickly wanders. I don't know how Zane pulled off that shit at the party. He's not in the frat. He wasn't even there at the party tonight. But if Sam didn't do it, and Mercy didn't do it, and *I* sure as shit didn't do it, then who the fuck else would have set everything up?

And who the hell is rotting in the back of Sam's truck?

I have more questions than answers, and unfortunately, the dead guy can't talk.

Once I stop fighting, Sam finally realizes that I'm serious. Although he doesn't punch me again, he glares like he's picturing my demise. I can hardly blame him. If he were coming after Zane the way that I'm coming after Mercy, I'd do the same—except I'd actually kill the bastard for it. Sam's too tame for that.

At least for now.

A smile curves on my lips. I'd pay good money to see Sam turned into a murdering bastard.

Regardless of what joys our bloodied future holds, however, he landed a solid hit. It's my fault for being distracted. But he didn't have to go in so goddamn hard. With a hiss, I touch the swollen flesh over my eye. It's gonna bruise. Fuck me. I'm gonna have a black eye.

My mind wars with itself as images of Zane and Mercy tending to my injury swarm in my vision. First, it's Mercy gently pressing an ice pack to my head, but then it's Zane brushing a kiss over the bruise before sweeping my lips against his, devouring my mouth like his life depends on it. Back and forth, one gentle, one fierce, until the fantasies blend together and they're both touching me, teasing me, driving me fucking wild.

It's heaven and hell wrapped in a nice little package... at first. Then, all of a sudden, Zane pulls out a knife and stabs Mercy in the gut, grinning as she bleeds out in front of me.

I can't let that happen. Mercy deserves a better death than what Zane would give her.

Taking a deep breath, I force myself to focus. The cold night air grounds me. There's a dead body, a damaged girl, and a big goddamn mess to clean up. Usually, I rely on Zane to help me, but my partner-in-crime isn't here.

Samson Wright is.

And he's fucking *smiling*.

I might regret making that bet, but for now, I have to deal with it. Clearing my throat, I address Sam. "Hey."

He tears his gaze off the exposed brick siding to glance at me. We were both lost in thought, and reality slaps like a bitch. We frown at each other, and I have to force myself to meet his eyes. They're bright green, practically glowing in the moonlight. Nothing like Mercy's. Nothing like Zane's. I hardly know the man—don't want to—and yet he might be my only lead for figuring out what happened tonight. Forming the words to ask, however, is hard as fuck. "Sam," I start, grinding my teeth.

His bushy fucking eyebrows pinch together. "Yeah?"

I rap my knuckles on the tailgate of his pickup, the metal cold to the touch. "Help me with this, and then—" I drag in a lungful of crisp autumn air. God, I don't want to believe that Zane is behind this. I want him to be at home, pacing the den, tearing his hair out as he waits up for me. Not sitting at his computer, grinning to himself over a triumphant night scheming to defile an innocent girl. He could be doing both, laughing under his breath as he paces the carpet, eager to see me but itching to know what happened at the party.

He never wanted me to leave the house.

Tried to get me to stay.

Practically begged me not to go to the party.

*Fuck.*

I lower the tailgate and drag the body to the edge by its ankles. If I find out that Zane had something to do with this— A growl catches in my throat. Sam won't be the only one with a price to fucking pay.

"Start from the beginning and tell me what happened tonight."

# CHAPTER 3

## MERCY

I'VE WATCHED my parents attend to the dead hundreds of times. I'm familiar with the ritual of it—lighting candles, choosing which record to play, honoring the life that's no longer with us. Under normal circumstances, I'm eager to help. Running around the morgue as a child was a favorite pastime of mine, and these weathered brick walls feel like home.

Preparing the body of a man who assaulted me feels wrong.

Still, I light the ancient candles decorating the corners of the room, choose a modern record with angry electric guitar and pounding bass beats, and for extra measure, I grab a chilled sangria from the wine cooler in the next room. Popping the top, I drink straight from the bottle as I stare at the cold, metal table awaiting his arrival. We usually wash the body and, depending on their religious affiliation, say a few words of prayer or at the very least, send well-wishes for his travels into whatever lies beyond a mortal death.

My heart wars with itself. Does someone like him deserve well-wishes after what he attempted to do? After what he's likely already done to others? Closing my eyes, I take a deep, calming breath and try to approach this situation logically.

I don't know the man. He could have been a kind brother, loyal son or a considerate friend. Maybe he was on the fast track to success in his field, or the top of his class, or—

His body appears in the blink of an eye, dropped onto the table without ceremony.

There's so much blood.

The scent hits me first, strong enough that I swallow a gag rising to my throat. What little body paint remains on his skin is marred by dried blood and scratch marks, and when I press my thumbnails beneath the tips of my fingernails, I feel it—the paint. The *skin*. Even though he didn't touch me *down there*, he got close enough that parts of his body are stuck to mine. I inhale quickly, a shallow little breath that hardly does anything, and feel stomach acid rising to the back of my throat.

"Mercy—"

I don't know who says my name, Kane or Sam, but it doesn't matter. I spin around so fast that I move by memory rather than sight, rushing to the sink to wash my hands and scrape as much of *him* out from my nails as I can. The water is scalding hot, but I don't care about that, either. I douse my hands in soap and scrub with a sponge, determined to remove every trace of him from my body.

This part—the furious scrubbing—isn't supposed to happen. It's not part of the Morningstar rituals. We prepare every body with the utmost respect. We're careful. Gentle, even, as we wash the body and remove any jewelry or metal. I scoff, a guilty burst of laughter catching inside my chest.

My first time prepping a body for burial or cremation on my own, and I'm fucking everything up.

Someone steps up behind me and wraps their arms around my waist, their breath warm on my neck as they nuzzle close. My mind blanks, unsure who to picture at my back, when bloodied hands join mine at the sink.

Kane.

He pumps a few dollops of soap into his palm before taking my hands in his and rubbing them down, much gentler than I had been as he caresses each knuckle and massages the mounts of my fingers. If my grandmother were here, she'd take this moment to remind me to study Kane's hands, to watch how they move, and compare our life lines and love lines to see if they match up. But I'm not a romantic like her—all I see are the pink suds in the sink.

"You lit candles," Kane muses, breaking the silence. He turns off the faucet and grabs a hand towel from the stack beside the sink. Patting my hands dry, he holds onto them as he waits for my response.

I don't know what he wants me to say. It's not like

I'm wishing that guy a happy trip to the afterlife. "It's tradition." My words ring hollow despite their truth.

"Fuck tradition," Kane rumbles in my ear, his voice sending a warm tingle down my spine. "Let's burn the bastard." He leads me back to the table when my legs refuse to work on their own. This is normally the part where we would wash the body and prepare it for cremation, but my stomach churns at the thought of touching him. In my hesitancy, Kane takes the lead, ordering Sam around as he checks the corpse for piercings or other identifiable markings. He takes pictures with his phone, like he's cataloguing another one of his kills, and scowls like he's unhappy with the results.

"I thought you liked killing," I murmur, unable to take my eyes off the body as he and Sam cart it towards the crematorium. It's been preheating for ages, it feels like, but it's finally up to temp to work its magic.

Kane side-eyes me as he pushes the body into the oven and locks the door. Pausing, he admires the mechanism before returning my gaze. "Depends on the person. The circumstances." Rubbing the back of his neck, he sighs. "Killing bastards is satisfying, sure, but..." He trails off, frowning again. "I should have made this one bleed more."

For the first time since they brought the body in, Sam speaks. "You can make the asshole responsible bleed." Arms crossed, gaze narrowed, Sam's body radiates tension, filling the air with it. His movements are controlled, as solid and sure as the tight muscles wrapping around his body, and the same thought from when he was on the phone with his father runs through my mind.

I hardly recognize the man standing in front of me.

He senses my stare and softens his posture, loosening his grip on his arms and relaxing his face. Taking a breath, he finally meets my eyes, and that's where I see the version of Sam that I know: in the emerald depths of his eyes, overflowing with concern. "Are you okay, Mercy?"

I'd forgotten about the wine, so I grab the bottle by its neck and barely contain a bitter laugh. No, I'm not okay. What a stupid question. I take a swig of wine, then another, and another, chugging as much as I can without spitting it back up. I'm not much of a drinker no matter the type of alcohol, so with enough wine, I'll pass out. Maybe that's better than living through shit like this.

It wasn't even *that bad*, considering the outcome, and I'm still miserable.

Sam frowns and tries to take the bottle from me. I hold fast, matching his frown with one of my own. "I deserve a drink after what I went through tonight."

"I'm not arguing against that," he murmurs, "but take it easy."

"Pahh." I tip back another swallow. Taking it easy is what got me into this mess. All of it. Kane's wicked game, the mess at the party, my situationship with Sam. My whole life has been spent alone, sheltered, *safe*. When I go out into the world, I'm not prepared for its twists and turns, and that's what spells disaster. I'm learning as I go and suffering the consequences.

What a fucking mess I've made of my life.

Kane stares at the bottle for a split second before glancing around the room. "Where'd you get that from?"

I gesture towards the door that opens into the back hallway. "First room on the right. We've got a wine cooler next to the fridge."

Muttering the word *sweet*, Kane disappears to ransack what little food and drink we have stashed for long nights like these. The cremation will take a few hours, and I don't like the idea of leaving the machine to cook on its own, so I grab a folding chair and drag it across the room. I can't watch the flames through the door, but I can pretend that I'm watching the fucker inside burn to ashes. Lifting my bottle, I murmur a sarcastic *cheers* and take another sip.

After I sit my ass down and stretch out my legs, Kane reappears with two bottles in his hands and one tucked into the crook of his arm. He sets all three on the floor beside me, then recruits Sam to bring in the couch from the other room. I watch from afar as they work together to angle the couch just right to avoid knocking the legs on the doorframe, Sam cursing aloud as he smashes his knuckles, while Kane laughs at his pain.

I can't help but crack a smile.

They both notice, the two of them zoning in on it immediately. Kane slides the couch the rest of the way across the floor and quickly steps up behind me. "I see that smile, Siren." He flashes a grin and grabs me from behind, reaching beneath my arms to drag me backwards out of the chair. It clatters to the floor as he hauls me against his chest, blindly plopping down on the couch and settling me into his lap. Snapping his fingers, he points at the bottles of wine. "Grab those for me, will ya, Sam?"

Frozen in place, Sam stares at the two of us. His gaze roves my face before dipping to my body, taking in the possessive way Kane's arms wrap around my middle as he leans back comfortably, pulling me with him. I've never sat in a man's lap before—unless straddling Kane in the cemetery that one time counts—and I can't say it's particularly comfortable. I shift in place, trying to get situated, when something hard suddenly digs into my ass.

"Kane!" I smack his hip while he grins against my neck, the scrape of his teeth matching the chuckle rumbling past his lips.

"Can't help it when you squirm like that, beautiful."

Grabbing a bottle of wine, Sam's mouth twists into a grimace as he sets it beside me and claims the one I left open on the floor. He picks up the metal folding chair one-handed and sits backwards, facing us as he untwists the cap of his wine. His gaze doesn't leave mine as he takes a swallow. I can't see the fire blazing in the oven behind him, but I can see one raging in his eyes. Flashing bright green as he licks his lips and takes another sip. "You shouldn't touch her," he murmurs moodily, frowning.

Kane hums in the back of his throat. "You're right. I shouldn't." That doesn't stop his hand from roaming my waist, his knuckles teasing the underside of my breasts. "But she likes it when I touch her. Right, Siren? You said so." His lips brush the shell of my ear. "And I'll never forget it."

Grabbing the bottle resting against my thigh, I crack the top and bring it to my lips, taking as many gulps as I can before the air rushes from my lungs and I gasp for air, nearly choking. I get a head rush, the edges of my vision going fuzzy as I catch my breath.

"Jesus, Mercy. Take it easy." Sam's brows pinch together and he takes a much slower, controlled sip from his bottle. I watch as a cut in his lip pulls, threatening to split open, and stare at the blackened ring around his eye. Swollen. Undoubtedly painful. Possibly my fault or, if you ask Kane, Sam's own fault.

"What happened to you?" I ask Sam, nudging Kane until he takes the bottle from me. He drinks just as greedily as me while we wait for Sam to answer my question.

Sam's jaw clenches and his gaze turns steely. "The fraternity thought I needed saving." He tips his head towards me. "From you."

"*Me?*" My chest aches as an old wound festers inside my heart. I shouldn't be surprised that people think the worst of me—like I've performed some kind of love spell to get Sam to like me enough to invite me to a party— but the assumption still hurts.

"Everyone was so friendly..." Shaking my head, I cut myself off, knowing that appearances can be deceiving. It doesn't matter how nice someone seems on the surface; they can be hiding ugly intentions behind practiced smiles. "Nevermind. It doesn't matter." I turn my face away to keep Sam from seeing how much this un-shocking revelation hurts.

The *one* time I step out of my comfort zone—meeting new people, trying to be social, having a good time—everything blows up in my face. Maybe it's like I told Sam before: I'm meant to be alone.

My chest caves in, and my next breath hurts. I wince. Both men notice, Kane's arms wrapping tighter around me while Sam quickly falls to his knees at my feet. Grabbing both of my hands, he peers up at me with such love in his eyes that it becomes impossible to breathe. I barely hear his voice over the sound of my own heartbeat. "Don't waste a second thinking about it, Mercy. I promise, you are not any of those negative things running through your head right now." He squeezes my fingers gently. "I will always choose you, no matter who or what we're up against. You are my number one priority."

Guilt tugs at my heart as I stare at the man who's always tried his best to give me what I want. Back rubs. A sleeping partner. Distance, even, when I ask for it. Aside from my siblings, I spent my childhood alone. When Sam appeared in my life and decided to stay, I never knew how to navigate our friendship. To this day, I doubt I fully comprehend the extent of his sacrifices to remain by my side—and knowing this, I've likely been taking him for granted.

I've been a shitty friend and, quite possibly, a terrible girlfriend, if we put a label on it. Not quite friends yet almost lovers. More than what we used to be, but not enough for either of us to be satisfied.

I don't know how to put this feeling into words. A disgusting cocktail of regret, guilt, shame, and embarrassment make my stomach churn. The bruises on Sam's face darken into shadows before my eyes, and I see them for what they are: a physical manifestation of both his feelings for me and others' wicked refusal of it. He shouldn't have to suffer on my behalf.

I bite my lip and pull my hand from his to run my fingertips over the swollen flesh above his eye. Gently, I graze every inch of bruised flesh on his face, and he allows it, clenching his teeth against the pain but never asking me to stop.

"Does it hurt?" My voice hangs in the air between us. What I really want to ask is "*Does it hurt to love me?*"

I have a feeling that the answer would be yes.

Sam would never admit that loving me is like willful drowning. He could come up for air, but then he would miss the ocean's deadly caress. That's likely what Sam craves—the darkest parts of me intertwined with the darkest parts of him, like drinking poison until you've *become* poison.

A better woman would pull him out before it's too late. Sacrifice her needs for his. Ensure that he lives and thrives in the light rather than suffer in her shadows. But I am not a better woman. I caress Sam's bruised cheek with the edge of my thumb, sweeping gently across the bone, knowing that his pain is proof of his devotion to me. It shouldn't excite me.

And yet.

I've never been someone's first choice. A priority.

Something to shelter and love and pour your heart into. But with Sam, maybe that's what I am. What I've become.

His first choice.

His *only* choice.

Cupping Sam's cheek, I dip my head and brush my lips over his, the split in his bottom lip scraping against mine. I swipe my tongue over the wound and shiver at the taste of his blood. "Thank you, Sam."

He clutches my wrist and keeps me still as his eyes search mine. "Mercy." Sam's next breath cracks inside his chest. He wheezes through the pain. "Don't thank me. I'm—" His emerald eyes shimmer with regret. "I'm so sorry." He kisses my wrist rather than my lips. "Everything that happened tonight is my fault. I should have—I shouldn't have—" Whatever he's trying to say gets lost in translation, and he clenches his eyes shut. "I should have been there when he—this is all my fault."

I don't blame Sam for what happened. I wish he wouldn't claim it all for himself, either.

Kane grunts, idly tapping my thigh as he enters the conversation. "Or," he murmurs, "there's more to it than Pretty Boy's failures." Sighing, he closes what little distance remains between us and digs his forehead into my shoulder, his chest tightening against my back as he works through whatever is on his mind. "Tell her what happened upstairs, Sam, in your room. Besides you getting your ass kicked."

The heat swirling in the air suddenly cools. I shiver. "What do you mean?"

Swallowing hard, Sam sits back on his haunches and creates some distance. "They had a video of us." Opening his eyes, he grabs his wine bottle and clutches the neck so tightly that his knuckles turn white. "At your house, before the party. We were outside."

It takes me a second to remember the conversation, but then it comes rushing back. Sam's pickup truck. Leaves swirling around us. The way he begged me not to make him watch me and Reaper together. How I asked anyway, knowing that it would hurt Sam but unwilling to compromise.

I wince. That was a shitty thing for me to ask.

After a few tugs on the wine label, Sam successfully tears off a corner and flicks it to the floor. "They heard us talk about Reaper. They assumed it meant that—" His scowl deepens. "That you—"

"That I wanted it." The words taste like ash in my mouth. "They thought I wanted to get fucked by The Reaper."

He sweeps his hand out in a small arc. "Yeah. But I don't know where that guy came from or who he is, Mercy, I swear. Or how anyone got the video. I didn't even know there was a video!"

Neither did I. I've adjusted to being monitored in my bedroom, but anywhere else? Are there cameras in the kitchen or living room or—I frown, picturing my grandmother minding her own business as she wanders the tombstones in the afternoon, or my father playing piano by himself late at night. Those are private moments. My conversation with Sam was personal. No one should be intercepting those—*no one.*

Reaching behind me, I weave my fingers through Kane's blonde hair and tug hard enough that he hisses, flecks of his spit hitting my shoulder. "Is the camera yours?"

Dread weaves through my ribs as I consider Kane's culpability in my assault. Would he have done this to me? My eyes narrow. No, that doesn't make sense. He would have bent over backwards if it meant getting in my pants. And he was *so angry* when he arrived at the frat house, he threw punches before he asked any questions. But who else would have a put a camera outside my house? Who else—

The answer rips through me like a bullet, leaving me gasping for air.

Our little trio is missing its fourth person.

The man who sticks by Kane's side like his shadow.

Who said he'd murder me if I got intimate with Kane.

*He fingered me so that Kane wouldn't find out I was a virgin.*

I clench my jaw at the same time Kane clenches his. I feel, rather than hear, the name that grinds past his teeth.

*Zane.*

The cameras are fucking Zane's.

# CHAPTER 4

## ZANE

STARING at the red GPS dot on my phone is murder on my eyes. I tell myself that I'm only checking where Kane is to make sure that he's safe, but as soon as my eyes move past the blinking little dot to the street name, my blood runs cold.

King Street, otherwise known as Frat House Row.

The place I explicitly asked Kane not to visit.

Considering Kane's history, I shouldn't be surprised that he disregarded my request, but it still fucking hurts. He could be balls deep inside of someone right now, fucking all of his pent-up frustration with me out of his system. Yeah, I kept the video of Mercy declaring her interest in Reaper a secret from him, but it's for his own good.

*Our* own good.

Clenching my fist, I slam it on my desk, then remove my glasses and rub my aching eyes. Nothing good will come from tonight. My week of self-indulgence, rolling around in the sheets with Kane and pretending the rest of the world doesn't exist, has clearly come to an end. It's everything I ever wanted, and yet...

Somehow, it doesn't feel like it's enough.

This feeling of *not enough* has been nagging me over the past few days. Maybe that's why I sent the video to Sam's fraternity—blowing everything up means that I don't have to confront the reality that what I always wanted might not be what I actually need.

But that's fucking stupid. Kane *is* what I need. He's always been the one thing keeping me grounded to this shitty experience called *life*. Without him, I'd be dust in the wind—too fragile to choose my own path and not strong enough to change anything. With him, I have purpose. My life has meaning because he gives it meaning.

That's all there is to it.

Blowing out a breath, I spin in my chair and stare up at the ceiling. Despite any unrest nagging at me, being locked away indoors has its perks. I don't have to talk to anyone. I don't have to worry about appearances or social etiquette. The worst of my troubles is keeping Kane from spending too much money online shopping or flirting with disaster for fun.

Disasters like a six foot, chronically depressed, cynical ball of anxiety like me.

Maybe I'm the problem. I should be happy. After years of pining for the man, he's finally mine. I wake up wrapped in his arms, warm and safe, his breath on my back and his scent on my sheets. Everything should be perfect...but this wriggling doubt in the back of my mind taints even the most tender moments. I lie awake and listen to Kane's breathing in the middle of the night, desperately ignoring the anxiety clawing at my eyes. I don't even know what's causing me to lose sleep—I just know that I'm uneasy *all the fucking time.*

Is Mercy the problem? Could it be that simple?

I clench my jaw as memories of her porcelain skin, silver in the moonlight, rise to the forefront of my mind. Does everything always have to come back to that fallen angel of a woman?

Something so ethereally beautiful shouldn't exist.

The front door suddenly creaks, and footsteps sound down the hall. My bedroom door is open, but Kane smacks its face anyway, slamming it into the wall as he stomps into the room. I sit up straight, anticipating a confrontation.

It never comes.

Kane pulls open my dresser drawers and grabs a duffel bag from my closet, shoving clothing inside without speaking to me. Without *looking at* me.

Nerves skitter down my arms. How long have I been staring at my computer? I glance at the clock in the corner of my monitor. It's past sunrise by now. Shit. He never called to check up on me, and I never called to check on him either. Is he mad about that? Or is this about Mercy again? Daggers stab the back of my eyes as I think of her and Kane together, the two of them canoodling in every sense of the word. Maybe he's going to leave me for her. But he's packing up my things, so he could be kicking me out instead.

Taking a breath, I try to calm my racing heart. I'm being paranoid when I have no reason to be. Calm down. *Calm the fuck down, Zane.*

While Kane rummages through my belongings and dips into the attached bathroom for God knows what, I click through his phone's tracking history. Sometime over the past few hours, I missed an entire detour across the city, curving around the mountainside to reach the Morningstar property. What was he doing there? Tucking Mercy into bed for the night?

Jealousy burns like magma in my gut as I picture him taking a bleeding, broken angel home, setting her down in the shower, and gently washing her battered and bruised skin. Wiping the tears off her cheeks. Kissing her swollen lips. Easing the ache inside her body by healing the cracks in her heart.

It should be *me* he tends to. *My* broken, aching heart.

Because if he saw Mercy tonight, I—

Sharp pain in my chest renders me speechless. I watch, barely breathing, while Kane doesn't so much as look at me. Why won't he look at me? Drawing a shallow breath, I clutch my chest. Each beat of my heart aches. Am I so disgusting to him that he can't stand the sight of me? The thought of living together gives him hives, so he's kicking me out without a word? Packing my bags and throwing them out the window?

"Kane—"

At the sound of my voice, his gaze snaps to mine. Fire burns hot in his eyes, but I can't tell its source. Fury? Desire? Obsession? Fuck, I've spent years watching him obsess over our targets as they fall apart beneath his touch. I've yearned to be the one he unravels. But that's not what this is. Kane's gaze is too intense —too sharp—and more dangerous than anything I've seen before. It's like the man I've fallen in love with has forgotten who I am. What we are to each other. He's not just my friend, but my brother. My lover. My *everything.*

I'll do anything to keep him.

"Kane," I start again, standing. "What's going on?" I hold my tongue to keep from asking something specific, like "Where have you been?" or "Are we in danger?" Or, worst of all, "How's Mercy?" The truth burns in my throat. I hope she's bleeding on the floor right now. I hope that Kane walked in on her being railed by another man and lost his shit. I hope that she's crying her eyes out, because her new favorite toy—*my man*—has lost all interest in her.

And yet.

Razor wire wraps tightly around my heart, squeezing, digging into the muscle, cutting deep and making me bleed. Picturing Mercy naked and alone with tears streaming down her face doesn't... feel right. It *sounds* right. It's what I've wanted. To get her out of the way so that Kane and I can finally be together, free from the binds of these stupid fucking games we play.

I've wanted this shit to end before it ever began. I'm the one who pulled the knife on her the first night we met. I wanted her dead and buried next to Forty-Three—barely a blip on our radar, underserving of the title Forty-Four, dead and gone in a heartbeat. That should be what I want now. It's what I've been preparing for. Fixing up that ridiculous chapel on her family property. Setting it up like a rustic love nest, ignoring all of its flaws, because I know that Kane salivates over that shit. The worn floorboards, the cobwebs hanging from the eaves, the smudged stained glass windows casting muted light across every dust-covered surface. It's dirty and awful and hardly romantic. But it's where I've imagined Kane killing her, when this shit is finally said and done.

Cutting our journey short before the grand finale has its consequences. I won't get to see how pretty of a corpse she is—bathed in ethereal moonlight, her perfect skin turned into a canvas of bruises, the rattle of her final breaths echoing in time with the flickering candlelight. I blink away the fantasy, knowing that it will never come true.

I can live with that disappointment so long as I have Kane.

Two long strides is all it takes for my lover to pounce. He barrels into my body, cupping my jaw and slamming his mouth over mine. The barest sound passes his lips—a hard, frustrated puff of air—as he backs me against the wall. Tearing at my clothes, he rips my t-shirt and attacks my neck at the same time, biting hard enough that I whimper.

"K-Kane," I stutter, my nerves unable to keep up with the rapid-fire beat of my heart. Anxiety pulses through my bloodstream, knowing that I want this—I want him—but something isn't right. We've spent the past week together in tender bliss, not *this*.

Not aggression.

He wraps his palm around my throat. "Shut up." Squeezing, he nips my jaw as he cuts off my airway. "I can't think with your voice in my head, so just—" A shiver rolls down his body. "Stop talking."

I grab the nape of his neck as I struggle with my next breath. "Safe word." We never came up with one. I didn't think I needed one. But *fuck*. This is too much, too sudden, too rough—

A growl rumbles inside Kane's chest. "This is what you want, isn't it?" He sucks a bruise into my skin, on the tip of my shoulder, and releases my neck, his hands dipping to roam my abdomen. "My attention." Lowering his palm, he cups my balls and massages, sparking desire in my blood. It burns painfully hot as he licks a stripe up the side of my neck and groans, his erection swollen against my hip. "Speak up, Zane. Is that what you want?"

I choke on the words tumbling around my brain. Yes. No. *Fuck*. My cock thickens, heavy and hot between my legs, and I moan.

Shoving his hand in my boxers and grabbing my shaft at the base, Kane rubs my length against his wrist, barely stroking, his voice rumbling in my ear. "Use your words, *lover.*" The endearment sounds wrong—harsh like cracking glass. Kane bites harder, the clench of his teeth on my throat painful.

I can't think like this. Can hardly breathe. I've spent hours wondering what he's doing, where he is, who he's with, but the sudden onslaught of attention renders me speechless. My body burns for him, but my heart aches.

Why? Why does this hurt?

Finally, I choke out a response. "Were you with her?" I feel the tension shift as Kane freezes in place, suddenly shaking from head to toe. "Were you?" Wedging my arms between us, I push him off of me. "Did you kiss her?" I shove him square in the chest. "Touch her?" My gaze rakes across his body, looking for signs that they've been together. He's shirtless. Hard as a rock, tenting his jeans so much that I'm sure it hurts. Jaw clenched. Eyes flashing like the sharpest shards of ice. "Did you kiss her —" I wipe my mouth on my forearm—"and come home to me after?"

Outrage roars in my ears, but I see it reflected in Kane's eyes. He's just as pissed as I am.

"You fucking asshole," he growls, grabbing my wrists. "You think this is fun for me?" Spinning us around, he tosses me onto the bed and crawls on top. By now, this is our normal. Kane likes to be in control. He likes feeling me squirm beneath him. But this time, he hovers over me, barely touching my body with his. Shaking. Gritting his teeth. Angry. Hurt. Trying to make me happy, I think, in his own way.

Our eyes lock, and we glare at each other.

"You want me to apologize?" I scoff, stretching my arms over my head. The sheets are soft, contrasting the man nearly pinning me down. My knuckles knock against the wall. Rigid, just like Kane. "I won't." Jutting my chin out, I hold my ground. "I'm not sorry for anything."

Not for his anger. Or what happened to Mercy. Or my role in everything. I'm not sorry about the years we've spent together—the people we've killed—the pain we've caused. Sometimes, when Kane is locked inside his studio finishing up a series of paintings, I visit the funerals of our victims. Studying their families. Feeling their grief. Forty-three kills, and I've been to at least half of their services, hiding in the shadows like a ghost. I can't bring myself to regret a single murder. I've tried—begging the twisted chambers of my heart to pump an ounce of remorse into my soul—but it hasn't worked.

Mercy is no different than the rest.

I don't have any regrets about that girl.

"You're not sorry for kissing her, so why should I be sorry for hurting her?" I know the answer. I know that I should say it, too. *Because hurting Mercy hurts Kane.* But I can't form the words when they're not true. I'm a twisted, fucked-up man for everything I've done. Our fallen angel makes no difference. She hasn't changed who I am—and she hasn't changed Kane, despite what he may think.

Kane's jaw clenches and unclenches repeatedly. His nostrils flare. His muscles twitch as he strains not to touch me. Blonde hair a mess, icy eyes wild, lips a darker shade of red than usual.

A speck of blood hiding under his chin.

He's fucking breathtaking.

No one deserves him more than me. I've been here by his side the entire time. The *only* constant in his life. Supporting all of his fucked-up fantasies, from the endless stream of murders to the black market art deals that follow. Reaper may be the face of the business, but I'm the one running it from the shadows.

Reaper wouldn't exist without me, and I can't breathe without the man behind the mask.

I close the distance between us slowly, running my palms up his biceps, across his shoulders, wrapping my body around his and tugging him down on top of me. He collapses with a shudder, holding me so tightly that my bones ache. The drag of his lips over mine is sensual but no less intoxicating, the two of us breathing in time with each other. I feel his heartbeat beneath my palm and wish that it beat for me—and only me.

But I know that isn't his truth, no matter how much I want it to be.

"I love you." He sighs against my lips as he fists the sheets over my head. "Why isn't that enough?"

Jealousy twists inside my chest, its thorns cutting into my heart. "I don't like seeing you with other people." I cling to him, scarcely able to breathe as I picture him and Mercy together. Panic rises like a tidal wave, threatening to take over. "I—" My voice catches. "I can't lose you."

Life without Kane is meaningless. I came to that realization long ago, when I nearly lost him to prison after our usual murder turned into a reckless double-homicide. I'd rather get locked up beside him than live free on my own. Shrinks would call it unhealthy, this dependency. I know that. But it doesn't change anything.

I want Kane more than I want life itself.

Maybe it's because I finally have him that I refuse to let go. After years of watching from the sidelines, my heart filled with a hunger that's impossible to satisfy. I don't just want Kane—I need him like oxygen.

And if he gives himself to Mercy, I'll have to survive off the leftover scraps. Clenching my fists, I scratch Kane's back with my fingernails. It's not fair that I have to share, so I won't. I refuse. Losing any part of him, no matter how small, will ruin me.

Kane pushes himself up on his forearms, his gaze gentle as it sweeps across my face. "I'm not going anywhere." The divot between his eyebrows makes me feel guilty for saying my fears aloud. He draws a steady breath and laces our fingers together, pressing my hand into the mattress. "Zane—" My name falls past his lips like a sigh.

Is he disappointed? Tired? Exhausted from whatever he and Mercy got up to tonight—

"You paranoid fucking bastard." He laughs, clocking me so accurately that I'm stunned. "You need to trust me." Squeezing my hand, he smiles. Some of the warmth returns to his eyes, but it's quickly doused by whatever he's keeping from me. The thing that's making him act all erratic like this.

Likely Mercy—or rather, what happened with her tonight. He still hasn't told me. Technically, I haven't asked. We dodge the issue, knowing that it exists, but unwilling to bring it to light.

I try not to let it get to me, but it does. He may claim that he loves me, but he likes her. I can see it, clear as day. He *really* likes her. Thinking of her puts this little wistful smile on his face, like he knows he shouldn't be so taken with her but can't help it. If he's still interested in her after how badly she's been broken, he's falling in love with her, just like I feared.

Is it possible to love more than one person at the same time? Kane makes it look as easy as breathing, like he's got more than enough love and affection for multiple people and himself. I barely have enough for him, let alone myself.

Maybe that's why he needs her. Because I can only give him a fraction of the love he needs to survive. But that doesn't answer the question of *why.*

Why does it have to be Mercy?

"I don't understand you." Gazing into Kane's eyes, I search for answers. "I don't know why you're so infatuated with her."

He returns my gaze but takes a moment to respond, thinking carefully about what to say. "Let me show you." Kissing the corner of my lips, he murmurs a gentle *please* that spells disaster.

Facing what I've done to Mercy doesn't scare me.

It's the consequences—a fallout with Kane, a fistfight with Sam, a confrontation with the girl herself—that do. Because no matter how black and white I try to make our situation out to be, everything falls into shades of gray. Our relationships. Our feelings. And all the empty spaces in between where unspoken truths lie, waiting for us to shine a light on them.

# CHAPTER 5

## SAM

THE FURNACE COOLS SLOWLY. For such an expensive machine, I'd expected more of a bang—a sudden *whoosh* as all of our sins are carried away on the wind, or something. But no, Mercy and I sit in silence as the crematorium does its work over the next hour, neither of us brave enough to speak the truth.

I fucked up tonight.

For some reason, Mercy doesn't seem upset about it.

I mean, she's clearly not okay—but she's not angry at me, and that's the part that confuses the hell out of me. Apologies weigh down my tongue, too many of them to voice at once. I say them in my head, one at a time, over and over and over like I'm practicing lines as a troubled school boy who got smacked with a ruler for daydreaming about the girl one row over instead of taking my quiz with any sense of urgency.

I'm sorry for taking you to the party.

I'm sorry for being in a fraternity.

I'm sorry that I'm not strong enough to keep you safe.

I'm sorry that in the end, I'm not enough to make you happy.

Which feels like complete bullshit, if I'm being honest. How could Kane—serial killer and professional fuckboy—be better than me? How could I *let* him be better than me?

Turmoil churns in my gut as I war with myself. A better man would let Mercy go, wouldn't he? Bow down to what she wants—because it clearly isn't me. She's been hugging a throw pillow for the past half hour, her eyes barely open as she drifts between reality and dreaming. Her head bobs, and she catches herself with a jolt, working hard to keep her eyes open and stare at the smooth stainless steel door between us and the body crumbling to ash inside.

This is stupid. Our situation. The uncomfortable tension between us. How she won't let herself relax.

Is it because of me?

Does she not trust me anymore?

Knives dig into my lungs, and I choke on my next breath. I wouldn't blame her if she didn't, but the possibility fucking hurts. If she doesn't think that I can keep her safe, then who does she trust?

Kane's arrogant smirk pops into my mind as I consider the possibility that Mercy trusts him more than me, and I want to punch the goddamn smile off his face. Not only does it suck that she might consider him her savior after he literally dragged that asshole off of her tonight, but he kissed her in front of me. Not once, but twice. First, before we left the frat house, and second, ten minutes ago as he rushed out the door. Without warning, he wriggled out from under Mercy, stole one hell of a kiss, and shouted something about *tying up loose ends.* He was gone in the blink of an eye, revving up his motorcycle outside and tearing down the street. If it weren't for the blush warming Mercy's cheeks, I'd have convinced myself that I imagined the kiss. That in my jealousy of their bond, I created a fantasy in which Kane was comfortable kissing her like he had a right to her lips.

The reality is just as grim.

He *does* feel entitled to her kiss.

Per our brief sparring match outside, it was *my* right to kiss her next. Not his. But he took it anyway, because that's who he is.

Selfish.

But the most important lesson isn't about Kane's ego; it's that he's a man who breaks his own rules. For people playing a game of life and death with the maniac, that is a *very* important lesson to learn.

Slowly, carefully, I slip from my folding chair and onto the couch beside Mercy. The cushion dips between us, and I wrap my arm around her shoulder and drag her against me: thighs touching, tiny hands curling around my t-shirt, cheek pressed against my shoulder and her soft breaths falling onto my chest. I drape a knit blanket over her bare legs and gently rub warmth into her thighs with my free hand. She must be freezing after so many hours without clothes. I should have gotten her a t-shirt or shorts or—

My thoughts derail as she settles into me like a cat seeking warmth, her eyes cracking open for the barest second. Peering up at me, she gives the barest smile before closing her eyes again. "Thanks for being here, Sam," she murmurs, sighing softly. "I don't know where I'd be without you."

I grit my teeth as waves of emotion roll over me, each one stronger than the last. Without me, Mercy might be at home, tucked in her bed, blissfully unaware of the dark corners of the world. The gun I stashed in the middle console of my truck. The spare in the glove box. The way blood splatter looks after a gunshot to the head—messy, pulpy, nothing like the movies—or how hard it is to clean afterwards. What it feels like to fight a man whose inner demons have taken over, and how easy it is to lose in a battle of physical strength.

Without me, she might be smiling at her sketchbook right this very instant, hunching over her desk with little more than a few taper candles to light each pencil stroke across the page.

Without me, she could be in so many places, doing so many better things than this.

But despite the overwhelming regret that's in my heart, it's hard to wish for anything other than holding Mercy close while she drifts to sleep. It's a familiar comfort that settles my lingering anxiety. My heart beats steadily, my nerves too shot for me to sleep alongside her.

I called Grey about the clean-up at my frat house, but

it's only a matter of time before word gets to my father. He could be halfway across the world, and it wouldn't matter—any word about his son makes it to his ears within a few minutes. Not that I'm expecting him to jump on a plane to see me. If he can't be bothered to take a car across town, he sure as shit won't be jumping for joy at the prospect of a thirteen-hour flight to see his son. Our reunion, no matter how dismal, is imminent. I've fended him off for a few years, citing my need for a college degree to delay my onboarding with the family business, but when he learns about this latest incident with the frat, he's bound to scoop me up in his talons and put me to work doing God knows what.

Whatever it is, it won't be good. For my father, the added bonus will be keeping me from Mercy and her family. It's no secret that I consider them more of my family than the man who raised me. It's one of the sticking points in our relationship that I'm sure irks him. Not because he wants to have a better father-son bond, but because it's proof of a battle that he's lost.

Thinking about my father puts me on edge, so I press my face to the top of Mercy's head and breathe in her scent. Lavender, like her pillow. Her breathing comes easy, and pride warms my chest. She's always fallen asleep best when I'm with her. Tonight's events didn't erase that. I close my eyes and whisper a prayer without meaning to, unable to stop the hushed words flowing past my lips.

*Stay with me, Mercy.* I press a kiss to her hair. *Forever.*

I don't know how long we sit in the dark, but the sun

rises and light shines through the windows. Mercy continues to sleep. The furnace completely cools and shuts off, awaiting the next steps. I don't actually know what to do. It's not like I read a manual or searched the internet for *how to cremate a body*. We could have buried him in the backyard and washed our hands of it by now. I guess this leaves less evidence than a fresh grave?

While I contemplate whether waking Mercy is worth it or not, the door to the hall creaks open, and Mr. Morningstar shuffles into the room. Coffee steaming from the travel mug in his hand, a yellow notepad tucked under his arm, dark hair falling into tired eyes, he turns to the right and starts checking things off of a list before noticing the antique velvet couch in the middle of the room or his daughter tucked beneath my arm.

He blinks, taken off guard, before coming over to check the crematorium. Holding his hand over the front, then the side, before checking the dials and switches that Mercy used to turn the machine on, he mutters a few things under his breath. After a minute of quiet contemplation, he moves to drop his notepad and pen onto the rolling cart before stopping midway, rethinking it, and tucking both into his back pocket. Then, he turns the cold metal folding chair around and takes a seat.

"Sir—"

Holding up his hand, Vinicius Morningstar gestures for me to remain silent. "Don't say any more than I need to know, son." He leans back in the chair and sighs. "Was it a dog?"

I blink. Should I tell him the truth?

"A cat?" Scratching off a dried patch of shaving cream on his cheek, he watches me closely. "Mercy knows how to bury animals," he murmurs, gaze narrowing at his daughter. "She wouldn't use the oven for something small... A cow?" Shaking his head, he answers his own question in his head. There's no farmland nearby, and a cow would be too heavy to move. Finally, his gaze flicks from Mercy's face to mine, and I have to stop myself from shrinking away. "You're looking worse for wear, Sam."

I clear my throat as quietly as I can. "I've been better."

The older man chuckles humorlessly. "No shit." Drawing a breath, taking his time, he asks another question. "Does this have anything to do with that man from the other night? Did he—" his voice hardens, deepening to an octave I've never heard from the jovial man, "hurt her?"

Of everyone I've ever met, Vinicius Morningstar has always been a polite, positive man. He has a quiet gentleness about him that makes him comfortable company. Short, thick around the middle, with kind eyes and a kinder soul, no one would mistake Mercy's father as anything other than a teddy bear you can confide your deepest regrets or darkest secrets to, and he'd never bat an eye. From what Mercy has told me, he eagerly took over the mortuary once his own father passed away. If he wasn't in the funerary business, he could easily be a counselor.

This side of him—a hardened man protecting his daughter—isn't one that I'm familiar with.

I guess we all have our multitudes.

"Kane didn't hurt her." I caress Mercy's upper arm with tiny sweeps of my thumb. She doesn't stir, passed the fuck out for once. I almost envy her. "This was someone else."

Vinicius—or Vinny, as most people call him—stares at me like he's searching for answers to questions he doesn't dare ask. Tension coils in the air around us. "Is it handled?"

I contemplate how to answer. By now, clean-up at the crime scene will be over. Someone from my father's expansive team of professionals should have contacted my fraternity brothers and gotten a list of all party attendees to begin payoffs and cover ups. Hospital staff may have been ordered to keep any visits from the injured fraternity president and his lackeys confidential. The police officers on my father's payroll have likely been advised of the situation, as well.

The body has been taken care of, too, thanks to Kane, Mercy, and me.

"Yes," I answer confidently. "Everything's been taken care of."

Nodding, Vinny relaxes. If he suspects that we murdered someone, he's being oddly chill about it. Then again, working as a mortician means that he's probably seen some shit I can't begin to imagine. Maybe it's a good thing that he takes the unexpected in stride.

"And you two?" He tips his head towards his daughter. "Have you mended things?"

The last time I saw Mr. Morningstar, Mercy was crying her eyes out in her bedroom. Kane and I were getting into a fight on his front porch. Of course, he'd be concerned about my relationship with his daughter. My heart yearns to say *yes, we're good*, but I know that nothing is that simple. I can't get too comfortable just because Mercy's letting me hold her right now. There's no telling what a clear head will bring when she wakes up.

She might resent me once the dust settles and reveals the fucking crater I've blown into our relationship.

"We're working things out." It's as much truth as I can give without cracking my chest open and pouring my heart out. Vinicius is like a father to me, but his concern is first and foremost for his daughter, not his almost-adoptive-son. I've relied on Mercy as my emotional anchor for years, but I can't place this burden on her, either, when she has just as much shit going on as I do. Going to one of my frat brothers to vent is out of the question, as is the football team. I'd rather die than go to a school counselor.

I haven't spoken with my therapist regularly since I was a teenager, but it might be time to give them a call.

Vinny exhales slowly. "Take things slowly if you need to. *Very* slowly." Holding my gaze, he makes sure that the message settles in. After a moment, he continues, "Do I need to know anything about that other boy? Kane?"

This time, I lie by omission. "He's rough around the

edges, but I think he genuinely likes Mercy." As much as it pains me to admit it...after seeing the aftermath of his anger—and how easily he shot and killed a man for touching Mercy—I have little doubt that he likes her as more than as a trophy kill to hang on his wall.

That's a problem.

We aren't playing a sexed up game of life and death anymore. Hearts are involved...and love makes people dangerous.

Zane is a perfect example of the lengths people will go to protect their loved ones from perceived threats. But if Kane has genuine feelings for Mercy, I can't help but wonder if that will be enough for him to change course. Instead of hurting her—*killing her*—could he fall hard enough to back out of the game entirely?

Could he spare her life instead of taking it?

I hold Mercy tight as fear flickers inside my heart. No matter what rules we create or who wins the game, I have a feeling that things are only going to get messier from here. With so many people grabbing hold of each other, cracks are bound to form. Bonds will break. And some-one's going to bleed.

Leaving Mr. Morningstar alone in the morgue to clean up our mess feels wrong, but the older man insists. "Take my baby girl home," he instructs, leveling me with a look that doesn't leave room for argument. "Clean her up and tuck her in so that she can get some actual rest. But, Sam

—" He pulls out a bottle of painkillers from a side cabinet and places it in my hand. "Stay with her. I don't want her to wake up alone."

The unspoken truth that passes between us is that Mercy has nightmares—we both know it—and that if she has a really bad one, she'll scream until she wakes herself up. I don't actually know what Mercy dreams about; she's mentioned something about shadows before, but by the time she wakes up, the images in her head turn fuzzy and indistinct.

I think that's why she took up drawing at such a young age; she was grasping at what flickers of her nightmares she could remember. Of course, if we believe what Grandma Star has to say, it was her mom who gifted her that first sketchbook many years before I ever met Mercy, which would mean that Mercy has been having nightmares since she was a preteen, if not earlier.

"She sees things that we can't," Star has always said, remaining mysterious about Mercy's affliction. But she's said that about Mercy's older brother Malachi, too—that he glimpses a realm beyond our own. I think their grandmother has wishful thinking about her family's alleged psychic abilities, conjuring up fantasies that suit her version of reality.

The truth about Malachi Morningstar isn't that he has psychic powers—it's that he hallucinated hard enough to attack his classmates. His mother had just passed away, and after enough sleepless nights, the lines between reality and fantasy began to blur. One short stint in a rehabilitation facility later, he was cleared to return to school on a trial basis. I don't know the full details of what happened next, but I know the aftermath: Malachi was sent to boarding school across the country. I never met him, and because of how long he's been away, I'm not sure that I ever will. He might not return to Harlin Heights... ever. Mercy doesn't talk about him much, and I'm never around their older sister Lilith long enough to ask. But Grandma Star will mention him from time to time, telling stories as though both he and her late husband are still around.

Sometimes, I worry that Mercy will follow a similar path as her brother and slip through my fingers like smoke.

Clutching her tightly to my chest, I carry her up the stairs to her bedroom. She stirs as we cross the threshold, like she can sense that she's finally safe and sound where she belongs. As I set her down on her bed, she cracks her eyes open and peers up at me. "Sam," she mumbles, sighing sleepily. "What time is it?"

I don't actually know. "Morning." Patting my pocket, I fish out my phone and check the time. Before I can read the numbers, however, my father's name screams at me from my lock screen, the text message icon beside his name ominous. Dread fills my gut like lead. What could he possibly want? Closing my eyes, I press the pads of my thumbs to the back of my eyelids. Stress ripples through my body. I knew he would contact me after I called in one hell of a favor last night, but I didn't anticipate it being so soon. Surely he can't know what he wants from me already...

Unless he's been waiting for the right opportunity to dig his claws into me. Shit.

Mercy's voice is still heavy with sleep. "What's wrong?" Kane's leather jacket slips from one of her shoulders as she sits up, exposing more skin and snagging my attention. Specks of blood paint her arm, creating freckles where there are none. I stare at the change in her appearance—mussed up hair, falling loose from her braid, wavy tendrils framing her puffy face. No doubt from crying. Stress. A lack of sleep or water or any number of things she needs to stay healthy.

This is all my fault.

I swallow my guilt and put on a smile. "It's nothing. Football stuff." I toss my phone onto her desk chair and hope that she doesn't pry, because I won't know what to say. My narcissistic father contacted me for the first time in a year, all because I used his influence and connections to cover up a murder we committed—no, not *we*. Kane.

Clenching my fists, I try not to pin *all* of the blame on him, but it's hard not to. If he never entered our lives, Mercy and I wouldn't be playing his stupid fucking murder game. We'd be back to normal, dancing around each other as friends but not *more than* friends. Would we be happy then? Playing pretend instead of whatever the fuck it is we're doing now?

Thankfully, Mercy's attention has already drifted, her gaze unfocused. I watch her for a few seconds before stepping in front of her. "Hey, you okay?" Frowning, I tuck a strand of hair behind her ear. I don't like the look in her eyes. It's like she's... haunted. I've seen it before, and it always gives me chills. Someone as young as the two of us shouldn't carry ghosts on our backs.

Grandma Star might claim that we all have demons —how heavy they are depends on how well equipped we are to handle them. I try not to picture a shadowy creature clinging to Mercy's shoulders and dragging her down into misery.

Mercy rubs her eyes. "Yeah. I'm just tired. And sticky." Peeling off Kane's jacket, she touches her arms and frowns. "I smell, too. Like beer." Her nose crinkles, and I imagine that she can smell the blood, too. A reddish smear trails down her chest from her collarbone to her breasts, disappearing between the valley of her tits. Another one is shaped like a handprint on her shoulder, but I don't think she's seen that one yet. I'd rather she didn't.

"I'll start the shower." Such a small gesture isn't nearly enough to make up for my sins, but it's a start. I turn on my heel to leave, but Mercy grabs my hand to stop me. I glance at her over my shoulder. "Do you want to come with me?" She nods, taking a quick breath and standing. We walk hand in hand to the shared bath in the hall. While I turn on the shower and test the temp, she stares at her reflection in the mirror. I'm sure that she thinks she looks like a fucking mess, but—

"You're beautiful, Mercy." Our eyes meet in the mirror's reflection. "No matter what you think you look like—" I pull my hand from the shower stream and shake the water off. "You're beautiful to me."

She bites her bottom lip, the barest hint of pink

dusting her cheeks. "I don't know..." Her gaze returns to her reflection, and she lets the leather jacket slide off her shoulders to the floor. Wearing only a black bra and panties, she scrutinizes her appearance. "I'm..." Taking a breath, she shakes her head. "Plain."

*What?*

Coming up behind her, I wrap my arms around her waist and stare at our reflection in the mirror. Her skin is as pale as the moon, softer than satin, and magnificent to touch. I resist the urge to run my hands along her body and settle for holding her. "You are anything but plain." By contrast, *I'm* the plain one. On the football field, I don't stand out amongst the other players. I'm not gifted athletically, and I could never make calls like a quarterback. My only job is to act as a wall to keep the other team from scoring. And my looks—compared to Mercy, I'm bathed in color, but that's merely because she's so extraordinary. My golden skin stands out against hers, making *me* look like the dirty one. I shouldn't touch her.

If anything here is ugly, it's me—the man who refuses to leave her alone now that I've decided to have her. It's not like I gave her much choice. I inserted myself into her life when we first met, and today is no different. I'm by her side because I choose to be, not because she's asked me to stay.

I always criticize Kane for being selfish, but when we stand side-by-side, I'm no better than him.

Mercy scrunches her nose like she disagrees with me. Rather than say anything, however, she slips away to check the shower temp. "Will you stay with me?" Facing the shower, she reaches behind her back to undo her bra strap, easily unclasping it and letting it fall to the floor. Her panties come next, sliding down her thighs to reveal the swell of her ass, bare and beautiful and—*holy shit, she's bending over.*

My nostrils flare as I catch a glimpse of her naked pussy, rosy pink and glistening, before she kicks away her panties and steps into the shower. The curtain closes, and I'm left to my imagination, picturing her naked body beneath the water. "Always," I murmur, clearing my throat when it comes out raspy. Fuck. She doesn't need a horn-dog right now. She needs a man who can control himself.

I'll be that and more.

Anything she needs.

I'm not going anywhere ever again.

# CHAPTER 6

## MERCY

STANDING beneath the shower's spray can remove the evidence of last night, but it won't erase the memory. As I scrub down my body and avoid looking at the bruises along my waist and hips, I take measured breaths to stay calm. Surprisingly, it's not difficult. I'm not freaking out. When I picture Fake Reaper's painted face, it crumbles to ash before my eyes.

The very ash that Sam and I poured into a ceramic urn after my father finalized the cremation process and unknowingly helped cover up our crime. Unless Sam told him something while I was asleep—but he won't fess up to anything, keeping suspiciously silent about their conversation this morning. Even now, I listen for any sign of him behind the shower curtain. Rummaging through the cabinet drawers. Fiddling with my makeup on the counter. Kicking the heel of his foot against the wall. When I don't hear anything, I peek around the curtain to find him reading the back of an ointment tube while sitting on the closed toilet seat, our family's first aid kit open on the counter next to him.

"You could let Grandma patch you up."

He chuffs and uncaps the tube before applying a dollop of ointment to his cut bottom lip. "Your grandma's hands shake when she drinks tea. I doubt she can stitch people up anymore." His emerald eyes flick over to me. "I'll be fine."

My body runs hot at his stare. It's not like I'm exposed since I'm standing behind the curtain, but the drop of water that trails down my neck might as well be his fingertip. *Or his tongue.* I bite my bottom lip and quickly retreat behind the curtain, determined not to go down that route. The sexy one. Sam's only here this morning because he's being overprotective and overly cautious—he's not here to slip his tongue into my mouth or his hand between my thighs.

As much as that might be nice.

*God*, what is wrong with me?

I clench my eyes shut and focus on shampooing my hair. The bottle wheezes as I squeeze out the last drop of soap, and while I'm unscrewing the top and fingering the bottle for what little soap remains, a new one appears from around the edge of the curtain, clutched tightly in Sam's fingers. "Thanks," I murmur, setting down the empty bottle to accept the gift. Before he can pull his hand away, I grab it. "Wait, Sam— Can you, um, wash my back?"

There's a beat of silence.

"Turn around."

Abandoning the shampoo, I do as instructed and turn to face the tile wall. A few seconds pass before I hear the curtain pull open, and the water spray shifts off of my body. I shiver from the sudden lack of heat, goosebumps trailing across my skin. "Use the—"

"Lavender," Sam finishes for me, although that's not what I was going to say. He ignores the loofa—my unspoken request—and pumps body wash into his palms before lathering up. Only when I'm damn near freezing does he touch me, starting at the tips of my shoulders and working his way down my body.

I thought he might haphazardly wash away any remnants of blood or booze before running away, but Sam's hands are gentle as he meticulously palms every square inch of my skin, slowly brushing his callouses over every bump of my spine and each ridge of my shoulder blades, even curving along my waist and taking extra care with the bruises. He thumbs a tender spot on my hip and I exhale through the discomfort, crossing my arms in front of my face and leaning into them on the wall.

A choked sound catches in Sam's throat as he wraps his hand around the mark and squeezes. The pressure hurts and I whimper, caught off guard. "W-what are you doing?" I stand perfectly still, suddenly feeling like a scared rabbit cornered by a predator. A fox is too slender and sly to be Sam, especially when he steps over the tub edge and pushes me into the shower wall. The stream of water hits my back and washes away the suds, heating my skin while the tile at my front makes me shiver. The contrast makes me dizzy. Sam's breath on my neck and his hands on my hips don't help. I take a breath, inhaling little more than steam. Did he turn up the water temp?

"Sam?"

"You have these—" Sam squeezes my hip again, making me gasp. "Marks."

My voice trembles. "I bruise easily." Fake Reaper wasn't exactly gentle when he tossed me around. It's no surprise that he left his mark on my body. I feel Sam's warm breath on my shoulder as he presses against me, the rough denim on his jeans chafing my ass.

"I *hate* them." Sam sweeps his hands up my waist, digging into my flesh until he touches the bottom rung of my ribs. Reaching around my body, he covers my abdomen with his touch, ensuring that no inch is unscathed, before grabbing my hips again, harder this time.

I gasp as pain blooms anew. That's going to leave an even bigger bruise than the one I had before. "T-then why are you—"

He suddenly backs off and his lips replace his hands, kissing the new bruise on my right side before doing the same to the left. I flush bright crimson and bury my face in my arms as he kneels beside me and attends to the remaining bruises on the backs of my thighs and calves, going so far as to lift my foot and kiss the bruise wrapping around my ankle, tenderly caressing each side before moving on to the next. Despite the alleged hate Sam holds for the marks on my skin, his touch isn't angry or violent as he explores my body and examines each of them. He presses down on the tender spots, reawakening the pain for a mere moment before attempting to sooth it with his mouth.

Blood pools in the affected areas, and I grow very hot, very quickly. "S-Sam." His name comes out as a whine, and I can feel him freeze in place. "I can't—" I drag in as much air as I can, but it's all steam. "I can't keep—" My knees buckle, and I collapse without warning. The room spins as I fall.

"Mercy!" Sam catches me easily and collapses onto the bottom of the tub, holding me on his lap. He reaches over and turns the temperature to cool, letting it wash over my chest and down my body. "You should have said something sooner."

Wrapping my arms around his shoulders, I bury my face in his neck and shut my eyes. The water glides across my back, easing the ache from Sam's touch. "It happened so fast." I take a shallow breath, already feeling a little better. "I don't know what you're doing."

"I'm—" Sam adjusts our position so that my knees don't press against the tub wall. The shower-tub combo isn't exactly built with muscled athletes and their pixie girlfriends in mind. He swallows. "It's nothing."

I peek at his face. "Are you blushing?" To sit up, I have to lean on his shoulders, but it's worth it to get the full effect of Sam's rugged beauty. When he clenches his jaw, overgrown stubble scrapes my wrist. As he avoids my gaze, I glimpse towering evergreens swaying in a thunderstorm, bending so far that they nearly break. The taut muscles beneath my hands are boulders baking in the sun, searing and solid to the touch. "Sam." Hooking my finger around his jaw, I turn his face back towards me. "You don't have to pretend with me. It's okay."

A muscle in his jaw tics. "You can't say that."

"Why not?" Combing my fingers through his damp hair, I pull it off his forehead. "You've seen some of the darkest parts of me, so why can't I see yours? Do you think it'll scare me?" Admittedly, finding out that he's a secret hit man or underling for his father might take some getting used to, but I can adjust. "I *like* dark things." Tugging his hair, I tilt his head back and stare into his storm cloud eyes. "Did you forget who you're talking to?"

His throat clicks on a swallow. "No. But—"

I press my finger to his lips, silencing him. "Let me decide for myself." Wrapping my arms around his neck, I cling tightly to him. "Show me? Please?"

It takes a minute for Sam to move. At first, he's cautious. Grazing his knuckles across my back, he mutters under his breath, too softly for me to hear over the splashing water. Then his lips find my neck and he sighs as he drags his fingers into my hair, tangling them in the wet strands. "You ruin me, Mercy Morningstar." The scrape of his stubble is replaced by the sting of his teeth as he bites down.

Pain blossoms, hot and sharp, and I dig my nails into his shoulders to keep from making a sound. I want to ask what he means, but my brain scrambles for the words as Sam's touch intensifies. He latches onto my neck, tugging my hair for better access to the column of my throat. Every pinprick of pain is followed by the swipe of his hot tongue as he moves along the column of my throat, marking his territory. In between breaths, I catch the faintest sound rumbling past his lips, growing louder with each passing second.

*Mine.*

A flash of desire burns through my body. Shutting my eyes, I bite my lip to keep from moaning. Sam doesn't stop, his hands roaming the rolls of my stomach, climbing the ladder of my ribs, grabbing my tiny breasts. He pants when he reaches my collarbone, sparing a glance up at my face.

"Who's blushing now?" He chuckles, deep and dark, and squeezes my tit hard enough to make me whimper. "Tell me to stop."

I shake my head. This is exactly what I asked for. "No."

He drags in a breath and cups my breast, tilting my nipple up to his mouth. "Alright, then."

The moment he latches on, sucking the bud into his mouth and rolling his tongue over the tip, my body convulses. I smack the wall as my back arches and a gasp catches in my throat. Electricity zings down my spine and settles between my thighs, intensifying the growing ache in my core. *Holy shit.* No one's ever touched my tits before. They're small and plain and—

Sam pops off my nipple with a wet smack, groaning as he switches to the other one. "So perfect."

I whine, feel it echo in the air, and try not to spontaneously combust. "S-Sam." God, I never knew this could feel so... *hot.* The cool water isn't touching my rising body temp, and I smack the handle to turn it off. Sam pays it no mind, perfectly content with teasing me like this and in no rush to move. "Please. *Sam.*" I don't know what I'm asking for, but my body wants *something*. Heat. Cold. Pressure. Air. Mixed desires war with each other. I shouldn't have to pick. Why can't I have it all?

Sam's willing to give me everything, right?

Groaning, he shudders. "Fuck, Mercy." Propping his chin on my chest, he peers up at me. "I want to lock you up, beautiful, so that no one can find you. You'll be *mine.*" His grip tightens on my ribs, making me flinch. "Forever. I'll treat you just like this." Blowing air onto my nipple, he chuckles as I shiver. "You'll be my pretty little plaything, won't you? Dressed up in ribbons and lace so that I can unwrap you every night." Biting the top of my breast, he sucks, pulling blood to the surface and leaving a fresh mark. When he pulls away, I catch a red smear on my skin, the cut on his lip bleeding again. The blood mixes with a water drop trailing down my chest, and Sam wipes it all away with his palm. "Let's dry you off."

I'm weightless as Sam lifts me out of the tub and sets me down on the bathroom counter. Mascara and eyeliner fall into the sink and on the floor, but when my eyes travel low, it's not the puddles of water or the fallen makeup that catches my attention. Sam's jeans are barely holding on. If it weren't for the massive tent in front, I'm pretty sure they'd fall right off. As he stands there soaking wet, they slide down his hips and reveal more muscle than I've ever seen on a man. Even the models for drawing class aren't built like Sam—he's cut from stone, resembling a Greek Adonis.

"Since when are you—" *fucking delicious* "—ripped?"

He barely hears me, too caught up in what he's seeing to answer. I blush once I realize that he's checking my body from head to toe and counting under his breath. It can't be that bad. I glance down and gasp at the bruises mapping my skin like constellations.

As a pale woman, I've always bruised easily. My veins aren't strong and the layers of my skin are thinner than tissue paper, so a little bruising is normal. But this is the worst I've ever seen. In addition to the bruises from last night, new ones have appeared over my stomach and hips, along my thighs, down my arms. Not all of them are deep, but because of my complexion, even the slightest difference stands out like watercolors on stark white paper.

I cross my arms over my chest and shiver. "Don't look." Emotions well inside my chest, too many to sift through and name, but the strongest one that punches through the surface is *shame*. Pretty girls don't bruise. Strong girls don't get thrown around by bullies. Smart girls avoid danger. Clearly, my ineptitude has resulted in this—this proof of my failures.

But Sam ignores my plea, grabbing a towel from the bar and holding it out for me. His eyes finally flick up to my face. "Come here."

Moving slowly to avoid more bruising, I slide off the countertop and step into the towel. Sam wraps it tight around me and tucks the ends in. Without warning, he engulfs me in a bear hug. Warmth seeps through the towel and into my bones, soothing some of the ugliness chafing at my heart.

"Those bruises are mine," he whispers, cradling the back of my head. "I put them there."

That's not true. I open my mouth, but he hushes me.

"I mean it, Mercy. Those are mine." The gravel in his voice rumbles inside his chest. "Any time you look in the mirror, you need to remember that." Pulling back just enough to peer into my eyes, he levels me with a serious look and taps one of the bruises on my chest. "I want you to think of me when you see them."

I don't know that rewiring my brain will be as easy as wishing it into existence, but for Sam, I can try. "Okay," I murmur, tucking my chin. "I'll try."

His lips brush the shell of my ear. "You *will*." He rubs warmth into my body through the towel. "C'mon, let's get you to bed." Sam carries me into my room and tucks me into bed. I watch as he drags his wet jeans down his legs, kicks them away, and hovers with his hands on the waistband of his boxers. A divot forms between his eyebrows.

"You can take them off." I turn onto my side and prop my head up on my hand. "I don't want you to get sick. If you need clothes, you can raid my brother's closet." It's not like Malachi needs them anytime soon. I don't know when he's coming home from boarding school. We haven't kept in touch since he's not allowed a cell phone and hates writing letters. The few phone calls he gets per month aren't wasted on his little sister.

Rolling onto my back, I stare up at the ceiling as Sam undresses. Rather than slip across the hall to find clothes, he pulls back my blankets and slides into bed beside me, quickly wrapping me in his arms and sighing into my hair. He relaxes instantly. "S'warm," he mumbles, burying his face in the crook of my neck.

It takes less than thirty seconds for him to pass out, but I lie awake, cocooned in his warmth and struggling to sleep. Normally, Sam would provide enough comfort for me to sleep peacefully, but my nap earlier this morning has taken its toll. I watch shadows dance around the room as they evade the barest whispers of sunlight filtering through the curtains. Each one tells its story with dramatic flair, flickering like obsidian flames crawling up the walls, dripping like candle wax over the windowsill, floating like ash in the wind, or writhing like a girl trapped in a nightmare that never ends.

# Chapter 7

## Kane

Samson fucking Wright is the shittiest communicator I've ever known. I send a barrage of messages his way, knowing that the bastard has his phone on him. He might hate my guts, but for possibly the first time in our lives, our interests align. I'm not trying to steal his girl. I'm trying to help her.

Is it so hard to believe that I fucking care?

ME

Hey, this is Kane. How is she?

Don't ignore me, Sam

Hey

HEY

SAM

She's awake. I think she's okay.

I'm fine, too.

Thanks for asking.

Jackass.

ME

> I'm going to get her phone from your place. Do you need anything?

I don't know why I'm asking; it's not like the grown-ass-man can't get things for himself. But he's with Mercy right now and I don't want him to leave. In fact, he shouldn't go back to his frat house at all. I doubt his fraternity brothers will be forgiving of what went down over some pussy. Clenching my jaw, I grind my teeth as I lace up my boots. I also need sleep, but caffeine is one hell of a drug and it's good enough to get me from point A to point B.

As I'm grabbing my keys, a floorboard in the hallway creaks. I glance over my shoulder to find my boyfriend peering at me from across the living room.

"You're leaving again?" Zane's crumpled t-shirt—*my* t-shirt, actually—is so fucking cute. It hangs low over his hips and slides off of one shoulder, exposing the hickey I gave him last night. Mmm. He rubs his bloodshot eyes and sighs. "Let me grab my shoes." Glancing down at his bare legs, he frowns. "Pants."

Sweeping into the room, I pull him in for a quick kiss. "I'll be right back. Get some rest."

"No." His frown deepens. "I'm going with you. Wait up for five fucking seconds." Slipping from my grasp, he grumbles under his breath while he dresses in yesterday's jeans and switches out my shirt for his own, quickly transforming into the grunge grump he is at heart. Hand-combing his hair and taking a quick piss counts for his morning routine, and he's good to go. "I'm driving. We're not taking your bike."

"Too fast for ya, gramps?" I tease.

He punches my ribcage as he pushes past me out the front door. "Too loud."

I guess I can agree with that. "Fiiiine. But we're going to Sam's frat, then to Mercy's house." I raise an eyebrow. "You cool with that?"

"Yeah." Avoiding my gaze, he unlocks his four-door snooze fest and slides into the driver's seat. "Get in."

The car ride is unbearable. Zane isn't fully awake, but I can practically taste his sour mood the closer we get to King Street. I refuse to humor him and put on my favorite music to drown out the angst. It only works so well. By the time we make it to Frat Row, I'm itching to get out of the car.

"Would you calm down?" Zane parks on the curb. "You're like a cat trying to claw its way out of a cage. Chill the fuck out."

Other than bouncing my knee, I've barely moved for the entire ride over. "I'm fine." I tear open the car door and walk as slowly and calmly as possible to the house, bouncing up the front steps and pushing inside without any resistance.

The place is completely empty. All of the furniture from last night—even the empty beer cans and red plastic cups—have been swept away. The floor's been professionally cleaned, too, damn near spotless for how old it is. I avoid the urge to explore the main floor and head up to the second story, eager to get this pit stop over with.

The faster we wrap up here, the faster I can check on Mercy.

Glancing at my phone, I make a mental note of Sam's wish list before checking the bedrooms. The first room is just like the main floor—completely fucking empty. Weird. The next room is the same. And the next. Even the bathroom has been gutted. "Are we at the right house?" I call out, knowing that Zane is nearby. My voice echoes in the empty space. I didn't exactly check the address, but this should be it. Where the fuck did everything go?

"The greek letters are out front." Zane huffs as he climbs the staircase. "Unless they moved overnight, this is the place." He follows my path through each room, going further than me and checking the closets. When he comes up empty, he returns just in time to watch me lower the attic stairs. "You've got to be kidding me. Nothing's here. We should go."

"Scared of the dark?"

A shadow crosses his face. "No. This is a waste of time. What did we even come for?"

"Mercy's phone. Her wallet." According to Sam's texts, she had a tiny purse with her. He also requested a change of clothes, but that's not gonna happen with the house suddenly abandoned. It's like Frat HQ picked up and left before they could be pinned for unauthorized brawling and first degree murder. Fucking weird.

The attic stairs slot into place and I climb up, turning on my phone's flashlight to check the dark, stuffy room. It's empty, too. Even the dust has been swept away, forgotten swirls and smudges of dirt the only clue that anything was ever stored here. Fucking *weirder*. "What the fuck?"

Who the hell played Cleaning Fairy overnight?

Zane watches me climb back down the attic stairs. He fiddles with a hangnail, looking bored out of his mind while I breeze past him to check all the rooms again. "Maybe you're right. This is the wrong house."

I try not to get annoyed, but the flip-flopping *is* annoying. "Make up your damn mind," I mutter under my breath, slamming a door shut. After I find nothing upstairs, we return to the main level. I retrace my steps from last night, envisioning the brawl, the weight of the gun in my hand, the body on the floor. "This is it, Zane, I'm telling you. Someone cleaned up."

His response is immediate. "Why would anyone care that much about a party?"

"It's not the party." Running a hand through my hair, I meet Zane's eyes. "It's the murder. I killed someone last night. We ran before the cops could arrive and took the body with us. And Mercy—" I stop myself and gauge Zane's reaction to her name, hoping for something, *anything*, that shows guilt or remorse. Hell, I'd take a confession so long as he purged himself of every fucked-up thought running through his head. Envy is a fucking poison. It'll kill him.

When Zane doesn't so much as twitch, I tear my gaze

away. *Fuck*, that hurts. I push my fist into my chest in a vain attempt to soothe the ache in my heart. Clearing my throat, I continue. "Sam called in a favor." I stare at the sliding glass door that Sam stood by when he made the phone call. "To Daddy Wright."

In the span of a single heartbeat, Zane goes from cool and collected to shitting a goddamn brick. "He got *Samuel Wright* involved?" Zane crumbles, crouching low and holding his head in his hands. "Shit. Fuck." His hands shake as he blows out a breath.

It's not the murder confession that makes Zane sweat —it's the enigma that's Sam's fucking father.

I shrug, not following Zane into a spiral about the news. "So what? He's just some fogey with money."

"Who knows how to wipe a scene." Zane pulls himself off the floor and grabs my hand. "We need to leave." He's insistent, pulling me away without his usual meticulousness. Each step is a flurry of anxiety as his natural rhythm goes out of wack. He damn near trips down the front porch steps. "Involving Sam is bad news. I told you this when you first invited him into the game."

I take the keys from Zane's shaking hands. "Hey. Easy." Inhaling deeply, I place my palm on Zane's chest and urge him to do the same. "Nice and slow. That's it. Just breathe, babe."

He shakes his head, a quick burst of nervous laughter making him even twitchier. "You don't understand." Zane glances around like he's checking our surroundings for threats. "Sam's an idiot, but his father's a menace. He doesn't destroy his enemies, he incinerates them. If anything is going to damage his reputation—a person, a city council vote, a competitor—he gets rid of them and wipes the evidence. Records have been falsified. I've seen literal newspapers get rewritten, Kane, within *hours* of publication." It only takes a few seconds for Zane's breathing to shallow again, and he fumbles with the door latch before stealing the keys back and unlocking the car. "We need to leave."

"What, you think Daddy's gonna erase—" I wrack my brain for what the fuck could be so scary but come up empty. "It's a good thing, right? He got rid of the evidence for us. That's less work and more playtime. Mercy's lost her phone, but hey, that's easy to replace." The wallet, not so much, but maybe she didn't have a lot in there. And who cares what happens to the frat? It's not like Sam loved being a member, anyway, from what I could tell.

I slip in front of Zane and claim the driver's seat before his anxious ass can attempt to drive. He quickly darts around the car and plops into the passenger seat, immediately starting his ritual for calming down. Bending in half and locking his hands behind his neck, he drops his head between his knees. "Drive," he groans, "fast."

That won't help him feel better. "I can drive slow—"

"*Fast*," he snaps, reaching over and clawing my thigh. "Now!"

"Okay, okay! Jeez!" I slam down the gas pedal and we speed away, blowing past a stop sign and damn near hitting a pedestrian.

"Is anyone following us?" Zane takes a quick breath before popping his head up to check. "We need to run. Pack our bags." I can see him start to calm down as he forms a plan. "Mine's already halfway packed. That's good. Really, I only need my computer. We can pick up everything else on the road—"

I slam on the breaks, and he nearly faceplants into the dash. "Kane! What the fuck!"

"We aren't running." I clench my fists around the steering wheel. "We have nothing to run from! We've killed dozens of people! That asshole from last night is no different." That last part is a lie; the asshole from last night is *way* different than anyone else I've ever killed. He fucking deserved it and worse. But for the sake of this argument, they're all the same. "I'm not leaving."

Zane huffs. "You're not leaving *her*." He glares out the window. "Great. We're risking our lives so you can *get some*." He spits out the last few words like a poison. "Samuel Wright cleans up his messes, and what exactly do you think a couple of black market dealers are to his empire?"

"We're not a threat." It's not like we sell a lot of things on the black market. A few untagged organs, some macabre paintings, that's all. "Besides, the Baranovas would protect us if we asked." If push comes to shove and I ask really nicely, they might. But our contacts within the bratva aren't exactly high up on the chain of command. Ever since Zane and I declined their invitation to join the mafia, they only contact us when their own guys are too busy to clean up their messes. We're contracted for dead body extraction on a case-by-case basis. It's not like they'll roll out the red carpet for a couple of grunts who aren't even official members. I doubt they'd spare the resources to help us at all.

Even then, it's not like we're in any real danger, right?

I try to understand Zane's panic. I *really* do. But I just don't see it. "Samuel Wright won't come after men like us. We're ants to him."

"Exactly." Zane blows out a breath. "We're *nothing*. Sam—our Sam—would be happy to have us killed and out of the picture."

"So he can have Mercy to himself." Like hell, that's gonna happen.

A beat of silence passes before Zane speaks. "I'm not so sure about that."

I roll my eyes. "Please. Sam would *love* to stash Mercy away somewhere as his secret little wifey."

"He might—but would his dad allow that? The heir to the Wright fortune, keeping a pet chained up in the basement?" Zane lifts an eyebrow. "At best, Mercy's an eyesore to her classmates. You know how important networking is in this city. Do you really think that Samuel Wright will let his son marry—breed—whatever you want to call it—someone without pedigree, money, or social status? It's easier to just—"

"Get rid of her." Anger flares in my veins. "Get rid of *us*."

We're the complication keeping Sam from ascending to his rightful place as King of the Dicks—or, well, King Jr. His father wouldn't give up the throne *that* easily.

With the right leverage, he could pry Sam's fingers from Mercy's cold, dead body and finally bring his son to heel.

Zane and I would be collateral damage.

...like Sam's fraternity. If the local chapter hasn't been disbanded, I bet all of its members are on suspension, or at the very least, paid off with fat wads of cash in their pockets. But to do that in, what, twelve hours? Daddy Wright must have people working within the college. Hell, maybe even higher up than that. I wouldn't be surprised if he's planted individuals on his payroll not just within Greek life but all major systems in the city for the sole purpose of sticking his fingers where they don't belong. Zane might call it tactical, but I call it splooging all over the map to lay claim on everything his cum touches.

What a fucking d-bag.

"I'm not running," I tell Zane, finally turning onto the road that winds around the city towards Mercy's house. "And I'm not letting Mercy get fucked over by some twat trying to control his son." I never thought I'd call Sam a rebel, but the day is full of surprises. "We need to get Mercy away from Sam." How we do that when the man is practically glued to her at the hip is... well. Surprisingly simple. Glancing at Zane, I study his face to gauge his reaction. "We have to kill him."

Zane sighs. The weight of it drags his body down until he slumps in his seat. "We can't kill him. That's like throwing gasoline on a dumpster fire. We'd never get away with it."

The prospect of prison doesn't scare me like it scares

Zane. I'm not sure if it's the criminal record part or the tough guys behind bars part that gets to him, but either way, he's never liked the idea of either of us getting locked up. It's hard for him to make friends, but his skillset would be invaluable to a prison gang. I know it would work out if we had no other option. But I don't think that's what's tying him in knots right now. "You still think we're gonna die."

I feel like I'm bashing my head against the wall. The caffeine I chugged this morning is hitting a nerve and giving me a headache. No matter what happens, Zane only sees one outcome: our deaths. It's like the Grim Reaper is following him around, hiding in his shadow, taunting him before the grand finale.

Fuck that.

"I'm not dying." I jab my finger at him. "You're not dying. Mercy's not dying." I leave Sam out, because killing him isn't off the table for me. As for Mercy... A frown tugs at my lips. Watching her life slip away is only fun if I'm the one stealing it. And even then, I—

I'm not sure if that's what I want anymore.

Shaking my head, I tune out the seed of uncertainty in the back of my mind and focus on what I *do* know. Mercy's in danger. Zane's in danger. Shit, we might all die if Zane's gloomy prediction is right. He might want to run away and live on borrowed time while the enemy hunts us down, but that's not my style. I'd rather live free, fight hard, and fuck even harder.

We might as well make the most of what time we have left.

# CHAPTER 8

## ZANE

"THIS IS A BAD IDEA." I watch as Kane hauls Mercy's duffel bag into the back of Sam's pickup truck. A dried mud puddle stuck in the grooves of the truck bed flakes onto her bag, staining the dark fabric a lighter maroon color. My nose crinkles. What an eyesore. Just like the rest of the rundown rust bucket. Why a millionaire's son is driving around this piece of junk is the question of the year.

No, actually—Kane's obsession with Mercy, *that's* the question of the goddamn year. Because we wouldn't be hauling her broken ass to a cabin retreat if Kane wasn't losing his mind. We're on Wright Senior's hit list. The last thing we should be doing is taking an expedited two-week holiday. We should be running as fast and far away from this fucked-up situation as we can get. Not *"camping out,"* as Kane cheerily puts it.

"This was your idea," he reminds me for the fifth

time, sliding his hand inside my front pocket and tugging me closer.

Yeah, *before* our world went to shit. I bite my tongue, though, because he's right. I invited Mercy to the cabin. I just didn't expect to see her so soon after last night—if at all. Truthfully, I'd hoped that she would become a thing of the past.

Maybe then she'll stop haunting me every waking hour.

"Relax. We're going off the grid. Wright won't be able to find us."

I can tell that Kane isn't fully convinced, but he's sure as hell pretending that he is. As for me, I'm trying equally as hard not to panic. Even with Kane pressing our bodies together, I can't stop fidgeting. Drumming my fingers on my thigh or against Kane's wrist, tapping my foot until I kick up gravel dust, ignoring the urge to scratch the prickly itch trailing down my arms. If it's not bad enough that a power-hungry sadist is plotting our deaths, I also have to face Mercy sooner than I thought.

Last night while I paced the apartment, I imagined what the morning might be like. I thought I'd be happy, smiling to myself as I cook eggs and bacon, sneaking glances at Kane while he dozes on the couch after his night out, the two of us waiting for a sob story text message from Mercy about how she'd been broken in mind, body, and spirit—or something like that. The details don't really matter. The most important part is that she'd be out of my hair and out of my life, once and for all, once she was no longer a shiny new toy for Kane to play with.

None of my predictions came true, though. I'm not at home making breakfast for my boyfriend. Kane is physically with me, sure, but I can tell that something's off. His mind keeps wandering to places that I can't follow. The worst part of all, however, has nothing to do with Kane and everything to do with Mercy. I thought I'd be eager to witness the carnage from last night—not the frat house, I don't give a shit about that—but the tears. The heartbreak. The ruin. I was going to drink in Mercy's misery like a fine wine, savoring every last drop. But now that we're here, I'm—

I draw in a breath and fight the bile rising to the back of my throat. I'm not elated like I thought I would be. My stomach churns as the version of Mercy in my head —a sad, broken girl peering up at me from beneath tear-soaked lashes—morphs into a raging hellcat trying to claw my eyes out. I don't know which I prefer: her anguish or her fury. Neither sounds appealing, if I'm being honest with myself. But that could be the anxiety talking. It ripples across my skin like the invisible threads of a spider's web I've been trapped in my entire life. I clench and unclench my shaking hands to fight the nervous tingles shooting through my fingers.

*Calm down*, I tell myself, repeating Kane's words in my head. Mercy doesn't know that I was involved in anything that happened last night. I was home all night. Scrolling on my phone, minding my own business, definitely *not* picturing a bullish bastard bending Mercy in half and slamming her tiny body onto his dick. No, not at all. Not even once. I also never imagined Kane burying his cock inside of her bleeding pussy, baring his fangs like a wolf claiming his mate under a full moon.

Nope, I never thought of that, either.

Clenching my eyes shut, I take a deep breath and hold it, counting down from ten. The problem isn't that Kane and Mercy are horrible together. It's that they're *not.* Polar opposites on the surface—him, golden and glowing; her, dark and dreary—but twisted inside. They both have that tortured artist thing going for them.

What do I have going for me?

I blow out a breath and try not to fall down that bottomless rabbit hole. Comparing myself to any of Kane's lovers, deceased or otherwise, drives me crazy. Lately, picturing Mercy in any capacity does the same. It doesn't matter if I'm remembering the silver glow of moonlight on her porcelain skin that night I crawled through her bedroom window or if I'm imagining a sharp-tipped blade kissing her pale thighs—if she's in my daydreams, I feel the knot inside my chest winding tighter.

Today, the coil of nerves in my body is wound unbearably tight. The lack of sleep makes things worse. I scrub my hand down my face and take another quick breath, knowing that it's too shallow but unable to take a deeper one. Fuck. Get a grip. This might be the worst day of my life, but it can easily drop even lower. I'm actually surprised that Kane hasn't lashed out about what allegedly happened to Mercy last night, *unless* whoever he killed took the brunt of his anger and saved me from it. I have a feeling that the body our little trio of misfits burned in the Morningstar crematorium is the guy that the fraternity president convinced to play Reaper for the night, and if so, that's the man that Kane killed. He hasn't told me as much, but it's the only plausible explanation for the random murder on his rap sheet.

Kane doesn't normally lash out like that because we keep to a schedule. *My* schedule. I've meticulously crafted it over the years, refining it as Kane's tastes evolve. Mercy's emergence as target forty-four, although annoying, isn't entirely unexpected. Just unfortunate. I'd hoped for a larger gap in between murders once we buried forty-three, Alejandro Carerra, but... it wouldn't have been a problem if we'd buried her with him.

Dragging a hand through my hair, I wonder how different our lives would be if Mercy hadn't stumbled upon us in the graveyard on Halloween. Where we'd be standing right this very instant. Not here, that's for sure. I can feel the protective streak radiating off of Kane as he eagerly stares at her front door, waiting for her to appear. It's reminiscent of Sam, really. The hero complex. Funny how one bad decision can fuck things up so astronomically. If Kane hadn't gone to the party and found Mercy in a compromising situation with another man, he would have never transitioned from someone craving her pain to someone saving her from it.

In the end, I guess I'm the one who fucked everything up. I meddled in their relationship. I've never done that with Kane and his targets before. Not like this. Not so directly. Not so personally.

But what she's doing to my relationship with Kane *is* personal... and unforgivable.

I won't let her take him from me.

The front door to Mercy's house creaks open, and my world narrows to the two square feet where Mercy is standing. If it weren't for the all black ensemble and the way she's tucked delicately beneath Sam's arm, I might not recognize her. The bold, black eyeliner has been washed away and replaced with puffy, pink rims around her eyes. The platform from her combat boots is missing, leaving at least an inch or two off of her normal height. Her raven hair is down but damp, clinging to her shoulders like vines inked beneath her skin. Sam releases her while another man—Mercy's father—slips her arms into a knit sweater. A scarf dangles from her neck, resembling a noose that's been cut free, while an invisible one tightens around mine.

I can't breathe.

Something sharp digs into my chest, radiating pain throughout my body. I gasp in a breath, but it does nothing to ease the hurt. This feeling is different than the burning I've grown accustomed to whenever Mercy is around. It's almost... cold. My head hurts as I try to dissect this new discomfort. What is it? What's the trigger?

And how the hell do I make it go away?

Kane's iron grip suddenly clamps onto the back of my neck. His breath is warm on my cheek as he steps in front of me and blocks Mercy from view. "Get in the car, Zane." Not giving me time to protest, he pushes me away from Sam's truck and to my car, nimbly pulling open the passenger door and pushing me down into the seat. Once the door slams shut, he presses the lock button on the key fob and walks away.

My heart sinks, joining the rest of my body in silent agony.

It's rare for Kane or I to upset each other. If anything arises, it's quickly resolved on account of how easily Kane forgives and forgets. He doesn't like to live with regrets or pent-up frustrations, so he lets shit go and moves on. But the flip-flopping between passive and active aggression is new. He's not normally one to hold a grudge, especially if whatever is wrong can be resolved.

We're in new territory, and I don't like it.

Not one bit.

# Chapter 9

## Sam

Ice cubes crack in my glass as Kane pours me a drink at the bar overlooking the lake. The room, which I assume used to be an office or library on account of the built-in shelves, has been transformed into a full-service drinking den, equipped with enough liquor and seats to support a family of alcoholics. My stomach growls, but I clink my glass against Kane's and drown my hunger in booze.

Today's been fucking weird.

I glance at the lump of fabric nestled into a window nook. Wisps of Mercy's dark hair peek out the top of the blanket, and she's kicked her boots off and left them on the floor behind her. She hasn't said a word since we stepped outside her front door. I was hoping that a change in scenery would help.

"This was a bad idea," I mutter, unstopping the bottle and pouring myself two fingers as soon as I down the first. I'd known about the cabin vacation since I'd read Mercy's text messages, but I hadn't expected her to want to go after everything she's been through. Everything *we've* been through.

I'm ready to strangle Zane every time I see him.

Kane groans. "Don't start that shit. You and Zane are killing the vibe."

"He didn't want to come either?" I scoff. Yeah, of course he didn't, the fucking coward. "What exactly did you say to him when you left last night?" All I've gotten from Kane today is a quick text saying *pack a bag* and *no phones*. Mercy didn't have a phone to relinquish since hers disappeared at the party, but I've left mine in my glovebox. There's no way in hell I'm traveling anywhere with these men without a fucking cell phone *or* a gun, but Kane didn't mention anything about firearms. I've got one stashed in the middle console of my truck and another in my bag. I convinced Mercy to carry a switchblade in her boot.

Not that it does her any good when it's out of reach on the floor.

A glimmer appears in Kane's icy blue eyes. "That's confidential."

Leaning in, I glance at the doorway to make sure Zane isn't eavesdropping. Even if I can't see him, the clang of pots and pans in the kitchen assures me that he's still cooking dinner. I meet Kane's eyes. "Nothing is confidential when it comes to Mercy's safety. What did you tell him? What did he say?" There's no excuse for what he tried to do to Mercy, but I still want to hear what reasons he came up with, no matter how pathetic.

I'll ask the psycho himself if I have to. Get him alone. Fuck him up a little. Make him talk. I clench my fist as frustration hits me in waves. It's one thing to attack Zane when his back is turned, but if Kane is here, I doubt he'll let me wander off with his brother. Hell, Zane wouldn't go anywhere with me voluntarily. Getting a punch in—much less answers—will be impossible unless Kane cooperates.

"I said enough." Kane claps a hand on my shoulder. "Relax, Wright. Have another drink. No one's holding a gun to your head." He busies himself with making a cocktail, something fruity red on ice, and brings it to Mercy. He leans over her and whispers something to get her to take it, smiling as she plants the bendy straw between her lips.

Her meds don't mix well with alcohol. She knows this. I know this. Kane, however, might not. I spin the bottles on the bar around and read the labels for what he put in her drink. The most damning ingredient is sparkling wine. I'm checking the alcohol content when Kane returns, a smirk playing on his face.

"Spying on me now?" He tuts. "I thought we were almost friends."

I say the most obvious truth that comes to mind. "You want to kill me."

Kane hums. "Don't hold it against me, Sam. There are only a few people I wouldn't kill." His gaze wanders back to Mercy as she puffs on the window and draws a spider in the condensation with her fingertip.

"What would it take?" I stare at the amber liquid in my glass so that I don't have to watch Kane go soft. It's subtle, the way his posture shifts. He does the same thing when he's near Zane, relaxing his shoulders, turning his torso in the other's direction, stealing glances whenever he isn't looking. Kane gets this goofy little smile on his face, and his eyes turn into liquid silver.

I caught him looking at Zane that way in the Morningstar's driveway before Mercy and I walked over. I had to do a double-take because I'd never seen him like that before. *Soft.* But here he is again, staring at Mercy like she's already his to admire. I swallow the lump in my throat and ask again. "What would it take, Kane? For you not to kill someone." Bargaining with a murderer feels stupid, but even if it doesn't work, at least I can say that I tried.

*I tried not to kill him*, I'll tell Mercy, begging, pleading, praying that she'll forgive me. I couldn't keep my promise to let him touch her. I couldn't stomach the thought of him pinning her to the mattress and burrowing inside her body. I couldn't watch him defile her, no matter how much she claims that she wants it.

Kane doesn't look at me, but he also doesn't answer. Lifting his drink, he downs the rest and slams the glass upside down on the bar. "Let's eat." He slips out from behind the counter and scoops Mercy into his arms, earning a giggle that claws inside my chest. I watch them leave the room before grabbing the knife from Mercy's forgotten boot and tucking it into my pocket.

This might be a cutesy vacation for the two of them, but for me, it's a battleground. Zane already made the first move when he set up that bullshit at the party. Kane, for whatever good it didn't do, allegedly made his when he talked to Zane. Now it's my turn.

I need some fucking answers.

# CHAPTER 10

## MERCY

Dinner is tense. The scrape of silverware on our plates might as well be gunfire for how often Zane tenses, making *me* jumpy. I'm not thrilled about being in the same room as him, but I was serious when I invited Sam to this little retreat. I need to look Zane in the eye and see how much he hates me. At least, that's what I told Sam.

In truth, I need to understand how he feels about me and if there's anything beyond the hatred, because we can't continue like this. We're hurting each other. All four of us. I don't think it's intentional, but sometimes our best intentions get muddied up in our feelings. With four people involved, it's no wonder that things are getting messy.

Part of me feels like I need to apologize, but I'm not sure where to start. Sam is the easiest to verbally apologize to, but it's the hardest confession to admit out loud. I know I haven't been kind to him, but it's not like he's been upset about it.

That still doesn't make it right.

I swallow another sip of water while the ice in my cocktail melts, diluting the flavor and hopefully, my desire to drink it. I had enough wine last night. I shouldn't overdo it just because I'm nervous. The men, however, don't seem to have a problem drinking to drown their feelings. All three of them have new glasses of amber liquid in front of them, the bottle left uncapped on the table within arm's reach.

In an attempt to cut the tension, I ask Zane about the pasta he prepared. "How did you make the sauce? Is it alfredo?"

He stabs a bowtie noodle with his fork. "I didn't." Glaring at his bite before putting it into his mouth, he chews slowly. "It was frozen."

"One of those one pot things," Kane clarifies as the only unbothered person in the room. "We didn't have time to go shopping on the way here."

"We normally order takeout."

Sam stares at his untouched plate before checking mine. "Trade with me," he murmurs, not waiting for my response before switching our plates and stealing my fork. Poking at his pasta, he nibbles on a bowtie before relaxing enough to hand me my fork back and let me eat. I eagerly down two forkfuls, my stomach growling loudly. I don't care if it's frozen pasta. I'm starving.

"It's not like I'm going to poison her, Sam," Zane grumbles from across the table, pulling a face as I inhale my food. "Or you."

"Forgive me if I have my doubts." Sam eats much

more slowly than me, going so far as to give me his plate once I finish mine in record time. "I half expected to find a razor blade embedded in the chicken."

Zane's smile is cold. "There's still time."

Kane rolls his eyes and throws a bite-size dinner roll at Zane's head. "Will you stop being such a dick?" The roll bounces off of Zane's skull and hits the table. "All of you suck right now. Except you, Siren; you're perfect." It's my turn to roll my eyes, but that does nothing to dampen the sparkle in Kane's eyes. "In fact—" He holds his drink in the air like he's about to make a toast. "I have an announcement." Silence fills the room as he takes his time making eye contact with each of us. Then he grins. "We need to get laid."

Sam chokes on his drink.

"I'm serious. There's so much goddamn tension in here—"

"Because we hate each other!"

"All the more reason to fuck. Everything feels better after sex." Kane winks at me. "Trust me."

My face flames while Sam ramps up his argument.

"We didn't come here to have an orgy."

"*You* might not have, but I've been looking forward to it for weeks. Even Zane's on board." Kane nudges his best friend. "Isn't that right, Zane?"

The sour look on Zane's face tells a different story. "I said that I'd think about it, not that I'd discuss it over dinner."

I stare at the way Kane's hand rests intimately on the back of Zane's neck. Something's different between them. Opening my mouth, I almost ask about it but stop myself as a more pressing question shoves its way to the forefront of my mind. Isn't an orgy... group sex? Biting my lip, I try to imagine what that would be like and inevitably picture myself lying on my back as three men hover over me. But the fantasy ends before it can begin; I don't know what comes next. My brain short-circuits as it overheats.

Grabbing my glass, I chug the rest of my water. "Um. But I haven't—" I start to sweat as three pairs of eyes lock onto me. "You know. Had sex." Cringing at my *fabulous* delivery of that line, I continue, "I don't know how to have sex with one person. How could I have sex with multiple people?"

"We could take turns—" Kane holds up his fingers as he rattles off a list of options. "One of us could watch. We could mutually masturbate. One person could kiss you while the other eats you out, like last time only better. Or if we get really freaky, we could DP you—"

Sam squeezes my knee under the table.

I know I'm going to regret this, but... "What's DP?"

"Double penetration. It's when two dicks are inside you at the same time," Kane says matter-of-factly. But the way he grins is one hundred percent devilish. "Or a toy, technically. With three men, though, we could triple penetrate if we coordinate properly. But let's not sprint to the finish line—"

"*Please*," Sam groans, "don't make up some cheesy metaphor."

"—when we haven't even warmed up yet."

Zane sighs as he pushes his full plate away. "I haven't agreed to anything. As it stands, Mercy is still a virgin." He purses his lips. "I don't have sex with virgins."

A part of me dies inside as he turns and walks away, leaving the three of us at the table in awkward silence. Deja vu hits as I recall the last time Kane said something like this at dinner—in fact, it might have been the exact same proposition. *Sharing*, I think he called it then.

That conversation went a lot smoother than this one.

Kane watches Zane leave, a tiny wrinkle of a frown playing on his lips. "I still think it's a good idea."

"That's a terrible idea," Sam hisses. "We still don't have any answers about the party! And you want to *fuck it out*, like we're in some romance movie!"

"That's called porn, Sam."

I crack a smile. "Porn can be romantic..."

Both men laser-focus on me again. "When have you watched porn?" Sam asks, his voice hushed.

I cross my arms. "I'm a virgin, Sam, not a nun."

Chuckling, Kane smirks across the table. "If you show me what you like, we can reenact your favorites."

"No, no, *no*. Not happening." Sam sighs and pinches the bridge of his nose. "I'm not here to fuck around, Kane. I'm here to keep Mercy safe from *your* psychopath brother."

Kane's smile darkens. "Careful, Sam. Call him names like that and he might gut you in your sleep."

"That's exactly my point."

This might be too much for one day. Closing my eyes, I fight a brewing headache. "I think I need to lie down." As I stand up, so does Sam. I try not to get annoyed. "I don't need an escort."

"It's a big house."

"Sam." Frowning, I grab my dinner plate. "Put this in the fridge for me. I've lost my appetite."

His frown mirrors my own as he takes my plate. "You skipped breakfast and lunch."

"I'm fine. I'll eat later." Right now, I need a break from the men. Taking a breath, I squeeze his hand for reassurance. "I promise." Before he can argue, I back out of the dining room. The short walk to my bedroom—next door to Sam's—gives me a moment to breathe. As fun as fooling around with the guys sounds, Sam's right. I don't have any concrete answers about what happened at the frat party, and until I do...

Orgies will have to wait.

Sometimes I imagine that shadows move. In the dark of my room, I see them stretching their fingers towards me, eager to touch the girl they've been haunting her entire life. It's a trick of the light—or lack thereof—and it doesn't bother me as much as it used to. I'm not scared of the dark.

It's what lurks within that frightens me.

I jolt awake at the pinprick sensation dancing across my body. Heart pounding, I sit up and stare at the unfamiliar shapes in the room: a stained glass lamp, a wicker dresser, an armchair sitting by the window. Not shadows. Not ghosts. Furniture.

The only scary thing is how none of them have any cohesion.

Voices slip beneath the closed bedroom door as two men argue about something. I listen close and quickly determine that Kane and Sam are disagreeing with each other—likely about what to do with me. In truth, I think they want the same thing, but Sam either doesn't want to admit it or Kane keeps waxing poetic about what it all means. Sex doesn't have to be complicated. Then again, what do I know?

It's not like I've ever done it before.

A wave of embarrassment washes over me as I replay what Zane said at dinner.

*I don't have sex with virgins.*

A frown tugs at my lips. It's not like I've been begging him to sleep with me. It's the opposite! I haven't come onto him once. He's the one with the problem, not me.

Besides, would having sex with me really be so bad?

I brush my fingertips across my lips, suddenly wondering if I really *am* the problem. All of these scenarios have one thing in common, and her name is Mercy Morningstar. Shit. What if I'm a bad kisser? What if Kane skipped home one day and told Zane how terrible I was at it, so now I'm the last person on earth he'll ever want to kiss... or fuck.

Groaning, I grab a pillow and hug it to my chest. My eyes and limbs are heavy, and I have to fight to stay upright. It only takes a few seconds for me to slump and close my eyes.

Maybe kissing Zane is overrated anyway. *He* could be the bad kisser or horrible lover in this scenario. Just because I'm a virgin doesn't mean that I'm the only one who's inexperienced. My nose crinkles at the infamous V-word. If I'd gotten rid of it a year ago when Sam and I were fooling around, I'd never have become Zane's—or Reaper's—target in the first place.

"I just need to get rid of it," I mumble, sighing. "Then everyone will stop obsessing over my vagina."

The hair on my arms rises as a deep chuckle emanates from the darkness. "People will always obsess over your pussy, Mercy." A shadow moves in the corner of the room. "It's made of liquid gold."

Frozen in fear, I watch as a figure materializes before my eyes. The sliver of light shining beneath the door catches on its body as it moves to the bed and kneels on the mattress. Slowly, it descends upon me, pushing me until I fall back onto the pillows. The sweet scent of bourbon fills my nose.

The shadow man—not Sam, I realize; this person is too thin—and not Kane, either; I catch his booming laughter in the distance—which only leaves...

"Zane," I breathe, pushing up onto my elbows. "What are you—"

"Shhh," he murmurs, suddenly dropping his entire body weight on top of me. One of his knees slots between mine, and he dips his head into the curve of my neck. "No more talking." A warm, wet swipe of his tongue makes me gasp. He chuckles again and nudges the wet spot with the nip of his nose. "You're annoying."

Um, what the hell?

Wedging my arm between us, I try to push him off me. "You're drunk."

"*You're* drunk," he slurs, sighing into my ear. "No, you're drugged, but you didn't eat enough for it to work right. You were supposed to pass out. Not wake up." He frowns against my neck. "Now I don't know what to doooooo."

I push harder against him, but he doesn't budge. I'm not sure if it's because I'm too weak or he's too heavy. "You drugged me?" That's impossible. Sam switched our plates at dinner. Zane couldn't have known that he'd do that. Did he drug both of us?

"Lover boy is predictable," Zane murmurs, "but you?" Lifting his hand, he taps my forehead. "I can't get inside your head. Which means—" He lifts himself onto his elbows and peers into my eyes. "You're so annoooying. With your tiny little tits—" His hand wraps around my breast and squeezes roughly. "And your stupid fucking mouth—" He lets go of my chest and grabs my chin, holding me still so that he can spit on my lips. But his touch doesn't last; he shoves his hand between us and grabs my pussy over my clothes. "And your golden—" His eyes narrow as he digs his fingers in, shoving my panties and the tips of his fingers inside of me. "*Wet* pussy."

My anger flares. I drag my mouth across his t-shirt to wipe off his spit and reach between his legs. He's hard as a rock. Grabbing onto him as best I can through his jeans, I squeeze until he hisses. "You're a dick."

"You like it?"

"No, that's—" I sigh in exasperation. "That's not what I said."

"But you *do* like it." To emphasize his point, Zane rolls his hips and grinds his erection into my palm. A soft whine catches in his throat. "I can tell because you're wet." His fingers rub my pussy lazily, like he can't be bothered to put any real effort into it. That's fine by me —I didn't ask for a late night hook up.

"I'm not wet," I snap, growing agitated. "That's vaginal discharge. It's normal."

There's a pause as Zane processes this. "So you're always wet?"

"No!" Pinching his dick, I growl. "Are you always hard?"

"Lately, yeah."

That's biologically impossible, but maybe for a drunk man, he thinks he's the exception to the rule.

"But it's not my fauuuult," Zane whines, grinding his hips again. He grunts, dropping back down to press his lips against my ear. "It's yours. And Kane's. He showed me his art. He *never* shows me until it's done, but this time, he made an exception. For me." Zane's bright smile presses into my neck. "Because he loves me."

My brain struggles to catch up. The only thing keeping Zane from grinding me into dust is the fact that he's too uncoordinated while drunk to do a good job of it. Every half-thrust slips from my palm to my thigh, and it's a struggle to keep him from notching himself between my legs. The strongest barrier to entry, however, happens to be his own hand as he absentmindedly strokes my clit through my panties.

He's also not doing a good job of that, but it's persistent enough to send tiny shocks of pleasure to my core. I bite my lip, hoping that this ends soon. If Zane passes out, I can roll him onto the floor and sleep in Sam's room tonight. But if Sam finds out that Zane drunkenly wandered into my bedroom, he'll be even more pissed than he already is. I wouldn't be surprised if he tosses me over his shoulder and drives me home after this, which is the last thing I want.

I've spent enough of my life hiding behind closed doors.

Telling Sam about this is out.

"He's so talented," Zane mumbles, continuing his monologue about Kane. I'd suspected that Zane at least had a crush on him, but the past twenty-four hours have taught me that Zane doesn't just like Kane—he loves him. "He painted you, you know. You and me and Kane and Sam—"

I inhale sharply as Zane suddenly presses a gentle kiss to the spot below my ear.

"It's really beautiful. The painting."

The sudden scrape of Zane's teeth contrasts the soft press of his lips and sends a shiver down my spine. His fist clenches around the edge of my pillow. "Which is why I fucking hate it." Dragging the pillow out from under me, he covers my face and holds it down.

Gasping, I taste cotton as he shoves the pillow harder over my face. My nose smushes. My hands, trapped between us, claw at his thighs. My eyes water. Through the fabric, I hear Zane's muffled voice.

"You're too beautiful," he growls, realigning our hips so that his cock presses against my center. He thrusts, snarling. "I can't get the picture out of my head. I knew I wanted to kill you, but now I want to kill you *and* fuck you." A bark of his laughter fills my ears as stars dance in my vision. I'm going to pass out. Zane is going to dry hump my unconscious body—maybe my *dead* body— into oblivion. My tears wet the pillowcase as I imagine Sam bursting through the door to find me exactly as he'd feared—raped and unconscious and desperately wishing she were dead.

"I'm so fucking confused," Zane mumbles, his grip slackening. "You make my head hurt, Mercy. And my—" he hiccups. "My heart."

Mustering all of my strength, I take advantage of Zane's waning resolve and *push*. He flails, dropping the pillow and wailing a high-pitched *whoa!* that would make me laugh if I wasn't so goddamn furious. My anger overpowers my panic as I snatch the pillow from him and slam it into his face. Growling, I smack him three more times with the pillow. "You—" *Smack.* "Piece—" *Smack.* "Of—" *Smack.* "Shit!" To my complete satisfaction, he sinks onto his back and takes each hit, not even lifting his hands to defend himself.

By the time I'm finished, I'm panting. Rage fuels my lizard-brain, and I'm half-tempted to straddle the bastard just so that he can feel how much *the virgin* turns him on. "You want to fuck me, Zane?" Leaning into my anger, I climb on top of him and hold the pillow to his face like he'd done to me. My heart pounds as he scrambles for purchase—not on my arms, like I expect, but on my hips.

With a muffled groan, he thrusts up into the cradle of my thighs. I cry out at the shock of heat that ignites in my core. Shit. *Shit.* I didn't think this through. My body trembles as I frantically abort mission and climb off of him.

He holds on tighter and pulls me back, jerking his head to the side to dump the pillow to the floor. The wicked twist of his lips shows his teeth as he snarls. "Don't you fucking move." A tremor courses through his body as he thrusts again, dragging the coarse denim of his jeans into the heat radiating from my pussy. "You dirty little virgin. You fucking slut. You like my cock, don't you?" Not waiting for an answer, he drags my hips over his and tosses his head back. It dangles over the edge of the bed so I can't see his face. "Fuuuuck, Mercy. Why do you feel so good? That's soooo—" He drags in a lungful of air. "*Annoying.*"

Electricity zings up my spine as the tip of his cock, straining against his jeans, nudges my clit. A cry catches in my throat. "Z-Zane, stop it." I shake my head but can't stop a tear from falling. This is so messed up on so many levels. "We can't."

He snorts, lifting his head to glare at me. "Kane would cream his pants if he saw this. Your boyfriend would, too." With a scoff, he grabs my hands and places them on his chest. "Put your hands here. Then you can lift your hips."

"I'm not—" My cheeks flush with embarrassment. "I'm not doing that!"

"Yes, you are," Zane huffs, holding my hands in place and dropping his head over the edge of the bed again. "I'm too tired. You do it. It's not that hard." His chest suddenly shakes as a bubble of drunken laughter passes his lips. "Not as hard as my dick!"

Okay, I am *so* done here.

Rolling off of him is easy while he's caught in a fit of laughter. He slides off the bed and bumps his head on the floor as he falls, mumbling an *ouch*. By the time he sits up and leans against the closet door, I'm already standing on the other side of the room. My heartbeat pounds between my legs as sticky heat gathers in my panties. I'm horny and frustrated and flustered and—

More tears gather in my eyes. Zane fucking *hurt* me, or tried to. Close enough, right? It's my turn to laugh as my adrenaline turns bitter. Storming to the other side of the room, I shove my finger in his face. "You don't get to touch me." My anger burns so hot that I have to stop myself from slapping him. He fucking deserves it, but I don't trust a drunk man with violence.

He blows out a breath and reaches for my hand.

I smack his away. "You don't get to touch me," I repeat, glaring. His stupid bulge has a dark spot on the tip, either from his cum or my desire. I tamp down the heat burning through my system and shove it into a box deep, deep down, where I can hide it forever. If I'm lucky, he won't remember anything about tonight. But just in case he does— With a snarl, I crush his dick beneath my heel. "You might not fuck virgins, Zane, but guess what?" Flipping him off, I put more weight onto his cock. "I don't fuck rapists."

The malicious grin curving on his lips falters. He wraps his fingers around my ankle, directly over the bruise another man created *when he tried to rape me.* "That's not fair. I'm not a—"

Pulling my foot free, I grab the pillow and throw in his face. "Fuck you, Zane." Not waiting for him to recover, I flee towards the door. I can't sleep here. Going to Sam means that he'll notice something is wrong and start a fight, so I can't sleep next door, either. The cabin is huge. I'll have to find somewhere else to curl up and cry.

"Mercy, wait—"

"Stay the fuck away from me."

I slam the door on my way out, hoping that it conceals the ugly sob I can't hold back anymore.

# CHAPTER 11

## KANE

PICKING my head up off the pillow is impossible. Drool clings to my cheek as I roll onto my back and stare up at the ceiling fan spinning, spinning, spinning... My stomach cramps and I quickly roll onto my side.

I'm gonna throw up.

Except the floor isn't where it's supposed to be. I reach out to grab the side of the bed and touch hardwood instead. In fact, I'm not even *in* bed. I'm on the fucking floor. My back is killing me as much as my head, and I have to swallow whatever threatens to come back up the wrong way. "Zane," I groan, dragging my gaze around the room. "What the fuck happened last night?"

My boyfriend is nowhere to be found, but Sam is passed out on a padded bench seat. He doesn't fit with such a large body; all four of his limbs dangle over the sides as he sleeps facedown on the seat. Another cursory glance around the room reveals that we're not even in a bedroom; we're at the bar overlooking the lake. Did we stay up all night? My head throbs as I try to catch the memory slipping through my fingers. Everything from last night is a blur after dinner. That blur turns into a void the later into the night I pry.

"Sam." Wetting my lips, I force myself to sit up. The room spins, and I have to shut my eyes or risk blowing chunks. Fucking hell. I went back to the fridge for Mercy's leftovers once it was clear she wasn't interested in finishing them, but clearly that was a mistake. What time was that? One? Two? The hours blur together like the half-empty bottles on the bar.

Oh. Yeah, that could be part of the problem. The alcohol.

Sam and I had waited for Zane to stop throwing a hissy fit and join us for drinks, but he never showed. Frowning, I wipe my mouth on my forearm and squint to gather my bearings. When Zane gets in one of his moods, he normally wants to brood alone, but I rarely let him. Why did that change last night? Because Sam was with me?

Or because I'm still mad at him?

Groaning, I rub my forehead. I'm not going to get any answers sitting on the floor. "Sam!" Standing takes way too much energy, but I force myself to my feet. There's no way in hell I'm crawling to Samson fucking Wright, no matter how unexpectedly chummy we are as drinking buddies. "Get the fuck up," I hiss, jabbing him with my fingertips. Jeez, even unconscious, he's ripped as fuck. The muscles on his back have a little give, but not like other guys. Damn.

It's no wonder Mercy salivates over getting him naked. Not that she's said as much, but I bet she does.

A smile curves on my lips as I think of our perfect little gloom girl. Even while on vacation, she clings to the color black like she's allergic to anything else. I wonder if she'd let me paint her in vibrant violets and radiant reds or if I'd have to tie her down to stroke a brush across her skin. A shiver of excitement runs down my spine. That's not a bad idea.

When I kick Sam's makeshift bed, he jolts awake, toppling over and hitting the floor with a grunt. "Shit," he groans, holding his head. I bet it's pounding as much as mine. "What the hell, Kane?"

At least he's using my real name now.

"Get up. Our people are missing."

"Where—" Sam holds his hand up to block the sunlight from hitting his face. "What happened last night?"

Yeah, it's fucking weird.

"Dunno," I answer honestly. "I've never passed out like that before." From the pensive expression on Sam's face, I'd guess that he hasn't, either. Swiping the closest bottle on the bar, I flip it around and dump its contents into the sink. I'm not tempting *that* devil again. "Shit must be strong."

Sam remains silent as he picks himself up. Shirtless, he rolls his shoulders back and shakes his head, scrunching his face once he realizes how much of a mistake that is. "Whatever. I'll find Mercy."

He doesn't wait for me to reply, but I do anyway. "I'll find Zane," I call out, frowning as I think of my lover all alone in a massive bed. I may not have gone to check on him last night, but he never came to check on me, either. That's like... boyfriend 101. We keep up with each other. Make sure we're safe and shit.

After drinking water straight from the tap, I clear my throat and make my way through the house. We've never been to this cabin before, and since our plans were escalated with the impending threat of Sam's dad, we couldn't stay at the one we'd actually rented for Thanksgiving week. Instead, we snuck into one whose owners have been away for a few months. It should provide enough coverage to keep us off Wright Senior's radar for a few days, at least. Maybe to get through the holiday, if we're lucky.

But what that means for me this morning is that it's easy to get turned around in a new place. The floor plan is circular for some goddamn reason, and I end up back at the bar before I round enough corners to find my way to the master bedroom. Opening the double doors, I grin at the lavish bedspread and white-curtained canopy. It's a perfect little nest for love birds like us.

The best part is that it's large enough to fit four people.

My smile freezes in place as I stare at the bed. Huge, fluffy, comfortable...

*Empty.*

No one slept here last night.

"Zane!" I call out, smacking the door frame. "Where'd you go?" A low-simmering panic creeps up my spine, all thanks to the bug Zane put in my ear about how well-equipped Samuel Wright is. If he wanted to sweep in unannounced and kidnap someone, he could. But I doubt that's his style when he wants to make a statement, and that's what Zane, Mercy, and me are to him—a direct statement to his rebellious son. Or our deaths will be.

*If* Zane's theory is right, but I'm not convinced—

A whimper reaches my ears from somewhere nearby. I hold my breath as I listen for another one, zeroing in on the source after a few missteps to the master closet and bathroom first. There's an attached suite through another set of doors, and I push my way inside without a moment's hesitation.

"Zane—" My gaze locks on a bundle of black fabric curled around itself. Dark hair covering their face. A knit blanket twisted around their legs. Sitting all alone in one of those swivel barrel chair things.

Not Zane.

Mercy.

"Siren," I whisper, carefully maneuvering around a coffee table to swoop in on her. She's unconscious but muttering in her sleep, her eyes rapidly darting back and forth behind closed eyelids. Are you supposed to wake someone from a nightmare, or does that make it worse? I puzzle over the best way to approach her when she inhales sharply, her mouth hanging open. No sound comes out, but her eyes squeeze tightly shut, and she stops breathing.

Fuck this bullshit.

"Mercy," I call out, quickly scooping her up and cradling her in my lap. The chair hasn't held her body heat, and she shivers the moment she comes into contact with my chest. Fuck. How long has she been here? All night? Why didn't she sleep in a bed? There have to be a half dozen scattered around this place. I'd made a mental note to check how many places I could enjoy her company this week, and the list was long.

Brushing my hand over her forehead, I grimace at the cold layer of sweat at her hairline. "Shhh, sweetheart. It's okay. I'm here." I don't know what she's dreaming about, but it must be bad if she won't wake up. Dark circles linger beneath her eyes, like she's had trouble sleeping for a while. It's not like I watch her twenty-four seven, but one of us has to have been paying attention while she was sleeping. Surely, *someone* knows that she gets nightmares.

Which means that someone knows the best way to wake her.

I grit my teeth as she trembles like a leaf. Is she cold? Scared? Shit. What do I do?

The only other person I've comforted is Zane, and that's not the same... or is it?

Carefully, I wrap her snugly in the blanket and haul her against my chest, brushing my fingers through her hair until she takes steadier breaths. Even then, she doesn't wake up. This is normally when Zane nervous talks himself to sleep to block out the roaring thunder shaking the windows, but there isn't a storm outside— it's inside Mercy's mind.

I swipe my thumbs over her cheeks and lean in to brush my lips over hers. A silly flare of—I don't know— something light and bubbly in my chest makes me smile. "I'll be your Prince Charming," I murmur, "just this once."

The kiss is gentle, but the explosion of sparks inside my heart isn't. I vibrate from head to toe as it over- whelms my senses, creating a buzz in my ear and a pitter- patter thump of my heart. Deepening the kiss, I swipe my tongue over Mercy's lips and hum into her mouth, craving more. Needing it like I need oxygen. This isn't healthy, whatever this is. A fuzzy feeling surges through my veins and crackles like candy, all from a single taste of her mouth.

It's not like this when I kiss Zane—that's a different kind of crescendo, starting in the marrow of my bones and building into an unbearable heat. I'm used to that with him: the slow burn that's as addictive as it is painful.

But kissing Mercy feels like... the softest shade of moonlight on a canvas, whose beauty sneaks up on you over time. It's always been pretty, but the longer you stare, the more you see its depth. A hint of lavender or a brushstroke of a royal blue. Subtle, majestic, captivating. Until all of a sudden, you've been staring at it for so long that you need more. One canvas isn't enough. You create a dozen, two dozen, *five dozen.* All with the same color palette. As excited for this painting as you were for the last. Dreaming of the composition, falling in love over and over again as you bring each one to life.

*That's* what kissing Mercy is like.

Realizing that you're falling in love.

## CHAPTER 12

## ZANE

I DON'T REMEMBER STUMBLING outside last night, but I remember jumping into the lake. Frigid water engulfed my body, numbing it to whatever the fuck Mercy's done to me. There's this... *thing* inside my chest. It prickles and stings like needles, digging into my lungs and making it difficult to breathe. I'm used to my anxiety spiking until I crash out and Kane comes to my rescue with gallons of water and handfuls of meds, but this is different. It's sharper. Impossible to grasp. Painful.

That's what she is to me.

Pain.

Whether it's my head or my heart, she knows how to fuck with it. Dancing in the dark corners of my mind, digging her talons into my tainted heart, making me miserable with every breath she takes.

As I lie on the shore in nothing but my boxers as the sun rises over the horizon, the numbness is a welcome change. Ever since she invaded my life, it's been one tumultuous feeling after another. Loathing. Desire. Agony. Confusion. Twisting my soul into knots. One second, I hate her, and the next, I don't mind what I see when I look at her. Of course, part of that could be Kane's influence. He's completely infatuated with the idea of her.

Whether or not the version in his head matches up to the real thing, I have no idea, but it's enough to make me wonder.

Would I be happier if I just... let go?

"Zane!" Even Sam's voice, faraway and unpleasant, isn't enough to rouse me. I stare up at the sky as its darkness fades away, completely overpowered by the oncoming morning. A laugh catches in my throat as, yet again, I think of her. Have I been fooled into believing Mercy is as empty as the night sky, when in reality, she's as bright as the blazing sun?

It would make sense since my world suddenly revolves around her.

Blowing out a breath, I ignore Sam as he trudges across the back lawn towards me.

"You're going to freeze out here," he huffs, hugging his arms closer to his body. Somewhere between taking shots at the bar with Kane and his descent towards the lake, he found a sweater two sizes too small. How cute. "What the hell are you doing?"

Dying.

"Existing."

Barely.

"Right," Sam murmurs, giving me the side-eye. "Do you remember what happened last night?"

All too well.

"No," I lie, wishing that he would go away. "What do you want, Sam?"

"I'm looking for Mercy." He shuffles his weight from foot to foot, appearing uncomfortable. "Have you seen her?"

"No." If I close my eyes, though, she's there. Beneath me, at first. Tears in her eyes. A flush on her cheeks. Then she's on top of me, and the flash of hatred burning through her body latches onto mine, clawing through my flesh to get to my heart. My lungs burn. "I haven't seen her."

Sam stares at me for a long moment. "You sure?"

"Positive."

His lips press tightly together. "Yeah, okay. Well if you see her, tell her to come find me. I need to talk to her."

Whatever. Not my problem. If I see Mercy—

I might finally kill her.

Lingering far longer than I like, Sam mumbles something under his breath. I don't bother answering, and then all of a sudden, he's stripping. Tossing his sweater onto my chest, he grumbles. "Put that on."

I don't think I could move my arms if I tried.

"Dammit," Sam hisses, dropping to his knees and shoving the sweater over my head. Then he finagles my limbs into the sleeves and tugs it on properly.

The warmth is uncomfortable, but it gets worse when Sam lifts me onto my feet. I shove him, or try to, but my coordination is off. I stumble and nearly crash in the mud.

Sam's right there to pick me back up. With a grunt, he tosses me over his shoulder and starts the long trek back to the house. I would fight him, but I'm too weak. Or too complacent. It's hard to care when every part of my body aches.

"Don't take this the wrong way," Sam huffs. "I'm not doing this for you. I'd rather throw you into that fucking lake and watch you drown after what you did to Mercy."

It seems that Sam's the only one with enough balls to speak the truth.

"But Mercy—" Sam shakes his head. "She has this thing for strays." Frowning, he pushes open the back patio door. "Against my better judgement, I think you're one of them."

Whatever he's saying isn't making any sense. "You think I'm like some... feral cat?"

"Yeah. More or less."

Laughing hurts. But, hey, I'm grateful for the honesty. Once we're inside the house, Sam drops me onto an armchair and rolls his shoulders once he's free from the burden of my body weight.

Crossing his arms over his chest, he glares at me. "Since we're alone... mind telling me *why* you tried to fuck my girlfriend?"

I've asked myself the same question over and over since I wandered out of Mercy's bedroom last night.

What was I doing there in the first place? How long were we locked together like two quarreling lovers? Did I imagine that she crushed my dick beneath her foot, or was she actually bold enough to threaten me? A twisted smile curves on my lips. Our little game is getting more interesting.

Kitten is learning to use her claws.

"You creepy motherfucker." Kicking my chair, Sam pushes it back against the window. "Stay the hell away from her."

"Or what?" I'm not afraid of Samson fucking Wright. His father, though... Running a hand down my face, I sigh. Nothing good is going to come out of this godforsaken cabin retreat. Being trapped in the same building as Sam is going to get us killed, no matter how optimistic Kane is about it. The no cell phone rule was my idea at salvaging the situation, but even then, I'm not convinced that it'll make that big of a difference. We're like an hour or two away from the city. If Samuel Wright wants to find us, he will.

It's only a matter of time.

A sigh passes my lips. I'm getting really tired of counting down the end of my days. They keep getting shorter and shorter, which means that my time with Kane is dwindling faster than I can keep up. I need to figure out how to save more time—

No, wait, I need to *steal it* from someone else.

"I'll trade you intel." Swallowing hard, I force the rest of that statement out of my mouth. "You tell me about your dad's investment in your future... and I'll tell you about my interest in Mercy."

Sam's forehead crinkles. "Why the hell do you care about my father?"

"I'm not dying because of your daddy issues, Sam."

If things go my way, I won't be the one dying, at all.

# CHAPTER 13

## SAM

THERE ISN'T much that I would put past my father. Zane's theory that my dad would wipe his existence off the face of the earth isn't that far-fetched. Money doesn't just open doors—it creates them, manifesting pathways that wouldn't have existed otherwise. That's how my father uses his wealth, as a tool to get what he wants.

"Destroying the frat is pointless, though."

"I don't care about your stupid fraternity," Zane snaps, pacing now that he's thawed out. The sweater I nabbed from the back of a dining room chair fits him perfectly; I bet it's his, after all, and not a random article of clothing like I'd initially thought. After I wore it for all of ten minutes, I'm shocked that he hasn't thrown it into the fireplace. I bet it still smells like my deodorant.

The cold must have addled his brain.

"You called in a favor," Zane repeats for the third time, scrubbing a hand down his face. "And your dad went overkill. That doesn't set off alarm bells for you?"

I can't confess to understanding my father's every whim. "I doubt he wanted anyone poking around about a murder his son may have been involved in, so no, not really. It makes sense to get rid of the evidence." Maybe we should have left the body there for my dad's team to handle, but it's too late for that. "It might not mean anything."

Zane swivels on his heel as he turns around to continue pacing in the opposite direction. The corner of the throw rug flips up. "Has he contacted you at all?"

"I don't know. I don't have my phone on me."

Nodding, Zane seems to accept the half-truth. "That's good. It buys us some time."

While he mutters to himself, I throw another log in the fire and make a mental note to check my phone for any more messages. I'll have to sneak out to my truck, but that's fine. I can say that I want to take a drive into town or something. If I'm alone, I could even charge it—

*No*, I reason, knowing that being alone is asking for trouble. That means that Mercy will be at Kane and Zane's, well, mercy. I'd have to take her with me, but then Kane might try to pile into the truck with us to ensure we don't drive away for good.

It's tempting, that's for sure.

Especially since I still haven't found Mercy. Stealing her away for a few hours—or a lifetime—would soothe the discomfort in my heart. I don't like the idea of my father coming after her for Kane's mistake. If he wants to *disappear* anyone, it should be Kane and Zane, not Mercy. She's innocent in all of this. But...

I hate to admit it, but Zane's right. The fraternity, the football team, my degree—they're all tying me to a life outside of my father's strict parameters. Football season is over, and I'm missing the final game to be at this lakeside cabin, so that's out. According to Zane, my fraternity is suspended. My degree, or lack thereof, doesn't matter when taking a position in Wright Industries or any of its subsidiaries. All that's keeping me from being squashed underneath my father's thumb is my own stubborn streak and the woman I'll do anything to keep away from my father's corruption.

If he could remove Mercy from the equation, my dad might think that he's won the argument against my staying away. It's not *that* far-fetched to believe.

Zane's smarter than I thought for putting that together.

Thankfully, that's as far as his conjecture goes; he doesn't know enough about my father's businesses to guess what kind of work I'd be involved with once absorbed into the Wright forces, and truth be told, neither do I. Despite sitting in on board meetings since I was ten years old, I've kept that part of my life as minimal as possible and blocked out anything unnecessary for immediate survival.

"I don't know what his plans are," I say honestly. "But I'm not interested, either way. He could offer me a mansion with a dozen wives, and I wouldn't take it." Frowning, I make sure that last part sinks in. That's not the life I want. Riches can't buy me happiness. "I don't want anything to do with my father's investments or business."

Scoffing, Zane turns a grumpy glare onto me. "I know very little about having a father, Sam, but I *do* understand power dynamics. When the time comes, your little fantasy of a normal life is over, and you'll be dragged into whatever position your dad's curated for you since birth. All of this —" He waves his hand dramatically. "Won't matter anymore." Closing the distance between us, he places his hand on my arm. "Mercy will become a ghost of your past, and so will we." Smiling wryly, he removes his hand. "The sooner you accept that, the easier this will be for everyone."

My eyebrows pinch together. "The easier what will be?"

Zane seems surprised that I ask. "The grand finale. You didn't think that Kane brought Mercy to this cabin for G-rated family fun, did you?"

No one could misinterpret Kane's intentions after his announcement at the dinner table last night. "But I thought—" Perhaps foolishly— "The game was already over." Anger and frustration surge through my veins. I grab Zane's collar and shove him against the wall. "You tried to *rape* her," I growl, slamming the back of Zane's head into the wall. The picture frames overhead clatter. "That breaks all kinds of rules. The game is fucking *over.*"

The shit-eating grin splitting across Zane's face makes any normal feelings I had for the man evaporate. "The game isn't over until someone dies," he laughs, coughing his way through the declaration. "And I didn't touch her," he counters, huffing indignantly. "So stop accusing me of something I didn't do."

"You hired someone to fuck her," I snarl, grabbing his throat, "against her will. That's fucking rape."

"Still," he wheezes, "not me. Didn't touch—"

I squeeze harder. His face turns a sickly shade of purple.

"—until last night."

*Last night?*

"You said you didn't see her!"

A sadistic smile flickers onto his stupid fucking face. "Oops."

My fist smashes his nose, and he sputters a laugh, his head bobbing as he struggles to hold it up. I hit him again, this time in the jaw, and drop him to the floor. I can't waste my time on trash like him. If he got to Mercy while Kane and I were passed out, I need to find her *now*.

Before this game actually ends.

# CHAPTER 14

## MERCY

Whenever I have a nightmare, I don't remember it when I wake up. The snippets that remain, mere flickers of the terror gripping me in my sleep, are easy to pour out into my sketchbook. I have multiple books filled with nightmarish shadows and glinting eyes watching me from the dark. These stay hidden beneath my bed, out of sight and out of mind. But maybe that's the problem—keeping them close means that they can still haunt me, even in my dreams.

This time, I dream about Zane.

The feel of his body lingers in my mind, warm and wanting and dangerous. *Tempting*, if I'm being honest with myself. Kane and Sam won't have anything to fight over if I give it up to Zane. It's not like Zane wants my virginity—if anything, I think he's repulsed by it. Our late night rendezvous was an alcohol-induced fluke.

There's no way that Zane *actually* wants to sleep with me.

But my dream self thinks that he does.

I feel myself running before the cemetery comes into view. Damp earth clings to the soles of my feet as I zig-zag through the headstones, out of breath and out of time. A full moon hangs heavy over the horizon, as vibrant orange as the monster's eyes. In my dream, Zane is coming for me.

If he catches me, he can do whatever he wants.

A wriggle of doubt snares somewhere in my mind. Those weren't the original terms of our agreement, but somehow, they feel accurate. I'm at the mercy of a man who hates me.

Another shadowy figure steps out from behind an ancient oak, his sharp fangs glowing in the moonlight. Blonde hair, glimmering blue eyes, a wicked smile. His body painted like a skeleton's, all the way from his head to his toes. Naked.

*Hard.*

I stumble backwards as Reaper advances, grinning wickedly, cock jutting out like a spear, *hungry.*

This one craves my body.

Muscled arms wrap around my waist from behind, pulling me into a hard chest. I can feel his breath on my neck as he trails his lips over my skin, groaning once he slots something long and hard against my ass.

*Won't you let me, Mercy?*

I gasp as Sam's voice plays inside my head.

*Won't you let me love you?*

Vines sprout from the earth and ensnare my legs, trapping me and Sam together. I open my mouth to scream, and Kane descends, groaning into my mouth and swallowing any sound that tries to escape. Then the cold press of steel against my throat makes me shiver. I open my eyes to find Zane holding a knife poised to cut both me and Kane at the same time, its two sides equally sharp.

*If I can't have you, no one can.*

As Kane's lips meet mine, I fall backwards into an ocean, suddenly cradled in its waves. Warmth envelops me from all sides, and Kane's voice carries on the breeze.

*Wake up.*

Gasping, I open my eyes to find Kane stroking my face, a wistful look in his eyes.

"Hey, beautiful."

"Kane. What—" Sitting up, I blink to bring our surroundings into focus. His arms are cocooning me to his body, making it difficult to move. With a huff, I settle back down and surmise that it doesn't matter where we are. It's not like anything has changed.

Three men still want me in their deadly game.

"What are you doing here?"

His thumb brushes over my bottom lip. "What are *you* doing here? Bed not comfortable?"

"More like occupied," I grumble, glaring into my lap. "Did you know that Zane drugged me at dinner? He came into my room last night to boast about it—" If you could call his drunken confessions that— "And smother me with a pillow!"

Kane's expression lifts. "He tried to *smother* you?" A smile makes him even more handsome. "That's new."

"Um, hello? He drugged me!"

"And he *still* didn't kill you." Kane laughs, light and airy and carefree. "He must really like you."

"*What?*" I gape at Kane's gleefulness. "You've got to be joking. He said that he hates me! Hates *us*," I clarify, smacking Kane's chest. "This isn't a good thing!"

"It's a great thing," Kane counters, still smiling. "There's a fine line between love and hate, Siren, and Zane is toeing that line. This is perfect."

I'm not following, but Kane doesn't elaborate. Scooping me up into his arms, he carries me out of the en-suite and into the master bathroom. "I've got a plan," he says cheerfully, setting me down on the counter. Tearing off his shirt, he tosses it to the floor and turns on the shower. "It'll be good for us to get some closure on the whole—" His gaze flicks to me. "Reaper thing."

Flashbacks from my dream make me shiver. The Reaper in my dream wasn't the one from the party, it was the one standing in front of me. "You haven't asked him about it?"

Pulling off his sweatpants, Kane is suddenly butt naked. Tanned skin stretches for miles along his torso, but so does a pale scar I've never seen before. It cuts from the right side of his ribs to belly button. He doesn't seem to notice my stare, too preoccupied with the plan forming in his mind as he tests the water temperature. "Not directly," he mumbles, avoiding my gaze. "But that's why you should."

I unwrap the blanket from my shoulders and hop

down onto the floor. "I'm not going anywhere near that asshole."

Before I can leave, Kane grabs my hand and tugs me closer to him. "What else did he say?"

Shit. I forgot how observant Kane is.

"Nothing," I lie, frowning. "He was drunk."

"Drunk people are usually honest."

I blow out a breath. "Not this one."

Lifting an eyebrow, Kane hums thoughtfully. "Well, if we want Zane to talk *without* alcohol, we have to make it so that he has no other choice." Taking both my hands in his, he leads me to the shower door. "You getting in with me, Siren?" A smirk curves on his lips. "I'd love to hear you sing."

A blush warms my cheeks. I can't get naked with Kane. He makes it seem so casual! "I don't sing for the living."

Humming again, Kane lets go of my hands to step into the shower. "Will you sing at my funeral, then?" The spray of water clings to the glass, obscuring Kane from view.

"Are you dying anytime soon?"

"Maybe," he murmurs, sounding way too depressed about it. "If I do, promise that you'll sing for me, Siren. That you'll miss me."

What a gloomy request. "Are you feeling okay?"

"Zane drugged me too. I'm washing it off. You should join me."

Rolling my eyes, I cross my arms over my chest. I can't deny that a hot shower sounds heavenly. But I'm not doing this because of Kane. I'm doing this for me. He just happens to be here. Stripping off my clothes, I stand in front of the steamed mirror. I can't see my reflection, but... maybe it's better this way.

I can pretend that night never happened.

As I open the shower door, the bathroom door follows, swinging open with a bang. I turn my head to find Sam staring wide-eyed at me, then I feel Kane's arm over my shoulder as he leans out of the shower to peek. "Sam!" he cheers, grinning. "Perfect timing. Get in."

Sam's emerald eyes are stormy. "What the hell are you doing?"

"*We're* showering," Kane answers easily, pointing between me and himself before pointing at Sam, too. "You're joining us. C'mon."

Kane drags me into the shower and holds me beneath the spray so that I can't watch Sam's reaction. Is he mad? Upset? Has he been looking for me?

"Relax," Kane murmurs, running his hands down my back. "Sam's not as scary as you think."

That remains to be seen.

The shower door opens again, and Sam crowds in with us. Broad shoulders, stubbled chin, brunette hair clinging to his forehead, he ducks his head to kiss me without warning. The warmth of his mouth matches the heat of the water, and I eagerly slide my hands up his chest.

"Are you okay?" Sam asks, sighing against my lips. "I couldn't find you, and then Zane said—"

Kane groans behind me. "Sam, your woman is naked. Stop talking."

Snapping his head up, Sam scowls. "*Why* is she naked? And with you? I don't—" He sighs. "I don't understand."

"I'll explain everything and then some," Kane vows, pulling me against his chest out of the water. "But right now, what matters is that the three of us are gonna have a little fun." Grabbing my chin, Kane tilts my head back until I can meet his eyes. "You wanna have fun, Mercy?"

I nod.

"Great. You gonna watch, Sam, or do you wanna join in?"

An illicit wave of heat radiates from my chest. All three of us together? What does that look like? I bite my lip and wonder... *what does that feel like?*

Sam meets my eyes and steps closer. "I'm not here to watch." Licking his lips, his gaze travels down my body. "You okay with that, Mercy?"

I have to stop myself from screaming *yes!* "I don't know what to do," I blurt out instead, immediately cringing. God, could I be any more lame? "But I'd like to try."

"Tell me if anything makes you uncomfortable," Sam murmurs, closing the distance between us. His hand travels up my ribcage until he cups my breast, giving it a gentle squeeze. "And we'll stop."

"We'll *try* to," Kane rumbles in my ear, "but no promises."

Desire burns deep inside my body. I can handle it.

Whatever they want to do to me, it's fine. More than fine. "I want this." Hooking my arm around Sam's neck, I pull him closer. "I want *you*."

Sam's breath catches. "Mercy..." He descends like lightning, surging into me and sending sparks throughout my entire body. Our lips collide as he pushes me into Kane's body, easily rolling my nipple between his knuckles and licking into my mouth. He groans, plucking my sensitive bud hard enough to make me squirm. Tingles of pleasure skate down my spine and pool between my thighs.

"Fuck yes," Kane rasps, grabbing my hips and grinding his erection on my ass. Water glides between our bodies, suctioning us together. "I love your ass." Grabbing my right cheek, he squeezes. "So fucking plump." Suddenly sliding down to his knees, he spreads my cheeks and groans. "Such a juicy little hole, too."

I don't have time to question what he's doing. He's already there, reaching between my legs to slide his fingers through my folds, then bringing those fingers to my butthole. Rimming it. Teasing it. Making me hot for something I thought was... I don't know, *not this*.

Sam latches onto my neck and slips his hand over my stomach, curving his fingers when he reaches my sex. "He might like your ass, but I love *this*." Pressing his fingers against my clit, he smiles when I cling to his shoulders. "You like that?"

I bury my face in his neck. "Y-yes. Please don't stop."

"Don't stop what?"

"Touching me," I gasp, trembling as he swirls his fingers around my clit.

"Touching you where?"

"There! Right there!"

Kane slips the tip of his finger inside my ass and groans. "So fucking tight. You gotta relax, sweetheart."

How can I relax when every part of my body is on fire?

Grunting, Sam dips his shoulder and slips two fingers inside my heat. "I'll get her to relax if you'd slow the fuck down."

"I need you to speed the fuck *up*," Kane growls, removing his finger. "Or I'm gonna—" Something wet and warm slides between my cheeks. "—come too soon."

"*Ah!*" I clench my eyes shut. *Holy shit*, Kane's licking my asshole, and he's not the least bit shy about it. It feels... different. I can't dwell on the sensation for too long because Sam thumbs my clit while pushing his fingers in and out of my pussy, dragging his knuckles against my walls, stroking me deeper than ever before. "Sam!"

With a groan, Sam slams his mouth over mine. "You're so fucking wet, Mercy. Dripping down my wrist." All at once, he pulls his hand free and holds it up in front of our faces. Something glistens on his fingers and strings two of them together. "Beautiful." He sucks his index finger into his mouth and groans again, his eyes sliding shut. "Delicious."

Ohmygod, why is that so hot?

"You try." Sam presses his middle finger against my lips. "Open up, baby."

I obey without hesitation, and Sam slides his middle finger into my mouth. It glides over my tongue, just as wet as promised, and I suck my desire from his knuckles. Tangy and erotic, making me burn even hotter.

He pulls his finger from my mouth with a *pop* and descends, licking into my mouth at the same moment he shoves his fingers back inside my pussy. I gush around him, hearing the wet sounds our bodies make, and whine with need.

Then Kane slips his finger into my ass.

I come in an explosion of heat, radiating from my core throughout my entire body. It sparks like embers across my skin, and I clamp down on both men's fingers, unable to stop myself.

Kane hisses, and something warm stripes my ankles.

"*Dude*," Sam huffs, "fucking aim that thing."

"Sorry," Kane chuckles, not sounding the least bit apologetic. "Guess you get to enjoy my cum, too. Lucky you." After a beat, he practically purrs. "Looks like you've still got a round in the chamber, Sam. What do you want to do with it?"

Sam bites his lip as he continues playing with my clit. "Will you swallow it for me, baby?"

I tremble as aftershocks of pleasure weaken my knees. "Yes," I answer, feeding off the raw need in his eyes.

"Good girl." Helping me down, Sam lowers me onto Kane's awaiting lap.

Grinning, Kane eagerly pulls my hair back and bands

his arm around my waist. "So fucking hot—" My pussy slides over Kane's dick, and he curses under his breath.

Stroking his cock in front of my face, Sam glares at Kane. "Put it in, and I kill you."

"Why, because it's *yours*?" Snickering, Kane nibbles on my earlobe. "Tell him that he doesn't own your pussy, Siren."

"Well—" Staring up at Sam, I grab the base of his cock and tease the tip with my tongue. Precum leaks onto my lips, and I lick it clean. It's saltier than I imagined. "He does."

With a slow thrust, Sam slides his cock into my mouth. "That's right," he groans, sliding his fingers into my hair. "Your pussy is *mine*. Your mouth is *mine*." Guiding me over his length, he buries himself as deep as he can and hits the back of my throat. His cock throbs and he moans as I suck, eager to please him, eager for his—

Hot liquid shoots into my mouth as he comes, each pulse of his cock sending another wave. I'm not ready, not even sure how to be ready, so I swallow without rhythm, struggling around the swollen appendage in my mouth. When he finally pulls his dick free, I gasp for air.

Kane's cock presses against my pussy. "Are you sure about that?" His teeth scrape against my cheek as he grins. "Because her pussy feels like it's mine, too." He rolls his hips, dragging his length through my slick folds, and laughs wickedly as I tremble in his arms. "See? She likes my cock just as much as yours."

I can't protest without it sounding fake, because

that's what it would be—a lie. I shake my head, though, and try to pull myself free. "We made an agreement—"

The tip of Kane's cock presses against my clit. "I never heard about it." Grabbing my hips, he thrusts, dragging the ridge of his cockhead over my throbbing clit. "Guess that means it doesn't apply to me."

Pleasure zings through my clit, making me cry out. "Kane!"

He groans. "I love my name on your lips. Say it again."

"No way—" Grabbing onto Sam's forearms, I pull myself up onto my knees. "Sam, help me up—" And get smacked with his dick. It presses against my cheek, just as hard as it was when it was in my mouth.

From the pained expression on Sam's face, I can tell that he's conflicted about it.

Kane barks a laugh. "I knew you were a freak, Sam. You're just as into this as I am. Let me fuck her first, and I'll even share her pussy with you sometime. We can both fit."

I sputter in disbelief. "What? That's impossible!"

"It's not," Sam breathes, staring past me to look at Kane.

Ohmygod. "You're both insane!"

"Insanely horny," Kane chuckles, smacking my ass. "From the look of Sam's cock, anyway."

"Shut up," Sam grinds out through clenched teeth. He finally pulls me off the floor and away from Kane's eager dick. "I'm fucking her first, so don't try it."

While Sam and I step out of the shower without even

having washed ourselves, Kane smacks the wet tile floor. "C'mon, why be shy about it? We can do it right here. There's plenty of room. You go first, and then I'll follow-up. She'll be dripping down her thighs within the hour."

I gape at his grinning face while Sam wraps me in a fluffy towel. "I'm not losing my virginity in the shower!"

"There are plenty of worse places." Kane picks himself up off the floor and grabs a bottle of body wash. I guess he was serious about taking a shower. "Look, all I'm saying is, we don't need to keep dancing around it. We're going to have sex." He meets my eyes, then Sam's. "All of us. So what's the hold up?"

Sam gently towel dries my hair. "Your boyfriend," he growls, remaining gentle with me despite the bite in his tone, "is a fucking problem."

Kane grunts as he lathers up his chest and arms. "He's misunderstood."

"*Seriously?*"

"Yeah, seriously." Turning around, he wets his hair. "We just need to get him to open up a little. He's stubborn, so we'll have to convince him."

"Convince him, how?" I ask. "I don't want to get him drunk."

"Not like that," Kane assures me. "But it's gonna take all three of us to make this work. I need your word that you won't hurt him." For this, Kane makes eye contact with Sam. "Especially yours, Wright. If you do anything behind my back, I'll strangle you. Slowly."

Holding Sam's hand, I lace our fingers together. "He won't," I promise for him. "We just want answers."

For starters, anyway. I can't speak to what comes after.

"Fine," Sam grumbles, squeezing my hand. "What is this master plan of yours?"

Kane turns off the water and faces us, his body glistening as he grins. "We tie him up. Then *she*—" he nods towards me— "gets our answers. He'll dodge my questions all day, but Mercy?" Whistling, he steps closer. Water drips down his body and pools at his feet. "She does something to him. Makes him vulnerable, or some shit. That's what we need if we're going to get through to him."

"Otherwise, we die." Sam scowls deeply. "I don't like it."

"You don't have to like it. You just have to go through with it."

I look to Kane, then to Sam. "Okay. I'll do it." I don't like the idea of waltzing up to Zane for anything right now, but maybe that's the point. To get to the other side of my discomfort, I have to blast through it. I can't sneak around it or pretend that he doesn't exist.

I have to confront our demons—both his and mine —head-on.

# Chapter 15

## Kane

Spending an entire day pretending that everything is normal isn't my fucking jam. It royally sucks. Whoever decided that lying made a person stronger was an idiot, because I feel like I'm about to jump out of my skin.

It doesn't help that Zane knows something is up.

"You're avoiding me," he says out of the blue, flicking his gaze up from the ice pack in my hand.

I place the pack over his nose as gently as possible. "I'm not." Sam got a few hits in while I was waking Mercy from her nightmare, the fucking prick. Yeah, Zane isn't faultless, but we're learning to use our words around here, not our fists. *Allegedly*, anyway. The learning curve is pretty steep. "Why did he punch you?"

A rare smile makes Zane wince. "I taunted him. Told him that I'd touched Mercy."

I press the ice pack down a little harder. Mercy left that tiny detail out of her report about last night. "Did you?"

Zane blows out a breath. "Hard to say. I think I tried to."

"You don't remember?"

"I was wasted, Kane. I'm trying to forget."

"Think harder."

Pulling my hand away from his face, Zane frowns. "Why do you care? Isn't this what you've been talking about? *Sharing*?"

Technically, yes, but... "I wish you would have told me that you were interested."

His answer is immediate. "I'm not."

Yeah, okay. Rather than press the issue, I move on. "They're gonna go grab lunch. Groceries and shit. So we have the house to ourselves if you wanna..." I brush my knuckles down his arm. "Hang out."

"You're letting them leave?" Zane narrows his eyes at me. "Sam's gonna run away with her."

"Shouldn't bother you," I murmur. "You've wanted her gone since day one." I run a hand through my hair and drop the ice pack onto the kitchen table. "But they'll be back." With a grin, I punch Zane's arm. "I begged her to get me orange chicken."

Along with rope, zip ties, and whatever else they can get their hands on at the one-stop shop next to the Chinese restaurant. There aren't a lot of stores this far up the mountain, but they'll manage, and then they'll come skipping right back. After that taste of how good things can be for us when we work together, neither of them will be able to resist the possibility of more.

I just need to get Zane in on it, too. He's close. Closer

than I thought, if he's drunkenly visiting her in the middle of the night. Sure, part of that could be murderous intent, but it'll make everything that much hotter between them.

I'm almost jealous. She's like putty in my hands, but in Zane's—

She'll fucking melt.

Drugging Zane doesn't feel right, but he started it. Crush up a few sleeping pills, and it's surprisingly effective. Between the two of us, we go through half the bottle in the cabinet.

"He should be out for a few hours?" I turn the bottle over in my hand to check the label. "Maybe?" I don't actually know how this shit works, but if he can slip pills into Mercy's pasta—that Sam and I happened to chow down on after the fact—I can put a few in his wonton soup. Tit for tat. He shouldn't be too mad.

It's the bondage that's gonna piss him off.

"Okay," I breathe, carefully setting my boyfriend down in an armchair we moved into the master bedroom. "Hand me the rope." Once I'm satisfied with my knot work, I brush his hair off his forehead and press a kiss there. Even unconscious, he's really fucking pretty.

The next part of my plan is harder to pull off. "Sam." Curling my finger, I beckon him closer. "Come here."

As expected, he hesitates. But he's moving slower than usual on account of the sleeping pills I slipped into his lo mein. Soup was easy—noodles were harder. When he stumbles, I throw an uppercut that hits him square in the jaw. Pain radiates down my arm, and I shake it out. "Damn, you've got a thick skull."

"Kane!" Mercy pushes between us. "What the hell are you doing?"

"Payback, sweetheart." The concern on her face is so adorable. "Don't worry, I'm just gonna tie him up. He'll be fine."

"We're not interrogating Sam!"

Sidestepping around Mercy, I hum in agreement. "We're not, but I don't want him getting any ideas while Zane can't fight back." I swipe the knife that Sam not-so-discreetly keeps in his pocket and toss it to Mercy. "Hold onto that for me."

Tying Sam up is easier after I get a few more hits in and he staggers to the ground. I wrap the canopy curtains hanging over the bed around his wrists and use a few zip ties to secure them to the headboard. It's not great work, but it's good enough. Slapping Sam's cheek, I grin.

This is gonna be fun.

My blood pumps hot through my veins as my plan comes to fruition before my eyes. Everything falls into place perfectly, and I have to stifle a groan at how goddamn exhilarating it feels. Is this why Zane's always planning shit? Because he gets off on it? I might understand the appeal if this electrifying thrill is his normal. I feel one thousand percent alive... and we're just getting started.

Now that Sam's fully awake and aware, however, he's aggravated to hell. "I will *kill* you," Sam hisses, flexing his muscles as he pulls at the restraints I lovingly tied around his wrists, "if she gets hurt." The curtains on the bed wouldn't hold him if I hadn't double-looped them and added a few zip ties to the mix, but it's sturdy enough for at least an hour. Plenty of time for Mercy to get every tantalizing question out of her system.

Still. My palms sweat as I test Zane's binds for a third time and avoid eye contact. I'm breaking his trust to ensure we get answers. She's the only one who can interrogate him the way I can't. It's silly, in a way. I've killed dozens of people—lovers, friends, genuinely *nice* people—and the one man I need to come clean is the one I don't trust myself to touch.

I'd never forgive myself if I hurt him.

Letting Mercy handle the tough questions is selfish, but if I look Zane in the eyes and he lies to my face, I don't know how I'll react. There's only so much I can forgive, and we're toeing a line that I don't want to cross. Mercy shouldn't have that kind of hold on my heart, but... here we are.

In the middle of this fucking mess.

I debate standing nearby while Mercy questions Zane, but in the end, I can't stomach the betrayal. I claim the big, empty space on the bed beside Sam. He glances over at me with disgust before turning his attention back to the other side of the room. The four of us are silent as Mercy decides what she wants to do. The knife I stole from Sam hangs limply from her fingertips. I'm not so sure she's going to go through with the interrogation. I should walk over there and encourage her, whisper promises in her ear about how everything is going to be okay and no one will be mad at her no matter what she says or does—not even Sam, despite how badly he's trembling. Jesus, the whole bed is shaking.

Clearing my throat, I extend a flimsy olive branch. "You okay?"

Sam's muscles tense, and the bed creaks as he pulls at his bindings. "You can't seriously be asking me that." He laughs, a short bark of a sound that makes Mercy jump. Quieting down, he watches closely as she takes a small, tentative step towards Zane.

He can't touch her, but she can touch him. It's perfect for bridging the divide between them. Zane may not realize it, but he craves physical intimacy like a cat, feigning independence while secretly envious of the golden retriever that gets all the attention.

Cautiously, she brushes the back of her knuckles against the swollen flesh over his jaw. "Did Sam do this?"

Zane doesn't reply, glaring a hole into the floor so that he doesn't have to look at her *or* at me. I know that he's fuming about being tied up and defenseless, but if I asked him directly about what happened the other night, I know he would lie. If not outright, then by omission. Or, he'd distract me with his body the same way I used to keep my targets from asking too many questions about me. It's an S-class move for manipulative bastards, but that's what Zane is.

The most manipulative bastard I know.

He doesn't seem like it when you first look at him. Quiet. Pretty. Cautious. To outsiders, he appears weak-bodied and meek, but to me, he's the strongest person in the world. He's the backbone of our entire illegal operation, keeping me in line while somehow sane and happy at the same time.

I don't think I've thanked him for all the years he's given me.

Sam exhales slowly and stops trying to break free. He taps his heel against the bedspread, antsy like Zane has been all day.

"It must be frustrating," I mutter, taking a deep breath. "Watching your girl fall for someone else."

His foot stops moving. "She's not falling for anyone."

We watch in silence as she links her arms around the back of Zane's neck and hooks her thighs over his, straddling him like a lover.

"Does that look like a woman resisting her heart?" Shaking my head, I can't stop a smile from curving on my lips. "She might not love him, but she feels for him in a way that you and I can't understand. I see him as my other half, and you—"

Sam's jaw clenches.

"You can't see past your possession kink to consider how anyone else feels. Not even her." I draw in a breath as the woman in question nuzzles Zane's cheek, likely whispering something that Sam and I are too far away to hear. "But there are other people involved in this. Me. You. Zane. We're like this..." I struggle to find the right analogy and fall silent.

"Mercy's like the night sky."

For once, I agree with Sam.

He draws a steady breath and exhales slowly. "She glitters, you know? In all that darkness, she glows with her own light. Even when you can't see her. Even when no one is paying attention. She doesn't do it for anyone else. She just... exists in her own universe."

Mercy embraces the man I love, enveloping him in a glow so soft that I'm suddenly speechless. A flicker of warmth inside my chest quickly turns into a flame, growing stronger with each beat of my heart. She may have been alone in the past, but that's not what I'm seeing now. The woman in front of me is expanding her universe the only way she knows how: by following her heart.

"Until she decides to let one of us in," I murmur, knowing that Sam can hear me.

"Yeah." Sam's voice catches. "Until she lets us in."

## SAM

Every muscle in my body winds tight as I watch Mercy climb into Zane's lap. He's tied up, so he can't touch her, but *she's* touching *him.* The last person on earth she should want to be around.

Why? Why does she do this to herself?

I've watched her take in strays from the side of the road. A bird with a broken wing. A dog whose head won't stop shaking. Feral cats who hiss when you get too close. She feeds them and brings treats and medicine and attempts to get them tagged as strays if she can't bring them home with her.

"It's not their fault," she told me once. "They're victims of a broken system." She calls it injustice while others call it survival of the fittest.

I see that same compassionate streak in her as she talks to Zane. I can't hear what they're saying, but I can imagine how she's trying to soothe him like she would a wounded animal. Coaxing them out of hiding. Treating their wounds. Making sure they feel safe and loved.

Zane has Kane for that. He doesn't need Mercy.

Still, she latches on. I don't think she can't help herself. When she sees someone in pain, her natural instinct is to identify the source and stop the bleeding. It's why she's so good with her family's business; their clients flock to her like doves whose wings need mending, and while Mercy's tending to them, she smoothes out their feathers and reminds them how beautiful they are, no matter the darkness dragging them down. Grief is natural. It ebbs and flows like the tide, receding one moment to return in full force the next.

That's what Vinicius Morningstar told me, anyway, at my first group counseling session. He hugged me without asking, breaking down a wall I hadn't known I'd built.

Mercy gets her bleeding heart from her father.

Kane drums his fingertips against his thigh, watching Zane and Mercy just as intently as I am. "You know," he says slowly, "I think they could be good together."

"You'd say that no matter what." Sighing, I roll my neck to relieve some of the tension. All this stress is killing me. "Besides, you don't know if he even wants that." Zane doesn't seem like the sharing type. Every vibe I've gotten from him has been dark and violent. He'd probably slit his own throat before letting Kane throw him around like a piece of meat.

Lifting an eyebrow, Kane turns his attention to me. "And you do?"

"I know about love." My eyes narrow as I try to get a better look at the unorthodox couple across the room. "It can make you do things you swore you never would."

"Speaking from experience?"

"Fuck off." Kane wasn't able to tie my left ankle down since it's near the middle of the bed, so I kick his leg. "You changed the plan without consulting me. We were supposed to tie *him* up, not me." I flex my arms and pull my bindings, but it's no use. Whatever he used to tie me up is stronger than I am.

I wiggle my jaw to test its movement. The only reason Kane could tie me up in the first place is because he hit me without warning. More than once. "That was a cheap shot."

Kane shrugs. "You punched him first. It's only fair that you got punched back."

"You hit me six times!"

"Whining about how badly I beat you, Sam? I never took you for a sore loser." He clicks his tongue. "What does Mercy see in you?"

A shard of ice digs into my heart. He's right, in a way. If I can't even win in a fight against Kane, what good am I? How can I protect Mercy if it's this easy to subdue me? Clenching my eyes shut, I swallow a groan and shudder as it settles in the pit of my stomach. I'm weaker than I thought. Pathetic. Useless.

My father's voice echoes in my head as he hurls those same exact insults at me, reminding me just how little he thinks of me as a son. But none of that matters so long as he stays the fuck out of my life. I don't need his approval.

I only need Mercy's.

But she's on the other side of the world right now, coaxing a stray to let down his guard and let her into his heart. Why, I'll never understand. It's not like she can save everyone. Trying is pointless, especially when we're talking about someone as broken as Zane. She shouldn't waste a second of her time or energy that she could be giving to me instead.

No matter how much love she pours into that man, he'll never love her back.

# CHAPTER 16

## ZANE

THE HEAT of Mercy's body is overwhelming. My thighs twitch as she settles deeper into my lap, making herself right at home. "What are you doing?" I hiss, clenching my fists uselessly. I've tried breaking out, but Kane zipped me in tight and left zero room for me to slip my wrists free. Of all the fucked up things he's done, this has to be the worst. The good news, if you can call it that, is that Kane might be able to pull the truth out of me, but Mercy stands no chance.

Not even when she wiggles in my lap like that.

"Stop it." My voice snaps, making her flinch. I close my eyes and breathe through my nose, determined to keep her out of my head. "Get the hell off me."

"No." Her voice is soft as satin, and her skin—I can't feel it, but I can see it, and that's damning enough. The scarf she wore this afternoon has disappeared, along with the sweater and long sleeves. There are bruises covering her body everywhere I look. Each one burns like a brand, searing into my mind. A handprint on her arm. Fingerprints dotting her neck. A hickey just above her collarbone. I keep my eyes closed, but it doesn't matter. It's too late to unsee them. The moment she walked into the room, I realized that I was doomed to suffer for my transgressions.

Those marks aren't love bites and bruises. They were made with hate.

Hate that *I* put into the world.

"Look at me," Mercy whispers, cupping my cheek.

"No," I parrot back, nearly laughing at how ridiculous this is. *God*, if I'd known what Kane was planning, I would have never come to this godforsaken cabin. A *vacation*, he'd said. Something fun and stress free. Like anything involving Mercy is stress free.

The desire to kill her and end my suffering wars with the trembling of my heart as she brushes her knuckles over the bruise forming around my eye, courtesy of her guard dog baring his fangs. He thinks that I'm encroaching on his territory—or he knows about the video I sent to his fraternity president—or both. Either way, I don't blame him for punching me. I'd do the same —or worse—if he pulled the same stunt on Kane.

Revenge is always sweeter than the initial attack.

Even with my eyes closed, I can sense the knife in Mercy's left hand. She's barely holding onto it, like she's afraid of its power. But if she were smart, she'd hold it to my throat and take revenge for every wicked thing I've done to her. Slice right through my carotid and bathe in my blood. I don't think that's Mercy's style, though.

A pity.

If I'd had a knife last night, I could have ended things. Sadly, hindsight is twenty-twenty, and I wasn't exactly sober enough to come up with a plan. I acted on instinct, and look where it's gotten me.

Between her thighs *again*.

Mercy wiggles her hips, applying pressure to my groin. Heat builds between us, and thoughts of death quickly fly out the window. I choke on my next breath. "Stop. It," I grind out, clenching my teeth. I don't want to feel this way, like every cell in my body is boiling. I swallow through the discomfort and finally open my eyes to glare at her for being such a—

My breath hitches as I tumble into endless amber fields, suddenly lost in the fathomless depths of her eyes. *What*— A choked sound catches in my throat. *What is she doing?*

So close.

She's so goddamn close to me.

Her voice echoes in my head, repeating what she said last night.

*Stay the fuck away from me.*

Oh, how the tables have turned.

Look who can't stay away now.

Gently cupping my cheek, Mercy removes what little distance remains between us. "Why did you do it?" she whispers, brushing the tip of her nose against mine. Her breath is soft and sweet as I breathe in, needing oxygen but tasting her instead.

Speaking pulls at my vocal cords, but I manage to rasp a response. "You'll have to be more specific, Kitten."

She hesitates for only a moment as she weaves her fingers into the hair at the nape of my neck. "Why did you try to rape me?"

Dread coils in my gut like a serpent. "I didn't."

"You did." She yanks my head back until my throat burns. "Even if it wasn't you with your dick out, you're the mastermind. You—" Her nails scrape my scalp. "Fucking—" Saliva flecks onto my face. "Coward."

I stare into Mercy's eyes, unable to look away as her anger crackles like golden lightning. This is what I was afraid of. Her magnetism. It latches on and pulls me in deeper despite the risk. Despite the pain. Kane's already addicted to her poison, and if I'm not careful, I'll bleed to death alongside him.

"Tell me why you did it."

I grind my teeth and wait for this nightmare to end. This is worse than what happened last night. At least then, I had the excuse of alcohol. Now, there is no barrier between my brain and my body, and it's reacting to her touch in ways that it shouldn't.

She frowns and digs her hips in. "Zane."

Warmth pools in my groin. I wish she would stop saying my name.

"*Zane.* Tell me."

Her body molds to mine on a sharp exhale that might as well be a moan for the shock it sends through my system. Electrified, I tremble beneath her as she purrs in my ear and pretends that this is what she wants. *Me.* I'm the last person on earth that she should be getting close to. Sitting in my lap must be some kind of game to her. A twisted tactic to make me reveal my secrets. I'm sure that on the inside, she must be revolted by me. As sick to her stomach as I am. My gaze latches onto a dark bruise on the side of her neck; a hickey, I think, and bile rises to the back of my throat.

Did Kane put it there, or was it Sam? Does it even matter which one's at fault anymore?

A voice screams inside my head. *Why do I care?*

I don't know. I don't know! Tearing my gaze away from her, I stare blankly over her shoulder as she makes herself comfortable, pressing her tits into my chest and damn near melting in my lap. On the inside, I'm burning alive.

"Go away, Mercy," I whisper. My body quivers like it recognizes that this is it: the end. She's barely touched me, and I feel like I'm dying—tearing apart at the seams so that she can take a peek at what's inside. If any one of us should be dubbed cruel, it's her. She toys with all three of us like we're nothing but playthings for her entertainment.

To be fair, I guess we toyed with her first.

Wincing, I can't stop the truth from tumbling out. "I'm not good for you." My breath hitches on the word *I.* Surely, I meant *we.* We're not good for her. Kane or me or Sam. We pretend to have her best interests at heart, but the reality is that every one of us is selfish. It doesn't matter who the bottle lands on when Mercy spins it—

her only options are men who can't wait to sink their teeth into her.

I draw in a ragged breath as a harsh tremor courses through my body. This entire time, I've thought that I'm better than Sam or Kane for giving into their baser desires. But... maybe I'm just like them, after all. That's why she should run. I'm not good for her, and she's not good for me.

She entices every one of my demons to come out and play.

Mercy falls silent for a single, blissful moment. If my arms were free, I'd snap them closed and catch her, the two of us tumbling to the floor and knocking our bones together, breathless and free to do whatever we want with the other.

My fingers itch for the knife.

One deep cut, and I'd break free from her bonds.

I could move out of the city and pretend that none of this ever happened. In a matter of weeks, I'd forget all about Mercy Morningstar and her ethereal beauty, haunting gaze, and broken heart. If we had to, Kane and I could run forever to be free from her memory. I'd do it for him. I'd do *anything* for him.

But that's precisely the problem. He's the reason we're trapped in Mercy's web, each of us dying for a taste of her ruby red lips.

Right?

The lines of blame criss-cross in my mind as Kane comes into focus across the room. It's his fault that we're in this mess to begin with. Then it's mine. Or it's Sam's.

I've spent so long blaming Mercy that even that doesn't feel right anymore, with her weight on my lap and her breath in my lungs. The poison of her lips hovering so close to mine, making me see things. Feel things. Fuck.

My vision blurs as my frustration mounts. Maybe we're all a little fucked up, and this is our punishment—circling the drain together as we fall to pieces one agonizing rotation at a time.

Mercy's delicate eyebrows furrow. "Okay, so you're not good for me. What else?"

Exasperated, I toss my head back and laugh. A twisted torrent of emotions swirl in my chest, each one darker than the last. Self-loathing clings to me like a second skin. "What do you want me to say?" Baring my teeth, I feel that hatred sink its fangs into the walls of my heart and rip it open. "That I hate myself? That I hate *you*?"

"I don't believe you." Mercy slides her palm between us and presses it flat against my chest, directly over my heart. It trills beneath her touch, aching and raw.

Kane never does this to me. He doesn't tear me apart to figure out why I do what I do, and I'd never dream of doing that to him, either. We work because we accept each other as we are, no questions asked. No questions *needed*. I love him exactly as he is. Why can't Mercy leave me alone if she doesn't like what she sees? If she's digging into my psyche for a redeeming quality, she's not going to find one.

"I think you're scared."

I lash out the only way I can: with words. "And I

think you're a dumb bitch." Even if it isn't true, she flinches like I've slapped her, but I'm too wound up to feel bad about it. I keep going. "You still wanna diagnose me? Try to fix me?" I scoff, thinking she'll finally get the fuck off of me, but she recovers and digs the tips of her fingers into my muscles. It hurts. Everything hurts when she's this close to me. "Stop touching me."

She blows out a breath. "Tell me the truth and I will." With a shake of her head, she flicks the thick curtain of her hair over her shoulder and sends a wave of lavender my way.

I choke on the scent as the memory of her sleeping like the dead flashes into my mind. I should have killed her that night in her bedroom. So many missed opportunities! I'd been tempted but too scared of pissing Kane off to go through with it.

"None of this would be happening if you'd just disappear." Meeting her gaze, I smile coldly up at her. The siren that lured the love of my life away from me. The woman haunting every dark corner of my life. "Every time I see you, I get this feeling in my chest." Pulling at my restraints, I hiss at the flare of pain as the ropes dig into my skin. "Kane won't let you go."

If there was ever any doubt, there isn't anymore.

We're going to die because of how much Kane wants her. Samuel Wright will kill us the moment he decides to reclaim his son, and I'll be tossed into a grave with both my lover and my ruin, forever stuck in the middle of their tragic love affair. "He chose *you*," I gasp, desperately trying to keep a sob at bay. "He chose you over me."

Fuck, it hurts even more to say it out loud.

"That's fucking stupid." Kane's face, red with rage, suddenly appears over Mercy's shoulder. "You went after Mercy because you threw a goddamn tantrum? Because you can't fucking share?" He runs his fingers through his honey hair and tugs on the ends. "I told you already. I love you. Mercy is never going to change that."

"She already has! You—" I blink away tears. A flush rises to my cheeks. Anger and embarrassment and *so much fear* make it hard to breathe. My breathing shallows, my pulse skyrockets, and my vision blurs. I can't fucking do this. I can't be here with them. But I can't leave Kane, either, or he'll die. Samuel will break down the door and hold a gun to Kane's head—

"Zane!" Mercy latches onto me and holds on impossibly tight. "You're hyperventilating."

From somewhere far away, Kane confirms that I'm having a panic attack. He grabs my hands and squeezes. "Get up, Mercy. I'm cutting him loose."

She ignores Kane and holds onto me even tighter. "I'm not letting go." Her cheek presses against mine. "You hear me, Zane? I'm not letting you do this. You're not allowed to self-destruct just because life doesn't go as planned."

"Fuck—" I hiss through clenched teeth—"you!" I can't breathe. I can't *fucking* breathe. What the hell does she know about anything? My life is far from perfect, but thanks to my tireless efforts over the years, I've managed. *We've* managed. Ever since Kane got out of juvie and we aged out of foster care, I've worked my ass off to keep us under the radar and out of trouble. That year apart was the worst year of my life. I sure as shit didn't plan on spiraling while he was away. Dropping out of high school wasn't planned, either, but we earned our GEDs and made it work. Murdering people for fun—that wasn't exactly on my bingo card, but do you see me crying about it? *No*, I roll with whatever punches Kane throws, because he's it for me. My past, present, and future. I don't need anyone else to survive. Especially not some meddling, sad-eyed angel of darkness who makes me feel so—

*So fucking unsure.*

I clench my eyes shut, but I can't block her out. A shiver of temptation threatens to unravel everything I've worked so hard to maintain. I shouldn't *want* anything else, because I don't *need* anything else. But the depths of my soul disagree. I quiver beneath Mercy's touch—all at once soothing and suffocating—and want to scream. I bite down on her shoulder and do just that, pouring my frustration into her bloodstream. The copper tang of her blood fills my mouth as I break the skin, but I don't let go. I sink my teeth in deeper, wanting her to feel my pain. Needing to let some of it go—to share it with whoever the fuck I can. Otherwise, I'll drown. I'll sink to the bottom of the ocean where Kane's light can't reach. He'll forget about the anchor that's been holding him down all these years and fly so high that he'll catch fire and burn alive, laughing as the flesh melts from his bones and he forgets how much I need him to survive.

Life isn't worth it if I have to walk alone.

Mercy's voice floats through the murky waters of my mind. "When my brother was first admitted to the hospital—" Her voice catches. "I fought the people who were trying to help him, because I'd already lost my mom, you know? I didn't want to lose him too. I was scared." She runs her fingers through my hair, soothing me as best she knows how. "So that feeling you have—the one that tells you to fight for Kane? It's okay. I understand what that's like."

A cruel bitterness creeps up my spine. I unlatch my teeth from her shoulder and lick the blood from my lips. What's the point in telling me any of that?

Mercy's smile is strained. "Zane, I—I forgive you."

Dark laughter crackles inside my chest. "You stupid girl. You stupid *fucking* whore." I can't help but snarl, spitting flecks of bloody saliva onto her skin. "I don't want your forgiveness!" I fight my bindings, not caring how badly it hurts. Mercy weighs me down enough to keep the chair from toppling over, but I crave the crash, knowing that I'll take her down with me. I don't deserve her compassion. I don't want her understanding. I want her pain and her fury and her anguish. That's what I've been waiting for. The punishment. All of my selfishness is bound to catch up with me, so why not now?

My eyes latch onto the darkness in Kane's gaze. "If you want to fuck her—" Bitterness seeps out of my pores as I start to sweat. "—go right ahead!"

Maybe *that's* the punishment I deserve. My entire world collapsing.

There's a roar from the other side of the room.

"*Don't you touch her!*" The four poster bed creaks as Sam struggles to free himself.

Laughing, I lean back far enough to stare into Mercy's eyes next. They're blown wide, the shock freezing her in place. "What's wrong, Kitten? Isn't that what you've wanted?" I lick my lips and swallow her blood on my tongue. "Kane's fat cock splitting you open?" Another laugh spills free, cracking the chambers of my heart apart. "I hope you choke, you fucking bitch."

A flash of pain, sharp and hot, hits me like lightning. My head whips to the side as Mercy slaps me. One of her fingernails cuts my cheek, and the sting makes me laugh even harder. That's right. Hate me. Make me bleed. Let me taste your fury so that I don't have to feel my own self-loathing. I drag in a lungful of air just in time for her to grab my face. Her fingers dig into my stinging cheek. I smile against the warmth of her hand.

"I forgive you." The fire in her eyes suggests otherwise, but she says the words anyway. Then repeats. "I forgive you, Zane."

My voice muffles. "Stop—"

"I forgive you."

"Shut up!"

"I forgive you."

"*Shut the hell up!*"

Kane's hand appears between us and covers Mercy's mouth. He hovers intimately behind her back, but his eyes don't leave mine for a single second. "You're an asshole," he grumbles, "but you're *my* fucking asshole. I know who you are, Zane Hunter. I've always known."

He brushes his lips across Mercy's cheek. "Now she does too. You scared, Siren?"

She shakes her head.

He grins. "See? You're a goddamn mess, but we can live with that."

Sam's voice rumbles across the room. "I fucking can't!"

"He'll come around."

"Like hell, I will!"

Kane rolls his eyes. "Shut the fuck up, Wright." Kissing Mercy's cheek, he backs up and lifts her off of my lap. "Go soothe your boyfriend, and I'll soothe mine."

I watch Mercy stand on her tiptoes and kiss Kane's jaw before she flits away to the other side of the room and climbs into Sam's lap, wrapping her body around his exactly like she had mine. I stare at them and see a mirror image of myself in Sam—muscles tight, face red, so fucking angry that he can't contain it anymore. His emotions radiate off of him so strongly that I'm convinced he's going to lash out... until all of a sudden, he goes perfectly still.

Mercy's kissing him so tenderly that he breaks.

"Eyes on me," Kane murmurs, grabbing my chin and forcing my gaze away. He kneels at my feet and places his warm palms on my trembling thighs, gently rubbing my tired muscles. "How do you feel?"

I choke on a sob as a wave of emotion crashes over me. Shaking my head rapidly, I stare at my partner until he blurs from the stupid tears in my eyes. "I can't—I can't keep doing this."

Kane uses the knife Mercy dropped to cut the ties around my ankles and rub my tender skin. "Then don't." Once he's satisfied, he moves on to the next set around my knees, slicing through them like butter. Then he unties a strip of knotted rope around my waist and pulls it away. "You're only miserable because you want to be."

"You're saying this is *my* fault?"

Our eyes meet. "Yeah. Kind of." Spreading my legs wider apart, he rests his cheek on my thigh. "You freak out when things don't go as planned. But that's life. You've just gotta... have faith." He reaches up and brushes a stray tear off my cheek.

"In what?" I whisper.

Kane's gentle smile takes my breath away. "In us." He snaps the ties around my wrists and drops the knife to the floor before crawling into my lap. The chair groans in protest at our combined weight, but Kane doesn't hesitate to tilt my chin up and claim my mouth. He sighs against my lips and licks the salty traces of my tears. "Things won't always look the same. We'll get messy and we'll fight and we'll have to make up all over again. But you know what?"

I hold my breath.

"There's no one else I'd rather fight with than you."

Grabbing Kane's hips, I scowl up at him. "Asshole."

"Dick."

"Bastard."

"Boyfriend," he murmurs, ducking his head to sigh against my lips. He trails kisses across my jawline and whispers in my ear. "Lover."

While his hands slip beneath my shirt and wander up my abdomen, I glance over at Mercy and Sam. "Not here," I wheeze, feeling my panic rise all over again. "Kane, not—"

"Shhh," he soothes, kissing my fluttering pulse point. "Relax. They're not even looking."

"They could."

Humoring me, Kane turns his head to watch them for a moment. "They're busy." He quickly returns his attention to me. "*We're* busy." His stubble scrapes across the curve of my neck as his lips travel lower. "Promise me something." He bites down and sucks a bruise onto my skin, making me squirm.

"W-what?"

Sitting up, Kane grabs my wandering hands and holds my gaze. "Don't ever hurt her again."

My lips tug into a frown. "She's—"

"Not the enemy."

I choke on a flash of anger, but it's short-lived. I know that he's right. She's not the one destroying us.

I am.

"Fine." I tear my gaze away from Kane to watch Mercy grind on Sam's lap, undoubtedly driving him into a frenzy. "I won't hurt her on purpose. But promise me something in return." Taking a breath, I tremble as my heart races all over again. "If you fall in love with her, tell me first." I return my gaze to my boyfriend, grateful that he's watching me instead of them.

Kane nods solemnly. "I promise, you'll be the first to know." He kisses me slowly, like he's savoring the taste of me—or Mercy's blood—on his tongue, and I willingly lose myself in the warmth of his touch. I'm tired of hurting. Of bleeding from the inside. Of driving myself crazy over Mercy Morningstar.

If she's here to stay, I'll have to learn to fight my inner demons... before they devour every last flicker of light I have left.

# CHAPTER 17

## SAM

As Mercy approaches me after whatever the fuck that was with Zane, I have to calm down before I lash out at the wrong person. The blood roaring in my ears makes it damn near impossible, but I swallow as much of my anger as I can, because it's not directed at her.

It's for the piece of shit who just called her a whore.

Mercy pauses at the side of the bed. "Hi."

I catch the unsteady tremble of her lip, and any residual anger in my body instantly fades away. "Hey." Drawing a breath, I nod towards my lap. "C'mere, baby. Tell me what happened."

She climbs onto the bed and straddles my lap before leaning her head against my chest. "I forgive you," she murmurs, inhaling sharply. "For what happened at the party. I wasn't going to tell you at first because I wanted you to forgive yourself, but..." With a shake of her head, she buries her face in my shirt. "I don't want you to hold onto any guilt. You didn't do anything wrong."

Her words hit me square in the chest. I wish I could hold her, but more than that, I wish that I agreed with her. Swallowing, I choose my next words carefully. "I shouldn't have left you alone."

"You didn't. We were pulled apart."

I find it hard not to argue, so I change the subject. "What did you ask Zane?" If I were running the interrogation, I would have beat the shit out of him before I asked any questions. That was my half of the plan, anyway, before Kane intervened. I understand his caution, especially now that I overheard Zane's shouting. I don't know that I would have stopped myself from giving Zane a broken nose or cracked tooth.

Mercy pushes herself up and wraps her arms around my neck. "That doesn't matter right now. I also need to... apologize." Biting her lip, she meets my gaze. "I realized while I was talking to Zane—no, before that, actually. For a while now." She takes a quick breath. "I... I haven't been fair to you, and I'm sorry. You've been trying to help me this entire time. You didn't even have to, you know? You could have walked away weeks ago." A tiny laugh floats past her lips. "Instead, you're wrapped up in all this... chaos. I wouldn't blame you for leaving."

Does she not understand how I feel about her?

As gently as I can, I lean forward and brush my lips over her cheek. "What kind of ideas did he put into your head?" Sighing, I press our foreheads together. "Do you remember the first thing you ever said to me? The day we met. You were wearing this..." I smile at the memory. "Frilly thing. Like a turtleneck. But see-through."

"A lace halter top?"

I don't know what it's called. I just know what I saw —an angel shepherding lost souls. My dad had just dropped me off for my first group counseling session, and as people wandered through the double-doors into the conference room, Mercy and her father were there greeting everyone. "Before the session started, you were handing out flyers for the Christmas party. You said, 'none of us want to be here, but sometimes, it's better than going home.' We'd only just met, and you pinged me on the spot. I never wanted to go home again. I wanted to be next to you."

In fact, every chance I got to sit by her during our sessions, I did. She didn't say much, but whenever her neighbors would share a personal story or challenge they were facing, she'd whisper to them afterwords and offer what few words she could. More than once, people cried. Mercy was a constant source of comfort for them, and she became a beacon of hope for me.

A light in the dark.

"So telling me that I should leave or that you haven't been fair to me isn't going to work. You can't push me away. I'm in this with you, Mercy." I brush my lips over hers, hoping that she's listening. "Life isn't fair, so why should we be?"

"Sam—"

I kissed Mercy in the shower this morning, but I wasn't paying enough attention. I should have been memorizing the taste of her lips. Counting the heartbeats. Anticipating the flutter of her eyelashes. Basking in the warmth of her skin. I can't touch her like I want right now, but I can *taste* her, and it will have to be enough.

Catching her off guard has its perks. She jumps like I've startled her, but all that does is make me chase her lips. The thrill of wanting and being unable to take is an unexpected rush. All I have are the barest of touches as our lips brush again and again. "Mercy," I rasp, kissing the far edge of her lips, the curve of her chin, the tip of her nose. "Mercy, baby, come here." I twist my wrists in a desperate attempt to pull them free. "I need you."

"You do?"

I smile against her cheek. She should know that by now. "I've always needed you. Even when we grew apart, I thought of you every day." The bruise I left on her neck is still there, but I suck on it to ensure it stays. Mercy gasps, trembling as she grinds down on my lap. I don't know if she realizes what she's doing, but she starts rolling her hips like she does, capturing my cock right where we both need it.

"I need you too." She cups my face and sighs against my lips. "Sam, I—I've been so scared that I'm going to lose you." Shaking her head, she nearly laughs. "That you'll realize I'm not worth the trouble. I know I ask a lot of you. Even this morning, in the shower, I—" Her breath catches. "I know that it isn't fair."

I've reached a point in my life where fairness is overrated.

"Fuck being fair." Finally, one of my wrists slips free.

I cup the back of Mercy's head and crash against her lips. She whimpers, and I greedily swallow the sound. *This kiss, I won't forget.* Her hands tug on my shirt until she pulls it over my head. When it gets stuck on my arm, she lifts onto her knees and reaches up to untie my wrist. As soon as I'm free, I cup her face and bring her back down onto my lips. She moans when I slip my tongue into her mouth and deepen our kiss.

I try to lift my knees and one of my legs snags on the tie around my ankle. Shit, I'm still tied down. What's worse: we have an audience. I don't sacrifice a single second of this moment to look at Kane or his psycho boyfriend, but I can feel the heat of their stares. They're going to see Mercy naked if we continue like this. I've had sex in front of a few of my fraternity brothers once on a dare, so it's not like I'm in completely foreign territory with two other men in the room—but for Mercy, all of this is new. She deserves rose petals and romance, not a lecherous late night show.

Even what happened in the shower this morning, despite the experience being new for all of us, was a step too far in the wrong direction. She deserves better than what we've given her so far.

"Mercy—" Her hands find my belt and she fiddles with the clasp. I have to grab her wrists to stop her. "Wait. We're not alone."

"We're not," she agrees immediately, "but it's okay, Sam." Abandoning my belt, she lifts onto her knees and climbs higher up my thighs, easily slotting her core against the length of my cock straining against my jeans.

Her breath ghosts across my cheek as she hooks her arms around my neck. Our eyes meet, and the sweetest lie falls past her lips. "I'm all yours."

Bittersweet agony claws at my heart, but I won't deny her what she wants a second time. I already regret how things went down in her bedroom after she begged me to sleep with her. I can't turn her down now. I'll do my best to make her feel like this moment is perfect.

If wrapping her in my arms is second nature to me, kissing her becomes my new ritual. I start at the hollow of her throat, taking my time as I pepper the barest of kisses along her collarbone, the tips of her breasts, the length of her jawline. Her breath catches as I brush my thumb over her nipple, teasing it into a tight bud beneath her shirt. This isn't how I imagined our first night together, but if this is it—if she can't wait anymore —I'll make the most of what I've been given and drag out every second as long as possible.

...which is made much more difficult when Mercy squirms on top of me. I hold my breath as I squeeze her breast, and she shudders from head to toe, wiggling her hips unconsciously. Is she trying to speed things along? Does she need me to touch her elsewhere? Am I hurting her?

Pinching her nipple, I revel in the way she whines.

No, she's not in pain. She's a needy little thing.

I can't help but smile as she winds her fingers in my hair and *pulls*. The pain is nothing compared to the heat of her lips on mine.

"Don't tease me," she pants, sucking my bottom lip into her mouth.

*Fucking hell*, that's hot. I groan as her tongue slips between my lips and she takes control, devouring me before I have a chance to devour her. Rocking my hips, I thrust into the cradle of her thighs. Electricity sparks in my fingertips and shoots down my spine as she thrusts back, matching my strength with her enthusiasm.

She's as tired of waiting as I am.

Tearing off our clothes becomes a matter of life or death. I rip her top down the middle and latch onto her breast the second it's free, greedily sucking her nipple into my mouth. She makes the prettiest sound as she winds her fingers in my hair.

"*Sam!*"

Fuck yes.

I yank the scraps of fabric down her arms and flip her onto her back so that I can drag her leggings down her thighs. Within seconds, she's completely naked. I toss her clothes in Kane's direction without watching where they land. Let the fucker sniff her panties as a consolation prize, because *I'm* the one feasting. Sliding between her thighs, I bury my face in her pussy. She squeals and kicks her heels, so I grab her ass and haul her against my mouth to keep her still. Grunting, I shove my tongue inside her molten core and drink her desire.

She's even wetter than when I ate her out at the restaurant.

"I need you," she whines, kicking her heels. "*Sam!*"

With one last kiss to her clit, I abandon her honey hole and rise onto my knees. Tugging my belt, I undo my jeans and shove them down my thighs, taking my boxers with them. My cock springs free and smacks my stomach, already turning an angry red at the tip. I haven't masturbated since Mercy touched me weeks ago, and as great as this morning's blow job was, I'm still raring to go. The evidence lies in how thick my cock is. I grab my shaft and give it a squeeze, knowing that it's girthier than usual. Shit.

I stare at Mercy's glistening pussy. She's soaking wet, but this is still gonna hurt. Maybe I should come first. Tame the beast, so to speak. Then I can clear my head, too, and take things slow. Make sure that she's okay before I rut her senseless.

Good idea, Sam.

I'm almost smiling about my genius plan when Mercy suddenly sits up and pushes me. I fall onto my ass and she climbs into my lap, not wasting any time. Alarm bells ring in my head—not just because of how big my dick is, but because I'm not wearing a condom. "Mercy, wai—*ohhh fuck.*" My eyes roll back as she drags her pussy over my cock with the sweetest cry on her lips. Her eyes flutter closed as she does it a second time, then a third, driving me into a frenzy within seconds. I'm drenched in her desire by the time she lifts her hips and bares down on the tip. Anchoring herself to my shoulders, she drags her bottom lip between her teeth.

Yeah, fuck the condom. I'm taking my girl bare.

Kissing her hard, I plant one hand on her hip and

one on the back of her neck to hold her steady. The heat of her core has me leaking precum all over her slit.

Shit. We're really doing this.

No more games.

No more waiting.

She sinks down slowly, her breath hitching once the tip is in. My body is on fire, screaming at me to thrust into her heat and take what's mine, but I wait... and then I watch, tilting my head to the side to catch a glimpse of the man who wanted this for himself. I always knew that sex with Mercy would be sweet victory, but witnessing the burning envy in Kane's eyes as she takes *me* into her body—willingly gifting me her virginity—is an unexpected rush. I damn near come when she's only halfway down my shaft, already throbbing as I slide even deeper.

"Take it slow if you need—" I choke on my words as she lifts her hips and suddenly slams back down, impaling herself with a shrill cry. She quivers for only a moment before rolling her hips, her pussy squeezing me so tightly that I can hardly breathe. Spots dance in my vision as I clench every muscle in my body and *beg* not to come. Not when this is everything I've ever wanted. Not until she's satisfied. Not here, not now, not yet—

My mind scrambles to latch on to something, anything, to keep my orgasm at bay. God must hate me, because, my eyes lock with Kane's at that precise moment.

At least it keeps me from coming.

Dragging my lips up the side of Mercy's neck, I maintain eye contact with him as I whisper in her ear. "Ready for more, baby?" She grabs my face and kisses me, putting my attention back where it belongs. I moan into her mouth as I wrap my arms around her waist. "Hold on tight." Pushing her down in time with my thrust, I bury my cock as deep inside of her as possible. We moan in unison. A shockwave of sparks zings through my entire body. And for the first time in weeks, I finally don't give a damn about what happens next.

# Chapter 18

## Mercy

WHATEVER POWER I thought I held by being on top is blown away by the sheer strength in Sam's thighs. He's the one putting in all the work, holding me so tightly that I can hardly meet his thrusts. Each one is as controlled as the last, building into a steady rhythm that drives me insane.

I'd imagined that sex would be a frenzy—a furious meeting of bodies over and over again—but Sam drives into me with steady purpose. Staring into my eyes, he watches every flicker of movement across my face and groans when I toss my head back and moan his name.

Overstimulated and overwhelmed, my body shudders with each drag of his cock against my walls. A heady mix of pleasure-pain each time he bottoms out makes me gasp, the wet slap of our bodies and the scent of sex quickly filling the air.

"Mercy, Mercy, Mercy," Sam pants, kissing a bead of sweat dripping down my neck. "All mine."

"*Ah!*" I shudder as he thrusts harder, slamming into my molten core with a groan.

"So fucking perfect," he drawls, nipping my collarbone. "So fucking *wet.* You're sucking me in, baby." He slams me down and holds me there, groaning as his thighs spasm. "You needed my cock." Another groan. "*Fuck,* you're tight."

"D-don't stop," I whine, cupping his jaw. Somehow, sitting still makes all the new aches and pains reappear. My pussy clenches around him, and I feel it—the girth of Sam's cock holding me open. The heat of him inside me soothes as much as it hurts. "You're so big," I can't help but whine. I'm stretched farther than I ever imagined possible. But when Sam moves, I can tell that I was made for this. He glides in and out seamlessly as my body makes room for him.

That makes Sam smile. "I'm not always this—*uhn*—size." The flush on his face spreads to his ears. "Had to go all out for you, baby; make your first time special." Sealing his mouth over mine, he kisses me hard. "But I'm about to—" Groaning, his entire body quivers. "*Fuck.*" His cock swells as he comes, each pulse of liquid heat making me twitch in response.

"*Ahh!*" I cling to him as his cum makes everything even hotter inside. Ohmygod. *Ohmygod.* I know we didn't use protection, but— "You didn't pull out." As if to emphasize this point, he rocks his hips like he can't help himself. Some of his cum leaks out around his cock, making an even bigger mess.

A satisfied smile curves on Sam's lips. "*Mmm,* yeah.

No. Your pussy's too good, baby, so fucking good." His muscles convulse as a final burst of cum paints my walls. "*Ohhhh,* yes, milk my cock."

My blush darkens at how dirty he makes it sound. "Sam!" I smack his arm. "Stop coming! We have to go back to the store!"

How long does it take before a morning after pill is no longer effective? Do they even sell them at the corner store? Is there a pharmacy in town?

"Hey," Sam murmurs, gently cupping my face. "We'll get whatever you need, I promise."

Biting my lip, I nod. "Okay." The knot of worry in my chest isn't gone, but kissing Sam helps ease my fears. I know that he'll take care of me.

The mattress suddenly dips behind me, and a deep rumble skitters across my skin. "*Tsk, tsk,* Sam. Filling up that pretty pussy like you own it? That takes balls." Kane's lips skim my shoulder blade. "Let me see how much of a mess you made."

Little shocks of surprise tingle down my limbs. "W-what?"

Kane lifts my hips and pulls me off of Sam's cock, pushing my body forward until Sam and I tumble onto the bed. My face smushes against Sam's pecs while Kane hoists my ass high in the air. Cum seeps out of my pussy, and a whisper of cool air blows across my sensitive flesh.

"Fuck, Siren," Kane groans, "your pussy's even prettier like this. All—" He slides a finger inside my core. "Used—" Then a second. "Up." And a third.

I whine as he explores with his fingers, rubbing the same places that Sam just did. The stretch burns, but the warmth—*the wetness*—makes my body tremble. I squirm, trying to pull away, but Kane loops his arm around my thigh and holds me in place.

"Kane," Sam growls, "what the fuck are you doing?"

"Enjoying your mess." He doesn't have to sound so pleased about it. "In *our* pussy."

My body convulses as Kane licks the cum leaking from my slit. "Kane!" I bury my face in Sam's chest. "S-stop! That's—you're not supposed to do that!"

"Says who?" Spreading my lips apart with his thumbs, he dives back in, groaning as he licks up Sam's release. "You taste good, Siren."

*Holy shit. Holyshitholyshitholyshit.*

The pads of his fingers find my swollen clit, and I cry out from the sudden spark of pleasure. He doesn't stop eating me out, and somehow it's... *really good.* Trembling, I hold my breath to keep from moaning. I shouldn't give into this. He didn't even ask first! Kane just decided on his own that this was what I'd want. I'm sure he'd call it *generosity*, but we all know that he has his own agenda.

He gets off on pushing my limits.

"That's right, beautiful. You want to come, don't you?"

My body spasms. *Yes*, I want to come. Obviously, I want to come. But this is— "Dirty," I whine.

Sam runs his fingers through my hair, a pensive

expression on his face. "If you like it, Mercy, then it's fine. It can be dirty *and* good."

"So good," Kane slurs, sucking my clit into his mouth.

A bolt of pleasure shoots through my core and I come hard, clenching my entire body against it. A tear slips free, and Sam brushes it away without hesitation. I shouldn't like this. My body shouldn't react this way. Having two men on me at the same time—*enjoying it*—does this make me a slut?

Zane's voice floats across the room, mocking me. "Looks like our dirty girl just came all over your face."

Shame fills my chest, making it hard to breathe.

What makes it *impossible,* however, is the wet smack of something long, hard, and hot against my pussy.

My body tenses. "No." I can't be fucked twice in one night by two men! Then I really *am* a slut. "Kane, don't—"

He drags his cock through my folds, thrusting towards my ass. His balls smack my clit, making me gasp. Pleasure breaks through the pain, turning my aching flesh against me. I moan.

"That's it," Kane grunts, "be our dirty girl for a little longer."

"She said no." Sam pushes onto his elbows only for Kane to shove the two of us back down, using his entire body weight to flatten me on Sam's chest. "Kane!"

"Didn't expect to hear you scream my name, Sam, but I don't hate it."

"Fuck you! Get off of her!"

"Only if she asks nicely." Smacking his dick against my ass, Kane kisses my shoulder blade. "Do you want me to stop, Siren, or do you want my cock, too?"

I whimper, not sure what I want anymore. My body is hot all over, sandwiched between two men. Would Kane really stop if I asked him to? Or is he just saying that so he doesn't seem like the bad guy?

"Until you decide—" Repositioning himself, Kane aligns his cock with my entrance and thrusts, missing the mark and sliding along my slit. "I'll be right here."

Clawing Sam's arms, I moan. Why does that feel good?

Something stirs against my thigh. "Shit," Sam hisses, clenching his jaw. "Goddammit."

My eyes widen. There's no way. *No way.*

Kane laughs hard enough that his rhythm falters. "See how dirty your boyfriend is, Mercy?"

"Just as dirty as you," Zane huffs from across the room. "The three of you are a fucking—" His voice catches. "Mess."

Is *everyone* in this room turned on?

Taking a breath, I plant my hands on the mattress. *Fine.* I'm turned on, too. I'm included in this—whatever this is. *Orgy,* a voice in my head reminds me. Or does this count as a threesome?

Pushing against Kane's weight is harder than I thought, but I slam my hips up when he pulls back, chasing his cock. "I want it," I admit aloud, shuddering as a wave of desire rolls through me.

Kane thrusts back, bumping my clit hard enough that I gasp. "What was that? I couldn't hear you."

"I want it!" I cry, desperately trying to meet his next thrust. His cock slips between my slick folds, teasing me with its length. I remember seeing it in his hand before—it's bigger than Sam's. Can something like that fit inside of me?

"You want *this*?" The tip nudges my entrance. My pussy clenches in anticipation.

"Yes!"

Humming as he pulls back, Kane nips the side of my neck. "Then beg for it."

My brain struggles to process his request. "Beg?"

"Beg," he rumbles, grabbing my right ass cheek and squeezing. "Beg for this cock you want so badly."

I choke on my saliva. He can't be serious.

*Smack!* Stinging pain makes me scream. Heat blossoms from his touch, and he rubs the spot lovingly. "Beg for me to stop, or beg for my cock."

"You're crazy!" But even as I say it, I realize that it doesn't matter. Crazy or not, Kane won't let up just because I call him names. "I'm *not* begging!"

"Then I guess we're at a stalemate," Kane chuckles, dragging his lips down my spine and kissing each vertebrae. "You have a beautiful body, Mercy." He rubs my stinging ass, then squeezes. "I'm glad that I finally get to see it in person."

*Smack!*

Gasping, I jerk away from Kane's palm and crash into Sam, who's lying completely still beneath me. I peek at his face to find him staring not at me, but at my ass hanging in the air. *Transfixed.* "Hey!" Scooting up Sam's body, I scowl at him. "What exactly are you staring at?"

His lips part, but no sound comes out. Swallowing, he tears his gaze away. "You don't want me to look?" Sam's jaw clenches as he turns his head and stares at the wall.

"I—" My brain short-circuits as Kane rubs my heated flesh, humming like he's enjoying himself. Maybe Sam's enjoying this too? Lifting my knee, I plant it between Sam's thighs and press down until I feel his cock—as hard as he was when we had sex—beneath my thigh. Face burning, I arch my back and lift my ass even higher. "You can look," I murmur, blushing. "If you want."

Sam meets my eyes before lifting his gaze over my head and sucking in a breath. "Your ass is *red*, baby. Damn." Snaking his arms down my body, he grabs my thigh and thrusts, rubbing his cock against my skin. "I never thought to—I mean, you've always had pretty skin, and you bruise easily—" He flushes crimson. "You look *really* good, Mercy."

"I think the word you're looking for is sexy," Kane huffs, rubbing his cock over the welt on my cheek. The heat and pressure combined with the prickle of pain sends shivers through my body. "You're fucking sexy, Siren." Glancing over his shoulder, he addresses Zane next. "Tell her that she's sexy, babe."

Zane's armchair creaks as he shifts his weight. "She'd look better with your cock in her ass."

Kane grunts. "Damn straight." As if considering the

idea, he spreads my cheeks and spits on my crack. Saliva drips over my hole, and he rubs it in with his fingertip. "But I want to fuck her pussy first." Realigning his cock, he pushes the tip between my lips, spreading them easily. With tiny thrusts, he teases the both of us, giving just enough for me to feel the burning stretch before pulling back out.

Biting my lip, I push back onto him as much as I can, struggling to breathe as another half inch slips inside. "Too big," I gasp, shaking my head. There's no way he'll fit. The tip alone stretches me as wide as I can go. "Kane, we can't. It won't fit."

"That doesn't sound like begging." Placing his hand on my lower back, he holds me steady as he pushes, driving another inch inside. The wet squelching sound makes me think that it's worked, he's in, but then he's slamming his palm on the burning mark on my ass, making me yelp with pain. Another half inch gives, and he groans. "I knew you'd be tight, but this is—*shit.*"

Sam slips his hand to my clit and rubs gentle circles around it, providing necessarily relief. "It's her first time, for fuck's sake," he growls, glaring over my head at Kane. "You'll have to work up to it."

"I don't *want* to work up to it," Kane snaps, grabbing my aching flesh. "I want her now!"

"Kane," Zane sighs, suddenly making an appearance beside the bed. He's staring directly into his lover's eyes and frowning. "You're above average. Even I can't take you all the time." Placing his hand over Kane's, he laces his fingers together and brings their joined hands to his lips, kissing Kane's knuckles. "You need to relax, or she never will."

While Kane's distracted, Sam makes good use of my clit, rubbing in exactly the right way to warm me back up. "You can say no," he murmurs, meeting my eyes. The concern reflecting back at me is touching. "Beg him to stop, and this will all be over."

Except it won't, will it? This is night one of however many we'll have together. I don't want it to end because *the virgin* can't handle her cock. "I want it," I reassure him, giving a watery smile. "I just don't know what I'm doing wrong."

Sam's brow pinches. "You're not doing anything wrong." With a jerk of his head, he gestures to Kane. "It's him. He's too impatient."

All of a sudden, the wet smack of lips meeting greets my ears. Curving my neck, I spy Kane absolutely *wrecking* Zane's mouth, sucking his boyfriend's bottom lip into his mouth and curling his tongue. My eyes widen as they makeout, unbothered by the fact that Sam and I are mere inches away. Staring. Intently.

"Mercy," Sam murmurs, gently thrusting his hips. "C'mere. I want to kiss you."

Leaning into Sam causes Kane's dick to slip free, but I'm relieved. As much as I want it to fit, I'm not sure that it will. While Kane pulls Zane onto the foot of the bed, I focus on Sam. Our kisses are gentle at first, as slow and steady as Sam's cock rubbing against my thigh, but they heat up fast. Panting, I grind my clit on Sam's pelvis, finding the perfect ridge for my pleasure. He smiles against my lips. "That's it, baby, use me."

As my pleasure builds, I sit up straighter. The ache inside my pussy subsides with each roll of my hips, and before long, I'm riding Sam's hip like I'm riding his cock.

"That's it," Sam repeats, grabbing his cock and stroking it fast. "Fuck, that's hot." With a moan, he tosses his head back as his body convulses. Warm stripes of his seed cover my ass and lower back, and within seconds, Sam's rubbing it into my skin. "Mine," he pants, digging his fingernails into my cheek.

I gasp at the sting. "Sam!"

"Don't stop." There's a hint of desperation in his voice. "I want to watch you come, baby."

The two men behind me moan, and curiosity gets the better of me. I curve my back to check on them, stalling my hips for just a moment.

Zane's lying on his back, face flushed as Kane cradles the back of his head and feeds him the tip of his cock. It slides in easily, like they've done this a thousand times before, and jealousy flares inside my heart. Both men stare intently at each other, paying no mind to Sam or me at all... until I gasp so loudly that Zane's eyes snap to mine. He widens his jaw as Kane slips half his dick inside, looking absolutely *smug* with himself. Like he's the better lover than me; which, honestly, is probably true with how little experience I have. But still! He doesn't have to rub it in so goddamn hard.

Sam finally notices the other pair. "Holy shit." Sitting up, he watches alongside me as Zane practically takes the entire thing, choking only on the last inch. Kane lets up, murmuring words of encouragement as he drives back in, deeper this time, groaning as he hits the back of Zane's throat. "Fuck, that's good. Such a greedy little cock slut. Get ready to swallow."

I watch in awe as Kane's ass clenches and Zane's throat bobs on multiple swallows, the pair working in sync to ensure that not a single drop is wasted. Anything that slips past Zane's lips is quickly shoved back inside until he swallows it all, eventually popping open his mouth and holding out his tongue as proof. Other than a subtlc shine to his lips, I wouldn't have known that he swallowed Kane's cum seconds before.

Grabbing Sam's hand, I squeeze his fingers. "I want to do that."

If I can't fit Kane in my pussy then surely I can fit him in my mouth, right? It opens wide. I already sucked Sam off once—surely giving Kane head can't be that different.

Zane hears me before Sam does. Smirking, he sits up as soon as Kane climbs off his chest. "You'll choke before you milk a single drop, Kitten."

Jealous indignation makes me reckless. I crawl across the bed to Zane, shove his face into the pillow, and grab the button of his jeans. Unsnapping it, I tug them over his hips and pull his cock free, squeezing his shaft the moment my fist wraps around him. "Wanna bet?" Smacking my lips, I lower my head and lick the precum beading from the tip.

His body seizes. "What the fuck do you think you're

doing?" he hisses, hips jerking off the bed as I stroke him from root to tip.

With a sugar sweet smile, I lie down on my stomach between his thighs. "Practicing." Licking beneath the head, I put Sam's mini-anatomy lesson to use and find a vein, enjoying the way it jumps beneath my tongue. "Think I can milk *you*, Zane?"

Fury sparks in the depths of his eyes, but it's overtaken by the raw hunger radiating from within. "I'd like to see you try." Huffing, he leans up on his forearms and glares at me. "I don't come for just anyone."

Maintaining eye contact, I suck the tip into my mouth.

A muscle along Zane's jaw jumps, but he's perfectly still otherwise.

"Fucking *hell*, Siren You're going to kill me with eyes like that."

"She's going to kill *Zane*." Sam sounds practically giddy about it.

"Show him how perfect your mouth feels, baby. I bet he'll come in five minutes."

"Three," Kane counters, bumping fists with Sam as they make a bet.

"Fuck off," Zane snaps, shaking with fury. "You can both go to he—" His voice catches as he swallows the rest of his sentence.

"Two. Final answer."

"Deal."

The men shake on it, and I laugh around Zane's cock in my mouth. He glares, but I catch the way his throat bobs. A bead of sweat drips down his temple. His fists clench the sheets.

A smirk curves on my lips as I suck on the tip, then bob my head lower, enjoying the way his breath catches as I give his balls a gentle squeeze. He may have won the battle over Kane's dick, but *his*—hot and heavy on my tongue—his dick is mine.

## CHAPTER 19

### ZANE

WHEN KANE first proposed the idea of sharing Mercy, I absolutely hated it. Every fiber of my being was on edge, because I knew that if he got a taste of her—alone or otherwise—I was fucked.

I never imagined *being* fucked.

Not by her.

It doesn't matter that it's her mouth instead of her pussy—she wields that hot hole like the weapon it is, licking and sucking my cock like her favorite lollipop. I didn't even know she had experience with dicks, because wasn't she a virgin until five minutes ago? Why the hell does she get off on *getting me off*?

I grit my teeth as she smirks up at me, completely smitten with herself and her dirty plan. I was already hard from swallowing Kane's load, and now she wants to show how good she is at swallowing *my* load. Is this a competition, or something?

How the hell do I forfeit, because—

Mercy hollows out her cheeks and I stop breathing. I can't. *I can't.* Pleasure radiates from the tip of my cock all the way through my shaft, drawing my balls up in record time. Fuck. *Fuck.* This can't be happening. I can't let Mercy fucking Morningstar *win*.

With a growl, I wrap her luscious locks around my fist and hold her down. Her cheeks puff out as she tries to breathe.

Yeah, you're not *that* experienced.

"You dirty slut. You want all your holes filled with cum, don't you?" I picture it now, Mercy lying on her back with cum leaking out of her ass, pussy, and mouth all at once—or we could stripe her entire body in white, coating her in our seed. I think I like that picture better, and I know that Kane would too. Painting her body as ours is poetic, in a filthy sort of way.

"Sam filled up your pussy, and now it's my turn to cover your tongue, isn't it?" I click my tongue against my teeth. "It's too bad that Kane can't fit in your ass, or we could fulfill your dirty little fantasy right now. Does that make you hot? Does it get you *wet*?"

I'm saying too much, but it's a distraction from the way her throat constricts around my head. I doubt she has experience deep throating anyone, so if I'm too rough with her, she might vomit.

If it wouldn't gross me out, I'd be tempted for the sheer fact that it would put her in her fucking place.

Trying to outdo *me* in a blow job?

Im-fucking-possible.

I've been training my throat for years, and what has

she been doing? Drawing pictures and mismanaging her sleep? Scoffing, I pull her head up to watch fat tears roll down her cheeks. That's better. The tension in my chest loosens enough that I can take a full breath. She may *want* to be better than me, but there's no fucking way she'll ever get there, especially not by practicing on my cock. I'm not as thick or as long as Kane, but I have a wicked curve that throws some people off their first time.

Mercy, however, doesn't have the experience to know otherwise. She bobs her head like a subservient little bitch, eager to please. I pull her hair to keep her from going back down. It's when she's too deep that I'll falter, and I don't want to give her the satisfaction of making me come. She's going to have to work for it.

Kane slides up behind me like a bitch in heat, ready to jump in on the action. I can feel his erection pressing against my spine, not as thick as earlier, but nearly. His refractory period is insanely short—it's one of the qualities that makes him popular at parties when there are more than enough holes to go around and not enough dicks to fill them.

"Stop," I swallow, turning my head to bump Kane's chest. "You're not involved in this."

He chuckles as he runs his hands beneath my shirt and up my chest. Teasing my nipples, he groans. "It's so hot watching someone else suck you off. Imagine if she had on lipstick. Cherry red, or burgundy—" He shivers, the sensation tickling my back. "I'd love to see your dick covered in red."

"Keep your blood kink away from my dick."

"*My* blood kink?" Nipping my neck, Kane chuckles deeper. "Look in the mirror, babe. I'm not the one who likes to carve people up."

"None of that—" I suck in a breath as Mercy descends, strategically using my waning attention to take me deeper into her throat. "Matters right now. You're gonna—" I pant. Mercy's hot hand massages my balls just the way I like, with a hard squeeze that makes my dick twitch. "Lose your bet."

"Don't care. I'd be happy if this lasted forever."

Rolling my eyes, I tune him out and focus on Mercy. "Someone's eager," I growl, cupping her flushed cheeks. She's hot to the touch, and her lips—swollen, red, *delicious*. Saliva drips from her open mouth and catches on my ballsack. Grinning, I pop her off my cock and shove her face in her mess. "Lick it up, Kitten."

Her whole body shudders. I can tell she doesn't want to. For a second, I believe that she's going to tap out, but then she swipes her tongue through the puddle of saliva and keeps going, drawing one of my balls into her mouth. Flicking her gaze up to meet mine, she sucks.

My hips jerk. Kane pinches my nipples. Mercy grabs my shaft and strokes *hard*, drawing up my flesh to tease the underside of my head. She must have seen that in a porn or something, but it does its job. An excessive amount of precum leaks from my slit, and she gathers it in her hand to stroke even faster.

"That's not a blow job," I remind her, clenching my jaw. *Shit*, but it's working. Before she can retort with some smart ass remark, I grab her hair and force her back onto my cock. The heat of her mouth makes me shiver. Sweat gathers at my hairline. It shouldn't feel this good to have someone else on my cock. Maybe it's because Kane's watching? He's clearly into it, rubbing his hard-on against my lower back while he looks over my shoulder. Even Sam, as possessive as he claims to be, is slack-jawed as he watches his girl swallow as much of my cock as she can, her eyes watering again.

Damn, that's a pretty sight.

Her tits jiggle as she raises her head, giving me a peek at her rosy nipples. I bet they'd feel good beneath my tongue. Taut, sensitive peaks craving my mouth. She'd cry out like the needy little thing she is and beg for my cock inside her dripping wet hole, all too eager for me to bury deep and fill her womb with my—

Mercy swallows the very tip of my cock, taking me deeper than I thought possible, and chokes. With a moan, I grab the back of her head and *push*, keeping her there while I come my fucking brains out. Hot spurts of my seed skip her tongue entirely and land inside her throat, forcing her to swallow.

*That's it, Kitten, drink my fucking milk.*

Silent tears drip down her scarlet cheeks as she struggles to breathe.

"Through your nose, sweetheart. Breathe through your nose." Kane reaches over me to rub the top of her head, like she really is a cat needing praise.

Sam joins in, swooping down to rub her throat and encourage her to swallow. "You're almost done. Good girl."

Once my balls are empty, I grab both sides of her face and pull her up, enjoying the way she gasps for air. Prying her mouth open with my fingers, I confirm that there isn't a single drop of semen remaining within. "You get an A," I tell her, "because you didn't scrape me with your teeth."

Kane rumbles behind me but doesn't say anything, thank God, because I'd hate for her to learn that I like that shit.

"Two minutes and forty-two seconds," Sam announces. Brushing Mercy's hair off her cheek, he kisses away her tears. "You did good, baby. That's fast."

"*And* you swallowed." Kane smacks my ribs. "This fucker didn't want me to swallow the first time."

Blushing is *not* how I wanted to end this experience. Cheeks flaming, I smack Kane back. "Keep that to yourself!"

Mercy stares up at me curiously. "Why didn't he want you to swallow?"

"Because at the time, Zane hadn't, y'know." Kane pretends to jerk off. "In a while."

Sam's lip curls. "TMI."

Kane rolls his eyes. "Like you were complaining this morning when she ate *your* load. I bet you hadn't jerked off since..." Scrunching his face, he starts counting back on his fingers. "When were we at Lucio's?"

That night feels like a lifetime ago.

Dragging a hand down my face, I take a breath before shoving my dick back in my pants. I want to say something snarky about how this was a *one time only* thing, but my heart isn't in it. If I say that, Kane will call me out on it, and I'll have to admit right here and now, *aloud*, that this wasn't... bad.

Despite the rough start to the evening, I feel lighter than I have in weeks. Completely sober, even. The voices in my head have gone quiet, allowing the others to filter in without their usual harsh edges and undertones. Instead, I'm left with the warmth of Kane's hand on my hip, the absentminded caress of Mercy's fingers on my ankle, and the simple, carefree banter between Sam and Kane as they debate the winnings from their blow job bet.

I'm not even that upset that I came.

While the other men argue, my gaze roams Mercy's naked body. The bruises on her skin are still as visible as they were earlier, but so is the sweat glistening across her shoulders, the delicate swell of her breasts, and the soft rolls of her stomach. The light in her eyes is brighter now, too. I listen as she joins the debate with the others, and she actually laughs, just as carefree as they are.

The moment is... happy.

I find myself trying to hide a smile, and to my surprise, Mercy wraps her hand around my ankle and smiles back. Not at Kane or at Sam, but at... me.

My heartbeat trips, and I quickly look away.

No matter how we remember tonight after dawn arrives, the fact remains that nothing has changed between us. The game is still on, as far as I'm concerned. Kane didn't fuck Mercy, and more importantly, *I* didn't fuck Mercy. Mouths don't count. Sam fucking Mercy was never part of the ruleset, so that's irrelevant.

As for falling in love...

I rest my head on Kane's shoulder and close my eyes, ignoring the unsteady beat of my heart.

Love can wait forever.

# CHAPTER 20

# KANE

THE TENSION in the house finally dissipates. Not completely—Zane is still awkward when Mercy walks in the room—but it's better, and that's what matters. "You should apologize," I tell him one evening as we pile chopped wood for a bonfire. It's been a few days since *the blow job that rocked his world*, as I affectionately call it, and it's about time that they move onto the next stage of their relationship. Preferably, one that involves more naked time between them.

Thinking about how willing Mercy was to make all three of us, the men—her men?—come brings a smile to my face every time.

Zane keeps calling me out about it.

"Stop smiling," he grumbles, half-heartedly glaring as he flicks the lighter on and off. "Pervert."

"You enjoyed it," I remind him for the dozenth time. It's one thing for me to catch Zane moaning in his sleep, but for him to admit it out loud? That he *actually* enjoyed our spontaneous love-fest?

It'll take an act of God to get those lips moving.

"You should still apologize." I peek at him from the corner of my eye. Admitting to any wrong-doing is another touchy subject for him. He doesn't like to be wrong. But orchestrating that bullshit at the party *and then* drugging all of us here at the cabin takes things to another level—a bad one. I don't give a shit if he torments other people, but *our* people?

If things are going to level out between the four of us and turn into something... *better*, we've got to nip that in the bud now, before Zane gets any other nefarious ideas.

"I'm not apologizing, because I'm not sorry." It's the same line Zane's been giving me for days. Every time he says it, he gets quieter and quieter. I don't think he one-hundred-percent believes that he was in the right for the shit he's pulled, but it's a lie that helps him sleep at night. Even though Mercy forgave him, it's a hard thing for him to swallow.

But *she* swallows like a champ.

Unable to stop myself from grinning, I smack Zane's arm as he spreads the kindling to start the fire. That whole day from start to finish feels like a fever dream. The morning kiss with Mercy, the hottest shower of my life, drugging my boyfriend and watching him get royally rocked by the *not-virgin*. Man, I can't make this shit up. I've been dying for another taste, but Mercy and Sam have been holed up in their bedroom—yes, *one* bedroom—for days while Zane and I canoodle on our own.

Being with Zane on his own is fun, sure, but I was hoping for a more open relationship between the four of us.

"That's my Thanksgiving wish," I say aloud, knowing that Zane is listening. "To keep this *thing* between us going."

"You don't make Thanksgiving wishes." Zane pinches the bridge of his nose. "That's Christmas."

Whatever. It's a holiday.

I poke him with a stick. "Don't you want to keep things going?"

"Keep what going?"

"I don't know, *things.*" I wave my stick around. "Between all of us." If I say that what we're building is more than sex, Zane might freak out, so instead, I call it what it is right now. "Like sex. Didn't you have fun the other night?"

Zane scrunches his cute fucking face like he's irritated. "Since when is being tied up against my will fun?"

"Since now." Smiling, I tug on the bottom of his shirt. We still haven't bought any clothes since we failed to bring our shit from home, so we're wearing whatever the fuckers in the cabin own. Today, Zane's rocking a navy flannel button up, khaki cargo pants, and brown work boots. Totally rustic. Not at all like the moody, grunge man I know and love.

Still, the "mountain man" look has its charm. Now I just need to get him to grow a beard and wear those slutty fucking glasses I love so much. Mmm.

Sliding my fingers beneath his shirt, I splay my palm

flat over his stomach. The happy trail leading down to his crotch is soft to the touch. "C'mon, admit that you loved it. I won't tell anyone."

Zane blushes. "I did not!"

"You were *so* hard for Mercy. How did she feel in your lap? I'm a little jealous she sat on you instead of me." Then again, I got to slide my cock through her soaking wet pussy, *sort of*, and that was heaven. "I'm gonna fuck her," I murmur, licking my lips. "You gonna watch, babe?"

The pink on Zane's cheeks darkens to crimson. "No!" He shoves more kindling beneath the stacked logs and struggles to light them. With a growl, he shuts his eyes and takes a deep breath. "Why do you have to fuck her?"

What kind of a question is that?

"I've always wanted to fuck her." Taking the lighter from him, I spark the igniter and light the kindling. After blowing on it for a second, I meet his eyes. "Don't you?"

He grits his teeth. "No."

I grab his chin. "Zane. Stop lying to me."

"I'm not lying."

"You are. You have been for a while now." I tighten my grip. "Why is it so hard to admit that you like her?"

A sound catches in his throat. "I don't like her!"

Taking a calming breath, I keep pushing. "You're scared to lose me. I get it. But what's the worst that can happen from sleeping with her? You have a good time? *We* have a good time?"

Zane remains silent for a long moment. "I don't want

to love someone else, Kane. I don't even want to *like* someone else. It doesn't matter who it is. They just…" He clenches and unclenches his fists repeatedly, wrinkling my long-sleeve shirt. "They disappear, and I can't—" He swallows. "I can't handle it, okay? I'm not like you."

Ducking my head, I press a gentle kiss to his lips. "Love hurts," I murmur, breathing in Zane's exhale. "But that ache in your chest—the one you think you can't handle? It's supposed to be there. It means that you have a heart." I thump my fist on Zane's chest, directly over his heart. "That's a beautiful thing, baby. That you can feel so much."

He stares into my eyes. "I don't want to feel this much, Kane."

I wish that I could kiss away all the pain he's ever felt in his lifetime—even the pain that hasn't happened yet. But for now, I'll settle for what I *can* soothe, and that's the doubt knocking around his chest. Sighing into his mouth, I cup the back of his neck and brush my eyelashes over his cheek. "Life is worth the pain," I remind him, quoting the very thing I tell my victims before they die. I give them one last chance to change their minds about dying before I slit their throats. But by then, the damage to their souls, their psyche, whatever you want to call it, has already been done. It doesn't matter how many flowers or smiles I bring—they've lost their will to live by the time I show up and remind them how good life can be. Any happiness we have together is temporary, on both sides.

But with Zane, our happiness is forever. I think that

with Mercy, we could expand that happiness tenfold. We can get out of the killing business if needed. Tell the bratva to *suck it* when they come calling about disposal jobs, and just—end the cycle. Stop the bleed inside Zane's heart.

"For what it's worth," I whisper, brushing my lips over my lover's, "I think you should follow wherever your heart leads, even if that's away from me."

Zane inhales sharply. "*Never—*"

"Shh. Listen." I meet his cautious eyes. "We won't step into our best lives if we stand still. We have to keep moving in the direction that feels best, even if it doesn't seem like it makes sense. And," I breathe, smiling softly, "I'll be right here with you the entire time. So if you decide that you don't want her, that's okay. And if you do, that's okay, too. I'm with you no matter what. But I want you to try it out for a bit. See how it feels." I kiss him gently, ecstatic when he kisses me back. "You don't even have to tell me how it goes. I promise."

"It won't go anywhere," he grumbles, frowning. "But for you, I'll... try. Only once." As Mercy and Sam emerge from the back porch with marshmallows and graham crackers tucked beneath their arms, Zane sighs. "Do we really have to do this?"

I wrap my arm around my grumpy bastard's waist. "Yeah. Try to enjoy it." Kissing his temple, I smile. "Nothing bad's going to happen if you live a little, Zane."

Scrunching his nose, he makes a sour face. "That's what everyone says before the sky falls." He glances up at the clear blue sky, its color rapidly shifting as sunset approaches.

"Okay, Mr. Doom and Gloom." I roll my eyes. He can be such a stick in the mud. "Hey! Mercy! Toss me some chocolate." I jab my thumb into Zane's shoulder. "He fucking needs it." Catching the candy bar she throws my way, I grin as I unwrap the chocolate and shove it into Zane's mouth. "Swallow that and keep the fire going. I'm gonna get us some drinks."

Having a bonfire is another fantastic idea of mine. Zane and I usually stick indoors during our cabin vacations, but this time, I want to try new things. Explore new people. Live a little.

The whiskey I nabbed from the bar pairs perfectly with the sticky sweet treats, and we all pass around the bottle as we take turns making smores. Sam gets melted marshmallow on his face, Mercy smears chocolate all over her fingers, and Zane—

Well, he's trying to be friendly.

It's fucking *hilarious*.

Scowling as he smashes a graham cracker onto a burnt marshmallow, he peels his sticky fingers away before shoving the smore at Mercy. "Here."

She blinks at him. "I've already got one." There's a half-eaten smore in one of her hands and a near-empty bag of marshmallows in the other. "But thanks."

Zane's jaw clenches. "I made it for you."

"Thank you?"

With a huff, Zane smacks her old smore—from Sam, I think—to the ground and places the new one in her hand. "Eat it." When she doesn't take the treat, he presses it against her lips. "I made it for you," he repeats, still frowning.

Not only did he make that one specifically for her, he fed me a half dozen of his first attempts, trying to create the perfect one to give to Mercy. Burning the marshmallow, although not everyone's preference, melted the chocolate the best.

Sure, his delivery could be ten times better, but he's not pretending to be charming. He's being himself.

I absolutely *love* that for him.

The burnt mallow cream oozes out from between the crackers and sticks to the seam of Mercy's lips. Relenting, she peels her mouth open only for Zane to shove half the smore inside. When she bites down, his fingers get in the way, but he doesn't pull them out.

"Should've known you'd suck at eating," he hisses. "If I hadn't shoved your head down, I bet you wouldn't have been able to swallow."

Sam spews his drink over the fire. "What the *fuck*, dude?"

I tamp down the urge to rescue Zane from himself. He's got to figure this out on his own. The whiskey, although great for warming our blood, has consequences... this being one of them. What little of Zane's filter exists rapidly deteriorates until he's either a cuddly mess or a grouchy one—and tonight, it seems that the grouch has come to play.

Mercy spits the smore out and grabs Zane's hand, ripping his fingers from her mouth. "At least this tastes better," she snaps, glaring at him. "Your cum was rancid."

"Was not!"

"Was too!"

Sighing, Sam frees himself from Mercy's death grip and trudges across the fire to me. "This was your idea, wasn't it?"

I smile as I take a sip of whiskey. "Guilty as charged."

"They're going to rip each other's throats out."

Grunting, I pass Sam the bottle. "Nahh. They just need to get it out of their system, and they'll be fine."

Sam's scowl mirrors Zane's. "Why push them together at all?"

"Zane needs it."

"But she doesn't."

"She *wants* it," I murmur, licking my lips. The pair are in each other's faces now, turning something as simple as holding hands into a death match between fingers. They fight for dominance without realizing it, grabbing the other roughly until they pull free. Back and forth they go, arguing over who had the upper hand during their blow job.

Sam takes a large swig from the bottle and sits down on the blanket beside me. "I'm only here because of her," he says after a moment. "She asked me to come with her, and I—"

"Couldn't say no?"

He rests the half-empty bottle against my knee. "Something like that."

Nodding towards the arguing couple, I ask Sam something I've been wondering over the past few days. "Have you guys been fucking?" Sam's good at keeping his emotions in check, and Mercy's been oddly tight-lipped in the mornings. I don't know what they've been doing every night, but it hasn't been loud—much to my disappointment.

There's only so much I can hear through the crack beneath their bedroom door.

"Yeah." A tender smile curves on Sam's lips as he stares at Mercy. "It's been... nice. Quiet."

Not rushed, I'm sure he means, which could mean that it's also passionless and boring. Two points for me and Zane, then. Our sex with Mercy will be anything but boring. I'm sure that's what she's missing, too—a good, hard fuck.

"Stretch her out for me," I murmur, unable to hide my smirk. Sam punches my arm and turns red like he's embarrassed, but at least he doesn't refuse or try to deny that he's warming her up for me. We both know that I'll get inside her sweet pussy before the week is over. Just...

I watch eagerly as Zane drops to his knees, face flushed as he drags Mercy onto his lap and kisses her senseless, groaning into her mouth as he weaves his fingers through her flowing hair.

...maybe after my boyfriend indulges himself first.

# CHAPTER 21

## SAM

I CAN'T KEEP SAYING that I didn't know things like this were going to happen. Bonfires were made for fireside makeouts—that's standard practice. Still, watching Mercy and Zane suck face is strange at first...

Until all of a sudden, it isn't.

Kane and I trade the whiskey bottle back and forth as we enjoy front row seats to their makeout session, the two of us silent as we watch our lovers tango with each other. I thought I'd be enraged to see Mercy enjoying herself with another man, but even the other night when all four of us somehow made it onto the bed together, I didn't get angry when I saw how into it she was. Sure, I got a little jealous when she declared, *loudly*, that she wanted to swallow Kane's dick like it was some kind of trophy, but jealousy is a far cry from hatred, and...

For some reason, I don't dislike this turn of events as much as I thought I would.

"I've never liked change," I admit slowly, rubbing my

chest. The alcohol burns on the way down, but with how chilly the evening air is getting, I don't mind it. Neither does anyone else, from the looks of it. Zane's got his hand up Mercy's shirt, and she's grinding down on his lap like a professional.

"Fuck, I need some of that," Kane grunts, completely ignoring my confession in favor of palming his erection through his pants. He glances at me, and I quickly shut that shit down before he can even *voice* whatever depraved thing is brewing inside his head.

"Not happening." Punching his arm, I scoff. "And stop doing that."

"What, *this*?"

I hear his fly unzip before I see his fat cock in his fist. "Jesus Christ!" Tearing my gaze away, I cringe. "Do you really have to do that next to me?"

"Does it really have to bother you?" Kane counters, rolling his eyes. "Get used to it, Sam. You're gonna see a lot more cock than you're used to from now on."

The sad thing is, Kane's not wrong. Mercy's shirt ends up on the ground, and Zane pops her tit out of her bra to suck on her nipple, earning himself a moan from Mercy that makes *me* get hard. I knew that Mercy wanted to have sex with Kane—I've come to terms with that fact—but the group dynamic between all four of us is still new to me. The shower was a surprisingly fun surprise, I'll admit, but everything after has been one mind-blowing experience after another.

Even the past few nights with Mercy—just the two of us—have taken a delicious turn.

She parts her lips and tips her head back, tossing her luscious locks over her shoulders so that they flow like water down her back. The rising moon reflects off the lake behind her and Zane, casting a silver-white haze on one side of their faces while the other is bathed in the warm glow of the fire.

My body temperature rises alongside my heartbeat. I swallow hard and ignore my twitching cock as much as I can… unlike Kane.

"Absolutely breathtaking," Kane murmurs, stroking his cock to the rhythm of Mercy's hips. "Did you teach her that?"

"Teach her—" *What* catches on my tongue as I watch Mercy dig her heels into the earth and grind harder, adjusting her angle on Zane's lap until she's practically riding him into the ground. My lips curve into a smirk. "I didn't teach her that." Mercy's acting on pure instinct.

It's fucking hot.

But she shouldn't undress outside in the cold, no matter how warm the fire is. Standing, I make my way over to her and Zane. The closer I get, the more my cock begs for attention, damn near punching through my zipper. As Mercy arches her back, our eyes meet over the tip of her nose.

"Sam!" She reaches for my hand and squeezes my fingers. "Is this—" Her breath catches as Zane tugs her nipple between his teeth before switching to the other one. "—okay?"

I smooth the hair off her forehead. "Yeah, baby," I assure her. "It's okay."

She smiles lopsidedly. "Okay, good, because—" A shudder rolls down her body. "I feel—*ah*—really good right now." Eyes wide, she pulls back far enough that Zane grumbles under his breath. "Kiss me?"

My heart clenches so tightly that it hurts. Despite being in an intimate position with Zane, Mercy still wants me. Smiling softly, I cup her throat and tip her back even farther. "Of course, baby. Whatever you want." Her lips taste like whiskey and chocolate, melting any resistance to this strange affair that I have left. "You look so good in Zane's lap," I murmur, cupping her breast and squeezing. "I bet you're soaking wet down there. Needy girl."

"Dirty girl," Zane corrects, staring at my hand kneading her breast. I pinch her nipple between my knuckles, and he lowers his head to lathe the rosy bud with his tongue. The wet swipe of his tongue sends a shiver down my spine.

*That's* a new sensation I never imagined before now.

Mercy cries out with pleasure. "Zaaaane!" Wiggling her hips, she huffs. "Touch me!"

"Oh, you're going to have to do better than that, Kitten. I distinctly remember Kane telling you to beg last time." With a smirk, Zane props his chin on Mercy's sternum and gazes up at her. "So beg."

Her eyes turn glassy as he rocks his hips into the cradle of her thighs. "W-what do I say?"

Dropping to my knees, I brush my lips across the

shell of her ear. "Tell us what you want." Kissing her neck steals all of my attention as she ponders what to say for far too long. "Don't overthink it."

Zane huffs irritably. "Seriously, Mercy, it's not that hard."

"Then why don't *you* beg?" Glaring at him, I grab Mercy's hips and hold her still. "Don't give it to him yet. Make him beg, baby."

She's still overthinking. A flush trails down her neck as she stares at Zane's smug face. "Um."

Kane chuckles from across the fire pit. "Zane's easy to rile up. He'll *definitely* beg if you make him wait long enough."

Zane growls at his boyfriend. "Shut up!"

I smile into the crook of Mercy's neck. This is more entertaining than I thought it would be.

Grabbing Zane's face, Mercy yanks his head back towards her. "Zane..." Taking a breath, she brushes her thumb over his bottom lip. "Don't you want to feel how wet I am?"

He swallows, his gaze lingering on her parted lips. "This won't work."

She takes his hand and dips it beneath the waistband of her leggings. "Zane," she exhales hotly. "I'm *so* wet. Can't you feel it?" Rocking her hips, she grinds on his fingers.

I can't see how deep they are inside of her, or if they are at all, but I can see Zane's reaction. His pupils dilate and his breathing shallows. A thin layer of sweat breaks out across his neck. He swallows hard.

I'm not faring much better. Holding onto Mercy's hips while she rocks them has consequences. My dick swells with the need to be the one trapped beneath her, and I have to hold back a groan. We've had sex for the past three nights—more than once a night, even, if I stay hard long enough—but apparently, that doesn't matter when it comes to my sex drive. I'm ready for night number four. Her pussy should be sore from all the pounding it's been taking, but Mercy doesn't show any signs of slowing down.

She speeds up, rocking her hips with fluttering lashes and a whine catching in her throat. When Zane doesn't reciprocate, she pouts. "If you don't want it—" Sliding off of Zane's lap, she collapses onto mine ass-first, engulfing my body in her heat. "Sam will take care of me. Won't you, Sam?"

"Yes," I moan, loving the way she presses her ass against my cock. Desire burns hot in my veins. *Yes*, she needs me. Fuck Zane. He can watch me claim her again and again, as many times as she wants. We've been using condoms, but I didn't bring any with me outside. What's one more cream pie? *Heaven?* Or would she ask me to pull out? Either way, it's a win. Sex with Mercy is *always* a win.

Her fingers slide into my hair and she pulls my mouth down to hers, eagerly flicking her tongue against my lips. Cupping her jaw, I give her the exact attention she wants, easily licking into her hot little mouth. She whines, matching me stroke for stroke, and rubs her ass over me. "Sam!"

"What is it, baby? You need more?"

She nods.

Unlike those two, I'm a gentleman. I won't make her beg for something we both want. Running my hand down her chest and over her stomach, I rub her needy pussy through her pants, enjoying the way she squirms. The heat of her burns straight through the fabric. I bet she really *is* soaking wet; tight and hot and creamy—

"Wait." Zane sits back on his haunches and purses his lips, the bright flush burning across his cheeks giving away his intentions. "We were just getting started." He clears his throat and looks away. "Mercy. Come here."

She exhales hotly across my neck and presses a kiss to my jaw. "No."

Zane clenches his fists. "*Mercy.*"

Ignoring him, Mercy curves her neck and nips my throat. I press the pads of my fingers against her clit and grin at Zane's heated glare. Rubbing in slow circles, I tease her while she sucks a hickey onto my neck. *Hell yes.* Mark me, baby. I moan as she bites down and pulls blood to the surface.

With a growl, Zane lunges forward and grab's Mercy's throat, pulling her teeth from my skin. "Fucking —*fuck me!*" He slides his fingers over mine and rubs lower, covering her pussy and scraping his nails over her clothes. "I'm so hard," he whines, clenching his eyes shut and thrusting his hips into the air. "It hurts."

*Pouting.*

Like a fucking dog.

I glance between him and Kane to find the latter man

grinning like an idiot at this latest development. Not only is his cock still in his fist, but his pants are crumpled in a pile on the ground beside him. Naked from the waist down, he winks at me. "Told you it would work."

"She didn't even have to touch him," I marvel, staring at the dark stain over Zane's crotch. He really *is* hard and hurting if that damp patch is his doing and not Mercy's. How often does he get off? Not enough?

Hard to believe with Kane as his partner.

Facing forward, Mercy follows my gaze to Zane's erection and turns her nose up. "You'll come too soon. Sam can last a long time." She pats my cheek, making *me* feel like a dog. "Isn't that right, babe?"

I've been trying my damndest to ensure that our nights together last as long as possible, going so far as to keep my socks on and only dig in my heels once her pussy is drenched. It's been an act of the utmost concentration and willpower, but apparently, it's paid off. She thinks I can last forever.

I'll be damned if I let her down. "Yeah," I rasp, clearing my throat. "I can make it last."

Unlike someone who came in under three minutes from a blow job.

Zane's jaw clenches as he tears at Mercy's leggings, ripping a hole in the crotch. We both dive for the access point at the same time, our knuckles colliding as he curves his fingers around her panties and I yank them aside. Her heady scent fills my nose as I brush my thumb over her clit, already coated in her arousal.

Yeah, she's fucking *wet.*

Moaning, Zane slides two fingers inside Mercy's molten core and plays with her, filling the air with the sound of her flesh sucking him in. He dips his shoulder and goes deeper, burying two—no, three—fingers as far as they can go. "You want me to beg, but I think your pussy's doing it for me. Hear that?" His wrist rubs the back of my hand as he presses harder against her walls. The distinct, wet gush of her arousal makes Mercy blush crimson and tremble violently in my arms.

"N-no it's not," she protests weakly. "That's just beca-*auuuuu*—" Her voice pitches and cuts her off mid-word. "*Zane! Ahh!*"

He's relentless, rubbing her G-spot with desperate precision. Panting against her mouth, he nearly kisses her. The wave of heat and desire burning through his body crashes through Mercy and onto me, and suddenly I feel like *I'm* the one intruding.

Mercy comes with a high-pitched cry that echoes across the lake and tumbles into the trees. Crows caw as they flee, scratching tree limbs and awakening the night. Crickets chirp nearby, the fire crackles and pops, and Mercy—

She stares into my eyes and steals the final piece of my soul. Cheeks flushed beautifully, lips puffy and pink, eyes alight with bright flames, she takes gasping breaths and drags my mouth over hers, kissing me with such reckless abandon that we nearly tumble onto Zane's lap.

With one hand on his fly and the other buried in Mercy's pussy, he quickly removes his pants, pulls out his cock, and finally abandons Mercy's body for his own, slicking his shaft with her arousal. Groaning, he strokes himself hard and fast, biting his bottom lip hard enough that it bleeds. "*Fuck,*" he hisses, quivering from head to foot. "You're soaking wet, Kitten. Creaming all over my fingers. And my—" he chokes—"dick."

Holding onto Mercy, I pour every ounce of my being into her body, needing her more than she needs me. I know that. I can accept it so long as she's happy and free and *alive.* So goddamn alive, gasping as I lick into her mouth and claim her saliva, her tongue, her teeth— needing more. Needing *everything.* I don't care that Zane or Kane are in the background; they're only background noise at this point. What I want—what I *need*—is her.

It's always been her.

"Mercy," I rasp, cupping her throat as she swallows. "Lie down for me, baby. I want to see the light dance across your body." Sitting behind her isn't enough. I need to be on top of her. Consuming her. Making her moan as she claws the earth beneath us and thrusts her hips in time with mine. Hair wild, body ablaze, heart on fire.

*Mine.*

She obeys beautifully, spinning around and lying on the cool earth. A blanket would be better, but if she's down for it, so am I. Dragging what little clothing she has left off her body and spreading her legs, I gaze at her glistening pussy and resist the urge to dive in. No, I want every last drop gushing around my dick more than I want her dripping down my chin. The firelight plays across her skin, transforming my moonlight girl into a golden goddess. She takes on the new color palette seamlessly, her usually pale complexion blending with the light until she's a beautiful caramel; soft and warm and fucking perfect.

While I throw my shirt to the ground and kick off my shoes, Zane fills the seconds with animalistic grunts and groans, his cock clenched tightly in his fist. Staring at Mercy's body, he licks a stripe across his teeth as he strokes mercilessly.

Tilting her head back as she arches her spine, Mercy stretches her arms over her head and pushes her tits out. "Zane," she purrs, the corner of her lips curving upwards, "I can warm you up, baby." Once he walks around me and starts to descend in my place, she pushes him back with her foot. "When you say please."

His eyes flash golden from the firelight, but he works his jaw like he's considering doing as she says. He might actually say please.

Too bad that it's still my fucking turn.

Shoving him away, I crawl on top of Mercy and settle between her thighs, easily aligning our hips and sliding my cock through her slick folds. She moans and wraps her arms around my neck, pulling me closer. "Sam," she breathes, peppering my neck with kisses. "Please fuck me. I need—" Her nipples brush against my chest, making her gasp. "I need you inside me."

Yeah, my girl begs—*for me.*

Kissing her hard, I take her just as roughly, punching my hips so that our bodies meet with a loud *slap* of skin-on-skin. Her pussy sucks me in, squeezing so tight that I can hardly move. She whines, clawing my shoulders as I stretch her wide. Every night, we've had to take things slow so that her body can adjust to my size, but tonight, she's feral. Moaning and panting in my ear, digging her nails into my back, lifting her hips off the ground. I let her be as wild as she needs, feeding off of her energy, needing this just as much as she does. My cock slides deeper, my hips slam harder, and the sound of her body accepting mine crescendos until it overpowers the scratch of our voices. I can't even hear my own heartbeat as I drive into her, the sound lost in the heat of our union.

"Mercy," I rasp, tasting her lips. "You feel so—" *Good* doesn't begin to describe it. Even Heaven, for all its alleged transcendence, isn't enough to describe how fucking perfect she feels right now. I kiss her instead, claiming her as fully as I can. My orgasm comes on fast, and I have to tighten every muscle in my body to keep from coming too soon.

Breathe. I just need to breathe.

In and out and—

"She's so fucking creamy. Look at it covering his cock. Gathering at the base, *fuck*. Such a pretty fucking pussy." A hand presses down at the base of my spine, pushing my cock as deep as it can go. "How does she feel, Sam? I bet she's gushing around your cock. It's dripping down her thighs." Kane's voice is raspy until he addresses Mercy, praising her with a gentleness I hadn't known he possessed. "You're making *such* a beautiful mess, Siren."

*Mine*, I want to snarl, but that wouldn't necessarily be true. She wasn't grinding all over my lap earlier—she was grinding on top of Zane's. For better or worse, we're sharing these moments of intimacy with Mercy.

Pride suddenly fills my heart until it overflows. We may be sharing the opening sequence, but I'm the only one reaping the benefits. She's creaming all over *my* cock. Her soft little moans and breathless pants are mine. The scratch of her nails on my back is mine. The pressure of her hips, the velvety cushion of her tits, the gaping wet hole between her thighs—mine.

*Mine-mine-mine.*

I come with a groan, the vibration of it coursing through my body. We weren't supposed to do this bare; she nearly freaked out over the first cream pie, and I doubt a second will soothe her fears of unplanned pregnancy. But it's too late now; I can't stop my dick from twitching as my cum spills free. At the absolute last second, I manage to pull out. Not fast enough, since I still cream all over her lips, but at least it's not buried deep inside her body.

*Where it belongs.*

My heart flips at the thought of Mercy taking my seed as deep as it can go, my cum painting her walls—her womb—white. I'd knock Mercy up in a heartbeat if she wanted it. Tie her to me. Bind her through blood first, then marriage, if she wants. Fuck. The raw desire for Mercy as my blushing, pregnant bride blinds me, and I bite down on her neck *hard*, groaning as another thick rope spurts from the tip of my cock and nestles between her warm thighs.

I'll give Mercy anything she needs to be happy, but

*this* craving—to fill her up over and over again until she's round with *my* child—is one hundred percent mine and mine alone. A dangerous wish. Too tempting. Burning inside my body like a demon clawing its way to the surface.

Carefully, I rock my hips and slide my dick through her folds, sweeping my cum as close to her womb as I dare. I absentmindedly rub her clit as I do, too focused on my task of not-penetrating to recognize her breathless little moans, the timid sway of her hips, the way she *pushes* just enough for me to—

Slip right in.

With a groan, I come a second time, filling up her channel exactly as I imagined. Painting her walls, rocking my hips to stroke deeper, pinning her down to keep her still as I carve my way inside her body, carefully extracting every last drop of my seed and securing it safely inside my woman where it belongs.

Not in her mouth or her throat or her stomach.

Inside her overflowing, soaking wet, dripping pussy.

*My* pussy.

*My* cum.

*My life.*

CHAPTER 22

## MERCY

IN THEORY, cooking a Thanksgiving meal should be a delight—both Sam and I have fond memories of gathering around the table with our families for holiday feasts—but the reality is that I simultaneously undercook and burn the mashed potatoes while Sam's roasted turkey is bland, pale, and unappetizing. The green beans, buttered and sautéed by Zane, and the fresh bread, purchased at the local grocer and baked by Kane, are what save the meal... if you can call it a meal at all.

Zane stares at the array of disappointing items set on the dining room table and sighs. "I'll call the Chinese place. We need an edible protein."

As he disappears into the kitchen to use the landline, Sam tears off a piece of turkey and pops it into his mouth, chewing slowly enough to make me cautious. Once he swallows, he chases the bite with a full glass of water. "That might be best." Coughing, he drinks my glass of water next. "Somehow it's both bland *and* salty."

With a grin, Kane smacks Sam on the back. "No sweat. We always order takeout. Zane's been humoring us with cooking, but I know he's been itching for a reason to give them a call."

"Chinese food must be your favorite." This will be the third time we've had Chinese all week. I don't know how many more wontons I can eat without turning into one.

"It's the only place that delivers up here."

Of course it is.

Frowning, Sam stands. "I can pick it up. It'll be faster than waiting for delivery."

"I'll come with you!" As I push my chair out, Kane's hand clamps down on my wrist.

"Where are you running off to, Siren? You've spent all day with Sam…" He brushes the pad of his thumb against the inside of my wrist. "Don't you want to spend time with me?"

A shiver runs down my spine, quickly followed by a wave of warmth. I'm both anxious and eager to hang out with Kane, primarily because he seems desperate to find ways to push me and Zane together. If he'd give me time to adjust to the idea of wanting yet another man—especially one who has harbored ill intent for me for weeks—then I'm sure things would progress smoothly.

Instead, it's like he's prying our mouths open and shoving medicine down our throats.

Pushing out his own chair, Kane grabs my hips and pulls me into his lap. His arms wind around my waist as he exhales into my back, relaxing once I'm settled in his arms. "Stay with me, Mercy."

Sam stares at me long and hard before turning away. "I'll be right back. Don't—" He swallows. "Don't do anything while I'm gone."

Kane's chuckle rumbles through his chest. "What could we possibly—"

"You know what!"

"I didn't take you as shy, Sam."

Emerald eyes flashing, Sam growls. "Don't fuck her, Reaper!"

"Don't worry, Wright, your precious girl is safe with me. I wouldn't dare try to seduce her without your watchful eye nearby. Isn't that your agreement?" Kane's hand snakes up my dress and slides between my thighs. I squeeze my legs shut and he chuckles in my ear. "That you watch while I finally..." He takes a small breath and murmurs so softly that only I can hear him. "Make you mine, beautiful... in the only way I know how." His arms tighten around me as he presses a tender kiss to the side of my neck. "If you still want me."

My heart does this funny little thing. A *ba-dum* that hits harder than the rest, making me lose my breath. Is Kane... giving me a choice? Would he walk away if I told him no?

There's *no way* he would leave. This is everything he's ever wanted, right? Me, naked, writhing beneath him as he pumps into my body and finally claims my body the way he's been yearning for ever since we first met. It's unfathomable that he would give that up just because I say something like *no thanks. Not interested. Time for you to go home. Goodbye forever.*

Yeah, right.

Except...

The smallest tremor courses through his body, ricocheting between his limbs like a stone skipping across the lake, growing weaker with time and distance, only for the next one to begin again in the middle of his chest where his heart resides.

Is he nervous about it? *The* Reaper—nervous about sex?

Reaching up and cupping his cheek, I turn his face towards mine and skim my lips along the length of his jaw. I'm a fool for wanting a man who vowed to kill me, and I'm an even bigger fool for closing the gap between us. "I'm looking forward to it," I whisper, answering honestly. "Be gentle with me, Kane."

He freezes, tensing up as he buries his face in the crook of my neck, but it's impossible to miss the curve of his smile against my skin. "Alright, Siren. I'll be gentle."

By the time I glance back up at Sam, his keys are in his hands. He stares intently at Kane and me, a glimmer of determination shining in his eyes. "Yeah. I'll be here." Before he leaves, he places his hand on my shoulder and bends to press a kiss to my lips. "Wait for me, Mercy."

I meet Sam's eyes. "I will."

He kisses me again, lingering to make it soft and sweet. "Promise?"

"I promise."

His smile is warm, catching me off guard. I grab his hand before he can pull away. "I love you," I murmur, "you know that?" My heartbeat trills as his smile grows and he leans in for another kiss, sliding his hand into my hair and pressing his body into mine. The chair creaks beneath our combined weight: mine, Kane's, and suddenly Sam's, the three of us testing its limits.

There's a sigh from across the room. "What are you three doing?" Something hits Sam's back and falls to the floor. A dishrag. I peer around Sam's shoulder to find Zane watching us, a divot between his eyebrows and soap suds clinging to his forearms. "You're going to break the chair."

"Don't care," Kane rumbles, pulling me higher up his lap. "I like when she's like this. Don't you like it, Sam?" Something pokes my butt, and I nearly roll my eyes.

*Men.*

"Mhm," Sam mumbles, licking the seam of my lips. "She's trapped." He doesn't have to chase my mouth, but he does anyway, cupping my jaw and sliding his lips over mine like he's determined to break in. Once I finally part my lips, he sighs into my mouth and slips his tongue inside, humming appreciatively as he tastes me. "You have such a sweet mouth, Mercy."

"So fucking sweet," Kane rumbles, rolling his hips beneath me. "I'm addicted."

"Me fucking too."

"Zane, come here. Have a taste."

*Mmm?* Pinned between two powerful men, I watch wide-eyed as a third shuffles closer, a hungry look in his eyes.

"Don't know if she's ready for me." Zane crosses his arms over his chest and raises an eyebrow. His white t-shirt, damp from whatever he was doing in the kitchen, clings to his chest and shows off a tattoo on his pec. A falcon, I think, or some other bird of prey. As dangerous as the man standing in front of me.

"Oh, she's ready. Aren't you, Siren?" Kane's hand travels higher up my dress, fondling my stomach before reaching my breast and squeezing. He thrusts his hips at the same moment, creating bittersweet friction in all the wrong places.

I lift my hips and adjust my position, easily arching my back and sitting back down with his cock pressed tightly against my core. With a tentative roll of my hips, I grind down on him and gasp at the pleasure that radiates through my body. "Oooh, that's—*good*." Biting my lip, I stare into Sam's eyes while Kane grabs my hips and uses me like his personal plaything, rubbing my pussy along the hard length of his shaft. The denim of his jeans scrapes against my sensitive thighs, contrasting the soft cotton of my panties keeping me somewhat modest. It isn't until Sam hikes up my dress that I'm exposed, blushing like a virgin as three sets of eyes stare at the lewd display between my thighs.

Sam holds my skirt in his hands like he's bewitched, unable to look away from how *thick* Kane's cock is as it tries to break through our clothing. His Adam's apple bobs as he swallows, and within seconds, he's tenting *his* jeans, too. "She's getting wet." Shoving my skirt into Kane's fists, he kneels, spreading my thighs wider so that he can slide between them. "That feels good, doesn't it, baby?"

I nod, having already said that, but maybe Sam was too engrossed in the moment to hear me. "So good."

Caressing my thighs, Sam glides his palms up my body until he reaches my panties, gently tugging them aside to reveal my pussy. He sucks in a breath and groans, eyes sparking like wildfire as he inches closer. "You're still creamy from this morning."

*Oh God.* Embarrassment floods my system, and I blush violently. We had sex this morning, but he didn't have to broadcast that fact! "We used protection," I remind him, biting my lip. I shouldn't be creamy since Sam didn't come inside me. I can tell that he wants to— he practically snarls every time he rips open a condom package—but ever since the accident by the bonfire, I've made him swear to always use protection.

We can't get carried away just because it feels good.

"I know. This is all you, baby." Sam's hot breath fans my thighs. "I want a taste."

Kane shoves Sam back with a boot square to his chest. My panties fall back into place. "It's not your turn," he grunts, nodding towards the other man in the room. "Zane. *Come. Here.*"

Without a beat of hesitation, Zane fills the space that Sam just occupied. Instead of kneeling, he cups my cheeks and tilts my face up, staring down at my lips with the most infuriating little frown on his face. "You better not bite me, Kitten." Licking his lips, he dips closer, his gaze flicking up to my eyes. "I bite back."

He descends without any ceremony, capturing my lips like a man on a mission. As soon as he's sure that I'm not going to attack him, he relaxes and softens his mouth, drinking me in with gentle plucks of his lips on mine. It's warm and wet and somehow sweet, the way he sucks my bottom lip or rolls his tongue, teasing my mouth and making me melt. Over and over again, he kisses me, seamlessly blending them together and humming with satisfaction every time I kiss him back.

Until there's a *rap rap* of someone's knuckles on the wall behind us.

I freeze, but the men jump into action. Someone pulls my dress down over my thighs while another grabs a steak knife from the table. Something crashes into the ground and I hear a body slam against the wall.

"What the hell are you doing here?" Sam. He's shouting. *At* someone. Oh, God, someone saw us making out. With my dress up and my body exposed and my—*my heart on fire.* It tumbles in a discordant rhythm, thrown off kilter by the sudden change in mood. The room crackles with electricity as all four of us stare at the intruder: dusty brown hair streaked with gray, a scowl carved on his otherwise perfectly sculpted face, bright green eyes that mirror the emergence of Spring without any of its warmth... and an eerie familiarity.

Kane grumbles as he lifts me out of his lap. "Fucking rich bitches. No goddamn respect." As he checks the perimeter for more men, he grabs the carving knife from the rejected turkey and hands it to me. "If anyone comes after you, stab them." He wraps my fingers around the handle and adjusts my grip for a firmer hold, then meets my eyes. "Even Sam."

I gape at him while he spins around and whispers something in Zane's ear. The other knife, the one plucked from the table before Kane and I stood up, is clutched tightly in Zane's fist. His grip doesn't relax even after Kane pries the knife away and claims it for himself. Looking back at me, he winks and mouths something to me. *He gets stab happy when cornered*—I think, unless that's me projecting. Zane wanted to stab *me* when we first met. It would make sense that a stranger barging in on us, on a holiday, no less, would make him jumpy.

The older man chokes out a response. "Is that any way to greet your father, young man? Put me down."

"No." Sam's entire body tenses.

"Put," his father snaps, "me," he grabs Sam's throat, "*down!*"

Sam shoves him against the wall before letting go. Unlike in the movies, Samuel Wright doesn't crumple to the ground. He lands on his feet and releases his son before casually dusting himself off like nothing happened. His pretentious white suit wrinkles at the collar, but he pretends that nothing is amiss. "Sit down, Samson. We have something important to discuss."

"Like hell, I'm sitting anywhere near you."

I stare at Sam's back, not believing my ears. Every time I saw Sam and his father when we were teenagers,

Sam always did as he was told without any hesitation. Now, he's like an agitated dog anticipating a beating. Practically snarling. On edge. Ready to snap at his master's fingers.

From what I hear, that's precisely what Samuel Wright is to most people: their master, controlling their lives with money and leverage. My dad doesn't talk poorly about people often, but the one time I caught him speaking about Samuel, he had this irritated glint in his eye as he told my grandmother what a snake Samuel was —and how much Sam and his mom deserved better. As far as I know, his opinion hasn't improved over the years.

I wonder what Sam and my dad know that I don't.

"You called in a favor, Samson, and not an insignificant one. So, either you sit down for a discussion like adults, or I drag you home like the boy you're proving to be."

"I'm not sitting anywhere near him." Zane snatches the steak knife back from Kane and aims the tip at Samuel's nose. "Get the fuck out of my house."

"Your house?" Lifting an eyebrow, he stares at his son rather than at Zane. "You're lucky you haven't been charged with breaking and entering. If I hadn't settled the dispute with the owners, you'd be at the station right this very minute."

"You're lying." Zane glares at Samuel. "There are no cameras on the property, and the security system is offline. No one knows we're here." Tipping the knife, he takes a step closer. "Except you. How did you find us?"

Ignoring Zane, Samuel sidesteps towards the table.

"Now, if that's settled—" A stripe of crimson blooms across his cheek. His eyes narrow as he turns his head and looks down his nose at Zane. "Samson, get control of your dog before I put him down."

It's Kane's turn to step closer. "What the fuck did you say, old man?"

Samuel smiles coldly at the two men. "I don't know how either of you came into contact with my son, but I assure you that whatever relationship you think you have with him ends today." Snapping his fingers, he returns his gaze to Sam. "Remove them."

Armed men appear from every entrance to the room, rushing towards us with expertise. They disarm Zane after he slices one of their arms, and two men grab Kane to keep him from swinging his fists. One man takes an elbow to the face and falls to one knee. As for me, I jab forward with a scream, using all of my strength and weight as adrenaline hits. The blade in my hand sinks into flesh, puncturing a soft spot in the man's neck. His eyes bulge as blood trickles from the wound, made worse when I jerk back and take the blade with me. He collapses to the ground, his body twitching as blood pours onto the carpet, staining it deep red.

Shit shit shit. *Shit.* Holy shit. What did I do? *What did I do?*

Someone hits me from behind and I stumble to the floor. The knife tumbles from my hands as I land beside the dead man, burning my palms on the carpet and staining my dress with his blood. I scream at his unseeing eyes, and someone kicks me in the stomach, knocking the air from my lungs and shutting me up.

Sam lunges, snarling like a demon as he tackles the man who kicked me. They knock into a china cabinet and break every dish inside, the clatter of cracking porcelain and splintering wood spilling into the air. But the man at Sam's mercy doesn't fight back; he lets Sam beat him bloody, barely holding his arms up to cover his head from serious injury, like he isn't taking the fight seriously.

Or he's been paid not to injure his employer's son.

Kane shouts as he shrugs off one of the men holding him, head-butting them in the nose and launching himself at the man keeping Zane hostage. They tumble to the floor in a tangle of limbs and fury, but unlike the man facing Sam's wrath, these two don't hold back. One of them pulls out a gun and shoots, missing Kane's head by an inch. I scream at the burst of gunfire and cover my ears.

The bastard responsible for everything sits at the table and uses a cloth napkin to dab the cut on his face, going so far as to dip a corner into a water glass to wipe away the blood. Then he takes the only knife remaining on the table and carves a slice of turkey for himself, unconcerned with the carnage taking place a few feet away. "Hold," he orders, sawing into the meat like a novice butcher. As the rest of his hired men pull out guns of their own, the room goes still... and Sam keeps punching. Once his victim finally falls unconscious, he drops the man to the ground and turns to face his father—no, to face *me.*

Falling at my feet, he scans my body for injuries. "Are you okay? Are you hurt?"

I grab Sam's hands and wince at his bloodied and bruised knuckles. "Are *you* okay?" This is the second time he's gotten into a fight over me, and each time seems to get worse. Guilt gnaws at my heart. It shouldn't be this way, not for normal people like us. We're not military or law enforcement or anyone remotely dangerous, and yet, bad things keep happening.

It's like we're cursed when we're together.

"Mercy," Sam murmurs, wiping away a silent tear tracking down my cheek. "Everything will be okay. I promise."

I shake my head. "You can't know that."

"I do." He smiles as he tries to reassure me. "Because I have you." Capturing my lips, he kisses me hard and fast, like he's trying to hold onto the belief that everything *is* okay and that he *does* have me. I cling to his shirt as he sweeps me into his arms and carries me to the dining room table, remaining calm despite the dead body on the floor and the armed guards surrounding us. Sam sits, keeping a wide berth from the table, and cradles me in his lap. "What do you want?"

"Respect." Samuel's smile is as cold as his eyes. "I did you a favor, Samson. The least you could do is return a phone call."

"I'm not coming home."

"Your fraternity is on suspension," Samuel says cooly. "The historic building you and your brothers have been vandalizing is on its way to demolition—at full fault of your own—and your membership has been revoked for infighting. You have also been summarily removed from any sports teams or clubs on campus, and your withdrawal from the school itself is pending approval, which will, of course, go through as soon as their offices reopen next week. I am not *suggesting* that you return home. I am demanding." He steeples his hands over the table. "Unruly children do not have the privilege of freedom. I will not have any son of mine ruin his life over some—" His lip curls. "Dead Girl."

Ice freezes inside my veins. I stop breathing. A harsh ringing fills my ears. How does he know that name? Why would Sam's father, mister moneybags, know anything about me?

Sam raises his voice. "She's the reason my life is better. All you've ever given me are ultimatums and broken promises. Ever since Mom died—"

"Do *not* speak of your mother!"

"Ever since Mom died," Sam shouts over his father, "you've been a fucking maniac. You can't control the world! You can't control *me!*"

Samuel folds his napkin and lays it on top of his untouched plate. "You will arrive home by midnight, alone, without another word."

The hairs on the back of my neck rise. Sam's dad is eerily calm, like he's five steps ahead of us on the board and everything is stacked in his favor. He who controls the landscape can shape the game and bend its rules, like a game master.

Yet another way Samuel Wright behaves like he owns the universe.

"I'm not going anywhere—"

"I'm not giving you a choice."

"You don't own me!"

"No," Samuel concedes, suddenly meeting my gaze instead of his son's. A pit opens up in the bottom of my stomach. "But I own Morningstar Mortuary, along with every one of its permanent residents." He lists my family members off with his fingers, like we're collectable cards. "A desperate father foolish enough to barter his family's lives away, a batty old woman better off dead than alive, a psychiatric patient abandoned by his own family, and a stupid girl who thinks her virginity is worth millions." Sneering, he glances down at my body. "I wouldn't touch her for free."

Kane or Zane, I'm not sure which, must throw a fit, because one of them gets punched in the face and thrown to the ground. I barely hear the *thud* over the ringing in my ears.

"Lilith," I breathe, my voice scratchy. "My sister." He didn't include her on the list. She must be safe.

"Ah, yes, the older sister." A look of longing appears on Samuel's face. "Now *that's* a body I could enjoy."

Bile rises to the back of my throat. What the hell is he saying? That he would—I swallow hard—*touch her*?

"Unfortunately, your sister's already bound to another man. Their contract is airtight, I'm afraid." Samuel tuts like he's disappointed about this. "It'll take a little more time to unravel that situation, but..." He licks his lips. "It's well worth the prize."

I'm going to be sick. My body quivers as equal parts anger and disgust roil within my gut. How dare he—*how dare he!*—treat us like toys for his amusement. "My family," I seethe, "is not for sale!"

Samuel clicks his tongue. "Everything has a price, Mercy Morningstar." A self-satisfied smirk makes him look like the devil himself. "And I've paid yours."

# CHAPTER 23

## KANE

SAMUEL WRIGHT DOESN'T JUST skyrocket to the top of my hit list, he wipes every other name from existence. All it takes is one disgusted look at my boyfriend and one stupid fucking decision to damn him to an early grave. After dropping the most bizarre info bomb I've ever heard, he gives one final order before finally leaving us alone: a parting gift for his son's unlikely bedfellows.

"Break his arm."

I fight against every man in the room. Every single one feels my fists, but it's not enough. The carving knife that Mercy dropped is lost in the chaos, and I'm shoved face-first to the ground to witness these men—*these demons without fucking souls*—break the man I love.

Zane doesn't scream, but Mercy does. Clawing to get to Wright's guards, she spews out curses that I've never heard of, more furious than I've ever seen her. Like a bat out of hell, she slips free from Sam's grasp and jumps on someone's back, scratching their face furiously enough to peel back their skin.

"Don't hurt her," Wright Senior orders, looking at Mercy much like he might stare at a rabid dog. "Yet."

"You fucking bastard!" Sam is kept at bay while his father looks between each of us, coldly calculating our worth like we're pigs at auction.

"Careful, now, Samson, or I might change my mind about your little toy." Once someone finally restrains Mercy, he grabs her chin and squeezes until her mouth pops open. "She's breakable, after all, much like that one." He glances at Zane lying motionless on the ground and *tuts*. "I was hoping he'd scream." Releasing Mercy, he suddenly steps on Zane's broken arm. "Come now, let's hear it. I want to know how badly it hurts." When Zane doesn't so much as whimper, Samuel snarls. "You stupid dog." He lifts his foot and slams it back down on Zane's swollen flesh. "Maybe we should break both your arms, hm?"

"Stop it!" Mercy tries to kick Samuel. "What is *wrong* with you?"

Ignoring her, Samuel sighs and backs off, finally turning to leave. "The fun will have to wait, however." He turns to his son. "Midnight, Samson. Don't be late."

Before he can escape, I make a promise. Speaking from the depths of my black heart, I ensure that the fucker can hear me. "I'm going to gut you, Samuel *fucking* Wright." Grinning, I stare at the bleeding cut on his cheek. That's only the beginning of his torment. "I will make you scream for a death that never comes. Your lungs will burn and your soul with whither and I will be your fucking God."

He pauses in the doorway and speaks with his back turned to us. "There is no God, only His forsaken children."

The armed guards quickly follow their employer, leaving the four of us to lick our wounds. Mercy crawls on her hands and knees to Zane's side, and I join her in time to help Zane sit up. His face is pale and cold sweat slicks his skin, but otherwise, he's sort of okay. When I touch his arm, he hisses in pain.

"I'm going to kill him," I growl, slamming my fist into the floor. "Fucking bastard."

"Let's get you to a hospital," Mercy suggests softly, her voice easing some of the tension crackling behind my eyes. Jesus, that hurts.

I shut my eyes and take a few deep breaths. "Not the hospital." We don't like having public records for this very reason—people like Samuel fucking Wright can track us down. "The Box." We may not be official members of the bratva, but the least they can do is patch us the fuck up on their dime.

"Medical facility," Zane explains for me, wincing as I lift him off the ground. "I can walk."

"Yeah, but—" I swallow the fury burning in my throat. If I don't carry Zane, I might charge after those bastards and get myself killed. That won't help anyone, least of all Zane.

He must understand where my thoughts are leading, because he brushes his hand over my forehead and smoothes out my brow. "Hey. We'll get him. There's not a single target we haven't put down."

Mercy hovers nearby and bites her bottom lip as we both turn our heads to face her. She's the exception to that rule—a permanent one, as far as I'm concerned. I give her as reassuring of a smile as I can. Now isn't the time to untangle my feelings about her, especially when I'm not even sure exactly *how* I'm feeling. Heart in my throat, oddly nervous, kind of excited?

Yeah, I'll keep all that to myself.

"What about—" Mercy looks over her shoulder at Sam, who's wound so tightly that he looks like he's about to blow. When she reaches for him, he flinches away.

"Don't touch me right now."

"Sam—"

"Don't. Please."

"But this isn't your fault."

He runs both hands through his hair and stares up at the ceiling. "I ignored my dad's calls and texts, Mercy. This is his way of punishing me for it."

Talk about a shitty fucking parent.

I shake my head. "Daddy issues aside, we gotta go." If I could snap my fingers, I would. "The Box. Now." The longer we wait to set Zane's break, the worse shape he'll be in. "Someone drive."

Mercy tears her gaze off Sam and nods at me. "I'll drive."

"Keys are on the nightstand in the master." While she disappears to grab Zane's car keys, I stare at Sam. "I don't blame you," I say honestly, "but it's not fucking okay, either way." Zane had warned me that Sam's dad was a dick, but I didn't anticipate Mega-Dick levels of cuntiness. I hadn't expected to run into the man at all, truth be told. He was supposed to be the boogeyman: scary in your head but harmless in reality, not a psychopathic control freak.

Zane growls in frustration. "*I* blame you, asshole!" Glaring at Sam, he huffs. "How did your dad find us, huh? What tipped him off?" His gaze travels down Sam's body like he's looking for a tracker. "What did you do?"

Sam's jaw clenches. "I already told you. I didn't answer his calls."

"Bullshit." Zane spits the word like venom. "There's something else; another reason why he's so pissed off. I'm alive after cutting his face, which means that he's playing with us. It's not efficient. He should have killed us and dragged you back with him."

I say the first thing that comes to mind. "He's a sick bastard who gets off on inflicting pain."

Zane huffs as he considers this. "Then why did he go after Mercy's family?"

"To hurt her." I roll my eyes. That's fucking obvious. "You're thinking too hard."

"You're not thinking hard enough."

"Sometimes," I rumble, nipping Zane's jaw, "you piss me the hell off."

He purses his lips. "The feeling's mutual." After a moment, he sighs and rests his head on my shoulder. "But I'd really appreciate if we could leave. Take me to the car?"

Little moments like these remind me that Zane, for all his posturing about the magnitude of his inner strength and intelligence, likes to be taken care of as much as the rest of us. "You got it, babe." I kiss his cheek. "Let's get you patched up." I glance at Sam before leaving. "What are you gonna do, Sam?"

Avoiding my gaze, Sam glares at the floor. "What I have to."

Right.

I nod. "Okay. Call us once you know something."

"Or have a plan," Zane mumbles, "for killing your father."

We don't need a plan for that, but whatever. I'll let my lover have something to focus on during our car ride across the city. Murder is a perfect distraction from his injury.

After spending the past week with Sam and arguing with him about Mercy for an entire month, walking away suddenly feels strange. My chest tightens like we're friends going through a breakup, and I don't exactly like it. Clearing my throat, I glance over my shoulder at him. "See ya, Sam."

He blinks, coming out of a fog to return my gaze. "Um. Yeah. See you."

Mercy appears right on time and falls into step behind me. "The roads should be clear because of the holiday—" She trails off once she realizes that Sam isn't following us into the hall. "What's wrong?" A divot appears between her pinched eyebrows as she takes a few steps back. "You're not coming with us?"

Sam looks damn near mournful as he rushes forward and sweeps her into his arms. "I need to find out what leverage he has on your family." Pressing his forehead against hers, he exhales slowly. "As soon as I do, I'll run back to you, I promise." Before she can protest, he slants his lips over hers and silences anything she's about to say. They linger in this stolen moment for what feels like eternity, each beat of my heart ticking like a clock. He's gentle when he touches her but no less insistent, determined to pour every ounce of himself into her body.

This isn't a short goodbye to last a few hours. It's meant for much longer—as long as it takes for Sam to complete his task.

When he comes up for air, he whispers something that I'm sure is meant for Mercy's ears only, but Zane and I hear anyway.

"I love you, Mercy Morningstar. I won't let anyone hurt our family."

He has the balls to say what I can't, and all of a sudden, I'm watching him run right past me to claim the final piece of Mercy's heart.

The game is over.

Samson fucking Wright has won.

# Chapter 24

## Zane

Witnessing someone's heart break is a funny thing.

I'm not sure how I'm supposed to feel about it—sympathetic or mournful, maybe—but in the end, I can't dictate my emotions. My heart does its own thing and lets me know, *hey, Zane, guess what?*

I'm fucking relieved, and I'm a shitty fucking person for it.

Our car ride to the bratva's hidden medical facility known colloquially as *The Box* is done in complete silence. Normally, this would be my preference. I don't have to listen to Kane prattle on about paint colors or Mercy whine about whatever is bothering her on this particular day, which leaves me to my thoughts. But between the shooting, intense pain in my arm and the weak flutter of relief in my chest, I hardly have any room left for coherent words, even inside my head.

What I do feel is *good* but also somehow *bad*.

As the medical staff whisks me away, I go through the motions of treatment. Gritting my teeth when they take x-rays, closing my eyes when they set the break, sighing with relief once they finally administer pain meds in an IV hooked to my arm. Took them long enough. I sit up in one of the beds lining the back wall of the facility and stare blankly at the partitions separating the triage and treatment areas. The Box has experienced doctors and state-of-the-art equipment, but keeping it under the feds' radar means that it has to sacrifice modern comforts like private rooms to remain discreet—much like how I've been running my life with Kane.

We keep our heads down, don't kick up too much trouble, and lay low so that we can continue living however we want.

In the span of—God, weeks?—Mercy and Sam have blown that lifestyle to pieces.

I still don't know how Samuel Wright found us at the cabin, but in the end, I guess it doesn't matter. The consequences have already begun. Sam's either neck-deep in his father's machinations right now or he's treading water as he tries to resist. I'm not holding my breath for Sam's success, nor am I delusional enough to think that he gives a rat's ass about me or Kane. Our lives, as far as I'm concerned, are forfeit. It was only a matter of time, sure, but I had been hoping to steal some time back from Mercy. Take a few years off of her life and add it to mine, or to Kane's, like I'm some sort of powerful deity or devil who can manipulate time and space like that. I scoff aloud at my idiocy. Going to the cabin and pretending we could somehow wring drops of life from Mercy's body was wishful thinking, after all, and not the least bit practical.

Nothing could save us once Samuel got involved.

Heavy footfalls approach from my right. I ignore them. Kane's likely pulling his hair out in a corner somewhere, and Mercy is trying to persuade one of the medical staff to let her use their phone to call her dad. Whoever else is around doesn't concern me.

But apparently, I concern them.

"I did not expect to see you here," a heavy Russian accent rumbles. I stare at the unlit cigarette Ezra Reinoff, *vor* to the Bratva's *pakhan*, rolls between his fingers. "Did prey fight back?"

This isn't a conversation I can ignore. I open my mouth and taste menthol on his breath. "Something like that."

Ezra grunts. "Is target dead?"

No, she's standing right over there.

He follows my gaze to Mercy. "She is Morningstar girl."

I'd be surprised that he knew who she was, except that's kind of his job as the official bodyguard for the bratva's king and queen—Baranova something or other. I don't keep up with criminal royalty well enough to remember their full names. Ezra, however, is the exception because he's the one who contracts Kane and me for clean-up jobs. Still, I don't want to think about Mercy more than I already do, so I steer the conversation another direction. "What are *you* doing here, Ezra?"

"Physical exam is important."

Lifting my gaze, I give him a once-over. He's not exactly old. "You worried about something?"

"No." After a moment, he taps the butt of his cigarette against his thigh. "But Morningstar girl is upset. Why?"

Do I really have to explain the downfall of my life to this fucking guy? I crinkle my nose. I guess I am in his territory and using his facility and its resources without explicit permission. Begrudgingly, I hold open the window for Ezra to peek into my life. "Samuel Wright has dirt on her family." I adjust my position to try and ease the ache in my arm, but nothing helps. Sighing, I watch as Mercy thanks the staff member and runs off with a cell phone in hand. "He says that he owns the Morningstars—all except Lilith. Not that he doesn't want her, too, but she's wrapped up in some other contract."

A contract. Legally binding. How would Wright have a document giving him ownership of people? It's illegal, for starters, and fucking weird on top of that. My thoughts drift to marriage and how binding that is, tying people's assets together under the guise of love. It's fucking stupid, is what it is. You don't have to sign your independence away to prove that you love someone.

Ezra scratches the stubble lining his jaw. The tattoos wrapped around his arm shift in the lowlight. "So he owns property. Maybe in illegal trade or fine print. Easy to change document of ownership, yes, but also easy to change back. Especially if won in card game. Then it is not binding."

I doubt Mercy's father gambled away their home. "Morningstar doesn't seem like the type."

"Does Vinicius have debts?"

"How should I know?"

"Debt," Ezra murmurs, "is pressure cooker. It builds until it explodes, and people become desperate to ease burden. But maybe not debt. Maybe..." He mumbles something under his breath, and I have to strain to hear him. "Exchange. Mutually beneficial."

The ache in my arm spreads to my chest, and I rub my sternum. "Mutually beneficial exchanges don't exist. Someone always gets fucked over."

There's a brief moment of silence. "You are bitter about girl?"

"What? No." My cheeks burn. "She doesn't matter."

Then why is my heart rate accelerating like I've been caught in a lie? It's *not* a lie. She doesn't matter. She isn't my end game.

Ezra flicks his gaze to mine. "If you like her, you must tell her. You will be eaten inside otherwise."

"Eaten *up* inside," I correct, scowling.

"You understand. Good."

No, I fucking don't, because that's not what's happening here. But Ezra's lack of comprehension isn't the problem. "We need to check who owns the mortuary." Maybe that will give us a clue as to what's going on. Property ownership is public record. Finding out should be easy. As for *person* ownership, Sam's on his own for that one. I may have a few black market connections, but we deal in detached body parts, not living human beings. The market is different.

"Strange business," Ezra murmurs offhandedly, "to keep the dead. For what? Sake of living?" He blows out a breath. "You cannot bring dead back to life. Holding memory is painful. You must let go."

My eyes widen as gears turn in my head. I understand dead bodies, and Samuel understands living ones. But who negotiates between the living and the dead? Who has an invested interest in both?

I stand as quickly as I can and walk carefully down the aisle. One of the medical staff calls out to me, but I ignore them and walk faster. Pushing open the exit, I search for Mercy and follow the sound of her voice. Around the corner, behind a stack of empty wooden pallets, I find her on the phone with someone. Kane paces back and forth in the middle of the alley and looks up at her every few steps, clearly not fully listening to her conversation, but invested enough to keep an eye on her. When he sees me, some of the melancholy clouding his aura dissipates.

"Hey," he murmurs, closing the distance between us. "I didn't realize you were done."

They haven't discharged me, but whatever. "Who is she talking to?"

"Her sister, I think." Kane immediately shifts gears

and takes my hand, pulling me to the side. "Can we talk?"

Anxiety prickles down my arms. "Not now."

"Soon?"

I meet Kane's soft blue eyes. Whatever he has to say must be important, because he's never this formal about anything. Tension pulls at my spine. I'm going to hate this conversation no matter what he wants to discuss. "Soon," I promise, pecking his lips. The little smile he gives soothes my aching heart more than should be possible.

Taking a quick breath, I press on. "I think I know why Samuel's interested in Mercy's family. Sort of." It's a long shot, but the theory makes sense in a roundabout way. "They met after Sam's mom died, right?"

"Yeah?"

"What if they conducted the funeral service?"

Kane presses his lips together. "Um, no offense to Mercy's family, but they aren't exactly..." He searches for the right word. "Rich. A job like that would pay a fuck ton."

"What if they were friends, then? Before Sam's mom died?"

There has to be something connecting their families; something that goes beyond Sam and Mercy's relationship. Wright shouldn't be interested in his son's girlfriends. There's something else. There *has* to be something else.

"You think *Samuel fucking Wright* is friends with Mercy's dad?"

"No, not Samuel. The mom. Ingrid and—" I forget Sam's mom's name. "—Mrs. Wright. Maybe she requested their services while she was sick in the hospital. Some people add funerary clauses to their wills."

Kane rubs the back of his neck. "I dunno, babe, that still doesn't explain why he would want to own the Morningstars."

Why does Samuel want to own anything? Leverage. Power. Possession. He's doing the same shit with his son, trying to take over his life. "Maybe he's trying to control Sam, then, and is using the Morningstars as collateral." That could work in the bastard's favor. "How close is Sam to Mercy's family?"

Something shifts in Kane's eyes. "Close, I think," Kane softly replies. "Sam called them *our* family. Not just hers, but *theirs*." He glances over at Mercy. "Like how you're mine." A gentleness in his gaze makes him appear ten years younger, like a boy falling in love for the first time.

My heartbeat stills. Seconds turn into minutes that feel like hours. We both stare. Kane at Mercy, and me at Kane. The way he glows for her—

I choke on frigid winter air when I try to take my next breath. While I've been falling in love with him, he's been falling in love with Mercy. I always knew he would, but the realization that it's happening now and not in the distant future makes me feel untethered. I'm not surprised, not really, because this is what Kane does—he falls fast and loves hard, no matter who he latches onto. That's just... who he is. How he's always been.

It's why I love him so goddamn much. His heart is ten times the size of mine and beats twice as loud.

"You love her."

He tries to cover it up, steeling his expression as he turns back to me. But the damage has been done; I saw his heart break in the dining room hours ago, only to witness him taping the pieces back together so that he can hold onto that love for her a little longer. I don't think he means to set himself up for failure or heartache; he's just... in love with love. No matter if it's for me or Mercy or both of us at once.

"It's okay," I tell him, trying to be supportive. My heart isn't fully on board, but I can suck up the pain if it helps him heal. "It's also okay to be sad that she loves someone else. That's... life." The smile I give is meant to be reassuring, but the tears stinging my eyes make it as watery and pathetic as I feel.

Of course Kane loves Mercy. She's perfect for him.

"I'm not leaving you." Sliding his hands into my hair, he pulls me close. "So don't you dare try to pull away. I can love more than one person."

But how much can he give either of us if his heart is split two ways?

Shaking my head, I close my eyes. I know that technically, he's right. He can love two people. If anyone has the capacity for it, it's him. I just don't want to lose him... and now, after all this time, he knows that.

God, I'm a terrible boyfriend. I'm supposed to be reassuring him, and he's the one reassuring me.

I rub the tips of our noses together and take a deep breath. "We're a mess, aren't we?"

"The messiest," Kane agrees, smiling against my lips. "But you're *my* mess, Zane Hunter, and I'm yours." The kiss is soft and sweet and a little sad, but maybe that's our new normal.

Soft touches, sweet whispers, and sad hearts.

# CHAPTER 25

## SAM

IN A PERFECT WORLD, I would have been born to your average American family. We'd have grown up with a white picket fence—or a chain link one; I'm not picky—and a yard big enough to play catch or have a dog or spend evenings grilling hot dogs and hamburgers with the neighbors. Our house wouldn't have to be large. Or fancy. Or even ours. Renting would be fine, too, not that I would have known the difference as a child. But we would have been happy. We could have been normal.

Just me, Mom, and Dad.

In a way, it's still the three of us in this house. My dad hasn't changed anything since Mom died; the decor is still hers, and the five foot tall family portrait hanging over the fireplace is frozen in time, reminiscent of the Romanovs before they fell. Sometimes, I wonder if there's a curse on families like ours, ones who extend their reach beyond mortal limits. The Wright family name shouldn't have as much power as it does, and yet, my father has enough sway to curb local elections and influence the city's growth, helping new storefronts he deems worthwhile and ignoring all the rest.

When my mother was alive, she was the chairwoman on a lot of different committees. They met in our dining room and drank tea from our finest chinaware. Together, my parents were an unstoppable force capable of bypassing red tape and creating change within the city. For a long time, I wanted to be just like them. Influential and well-liked among both peers and professional adversaries, with a doting wife and loving family.

Until I realized that it was all a lie.

I have no doubt that my father loved my mother, and I believe that when they first met, she fell head over heels for the confident, multi-million dollar heir to the Wright legacy. They began working together philanthropically before they ever got married, I've been told, and I think that seeded their interest in each other. Everything I've seen or heard about my parents' sparkling reputation has been through the rose-tinted glasses of the public eye, which misses the heart of their relationship... or lack thereof.

My mother was as much a prisoner in my father's world as I am today. Which, suddenly, is suffocating.

I've spent years pretending that I have autonomy—attending a local college instead of an Ivy League, driving around a beat-up old pickup truck that a friend sold me for dirt cheap, playing football and spending hours on the practice field to avoid *ever* going home. But the reality is that no matter how far I think I've pulled away from my father, with one snap of his fingers, he can rope me back in and tighten the knots.

Standing in his office while he stares disapprovingly at me feels a lot like being a cockroach under his shoe. He's waiting for the moment I sense freedom lurking just out of reach—for that tiny, glimmer of hope—before he breaks me.

Despite the hour of night, my father is dressed as though he's come directly from a board meeting. For all I know, he may have just finished berating some poor employees who didn't meet their monthly quota, and I'm next in line for a verbal lashing. When he finally speaks, I brace myself for the worst.

"Do you know why I've allowed you to entertain this fantasy of yours for so long?"

The best response is silence, but I can't help myself. "And what fantasy would that be?"

My father's perfect smile turns cruel. "That you have a choice, son. In any of this." He stands and slowly makes his way to the built-in bar beside the unlit fireplace. "There are things outside of our control. Your birthright is one of them. You cannot deny it, much like I can't deny it from you."

"I'm sure you could find an all-too-eager replacement." The glassware clinks as my father pours himself a drink. "I don't want your money or your legacy, and I sure as hell don't want your name."

He turns around and walks closer. With one hand gripped tightly around his glass, he slaps me with the other. The liquid sloshes over the side and stains the rug, joining the red welt on my cheek as the only evidence of my provocation. "Neither of us has a choice in this, Samson." He leans on the edge of his white marble desk as he takes a sip of his drink. "Your mother died before she could produce a more suitable heir, so as regrettable as it is, you are all I have."

I was sixteen when mom died. They should have had plenty of time to procreate. "I bet you suck in bed, don't you?"

My father stops breathing.

"Can't get it up anymore? Or maybe that was the problem all along. I'm your miracle child, born from the one time you could actually finish. What, did she deny you, too? Is that why you're so fucking frigid? Couldn't even get it on with your own wife—"

This time, he throws his drink at my face. I dodge, and the sound of shattering glass fills the room. Both of us fall silent and still. I need to play nice in order to figure out what he has on Mercy's family, and he needs to play nice-ish so that I don't burn his entire legacy to the ground. We're at a stalemate, and we both know it.

He clasps his hands together and looks me in the eye. "You know what's at stake, don't you? That girl you've been watching, her family—" His eyes flash silver in the moonlight. "They're inconsequential compared to the bigger picture. I'm providing you with a future." Glancing at my mother's portrait hanging over the mantle, he frowns. "All they can give you is a family that's just as broken as ours."

I follow his gaze and study my mother's face. She

looks elegant in a white gown and pearls, with a subtle smile that illuminates her vibrant eyes. My father believes that we're broken because my mother is missing. I could yell myself hoarse proving him wrong, but it won't matter. To him, I'm the shitty consolation prize he got for loving a woman as radiant as the sun. She burned so brightly that her body gave out long before any of us were ready.

But I'm not planning on marrying the sun.

I'm in love with the gentle pull of the moon.

Drawing a breath, I swallow my feelings and lock them away in a box inside my chest. If I'm going to play my father's game, I have to stay sharp. The only way I can help Mercy now is to undo whatever contracts my father holds over the Morningstars. It will take time. Precious time that I'd rather spend with the woman I love. But...

If I have to sacrifice my desires to keep her safe, so be it.

I'll become the son my father always wanted.

It's a price that only I can pay.

CHAPTER 26

## MERCY

The days blur together. Somehow, I pull together a project worthy of a B for my painting class, and then the fall bleeds into winter.

I don't hear from Sam at all.

Keeping busy around the house helps. With my siblings' absence and my dad's impossible schedule keeping the morgue running, things have fallen into disarray. The dishes keep piling up. My grandmother's run out of tea and no one has restocked for her. We haven't switched out our summer blankets for the winter ones, and squirrels keep breaking into the attic. I'm on the roof to assess the damage and find their hidey-hole when Kane's motorcycle roars down the driveway. He jumps off after skidding to a halt and kicking up gravel dust.

Throwing off his helmet, he lunges for the ladder. "What the hell are you doing?" He climbs the rungs in record time and unsnaps the belt around my waist to claim my tools for himself. "Get down. I'll fix it. Where's the leak?"

"It's not a leak," I sigh, staring at the blocked gutters. "It's an infestation. We have friends in the attic, and the gutters—" Stress builds quickly, and I feel it pull at my spine. "I should have been paying more attention. I'll fix it."

Kane hooks my belt around his forearm and grabs me by the shoulders. "No, *I'll* fix it. Go back inside." He glances down at the ice clinging to the roof. "It's not safe up here."

Scoffing, I puff out a breath. It clouds the air around us. "It's not safe anywhere, Kane."

A muscle in his jaw twitches. "You've been listening to Zane."

"It's hard to ignore when he keeps spiraling." I rub my tired eyes. "I thought you talked to him."

"I *did.* He's stressed the fuck out. Again."

Even with a broken arm, Zane hasn't slowed down. If anything, he's gotten more manic, pacing the kitchen and ranting to my poor grandmother. She plys him with tea and manages to make him sit before he hurts himself, but there's only so much any of us can do. He needs professional help.

I contacted my psychiatrist a week ago and squeezed Zane in for an introductory appointment. He doesn't know about it yet, but Kane and I have been working up to telling him... Sighing, I pull Kane's phone from his pocket to check the time. "His appointment is in two hours. Are you taking him?"

Kane's forehead wrinkles. "Yeah, but..." He turns his head towards the old church they've claimed as a temporary base of operations. Zane hasn't come out yet this morning. "I think you should take him instead."

"Are you crazy?" My foot slips, and I hold onto Kane to keep from falling. "He doesn't even like me!"

Cursing aloud, Kane shuffles us away from the edge of the roof. "Shit, Mercy, you're gonna to break your neck up here." He sighs. "Look, I'll work on the house today if you promise to take care of Zane for me. You know the doctor and what to expect. I don't. This is out of my wheelhouse." Meeting my gaze, he smiles wryly. "Zane isn't nearly as prickly as you think he is. He's just been in a bad mood lately."

"Ever since he met me," I grumble, brushing the hair from my eyes and tucking it behind my ear. "Fine, I'll take him, but you need someone to help you up here. My dad's got an address book with local businesses and people we know who owe us favors. Ask him where it is, or Grandma might know?"

While I'm rattling off instructions, Kane helps me get to the ladder. "I've got it. Go wake Zane."

"He's not up yet?"

Kane descends after me and jumps down the last two rungs. "Trouble sleeping."

That must be going around. I've hardly gotten a good night's sleep in God knows how long. "If you slept inside the house instead of out in the cold—"

"No."

"My dad said you could stay in Malachi's room."

"We're fine where we are, Siren. Don't worry about us."

I frown as he lengthens the tool belt and clips it around his waist. "The church is falling apart. Does it even have insulation? Or a roof?"

Kane chuckles and hooks his fingers over mine. "See for yourself." Kissing my forehead, he pushes me towards the church. "Bring him some coffee and he might actually smile."

That's not a bad idea. While Kane hunts for my dad's address book, I pour fresh coffee into a thermos and grab the last remaining blanket from the hall closet. We reaaaally need to weather-proof the house, or it'll be a terrible season. The fireplace needs emptied, the chimney swept, firewood gathered—the list is endless, and my eye twitches as I think about it. "While you're in the attic, Kane, can you check for the box labeled *Winter*? It should have blankets and decorations, maybe some fire starter logs? If it's not there, it might be in the storage room at the mortuary. Dad's working, so he can let you in—"

Kane sneaks up behind me and wraps me in a bear hug. "Mercy—" He presses his face to the top of my head and takes a deep breath. "You're an angel."

Butterflies flutter inside my chest. "Are you okay? Did something happen?"

He shakes his head with a soft laugh. "I'm trying to give you a compliment. Why does something have to be wrong?"

Because something's always wrong.

"I dunno, I just..." I shrug. "Worry."

About Zane's mental health. Kane's intentions, although sweet on the outside, and what ulterior motives he might have. Sam's sudden disappearance. My grandmother's age. My dad's stress levels. My sister Lilith, locked in some mysterious contract, and my brother Malachi, wreaking all kinds of havoc in boarding school across the country. None of us have heard from him in months, and he's not returning our phone calls.

Hopefully he hasn't been admitted to the hospital for psychosis again. Once he turned eighteen, they stopped calling us when he'd have episodes. Like Sam, he's pretty much vanished.

I bite my lip as Sam's dad's assessment of my family echoes in my head. *A psychiatric patient abandoned by his own family.* My mood plummets as his statement rings true. Malachi is my little brother, and I haven't been taking care of him.

I haven't been taking care of anyone but myself.

Sighing, I drop my head onto Kane's chest. "I need to do better."

He brushes his hand through my hair. "You're doing fine. Besides," he murmurs, leaning back to meet my eyes. "You've got me now." A small smile graces his lips as he pulls me in for a chaste kiss. "I won't let you fall, Siren."

My cheeks flush as he presses another kiss to my lips, this one just as soft as the last. "Thanks," I murmur, not sure what else to say. "I'll, um, get going." I feel his burning gaze on my back as I gather my things and hop down the front steps, making a circuit through the tombstones on my way to the church. These could be cleaned up, too, although the ones closest to the church have been cleared of leaves and what little snow sticks to the ground. Is that Kane's doing, or is Zane doing yard work to cope with his anxiety?

I push open the heavy chapel doors without knocking. I haven't been inside in a long time, and the transformation is shocking. Most of the pews have been broken down into planks and used to repair the walls or patch the hole in the roof, while a select few remain untouched near the pulpit. The floor, although dated, has been sanded and scaled while the rotted boards have been replaced entirely. Although there is no electrical wired to the building, a generator hums just outside a long stretch of windows, with cords snaked through a broken pane to power the string lights criss-crossing through the rafters, Zane's computer system, and various hookups for charging cell phones and running space heaters.

It's a nightmare for any fire department.

"Zane?" I wipe my feet on a brand new door mat covered in bright pink hearts and a bright orange sticker declaring *75% off!* stuck to the corner. No one responds to my call, but I catch a flicker of movement behind a computer station stacked with four monitors and a whirring desktop. Beneath the tabletop, I spy slippered feet tapping incessantly. "I brought coffee," I proclaim loudly, hoping to rouse Zane's attention. "I don't have any sugar or cream—"

Dark eyes and tangled bed head peer around the edge of the closest set of monitors. "I'll take it black."

I walk over and pour a generous helping into the thermos lid before handing it over. Zane doesn't wait for it to cool before taking a sip, grunting the moment it hits his tongue. "Tastes like shit. How old is this?"

I don't know. Does coffee go bad? "You could say thanks." Setting down the thermos on his desk, I cross my arms over my chest and stare over his shoulder at the computer screens. All four of them have different projects pulled up, with two being devoted to fuzzy camera feeds of a bustling office and a conference room while another is rapidly auto-sorting emails. The final monitor is a crisp video feed of Kane crouching off the rooftop with a flashlight stuck between his teeth and a hammer in hand. "You were watching me?" Goosebumps trail down my arms. "For how long?"

"Since you got up this morning." Zane takes another sip of coffee. "You don't linger in bed anymore, do you?" He hums softly. "You used to sketch in the mornings before class."

My dreams have been too erratic to try and pin down, so there's no point in trying to sketch what I can't see. Rather than tell Zane this, I offer another explanation. "There's too much to do."

"Like pretending you're a carpenter?"

"Like fix up the house!" I smack his arm. "What are *you* doing, anyway? Playing solitaire?"

Zane stares at me with dead eyes. "Does this look like solitaire to you?" Sighing, he presses his thumbs to the backs of his eyelids. "I'm keeping an eye on Sam, okay? Butt out or I might miss something."

"Sam?" I push Zane and roll him out of the way so that I can step in front of the screens. "How is he? What's he doing?" I look between all four screens, but the only person I can definitively make out is Kane. Grabbing the mouse, I move the cursor to the top right monitor and click to zoom in on the conference room. A meeting is going on, and maybe that's Sam at the front—

With a growl, Zane drops the thermos lid and wraps an arm around my waist to pull me into his lap. Then he grabs my hand and wrestles the mouse from me. "Will you—stop!" The mouse bounces on the desk after he throws it out of reach. "You'll fuck everything up!"

"How could you keep this a secret from me?" I elbow him in the ribs, but he doesn't let go. "You know that I've been worried sick!"

"That's why I'm doing this," Zane hisses in my ear, "because you won't shut up about Sam!"

Indignation flares hot inside my chest. "Excuse me? Since when have I—"

"In your sleep, Mercy." The tip of Zane's nose nudges the side of my neck. He sighs heavily. "You won't shut up about him in your sleep."

A flicker of embarrassment makes me blush. "You're watching me sleep now?"

He huffs. "Hardly. You toss and turn all night." His lips skim my bare shoulder as my sweater slips down my arm. He pulls it lower with his teeth, snapping the neckline with a grunt. "Kane snores, you have nightmares, and Sam—" Zane nips my skin. "Mmm. You taste like lavender, Kitten."

I take a shallow breath as my heart skips a beat. "Focus, Zane, what about Sam?"

"Sam, Sam, Sam," he rumbles, slipping his cold hands beneath my sweater. "All you care about is Sam, and it's getting pretty fucking old."

"That—that's not true!"

A shiver runs down my spine as Zane splays his hands flat against my stomach, then drags his knuckles up the ladder of my ribs. Once he reaches my bra, he grunts and grabs my boobs. "You're really warm," he murmurs, lightly squeezing. "It's nice."

"I brought you a blanket," I choke out, ignoring the tingles of pleasure as he idly rubs my nipples through the fabric. "It's over there, um—" Shit, where did I drop it? "I'll get it!"

Zane pinches my nipples and pants in my ear. "Don't you want to hear about your precious boyfriend?"

"Yes, of course, I—" My breath catches as heat pools between my thighs. "Zane, stop," I plead, trembling. "You're not thinking straight."

"I'm thinking just fine, Kitten." He kisses a tender spot below my ear. "Sit still, and I'll show you Sam."

This is fucked up.

"I came here to help you." Reaching beneath my shirt, I claw at his wrists. "Stop being a fucking dick!"

Growling, Zane lets go of my breasts and grabs my hands. "Then stop being a bitch!"

"What are you talking about?" I've been nothing but kind to both Kane *and* Zane since they arrived. Cooking meals for my family, plus two, and not complaining when they use my body wash and shampoo. Even my tooth-paste! "You're the ones taking advantage of my family! You moved in without even asking me!"

Ever since we got back from the cabin, they've been hanging around the house like we run an inn instead of a morgue. I've overlooked a lot of things because of how happy it's made my dad to have someone interested in the family business, and Kane is all too eager of a pupil—more eager than me or my siblings have ever been, truth-fully. Zane has been antsy, yes, but he keeps my grand-mother occupied by playing cards and overlooking when she cheats, even going so far as to try her daily tea concoc-tions without spitting them out if they taste like dirt.

Having them around hasn't been all bad, but it's one hell of an adjustment.

Now, he's calling *me* a bitch?

"We didn't want you to get lonely without Sam," Zane says slowly, easing his grip. "And if we asked, you would have said no and insisted that you were fine. You're not fine, Mercy, no matter how much you pretend to be." He laces our fingers together and rests them on my stomach. "So yes, you've been a little bitchy, but it's not your fault. I get that we're—" His lips quirk into a half-smile. "An acquired taste."

That's an understatement.

He takes a deep breath and reaches for the mouse. "If I do this for you," he murmurs, "if I keep you updated about Sam, could you..." His lips skim the shell of my ear. "Hang out more?"

Now I *know* that Zane's not getting enough sleep.

Curving my spine, I turn around and flatten my palm against his forehead. "Are you feeling okay? Chills, cold sweats—" The sour look on his face makes me laugh, and his expression instantly lightens.

"Don't make me bite you," he teases, smirking. "I might be infectious." He dives into the crook of my neck and chomps down, a deep laugh rumbling in his chest as I squeal.

"Zane!" I pull on the hair at the base of his neck. It's gotten longer since we met, making it easier to yank. "Be serious!"

Two words I never thought I'd have to say when it comes to Zane.

He sighs against my skin and drags his lips up the column of my throat. "I am serious, Mercy."

My heartbeat stutters as his tone shifts.

Kissing a trail along my jawline, he hums softly. "I'm always serious when it comes to you."

I stare at the screen as Zane clicks to enhance the image of the conference room. It takes a few seconds, but then the men at the twelve-foot long table come into focus. I only recognize two of them: Samuel Wright, CEO and founder of some of the largest corporations in the city, and a younger carbon copy of him. Dressed in a tailored black suit, brunette hair perfectly styled, summer eyes shining in the sunlight beaming through the window.

Sam looks like he's exactly where he belongs.

But then he turns away from the room and faces the camera for one second, maybe two, as he takes a calming breath, and beyond the charming facade is a man whose eyes betray just how exhausted he actually is, down to the marrow of his bones.

"We have to help him." My heart beats rapidly as I get worked up, my nervous system flailing in response to Sam's distress. "What can we do?"

Zane nuzzles my neck and presses his lips to my fluttering pulse. "That's the problem, Mercy." He taps something on his keyboard to take a screenshot. "He walked into that wolf den on his own. Now it's up to him to find a way out."

I think back to what Sam told me before we separated. "He's choosing to stay," I realize, my heart breaking. "He's not leaving, because he hasn't found what he's looking for yet. He's trying to save me. Save *us.*" My voice catches. All this time, I've been wondering if he's finally realized how much of a burden I am—how much he doesn't need me. When in reality, I'm still as much of a burden as always, and he's going through hell to make it work.

Zane is, too, in his own way. I tear my gaze off the monitor and scan Zane's face. The paleness of his complexion. The dark circles under his eyes. The way his bones jut out more than I remember. He isn't taking care of himself, because he's too busy worrying about everyone else.

"Let's get some fresh air, okay?" I cup Zane's cheek. It's cold to the touch. "We can spend the day together. Just you and me."

Something flickers in the depths of Zane's eyes, like

dying embers struggling to light. "Okay." He licks his dry lips. "What do you want to do?"

I catch him off guard by pressing the barest kiss to his lips. His muscles tighten as his entire body goes stiff. Dragging in a breath, he bumps my forehead with his and closes his eyes, exhaling slowly. "That's not fair," he murmurs, sliding his hand into my hair. "I didn't say you could kiss me."

This man has never asked for permission to touch me, and *now* he has a problem when I touch him back?

"You're a hypocrite." I shake my head and his fingers snag in my hair. "You've been kissing me this whole time."

His gaze flicks to my lips before returning to my eyes. "I like kissing you, Mercy." Tilting his head up, he kisses the corner of my mouth. "Is that a problem?"

Warmth spreads through my veins. My heartbeat suddenly races. This feels important. Like we're... testing a boundary, or creating new ones. I take a shaky breath. "It's only a problem if I can't kiss you back."

A smile curves on his lips. "You want to kiss me?"

"Don't let it go to your head."

He laughs, the sound rich and full of life. I find myself smiling alongside him. "Alright, Kitten. You can kiss me whenever you want." His arm tightens around my waist as he pulls me closer. "Don't hold back."

# CHAPTER 27

# KANE

IT TURNS out that asking Mercy to take Zane to his appointment is the best fucking idea I've ever had, not only because the two of them are stuck together for half the day, but because it gives me unfettered access to Mercy's father: the one and only Vinicius Morningstar. Every free moment I've had over the past few days has been spent under his direct tutelage. Learning about the machines and instruments in the morgue, watching him catalogue inventory and expenses, assisting him with heavy lifting when the time calls for it and, occasionally, catching up on his emails. Vinny is *definitely* struggling to run the place on his own, and that's exactly why he needs a guy like me.

Enthusiastic, funny, gorgeous—and head over heels for his daughter. I'm *invested*. It makes me the perfect right-hand-man.

While Vinny rubs the back of his neck at a lopsided

table in the break room, I crack open a soda for him. He gives me a tired but grateful smile.

"Someone as young as you shouldn't be cooped up in a place like this all day." He slides the can towards himself but doesn't take a sip. "I'm not naive. I know that you're only here for Mercy's sake. She asked you to keep an eye on me, didn't she?" Vinny shakes his head. "I'm not *that* old. I can take care of myself."

I've seen how often he forgets to take breaks and eat a real meal, opting for packs of dry crackers or frozen breakfast sandwiches rather than eat the lunches Mercy packs for him. They sit in the fridge at the house until someone—usually Granny, I think—takes them for herself. That could be why he leaves them, but still. The man's gotta take better care of himself or he'll end up in one of the plots out back.

"She didn't send me." Sitting opposite him, I put on my most charming smile. The best part is that I don't have to fake it. I *like* Mercy's dad. Ever since he held a shotgun to my face for allegedly making his daughter cry, I knew that I was gonna like the guy. Working under him during the day and sitting at his dinner table every night has been nice. He smiles when the table gets rowdy over a deck of cards before bed.

I think he misses having a full house.

"I'm gonna take the business from you, old man." Rapping my knuckles on the table edge, I barely hold back a grin. Yeah, *Kane Morningstar* has a nice ring to it. "I like it here, and I'd like to stay."

He stares at me for a long, silent moment. "Is that

what you're doing with my daughter? Using her to absorb the business? There's no money in it. If you want a lavish lifestyle, you'll have to look elsewhere."

The implication that I'm using Mercy rubs me the wrong way. My smile sharpens. "I'm living in an abandoned building. Do I look like I care for luxury?"

"You look like you're in love with my daughter."

I hadn't realized it was that obvious. "I am," I admit slowly, trying to gauge his reaction. But unlike his daughter, Vinicius has one hell of a poker face. I can't read him at all. "But I haven't told her yet, so I'd appreciate if you kept that to yourself."

Another moment of silence passes between us. "You're also in love with that other boy."

I nod. "They both mean a lot to me, and I want to make them happy." To do that, I need to make some lifestyle changes, starting with my profession. If I can't kill people anymore, at least I can stick to what I know. Besides, being with Mercy guarantees that I'll always have a creative outlet. "I think the three of us could be good together. We're still figuring things out, obviously, but..." A small smile curves on my lips. "I want this to work, and I'm willing to put in the work to ensure that it does." I meet Vinny's steady gaze. "That's why I'm here. I'd like to run the business with Mercy. I know she hasn't talked about it, and I haven't brought it up with her yet, but—"

Vinicius holds up his hand to stop me. "That's a conversation you'll have to have with my daughter. She's..." He searches for the right word. "Hesitant. But you have to understand—this place may hold memories of both the dead and the living, but it's the dead who prevail. That's why my eldest daughter doesn't come around much. Everything you see in this room, in this building, was put here by my late wife."

Mercy doesn't talk about her mom. I perk up at the mention of her.

He brushes his hand across the tabletop lovingly. "She thrifted many of the pieces here, along with what you'll find in the house. What hasn't been inherited, that is."

Something about the Morningstars' lack of funds has been bothering Zane. He's been driving himself crazy looking at their bookkeeping, tracking their payment history, and hunting down their investments. I suspect that it has everything to do with Samuel Wright and his claim of ownership on the property and its people—but I'll admit, the details go over my head.

If I'm going to take care of Mercy from now on, I need to step up, too, but in my own way. I thought that handling the business would be a proper contribution, but if it goes under, then what's the point?

I need to figure out how to save Morningstar Mortuary, and to do that, I need to understand where the bleed is. Zane can track leads and mutter to his keyboard all he wants. I'll ask the source.

"How is it that you're busy as fuck but not making bank?"

Vinicius cracks a genuine smile. "You're not one to mince words, are you?"

I match his smile. "I don't like to waste time."

Shaking his head, he chuckles under his breath. "That'll be a welcome change around here." His gaze roams the room before he stands. "This is hardly the place for me to dredge up bad memories. Let's take a walk."

We step out the back door and into the crisp afternoon air. Sunlight warms our skin but proves just how sickly Vinicius' pallor is. Thinning hair, tired eyes, but harboring a sense of inner peace the moment we step onto the back lot. A sprawling meadow, complete with knee-high weeds and thorny twigs, stretches for at least half a mile until it hits a dense evergreen forest. Vinicius steps over briars and makes a beeline for an old, cement picnic table. A mossy birdbath, long abandoned by its avian friends, sits beside it.

Vinny takes a seat while I opt to stand and face the road in case someone drives up.

"My wife and I," he begins after a moment, "made a risky business decision long ago. It turned out to be a bad deal, and Ingrid..." His eyes cloud as his mind drifts into the past. "Well, she was more than happy to make the most of a sour situation. Turn lemons into lemonade, and all that. We were newly married, and she was invested in our business." He flicks his gaze towards me. "Sort of like you."

Pride swells inside my chest. That's one more point in my favor. I have a feeling that Vinny's ready to move on to the next part of his story, so I circle back around to the important details. "What kind of deal was it?"

If he's suspicious, he doesn't let on. "An investor.

Ingrid was convinced that if we could breathe more life into the business, create a few newspaper ads, put our faces on a billboard, that the clients would roll in. So that's what we did: found an investor who promised that we'd see a turn-around. With his financial support and connections, we were supposed to be set for life and ensure that our children would have equity once we eventually passed. I'm sure you can see where I'm going with this."

"The clients never came."

"The opposite, actually. They disappeared altogether. A few families that have worked with us for generations have stayed loyal, but as they grow older and their children move away, there aren't many left for us to bury. As for attracting new clients, well, most people live within the city limits, so they look for services closer to home. We live on the outskirts; it's harder to drum up business when no one knows who we are. I'd thought that Lilith could help with that since she lives in the city, but I don't think her heart is in it, and Mercy's been focusing on her studies. I don't have staff to run our daily operations or handle the marketing for me, so I'm left to handle everything on my own. If it weren't for what few jobs Samuel brings each month, we'd close for good."

Alarm bells ring inside my head. "Your investor is Samuel Wright?"

I'm not sure that he hears me. "They're just enough to keep us afloat but not enough for us to thrive. For years, he's fed us table scraps." Vinny clenches his jaw. "Even if Mercy were interested in taking over, I can't—"

His voice shakes. "I can't give it to her like this. I won't ask her to suffer for the sake of preserving a dying legacy."

Well, shit. I hadn't realized how fucking bad it was. A new coat of paint and a sign in the yard aren't gonna cut it. We need an intervention—*or,* a smart as fuck techie who can work his magic and drum up business. Good thing I have one in my back pocket.

"I can help. Zane and me, we can figure it out. I'll be the face and he'll be the logistics. You shouldn't have to do everything on your own." Mercy can fit in wherever she damn well pleases. As far as I'm concerned, it's her company, not mine. Whatever she wants to do within it, run the damn thing, paint a mural on the walls, maintain communications with clients—I don't give a damn so long as she's with us. "Do you have a contract or something? With Wright, I mean. Surely it's expired by now." I can't fathom a document living longer than Mercy's been alive. "We can pick up where you and your wife first began."

"That's not possible."

Is he going to dispute every fucking thing I say? "Why the hell not?"

"Because—" He glares into the distance. "My wife handled everything. The legal fees. The signatures. Whatever she agreed to with Samuel, she took to her grave, and I haven't been able to get a single word out of Samuel or his legal team. They won't budge, and I can't find a lawyer in the state who will take my case, because Samuel's paying them all off." The fury for the fight dies as quickly as it sparks, engulfed by a bone-weary sigh that makes *me* feel depressed.

"There has to be a physical copy somewhere. Your wife must have kept one. She wouldn't have—"

"Fucked us over?" A bitter smile curves on his lips. "I used to think so, too; that she loved us as unconditionally as we loved her. But now, I... I'm not sure anymore." He draws a shaky breath. "It was her idea to seek an investor. She's the one who introduced me to Samuel in the first place. We didn't pursue any others, because she insisted that he was the right choice. I trusted her with my life, so letting her handle everything was the easiest decision I ever made. It was a weight off my shoulders, truthfully." Staring up at the clear blue skies over our heads, he swallows hard. "But now it's the biggest burden I carry."

The overwhelming sorrow radiating off of him makes my heart ache. Taking a breath, I sit next to him on the bench seat. "Scoot over, Pops; make some room." When he gives me a bewildered look, I throw my arm over his shoulder. Half my ass cheek is hanging off the edge, but whatever. It's fine. "We're in this shit together, now, so don't get all mopey on me. I can only handle so much emo energy, and Zane's got that position covered, believe me."

I hope Zane's appointment is going well and that Mercy can handle his mood once it's over. I don't envy her one bit.

"I can't give you my company, son."

"Don't worry about it." So what if I can't put my name on it? Big whoop. "Lucky for you, I *am* interested in your daughter, so I'm sticking around for good, business or no business."

But unlike Vinicius, I have hope for the future of Morningstar Mortuary. What he doesn't know is that I've got an inside man working the scene to figure out exactly what shit Vinny and Ingrid stepped in when they tangoed with Samuel Wright. It's only a matter of time before Sam comes crawling back home to kneel at Mercy's feet and beg for her forgiveness for taking so long —but that won't matter, because he'll bring the answer to all our problems with him.

Samson fucking Wright is our ticket out of this mess with his father, and I never thought I'd say this, but I'm actually fucking grateful to have the bastard in our corner.

"If you're sticking around, there's one thing you need to remember." Vinicius nods towards the expanse of land around us. "If you hurt my daughter, I have plenty of space to bury you out back."

The biggest grin stretches across my face. "You promise?" Spending eternity on this gorgeous plot of land sounds like the perfect resting place. "Because there's nowhere else I'd rather be buried than right fucking here."

He glances at me from the corner of his eye. "You're a weird fucking kid."

I laugh as he elbows me in the ribs. "Get used to it, Pops."

If I have my way, I'm not going anywhere anytime soon.

# CHAPTER 28

## ZANE

I SHOULD HAVE KNOWN NOT to trust Mercy and Kane. They were all too eager to get me out of the house —church—whatever you want to call it, citing *spending time together* and *getting fresh air* as their reasons for dragging me out into the sunlight.

The reality is that they've been scheming to get me to see a therapist.

"Grandma Star is paying," Mercy murmurs softly, like anyone in the lobby is actually listening to us. "And she said you can't refuse!"

"That's even worse," I groan, rubbing my aching head. The throbbing behind my eyes has been killer ever since we walked into the building. Huge paneled windows give us a terrifying view of the busy streets below, and I have to tear my gaze away or risk being blinded. Whoever did the tint job needs to be fucking eviscerated.

I'm not having a good fucking day.

"I can't take money from your grandmother." She's old and feeble and probably gonna die soon; she should spend it on whatever is gonna make her happy, not on getting me to see a shrink.

"She *insisted*," Mercy huffs, grabbing my hand. "Just sit still and wait until they call you." She fiddles with my fingers, pinching the webbing between them and running her thumb along the middle of my palm.

"What are you doing?"

Her cheeks flush a pretty shade of pink. "I'm nervous. Doctors offices—" She inhales sharply as a door opens down the hall. "They're not always happy places, okay?"

"How reassuring."

Blanching, she immediately backpedals. "I mean, you're going to be fine. Dr. Schwartz is fantastic. She's been working with me since I was a kid."

How long has Mercy been attending sessions?

Frowning, I dig a little deeper to see what I can learn. "What do you talk about during your sessions?"

Mercy scoffs and pinches my thumb. "That's confidential."

"Mhm. It would make me feel more at ease, though, seeing as how you tricked me into coming. I'm sure Dr. Schwartz would love to hear about how you and your grandmother forced a man into this appointment. She's going to *love* analyzing that little detail about your life. I'm sure it'll be an extensive talk the next time you see her—"

Growling with frustration, Mercy clamps her hand

over my mouth. "We talk about a lot of things, okay! My parents, my nightmares, what drives me, and *yes*, even my relationships. But I've been a little busy, so I haven't had the chance to tell her about you. This is the perfect opportunity for you to get an outside perspective on your life and figure out what truly motivates you—because pushing yourself through life off of the fear that Kane's going to leave you if you're suddenly not good enough anymore?" She blows out a breath. "That's not gonna last, Zane. You need another reason to live, and I bet Dr. Schwartz can help you see what's inside your heart; what you *really* want out of life."

I gently grab her wrist and pull her hand into my lap. "You know, Mercy, it almost sounds like you're speaking from experience."

She smiles wryly. "I know a thing or two."

One of the staff calls my name to the front. "Hunter!"

Mercy's way too enthusiastic as she jumps up and drags me with her to the counter. "Yes, he's here. We're ready."

"You can wait here, ma'am. Come with me, sir. Dr. Schwartz is waiting."

I watch Mercy's face fall and sigh. "You can borrow my phone," I tell her, pulling my cell from my pocket and placing it in her hand. "Text Kane if you want, but don't download any games." A laugh catches in my chest. "Unless it's solitaire. We can see who gets the highest score." I drop her hand and walk away.

Having an impromptu appointment sucks, but

Granny's been pretty okay company. I'd hate for her to think I'm not appreciative of what she and Mercy's dad have been doing for us.

Shit, I'm going soft.

The staffer opens the door to Dr. Schwartz' office and closes it behind me. There's no one sitting at the obnoxious brown desk taking up a quarter the room, and the zen garden resting in front of the chair I'm supposed to take hasn't even been raked clean. Frowning, I shove my hands in my pockets and glance around the room. Kind of unprofessional to say that she's waiting and then find out that she's not even here.

The hair on the back of my neck rises, and I spin on my heel just in time for a man in a suit to jump me. He slams his palm over my mouth and pushes me until I stumble onto the edge of the desk. Lifting my foot, I slam it into his crotch, and he wheezes, doubling over in pain.

"You piece of shit, *it's me!*"

I hold a ballpoint pen like a knife. "Who the fuck—" I stop short as I realize who the idiot holding his ballsack is.

Samson goddamn Wright.

Wearing a navy suit and expensive cufflinks, he looks like a filthy rich asshole I'd stay the fuck away from if I had a choice. But there's a nervousness about him that I'm not used to seeing; he's jittery, quick to fidget, and his eyes—bloodshot to hell and back. As if hearing my thoughts, he pulls out eye drops and puts a few in each of his eyes.

"You look like hell, Sam."

He laughs darkly and rakes his fingertips over the fresh fade along the side of his head. "I've felt better, thanks." Giving me a once-over, he clenches his jaw. "I know why *I* look like shit, but why do you look like you've just come out of hibernation?"

I scratch the patch of facial hair on my cheek. "It's not that bad." I bet I've looked worse. The sweatpants probably don't help, though.

Sighing, Sam drags one of the chairs away from Dr. Shwartz' desk and sits down. "Look, I called in a lot of favors to make this happen. We don't have much time." He glances at the fancy watch on his wrist. "My dad will notice that I'm gone once he's done on the shitter."

I roll my eyes. "Paint a picture, why don't you."

"I gave him laxatives." Sam bounces his knee and stares at me for a second, but his attention darts around the room, either too nervous or too hyped up on some kind of drug to sit still. "I had to rearrange our meetings, too, but that's not the point. How's Mercy?"

Keeping a straight face, I shrug. "Why don't you ask her yourself? She's right outside."

Sam's gaze flicks to the door. "I can't."

"You should." I walk over to Sam and get in his face. "She can't sleep because of you."

Guilt cuts across his features. "I *can't*, Zane."

"Why the hell not?" My anger flares hot as I pace in front of him. "What's stopping you? *Daddy*?" I scoff aloud. "Didn't know he had his dick up your ass."

Taking a breath, Sam collects himself. It's like watching a curtain fall over a stage, distracting viewers with its soft velvet that makes the theater look opulent when in reality, there are rats living in the walls and mold hiding beneath the floorboards. I've been watching Sam ever since I hooked into his dad's camera feeds; he's risking burn out by running so hard from one project to the next.

"What does he even have you doing?"

Sam shakes his head, dismissing my question. "I need to know if Vinny's having their annual Christmas party."

I damn near throw a paperweight at him. "Why the hell does that matter?"

"Because if he is, I can convince my father to attend. He loves to gloat, and it's the perfect opportunity for him to examine how much damage he's done."

"I don't want to be anywhere near your fucking father." My arm twinges at the memory of his heel on my broken bone. "I'll kill him."

Sam's eyes brighten. "Good. That's the point." He stands and steps in front of me, cutting off my erratic pacing. "I want you and Kane to get rid of him. You're good at this kind of thing, aren't you?"

My heart races. Killing Samuel Wright, although gratifying as fuck, isn't a walk in the park. "I'll never be able to get close to him." What's more, my kills with Kane were planned down to the minute. We spent months setting everything up for a perfect finale. We don't have that kind of time with Samuel.

If he attends the party, he'll be on our doorstep within weeks.

"You will," Sam insists, grabbing my arm. "I promise.

I'll create an opening. The party is the perfect place." He releases me and fidgets with his watch band, tugging on the end repeatedly. Raw, red skin peeks out from beneath. "He doesn't usually bring security. Thanksgiving was an anomaly."

"I'm not going against a group of armed guards."

Sam frowns. "He won't have any."

I cross my arms. "You've got to be joking. He won't come anywhere near us after that stunt he pulled. He knows we'll be out for blood"

"That's the thing—he's overconfident. It's his biggest flaw."

If I tell Kane that Sam's on board for murder, my boyfriend will be a bundle of incessant energy as we count down the days. It'll be unbearable. But, I can't pull this off on my own. I need his crazy ideas to come up with a solid plan. So how can I tell him without getting him too riled up? Or, worse yet, without Mercy finding out?

I doubt she'd be willing to ruin her family's party—the one good tradition they have going for them—for a little throat-slitting.

The bigger question is why does Sam want to kill his father all of a sudden?

"What's in it for you?" I narrow my eyes as Sam swallows. "Inheritance? If the cops sniff around, you'll be suspect number one. Golden child finally reunites with his rich bitch father, only for dad to keel over within a month. It's suspicious as hell, Sam, and not the kind of court battle you want to go through."

"I don't care about the money!" Tearing his watch off, he throws it to the ground and scratches the irritated skin on his wrist. "All I care about is Mercy. How is she?"

I repeat myself from earlier. "See for yourself. Go talk to her."

"I can't," Sam grimaces, grinding his jaw. "I already told you."

"Why not? Because Daddy's watching?" I pick up the watch and turn it over to inspect it. "Is this thing bugged?"

"No, I had it checked. It's a normal watch."

Shoving the watch into his chest, I snarl. "Then what's your fucking problem?" I throw my arm out towards the lobby where Mercy's waiting. "She's *right there*, Sam, completely unaware that you're here. She's been crying herself to sleep, did you know that? Can't remember a damn thing she dreams about, but I hear it every night. *Sam, don't leave; Sam, where did you go?; Sam, why did you abandon us?* Over and over and over again. It's enough to make me—" I laugh bitterly as I tug on the ends of my hair, the searing pain in my scalp keeping me grounded. I could get lost in the sound of Mercy's cries.

"Because if I go out there, I won't leave!" Sam shoves me back. "If I see her face, even once, I won't be able to walk away. And right now, she needs me. Not in her arms where I want to be, but where I can be useful. Out here," he spits, slamming the heel of his palm over my heart. "Where I can't fucking touch her!" He snarls like an animal and clenches his eyes shut. "I'm doing this for her. The only way to rip his claws out of her is to transfer ownership. That's the bull-shit I'm dealing with. This contract was written in fucking blood. It's like some—" His face twists. "Underworld shit. He's the king of hell, and we're souls for him to collect."

"He doesn't *own* people, Sam. That's illegal."

Sam scoffs. "So is killing people, but that's never stopped you before. Forty-three people, Zane? Are you fucking crazy?"

Dread fills my gut like lead. "How do you know that?"

"Because that's his latest punishment." Sam's sneer is ugly as hell. "Tallying up how many people you've killed and how they died. Don't ask me how he has the resources. I just know that there's only so many dismem-berment videos that I can take before I fucking crack."

There shouldn't have been any recording devices on site for *any* of our kills. "It has to be doctored footage. That's impossible." Yet, Sam knows our exact number of kills. A wave of anxiety ripples through my body like an undeniable current, easily sweeping me into a panic. If Sam already knows that much about Kane and me, what else can he find out? Are our whole lives on record in some billionaire's basement for him to laugh at whenever he damn well pleases?

Does power like that even exist?

"Mercy's forty-four, isn't she?" Sitting in one of the patient chairs, Sam puts his head in his hands. "Just another number for you two. I can't fucking believe it."

"Oh, don't act all high and mighty. You know if the

roles were reversed and Mercy wanted to kill people, you'd be lining up victims for her." I hold my head high. "I have no fucking regrets, because I'd do it all over again in a heartbeat. And you, Sam, are no different than me. Don't you dare pretend to be shocked and disgusted about what we've done until you've had a good, hard look in the mirror, because I promise you, the minute she looks you in the eyes and whispers her greatest desires, you'll do whatever it takes to make her happy. No matter the cost."

Sam takes a deep breath and meets my eyes. "I can't do that with a leash around my neck." He pulls at his collar next, loosening his tie when that doesn't satisfy him. "Getting rid of my father serves two purposes. It ensures that I have enough assets to do whatever the hell I want with my life, and—" He stares at the wall between him and Mercy. "It passes ownership of every fucked-up contract my father owns to me, including the one with Ingrid Morningstar's name on it."

I stare at Sam as he clasps his watch onto his wrist. "What does Mercy's mom have to do with anything? I thought her dad's the one who sold her family away?" How far back does this shit with Samuel go?

"No," he replies, fixing his tie next. The man's a mess. "Ingrid's the mastermind. It's why my father had her killed. She knew too much and gave little in return after my dad got what he wanted."

A shiver runs down my spine. "Which was?"

"That's... complicated."

"How complicated can it be?" I stop him from leaving. "Tell me."

Sam's eyebrows pinch together, but he relents with barely any coercion. He likely needs someone to talk to about everything he's uncovered.

Ironic that we're in a shrink's office.

"Dad wanted the mortuary for easy body disposal. That part's obvious. But he didn't want the Morningstars to get 'above themselves'—" Sam's frown deepens. "So not only has he been sabotaging their business for years, he added a clause in the contract about body ownership that Ingrid's lawyer must have missed or willingly overlooked."

My money's on the latter.

"Everyone who has the Morningstar name, whether maiden or married, along with every single person buried on the property, Morningstar or not, belongs to him. Which means..." He clears his throat. "Even in death, he's trying to control my mother."

I try to understand, but I'm missing the full picture. "I thought your mom was buried at that Catholic Church in the center of the city." News outlets would not shut up about Mrs. Wright's funeral the week that it happened. White rose petals filled the streets as her casket was transferred to the church.

"That's what everyone thinks, but the Catholic Church is one of the few places my father doesn't have a foothold. She was baptized Catholic at birth, so he thought he'd win points with the local diocese by holding her funerary service there. But she isn't buried at *that* church; she's buried at the one on the Morningstar property. Right out front, if the pictures are to be believed."

"You're telling me that you had no clue your mom was buried with the Morningstars?"

"My dad didn't exactly invite me to her second burial after I cried my eyes out at the first one. I was already enough of an embarrassment. Besides," Sam sighs, "we'd been fighting ever since Mom first got sick. This was another way he'd have one up on me."

I clap my hand on Sam's shoulder. "That's fucked up."

His smile doesn't reach his eyes. "Yeah, well, that's what it's like to be a Wright. Be glad you have a different last name." He gets a faraway look in his eye. "If I ever marry Mercy, I'm changing my name to Morningstar. They've been more of a family to me than my own ever has."

A smile curves on my lips, but Sam's slipped out the door and disappeared before he can notice. *Thank God,* too, because I don't want to be the one to tell him that he's gonna have to fight Kane for Mercy's hand—or for her last name, at least. Because if I know my boyfriend like I think I do, he's a total sap for that shit.

Warmth spreads from my chest to my fingertips, and I shake my head to knock the smile off my face. If I'm not careful, I might start to fall for that kind of shit, too, and the last thing we need are three men sharing last names.

I sure as hell don't want to look like I'm married to Sam.

Imagining Kane and Sam bickering about it, though?

Fucking priceless.

# CHAPTER 29

# MERCY

"THANK you for taking care of the house today. Did you find my dad's appointment book?" I slip my hand into Kane's as he says goodnight on my front porch. It would be like a scene from a romance movie if he wasn't walking across the lot to sleep in the old church afterwards. I'm pretty sure no one in a movie's ever done that before. They go home to giggle in bed about their crush, not watch them through the window across the street.

"I found a lot of things," Kane muses, twirling a strand of my hair around his finger. "Like your family photo album. Never knew black was a staple color for children."

"Your family didn't wear matching ensembles?"

"My family wasn't a family at all, Mercy." His smile falls for a split second before it grows twice in size. "Zane became the only family that mattered, and now I can confidently say that I have *your* family, too." He chuckles. "Your dad likes me."

First Zane says it, and now Kane?

"Trying to take my family from me?"

"Trying to steal your heart, Siren." He grins into the curve of my neck. "Is it working?"

I bite my lip as butterflies flutter around my heart. "Maybe," I murmur, deciding to play along.

"*Maybe?*" He hums in my ear. "I'm gonna have to try harder, then." His hands wind around my waist as he kisses my lips, beginning our goodnight ritual the same way he always does: by taking my breath away one delicate kiss at a time. What used to be a heated battle of wills has cooled with the winter, and Kane kisses me like he's making a thousand wishes on every single sparkling star in the sky. Something about the way he holds me feels more intimate than anything else we've done in the past.

I can't help but wonder if he feels it too.

"I could stay here forever," he whispers, enjoying himself far too much for a man who's in love with someone else.

My heart flutters. I don't think I'm supposed to feel this way about a murderer, let alone *two* murderers. Unless, of course, I've joined the club after killing that guy with the carving knife. I try not to think about it, but maybe that's what's changed. There's a black spot on my soul, and like attracts like. I've become less of the woman I was and more like the woman they want me to be.

A killer, just like them.

Yet in moments like these, I find it hard to believe that any of us have blood on our hands.

Forcing a smile, I push Kane away and take a step back. "Zane would kill you. He'd kill *me*."

Something warm glows in the depths of Kane's eyes. "A double-homicide sounds pretty romantic."

"It does not!" Laughing, I clutch the blanket draped around my shoulders. "Aren't you freezing?"

He dusts fresh snow from his blonde hair. "Nah. You warm me up, beautiful." A smile curves on his lips as I blush bright pink. "Just like that."

I avoid his gaze as I clear my throat. That's another thing Kane's been doing lately. *Flirting*. Now that Sam's gone, things are actually... normal-ish, or as normal as they can be. I wouldn't say that anything is *better* since there's a gaping hole in my chest where Sam used to be, but the world feels different. There's less tension between Kane and Zane now that they've come to terms with whatever *this* is between the three of us, and I...

Well, I'm having trouble sleeping, and it's giving me headaches.

"You shouldn't be so nice to me." I rub my tired eyes and take a quick breath. "I'm not so easily won over."

Except, when Kane ducks his head and gets that sugar sweet look in his eyes as he tilts my chin up for a kiss, every cell in my body melts.

He's stealing parts of me that I didn't know he could.

"You like it when I'm mean, Siren?" Kane tugs on the end of my blanket so that I tumble into his chest. His teeth scrape my jaw as he slips his frozen fingers beneath the hem of my sweater. "I can be *really* mean and make you cream all over my fingers. Shove your cute fucking hat in your mouth so no one hears you scream." Swallowing hard, he drags in a lungful of air. "I know you'll love it, Mercy." He kisses the column of my throat. "I promise."

Heat blooms inside my chest and settles between my thighs. I'd be lying if I said I hadn't thought about it, about being with Kane. Or Zane, if I'm being honest. I've replayed the memory of them kissing each other over and over in my head, and I wonder... if things are good with one partner, how good could it be with two?

I know that Sam was supposed to be here when I slept with Kane, but he's disappeared, and I'm not sure when he's coming back.

I don't want to wait anymore.

"How about I stay the night with you? You and Zane." I nod towards the church. "We could have..." I bite my bottom lip. "A sleepover?"

It sounds stupid as hell now that the words are out of my mouth.

"A sleepover?" Kane chuckles as he digs his thumb into the dip beneath my hip bone. "And what would you like to do at this sleepover?"

I swallow. "Um." His hand slides around my waist until he's cupping my ass. "W-watch a movie? It's nearly Christmas. We could watch a—" My voice shakes as he squeezes my bare cheek beneath my panties. "—rom-com."

A laugh rumbles deep in his chest. "Not the rom-com type. But tell you what. You watch the movie..."

Kane's breath is warm against my ear. "And I'll enjoy the sweets."

"Turn off the surveillance, babe! It's movie time." Kane shakes a bag of homemade cookies as he pushes through the front doors to the church—the *ajar* front doors— and leads me inside. "Grandma hooked us up."

Zane looks up from his computer system, four monitors and a whirring, multicolored black box set on top of a folding table, and scowls. "You know how important —" He stops himself when he notices me. "She has a sleeping bag."

I walk toward the unkempt mattress hiding behind the pulpit and throw my sleeping bag on top. "*She* is staying the night."

"*What?*" Glaring up at Kane as he swoops down to kiss his forehead, Zane takes off his glasses and rubs his eyes. "That's not what we agreed to, Kane."

"Agreements can change."

"When they're discussed, not—" He opens his eyes and stares at me. "Trampled on." Sighing, he turns back to his monitors and rapidly clicks his mouse. "Give me a minute to wrap this up. Go entertain her." With a grin, Kane ruffles his lover's unkempt hair and stomps over to me.

Seeing the chapel at night gives it a whole new vibe. In addition to the string lights criss-crossing over our heads, there's the sound of crickets outside and the hum of multiple space heaters turned on full blast. The chill of winter keeps its distance.

"Love what you've done with the place." The mattress is soft under my feet, so I plop down and shove my legs under the blankets. It's warmer in this little alcove than the rest of the room, with the string lights providing a soft glow of both light and heat from above. *Definitely* a fire hazard. I'll have to keep the Marshall away from this particular location when he comes for our annual inspection.

Despite my sarcasm about the venue, the longer I take in the view, the more I appreciate it. The stained glass windows twinkle from the bare bulbs scattered around the room, their soft sway from an invisible draft in the rafters making everything sort of... cozy. In a run-down, homey kind of way.

"It's definitely an upgrade from the apartment," Kane murmurs, "no matter what Zane says." Holding out his hand, he smiles sweetly at me. "C'mon, I want to show you something." He pulls me to my feet and waits for me to slide on my slippers. "I've been waiting for you to get curious," he admits as he laces our fingers together. "Took you long enough."

My face warms. "I've been busy!"

His smile curves into a smirk. "Mhm. Busy avoiding me and Zane."

I sputter. "That's not true! I see you all the time!"

"Yeah, because *we* come to *you*. Why do you think Zane spends so much time in your house? He doesn't actually believe in tarot, you know. He's been waiting for you to sit with him. Damn near bites my ear off about it every night. I don't know how many more times he can draw The Hanged Man without going insane."

"He's been drawing the same card?"

Kane nods. "He's convinced that your grandma's stacking the deck, but I don't think she has the dexterity to pull that off."

What Grandma Star lacks in finesse, she makes up for with experience. I wouldn't put anything past her when it comes to her tarot or her tea.

There's a door near the back of the chapel that leads to the only other section of the church, the room where the pastor used to live. When Kane swings open the door, I'm expecting to find an empty dust den, but it's even brighter than inside the chapel. Lamps of all shapes and sizes fill the space, with dozens of canvases and sketchbooks leaning against the walls or stacked on the floor. Art supplies of all kinds litter the room in organized chaos, separated by type first, then by color. Stacks of clean towels and buckets of water, some dirty with paint and others clean and clear, sit closest to the only window in the room. A single easel stands beneath a warm spotlight created from multiple lamps with overturned shades, its canvas the largest in the room.

"I've been painting," Kane informs me, "at night when I can't sleep. I've reworked this scene over and over again, but I can't figure out what's missing." He lifts me over a spilled patch of paint before walking through it himself, uncaring of the muted lavender footprints he leaves behind. Standing behind me, he wraps his arms around my waist and rests his chin on the top of my head. "I need your eyes, Siren."

Warmth envelops my body along with the familiar scent of an art studio tinged with something smokey and earthy. *Kane*, I tell myself, snuggling into his chest. Sam's absence has been strange, but Kane's been present the entire time. Zane, too, honestly, the two of them attempting to fill a void that Sam left.

The fact that he hasn't said a word or sent a note or anything makes me anxious.

"I thought that Sam loved me," I murmur softly. "He said that he loved me." The colors on the canvas bleed together as my focus slips. "But how can he love me if he isn't here?"

Kane's chest expands against my back as he takes a deep breath. "Love can't be defined that easily, Mercy. It's like..." He dips his fingers into a fresh blob of burgundy on a nearby palette. "Paint." Rubbing the pads of his thumb and index fingers together, he spreads the paint between them. "When you mix the colors together—" He dabs three of his fingers in a pure white. "—the composition changes. No two loves are the same." Tracing a flower bud on the back of my hand, Kane separates the colors until they reach the center, where they combine into a dusty rose. "And when you add a third —" Deep indigo blends into the petals, quickly followed by a sudden swipe of vibrant orange highlights. "Or a fourth, that love is unique."

"It's complicated," I murmur, brushing my fingertips across the palette to gather paint. I draw a white diamond on the back of Kane's hand. "It should be easy." My heart catches in my throat. My parents' love was always easy; they were in sync every step of the way, from sunrise of their first day together until their final sunset when they parted for different realms. My dad misses her every day.

I miss Sam every day, too.

Kane takes my hand and gently spins me around to face him. "Loving you *is* easy." His eyes reflect the bright lights, sparkling and intense as he holds my gaze. "It's the easiest thing I've ever done, Mercy." Taking a breath, he laces our fingers together. "I know that Sam feels the same. Don't give up on him... or on me." A faint blush dusts his cheeks. "I've never done this before, and I want to do it right. I normally rush into everything since I get so—" He scrunches his face. "—*excited*, you know? You excite me, Mercy, but you also have this calming effect. Like you can anchor me back to earth. I need that sometimes." He steps closer. "I need *you*."

Now *I'm* the one blushing. "You've never done... what before?"

His gaze remains steady as he brushes warm knuckles across my rosy cheek. "Fallen in love like this."

I bite my lip as nerves tingle down my arms. My heart skips once, twice, *three* times as I hold Kane's gaze. The spotlight behind him damn near makes him glow, turning his blonde hair golden and his eyes warmer and brighter than I've ever seen.

He doesn't look like a man who wants to kill me.

He looks like a man who...

*Loves me.*

"But I thought—" My mind whirls as I try to come up with a reason why *we can't*. I'm not supposed to like two men at the same time, let alone love more than one person. Sam makes sense. Kane makes my world spin.

I take a step back and stumble on a stack of canvases. Kane catches me, but rather than pull me back up, he holds me close and falls right along with me. He takes the brunt of the fall as he slams into the floor, grinning like an idiot as he gazes up at me. "You're beautiful," he breathes, tossing his head back. "God, you look good with my art." Grabbing my shoulder, he pulls my sweater down to expose my collar bone and smears black paint across my skin. "Should've brought you here sooner."

As he grabs a bottle of sunflower yellow and squeezes it into his palm, I scoot back. "Wait! Kane!" We haven't talked about anything he just said, and covering me in paint all of a sudden is the kind of crazy spontaneity that makes him unpredictable. He follows his heart, no matter where it leads.

"You love Zane! You can't possibly love me too!"

Sitting up, he hums as he tosses the paint bottle away. "I can, and I do. Come back here. I wanna paint you."

"Use a canvas!"

He licks a stripe across his front teeth. "Your body is better."

I scramble to my feet and run for the door, only able to turn the knob before Kane snatches me from behind. He lifts my sweater over my head with one hand and smacks my stomach with the other, smudging a yellow-black handprint on my skin. I gasp at how cold the paint is and squeal when Kane slides his hand beneath the waistband of my leggings and grabs my hip, expertly smearing paint in a sticky wet line down my body.

Laughing, he peppers open-mouthed kisses along my neck as he yanks at my pants. "Take these off, Siren, c'mon. Work with me." He snaps the waistband and laughs again, the sound full and rich and just as warm as his body heat.

Bending at the waist, I dig my ass into his crotch and stall for time as I reach for a bottle of royal blue nearby. Once it's in my hand, I pop the cap and whirl around, squeezing paint all over Kane's chest. He laughs, grinning as he strips off his t-shirt and steps into the paint stream. "Gotta get dirty with me, sweetheart." With a wet smack, he slams my palm onto his chest and smears paint across his torso, the smooth glide over his skin more satisfying than it has any right to be. I grab his waist and leave a handprint, and he does the same to me. The yellow from his hand mixes with the blue on mine, creating a vibrant green as he eagerly palms my ribs on the way up to my breasts.

I jump back before he can ruin my bra, although I'm sure the damage has already been done to the rest of my clothes. I'll have to throw this entire outfit away. Paint will never come out.

The door creaks open. "I'm done with my—" Pausing, Zane quickly assesses the scene before stepping up behind me. His voice purrs in my ear as he reaches for my bra. "Allow me, Kitten." The frustrated puff of his breath warms the back of my neck as he unclasps my bra one-handed... on the fourth try. As soon as my breasts spill free and my bra hits the floor, that same hand grabs my waistband and pulls down my leggings. My panties are next, rolling as they slide down my thighs. When they get caught around my ankles, Zane kneels by my feet to help me step out of them. "There we go," he murmurs, brushing his lips across the back of my thighs. "A perfect canvas."

While Zane touches me from behind, Kane watches, completely enraptured. If he were religious, I imagine that he'd fall to his knees in prayer, thanking whichever god put us on this lecherous path. As it stands, however, he clenches and unclenches his painted fists while his dick swells, creating a massive imprint down one side of his jeans.

I try not to stare, but heat pools between my thighs as I remember the feel of his thick cock sliding against my aching pussy, desperate to fit inside. I'm still not sure that it would fit, but...

I want to try.

*Sam isn't here*, the voice in my head reminds me. An ugly scar on my heart throbs. He promised that he'd be here when I have sex with Kane. I fulfilled my end of the bargain—Sam took my virginity. Now that it's his turn to ante up, he's gone, and I'm painfully alone.

So much more alone than I was before he came back into my life.

Closing my eyes, I throw thoughts of Sam to the back of my mind. He might not want me anymore, but there are two men who do. Kane could fall in love with me any minute now, and Zane...

His touch sets my body on fire.

He slips his hand between my thighs. "You're warm," he murmurs, pushing my legs farther apart. "Right—" He kisses the globe of my ass while his hand wanders north. "*Here.*"

I gasp as he rubs my pussy with his knuckles. A moan catches in my throat as he teases my slit with his fingertips. "Z-Zane," I whimper, fisting his hair. "Stop that."

Humming happily, he bites my ass. "No."

Kane quickly strips, tossing his remaining clothes to the floor and sitting his bare ass on a tarp. "Bring her here," he rasps, motioning for us to come closer. "I need to taste her."

Grunting, Zane smacks the meatiest part of my thigh. "Don't get paint on her cunt."

Kane grins cheekily but doesn't argue. "I'll be careful with my hands." He pats the tops of his shoulders and carelessly spreads more paint across his body. There's no way I'm coming out of this unscathed. "Come here, Siren. Hook your legs over my shoulders."

I stare at him without comprehending his request. "I'll fall."

"You won't." Kane licks his lips as I shuffle closer. But before he can grab me, Zane reaches around and holds his fingers to Kane's lips. Without prompting, Kane pops them into his mouth and sucks my desire from Zane's fingers, the two of them groaning in unison at the sight.

Arousal drips down my thighs. I bite my lip and squeeze my legs together. Seeing the two of them together has no business being that hot, but for some reason, it turns me on just as much as when one of them touches me. Kane's gaze flicks to mine as he hollows out his cheeks, sucking hard enough that Zane shivers.

That's hot as fuck.

I blush scarlet as Kane winks at me, then licks his lips as his lover pulls his fingers free. But Zane doesn't linger in the moment; he grabs the back of my knee and lifts my leg so that my calf hangs over Kane's shoulder. My pussy throbs as Kane's nostrils flare and his eyes dilate, his attention zeroing in on my molten core. "Ohhh, *fuck*," he groans, panting against my thighs. "You're so wet, sweetheart."

"Dripping," Zane purrs in my ear. "You're a filthy fucking girl, aren't you? Desperate for his tongue inside your needy, wet cunt."

I gasp as a wave of heat courses through me. That sounds like something out of a porno, but... *God*, I kind of like it. "Yes," I mutter, blushing furiously. "Please."

Chuckling, Zane pats the back of my other thigh. "When I lift you, I need you to jump with it and swing this leg over his shoulder for me." He takes a short breath. "I'd do it myself, but I'm a little... handicapped." The velcro from his sling scratches my shoulder. The doctor put Zane in a soft cast so long as he promised to stay idle, but this plan goes directly against those orders.

Nothing about what we're doing is *idle* work.

"You shouldn't move so much—"

"Hush." He smacks my ass. "You ready, Kane?"

Kane grins wickedly. "Born ready, baby."

Heat blossoms deep inside my body as it submits to their crazy idea. But it's also ridiculous—Kane can't possibly want me to straddle his face. He won't be able to breathe! "Won't he—" I squeak as Zane lifts me and practically shoves my crotch in his boyfriend's face, smothering Kane between my thighs. With Kane's blind help as he grabs my ankle, we manage to hook my other leg over his shoulder, and I'm suddenly at their complete mercy. Both men are supporting my entire body weight. The word *suffocate* gets lost in my brain as Kane dives in, kissing and licking and sucking, grabbing my ass to hold me in place.

There's no way he can breathe, but he must not care. Every flick of his tongue sends electricity down my spine, especially when he swirls the tip around my clit and digs his nails into my ass. The pleasure-pain makes me cry out, and I hold onto the back of Kane's head for dear life. My pussy throbs, aching and needy just like Zane said.

I *am* a filthy girl.

I fucking love this.

A moan, low and deep, fills my ear. Zane's hand roams my waist before reaching up to massage my tits. With my back resting against his chest, he gropes and squeezes freely, tugging at my nipples and panting in my ear. "Look at you, grinding on his face. Such a dirty fucking girl."

*Oh God,* he's right. I'm grinding all over Kane's mouth and nose with reckless abandon; flashes of glistening wet skin peek out from between my thighs, Kane's face absolutely covered with my arousal.

I've been touch-starved since we left the cabin, but I didn't realize it was *this* bad. Still, without Sam here as an intermediary, I'm not sure what to expect from these two. Then again, I've never been able to predict their movements. The way Kane's looking at me, equal parts hunger and *something more*, makes my heart flutter the same way it does when I'm with Sam, and I'm not—I can't—I don't know what to do!

A flare of white-hot panic chases my mounting plea-sure. When we first set the boundaries for the game and I said that I'd make Kane fall in love with me, I hadn't imagined feeling like this when it happened. Triumphant, maybe, or a little arrogant, but not *this*.

I'm in danger of falling alongside him.

I struggle against their hold, suddenly desperate to escape the bubbly, bright feeling inside my chest, but all that does is push Kane's tongue deeper. He groans, and the vibration ripples against my clit and makes me squeal. Clenching my eyes shut, I drag in a lungful of air and claw at his scalp. "*Please* put me down. This is—we can't —" I struggle to find the right words, but maybe that's the problem.

There are none to describe our complex, fucked-up situation.

I fall for him, he falls for me, add a little tongue, a sprinkle of sex, a few more hearts to break, and voila! You've got a disaster in the making. I'm such an idiot for thinking that I could come out of this unscathed.

I flail around long enough that our fragile equilibrium shatters. In an instant, the three of us tumble to the ground in a pile of naked limbs. While I catch my breath, Kane is already in motion. He tears Zane's shirt over his head, barely heeding the other man's injury, and slathers his chest in a homemade black paint. As Zane moves, it shimmers in a cool violet hue that makes the veins snaking down his arms and chest pop. Goosebumps break out across his pale skin and his nipples pebble into hard peaks. Despite the way he leers and hisses Kane's name, Zane snatches his boyfriend and slams their lips together. "You'll pay for that," he rasps, trapping Kane's bottom lip between his teeth and clawing his chest.

Angry red marks appear, but Kane merely grins and grabs Zane's ass. "Make it hurt, baby." They make out while Kane covers them both in paint. He drags his messy hands down Zane's good arm and across his stomach until he reaches the promised land, eagerly palming Zane's dick through his sweatpants.

Zane bites Kane's shoulder as a shudder courses through his body. "W-wait," he gasps, grabbing Kane's wrist as he reaches for the waistband. "We are *not* painting our dicks."

"It'll wash off."

"I'm not risking a chemical burn so you can get your rocks off!"

I read one of the paint tube labels while they bicker. It's definitely washable—with an adhesive sponge and dish soap. Best not to get it on anyone's pubes. The paint on my skin is already drying and pulling at the little hairs on my body; I can't imagine it sticking somewhere more sensitive. Clearing my throat, I grab their attention. "I'm with Zane. No more paint."

After a shared look, they turn to me. "We'll be careful," Kane promises, a slow smile curving on his lips. "Won't we, babe?"

Zane runs a hand through his dark hair and creates silver streaks from the paint stuck between his fingers. He frowns when he notices. "You don't know the meaning of the word."

"That's why I have you."

They share another look, this one softer than the last, before helping each other to their feet. "We're already dirty," Kane reasons, licking his lips. "And we need to keep each other warm. It's supposed to freeze tonight."

I take a step back as they take one forward. "Can't we shower first?" My heart races at the hunger in their eyes. "Then we can climb into bed for the movie."

"Mmmm..." Kane taps his chin. "No shower here, Siren. We'd have to go inside for that."

"Too far," Zane murmurs, sliding his hands into his pockets. "And you know how Kane is. Once he gets an idea into his head, it's impossible to talk him out of it." A small smile graces his lips. "Stubborn bastard."

Kane grunts in agreement.

"But the paint—"

"Isn't a problem," Kane interrupts, holding his palms up. They're absolutely covered in paint. "I don't have to touch you." Inclining his head, he motions to Zane. "He does."

Dark eyes smoldering with heat, Zane takes one step closer, then another, and another, quickly eliminating the distance between us. He grabs my chin and tilts my head back to stare into my eyes. "I don't fuck just anyone." His grip tightens as his gaze roams my face. "They have to be important to me, or I don't... I can't..." Swallowing hard, he clenches his eyes shut. "But you *are* important to me."

I bite my bottom lip. Nothing about the way he's holding my face hostage makes me feel important. "Are... are you sure?"

Zane takes a deep breath and holds it. Slowly, *so slowly*, he lowers his forehead onto mine and releases his breath, dissipating the tension lingering inside his body. "Yeah," he murmurs, sliding his palm to my cheek. Our noses brush as he caresses my face. "I'm sure."

# Chapter 30

## Zane

I've spent more hours stressing over Sam's new schedule than I can count. From the video footage and tracking I've done online, I've come to the conclusion that he isn't just busy—he's being run ragged at his father's behest, likely as some twisted form of punishment for disobeying him over the past few years. Seeing him at the psychiatrist's office today only solidifies my theory.

His dad's a fucking maniac.

It begs the question, though: why did he let Sam loose at all? Why not cage his son before he ran amok and tasted freedom?

I've turned those questions over in my head night after night, wondering what exactly Samuel Wright has been waiting for. His arrival at the cabin wasn't random; it was planned, much like the way he's been stringing Vinicius Morningstar along ever since the day they met. Everything Samuel does is calculated with precision, so why—why did he wait until now to rein in Sam's leash?

It isn't until I'm weaving my fingers through the soft waves of Mercy's hair, breathing in her every exhale, feeling the unsteady beat of her heart beneath my palm, aching for the taste of her lips... that I begin to understand.

Samuel Wright was waiting for his son to fall in love.

Even as the realization dawns on me, I'm too distracted to recognize it for what it is, too wrapped up in the warmth of her skin and the tinkle of laughter that falls past her lips. She's nervous, but so am I. Excited, a little scared, but ready.

It's time to try something new.

Mercy shivers as I walk her backwards through the studio doorway and into the chapel. For once, I don't have a plan. All I know is that I'm not some heathen that's going to touch her—fuck her—*love her*—on the dirty floor; if we have a mattress, we might as well use it.

The string lights hanging in the rafters sparkle like stars as I steer Mercy across the empty pews to the mattress lying on the floor behind the pulpit. I've spent countless hours in this church cleaning the place up, dusting twice a day, sweeping out crinkling leaves and abandoned bird nests, patching the holes in the roof, and the end result has been good enough for Kane and I to pack up our entire lives and rough it until tensions with Samuel Wright die down. With Kane, things have felt perfect because he makes them perfect. Smiling at me over lukewarm coffee in the mornings, traipsing the short distance across the cemetery to visit his new favorite family in the evenings, making love to me every night until neither of us can catch our breath. To my complete and utter surprise, I have few complaints about this new chapter in our lives.

But as I stand hand in hand with Mercy and glimpse the bare-bones essentials surrounding us, I can't help but feel that it's inadequate. She won't want to brush out her bed head without a mirror or pee in the woods when nature calls in the middle of the night. Expecting anything more from her when I can offer so little is asking for disappointment.

Her smile is a comfort I don't deserve, yet she gives it anyway. The brush of her lips over mine, shy and sweet and so fucking patient, is a balm to my soul.

I don't deserve any of this.

I don't deserve *her.*

"I've hurt you," I whisper, unable to stop the words from tumbling out. There are few things in life that I regret, but Mercy is the biggest of all. How I've treated her. How I've touched her. How I've hurt both her and the man I love by holding on so tightly. How I've hurt *myself.* I cup her cheek and say the words that I've been holding onto ever since she first welcomed us into her home. "I'm sorry."

She places her hand over mine and leans into my touch. "I'm sorry, too."

The warmth of Mercy's heart is so gentle that it burns, leaving me breathless and aching. For more, for less—the push and pull between us so familiar by now that I'm not sure which lead to follow. She brushes the tip of her nose against my jawline and exhales shakily, visibly nervous. That, I understand all too well.

I'm trembling more than she is.

We hold each other's gaze for as long as we dare, both of us breaking away at the same time. My face flushes, and I bite the inside of my cheek to keep from smiling. Weeks I've spent at her kitchen table, brushing elbows with her at the sink, fapping in her shower to the scent of her shampoo, watching her and Kane dance around their feelings, pretending that I'm not as taken with her as I am. And now, here she is.

I'll have to thank Kane for inviting her over.

"We don't have to... you know," she mumbles, her cheeks turning pink. "We can stop here."

I swallow the lump stuck in my throat and force my vocal cords to work. "Do you want to stop?"

She gazes up at me from beneath long lashes. "Only if... you do?"

My heart pounds in an unsteady rhythm, thrown off by the contrast between Mercy and Kane. With Kane, I knew from the start that our love would be as painful as it is precious, but with Mercy, everything is new. Her body is soft—so much softer than Kane's—and fragile, easy to break if I'm not careful.

I trace her bare collarbone with my fingertips. There was a time when I wanted nothing more than to watch her suffocate beneath my hands. To slice into her flesh and sense death looming nearby, the two of us eager for the moment she slipped unconscious and fell from my arms into his.

So many fantasies I've played in my head, yet none of them have come true.

Maybe it's better not to dream at all. Then, I won't be burdened by unfulfilled promises and evolving desires. I'll take each moment as it comes instead of planning for the crash and hoping for the windfall.

I rub my thumb across a drying streak of paint on her shoulder. It flakes off to reveal unblemished skin underneath, pale and pretty and perfect. If Kane holds the warmth of the radiant sun, Mercy holds the subtle glow of the moon. Two halves that fit together perfectly.

There isn't any room for me unless I make room between them.

"I want—" My voice catches. I start again. "I *want* —" Squeezing my eyes shut, I take a deep breath. "I want you!"

Those three little words fall like dominos, crashing into every turbulent emotion ricocheting inside my chest. My heart vibrates as I come to terms with the chaos, knowing that I can't suppress it. I need to embrace it. "I want you," I gasp, grabbing Mercy's arm. Her waist. Her throat. Her breast. Everything that I can touch, I take, gasping as I drop to my knees on the mattress and take her with me. She lies down on her back while I explore her body piece by perfect piece, familiarizing myself with the arch of her foot, the warmth of her thighs, the exact distance between her hip and the bottom rung of her ribcage, how many seconds it takes for her back to arch as I knead her breast and suck its taut peak, which of her hands grabs for mine first, how eager she is to meet my lips.

Our kiss should be a shy, sweet, gentle thing, but she claws my scalp and pulls me in, moaning the moment our lips meet. Sucking on my bottom lip, teasing my tongue with hers, breathing me in as much as I am her. She wraps her arms around my neck and her legs around my waist, pulling me into the cradle of her thighs.

"I'm ready," she breathes, holding my gaze. "Except —" Her eyes widen. "Condom! Oh, crap!"

I can't hold my laugh. "Kane," I call out, looking up to find the man gaping slack-jawed at us, "could you grab them?"

He hardly blinks as he rummages around for our boxes of condoms, moving on autopilot as he tosses two at me. Mercy releases me so that I can take off my sweatpants and tear open a package, but as soon as I do, I realize our mistake.

"These are yours, love." I roll the condom on anyway, hoping it'll magically suction at the base or that I've grown an extra inch in girth since I last checked, but neither of those occur. "Where are mine?"

Chuffing, Kane starts throwing pillows and blankets around. "Maybe we're out."

"We just bought a new box last week."

He lifts an eyebrow, daring me to do the math. I quickly run the numbers in my head and crinkle my nose. "Okay, we have a lot of sex. But we shouldn't be *out-out*."

Mercy stares at my dick and bites her lip. "It doesn't fit?"

Sighing, I run my hand through my hair. "No, it doesn't." Running to the store will kill the mood. Fuck. I pull off the condom and toss it into the waste basket. She might let me fuck her without a condom, but I won't pull a Sam and assume she's okay with it. I saw how anxious she was after that last cream pie; I won't risk putting her through that if she isn't one hundred percent comfortable with the consequences. "It's okay; we don't have to have sex."

It just really fucking sucks.

Mercy's face falls. "Oh. Okay." She pulls her legs up and grabs a blanket. "I guess we can watch the movie then?"

God, I hate this.

"Wait." Grabbing the second condom, I hold it out to Kane. "He can do it. I can facilitate." Once Kane takes the condom from me, I grab Mercy's hand and press a kiss to her wrist. "I know you wanted Sam here for this, but this is even better. It's safer." I feel like a fucking genius. "I know Kane better than Sam does. He'll listen if I tell him to back off. If Sam told him to stop, he'd take it as a challenge and keep going."

Or go harder.

Kane grabs my shoulders and gives me a shake, agitating my broken arm. "I fucking love you," he rasps, tipping my head back and kissing me upside-down. He drops to his knees and places the condom in my hand. "Put it on for me?"

"H-hold on!" Mercy covers her blushing face as I tear open the package with my teeth and carefully roll the condom on Kane's dick. He twitches in my palm, so I give him a gentle tug to test his response. A full-bodied shudder rolls down his spine.

He's fucking ready.

We both turn to Mercy. "If you don't want to, Kitten, he can fuck me instead. Maybe it'll help if you watch first." It won't be the same because I don't have a pussy, but it'll give her an idea of the stretch needed to fit him. We had to practice before I could take him all the way. Mercy might not be able to fit him inside all at once.

She needs to understand that or she'll risk crushing disappointment if it doesn't happen on the first try.

Biting the inside of her cheeks, she puffs out a breath. "I want to, okay!" She pushes herself up onto her elbows. "But I've never—I mean, I've only ever been with Sam, and he's not... as big." Her gaze flits between both of our dicks. "Zane's is closer in size, so that should be fine, but Kane's—" The flush on her cheeks spreads down the side of her neck. "I've never seen one that big before."

I doubt she's seen many dicks in her lifetime.

"Don't inflate his ego too much," I tease, smacking Kane's back. "Or his dick will get even bigger."

Mercy squeaks like a goddamn church mouse.

I bust out laughing. "I'm joking! It won't grow any more!" Until he's about to come, but she doesn't need to know that part.

Kane pulls me in for a heated kiss, throwing me completely off guard. He takes advantage of my surprise and pulls me into his lap, quickly grinding his erection against my ass. "Want me to take care of you first?" He kneads my cheeks and presses the tip of his cock to my hole without giving me any time to adjust. Fire courses through my veins as he sucks a bruise onto my neck.

That doesn't sound too bad, actually, except—"Your fucking hands," I hiss, smacking his arm. "Did you get the paint off?"

He chuckles.

That's a fucking no.

"You like when I mark you," he teases, nipping my shoulder. "He likes a little pain with his pleasure."

My face flames bright red. "Don't tell her that!"

"But it's true."

Shoving Kane's forehead, I push him away so that I can get some air. "Mercy," I gasp, arching my back to check over my shoulder. "What do you want to—"

*Oh, fuck.*

She's rubbing her thighs together and clutching her breasts in both hands, her skin flushed a pretty pink from her hairline to her chest. The splotches of paint on her body are as stubborn as the man who put them there. I choke on my next breath as Kane smacks my ass and growls.

"Let me fuck you, Zane. She likes it."

No one can argue with that astute observation.

While Kane grabs the lube, I crawl back over to Mercy. "Don't think that we've forgotten about you." Her eyes widen as I climb on top of her and pin her to the mattress with my forearm. "Kane's just excited that you're here."

He smacks my ass as he pushes up onto his knees behind me. "You're excited too, jackass."

I can't deny it. I'm damn near breathless from the adrenaline rushing through my body.

Mercy stares up at me, her honeyed eyes darker than I've ever seen before. "Your arm," she murmurs, touching my elbow. "Doesn't it hurt?"

There's enough going on that I can ignore the ache. Besides, the break wasn't *that* bad. "I'm fine," I assure her, repositioning myself so that I'm a little more comfortable. But with a woman beneath me and a man lining up behind me, there isn't much room for me to maneuver.

"We can switch places," she offers, trying to sit up. "Lie down."

How sweet.

Ignoring her, I drag my fingertips down her chest and carefully avoid touching her tits. She's burning up, and we've barely gotten started. I bet if I reach lower... Sliding my hand down her body, I push her thighs apart, eager to feel how turned on she is.

My fingertips slip right over her swollen clit, making it impossible not to play with her. She's *soaked* down there.

"Zane!" she gasps, grabbing my good arm. "*Ah!*"

Kane rumbles behind me. "Get her nice and wet for me." Spreading my cheeks, he drips lube down my crack and rubs it in with the tip of his dick. "Need me to eat you out?"

"No." I shiver as he teases my hole. "I'm ready."

So fucking ready.

As he pushes the first inch inside, he adds a generous amount of lube to ease the glide. "I could use my fingers," he offers, caressing my lower back. "I can clean the paint off."

"No." I take a deep breath. "I want your dick." As I adjust to his size, I bury my face in Mercy's tits and groan. Kane pulls back only to push another inch in, then another, slowly building into a rhythm.

"*Ohhh*," Kane moans, holding me still. "Look at her face, babe. Look."

I take a deep breath and tilt my face up. Sometime between when Kane first thrust inside of me until now, Mercy started rubbing her clit on the heel of my palm. Head tossed back, raven locks spread like a dark halo on the pillow, she parts her lips on a silent *O* as she shimmies her hips and stares directly into Kane's eyes.

Moving my wrist, I slip two fingers inside her heat. "Imagine that he's fucking you, Kitten," I rasp, plunging my fingers in time with Kane's shallow thrusts. "He's being so gentle." My cock leaks onto the bedsheet, rubbing the soft fabric every time Kane pushes forward. I wish I were inside of her. She's molten to the core, smoldering hot and so wet that it's dripping down her crack. I play with her pussy until I can hear how wet she is, curling my fingers and finding that spot that makes her squirm.

Kane picks up the pace, spurred on by Mercy's frantic moaning. I push back onto him, gasping as he hits *my* perfect spot. "Fuck," I whimper, clenching my eyes shut. Pleasure shoots down my spine with each drag of his cock, and I bite down on Mercy's breast to stifle my moans. I come first, pumping thick ropes of cum onto the sheets. It sticks to my skin and makes a huge mess, but Mercy's just as dirty as I am, sweating from head to toe and trembling so hard that I can't hold her still.

"Fuck, Siren, *fuck*," Kane groans, shoving his cock all the way inside my ass. I cry out at the sudden stretch, but it's Mercy who convulses, whimpering as my hand plunges deeper inside of her pussy. With a groan, I sweep the pad of my thumb across her clit and jerk my wrist, knowing that she's close, needing to watch her come, aching to feel her wrap around my fingers—

The moment Mercy comes, she holds her breath. Her thighs convulse and she claws my shoulders, scratching angry red marks into my skin. Kane slams his cock inside of me and grunts as he blows his load immediately after her, burying his seed as deep as it will go.

All three of us are a panting, sweaty mess as we collapse on top of each other, my boyfriend careful to roll onto his back and pull me with him. He doesn't speak, but he trails his palm down my broken arm in a silent question: does it hurt?

I kiss his shoulder. Yeah, it hurts, but everything else feels so fucking good that a little pain can't eclipse how light my heart feels. Mercy reaches for me and takes my hand, holding my gaze as she smiles sweetly. Strands of her hair stick to her forehead and neck like spiderwebs, weaving the story of tonight across her skin.

Kane takes Mercy's hand and pulls her into my side, reaching over me to cradle the back of her head and kiss her hard, groaning into her mouth. He's still thinking about round two.

My cock twitches.

*I'm* still thinking about round two.

"Shower first," I grumble, pinching Kane's thigh. "And new sheets." I am *not* sleeping in cum tonight. Not when we have a guest.

Grinning as he pulls away from Mercy, Kane chuckles. "Fine. We'll shower, then we'll fuck." He presses a tender kiss to Mercy's cheek before leaning down to kiss my lips. "We have all night together."

I stare into my lover's eyes, knowing that this one night could easily turn into more exactly like this one. It's a dangerous path—one that we've never gone down before. I squeeze his hand, and he squeezes mine back.

"Yeah," I agree. "We can take our time."

Kane's smile, radiant and warm and so full of life, takes my breath away. He kisses me soft and slow before turning to Mercy and doing the same, humming happily as we both reciprocate. A blush dusts my cheeks as I watch them linger in the kiss, drawing out the moment as much as possible.

The pressure in my chest, that feeling of something heavy building and building until it explodes, is decidedly quiet. I don't know when the change happened or how, but I understand that it's because of Mercy—or more accurately, because of how she handles Kane. There's a softness to her gaze, her touch, that he deserves more than anyone.

I used to think that she would eclipse me entirely. Block me out like the moon overlapping the sun. But then they both turn to me and drag me into their orbit. Not pushing me out or throwing me down, but making room so that their love can overflow onto me, too.

Everything clicks into place. The reason why Kane can't let Mercy go. Why Sam's been insufferable about keeping her safe. How Samuel could wait years before making a move. Why I've been so painfully jealous every time Mercy walks into the room.

Love is a double-edged sword.

It's the one thing no one wants to lose. The one thing worth fighting for. The one thing people will go to any lengths to protect.

A weakness. A strength.

Or even a liability, wrapped in pretty red ribbon, soft sighs, and starlight eyes.

## CHAPTER 31

### SAM

THE MORNINGSTARS' annual holiday party is my favorite event of the year. I've been attending ever since I met their family, after Vinny insisted that everyone who attends their grief support group *is* family. At the time, I was still reeling from the loss of my mother, and my dad was being as cold as ever, so I didn't have anything happy to go home to.

That's why being around Mercy and her family—sharing the warmth of their company and eating way too many cookies than should be legal—has always meant so much to me.

They're the family that I always wanted.

But this year, I'm nervous. I play it off as excitement when my dad's looking, but every time he turns his back, I dig my fist into the bruise on my thigh so that the pain keeps me grounded. I can't afford to make any mistakes tonight.

If we fail and my father lives, he won't show us any mercy.

The first person he kills will be the one I care about most.

I've played this scenario over and over in my head ever since I came up with the idea. At first, it was a wishful, frantic thing muttered in the dark of my bedroom, but the longer I sat with it, the more it made sense. The best way for me to protect Mercy is to ensure that my father can't touch her, and the only way to do that is to kill him.

Taking over his contracts and heading the dozens of companies he's founded is a nightmare. I'll have to untangle, but it'll be worth it if I can have Mercy.

I'll do anything to keep her by my side.

Now that the day is finally here, everything is falling into place. Our gift is as ostentatious as it can get—a serif relief of the letter M that suspiciously looks like a W at the same time—and a case of the most expensive wine on the market. It's not so expensive that no normal person has heard of it, but it's well-known enough to prove just how much money the Wright family has.

A fuck ton.

I used to believe that my mother's charitable efforts were what garnered so much finances, but the reality is much more grim. Working under my father has proven that behind the veneer of charitable deeds and fundraisers, he has innumerable underground contacts for drug smuggling, weapons deals, and laundering money.

It's no wonder my mom grew to hate him.

The party is being held inside the mortuary itself; the few back rooms that aren't used for storage are transformed into a quaint setting for mourners to gather for a rare moment of peace. A Christmas tree, decorated with homemade ornaments and a variety of gifted ones over the years, sits in the lobby for guests to enjoy with hot cocoa and a round of holiday bingo. This is the first time in years that I haven't helped set up for the event. Knowing that Kane and Zane likely took over that duty makes me sadder than I realized it would. Next year, I'll have to string the whole place in lights and set sparkling reindeer out front.

I can't be outdone if I'm going to become the man of the house.

This year, however, I have an even greater surprise—something that I'll never be able to top again.

"Are you ready?" I glance over at my special guest, noting the way he didn't bother to dress up. I'd set out my best outfits for him to choose from, but he decided to wear what he arrived in this morning: a black denim jacket, heavy combat boots, a worn long-sleeve t-shirt, and ripped jeans. Playing with his lip piercing as he stares at the mortuary, he doesn't respond.

"I know you haven't been home in a while—"

A flash of anger in his eyes makes me pause. Maybe bringing him wasn't a good idea after all. Then again, if anyone's got a grudge against my father, it's him. We need that kind of energy if we're going to win tonight.

"Stay behind me," I instruct, stepping up to the front door. "They need to see me first."

He chuffs. "Whatever, dude. Like I care who goes first."

My father is actually the one who enters first, drawing eyes as he sweeps dramatically in front of our gifts—delivered this afternoon—and makes a show about checking them. When his gaze lands on Vinicius Morningstar, Mercy's father, he smiles at the other man and inclines his head. They'll speak at some point tonight, but my dad will take his time with the approach, luring Vinny with a slow pull rather than a direct approach. That's usually how he handles things—pretending to be indirect while secretly aligning the pieces on the board until he's the last person standing.

Ignoring him is easy. I follow him into the lobby and avoid the urge to look for Mercy. I'm starving for a glimpse of her, my stomach tying itself into knots. But this moment, for all of the planning that went into it, isn't about me.

It's about the man walking in behind me.

There aren't many guests, but a whisper spreads around the room like smoke. It takes a moment for Vinicius to recognize the words rumbling around him, but when he does, he drops his glass of wine.

A gasp catches my attention, and I turn my head to find Mercy struggling to hold back tears from across the room, but she isn't crying at the sight of me.

She's speechless at the sight of her younger brother Malachi.

The boy who's been 'at boarding school' for years.

With a strangled cry, she rushes to him, barreling into

his chest so hard that he stumbles. "Hey, Sis," he mumbles, hiding his face in her raven hair. They wrap their arms around each other and share a private moment that the rest of the room politely ignores... but I can't.

Staring at Mercy's back is a kind of torture I've never experienced. Her chest rises with a sob that I long to soothe, and I clench my fist in my pocket to keep from reaching for her. Bringing Malachi here took groveling to my father to make it happen, but the payoff is a thousand times worth it.

Especially since it means we have another man in our corner when the time comes to kill my dad.

Someone punches my arm. "Sam, you fucking bastard. You made it."

"Kane," I greet numbly, refusing to look away from Mercy. She pulls away from her brother and futilely wipes the damp patch of tears on his jacket, or maybe it's the makeup. At least he's wearing black so it blends in.

Time slows to a crawl as she grips her brother's hand tightly in hers and turns around, her watery eyes finally landing on me.

I hold my breath as another silent tear slides down her cheek. She's curled her hair for the evening, two long strands framing her angelic face. Dark red lipstick matches the color of her blouse and the laces on her boots, but the tights, ruffled skirt, and leather on her shoes is pitch black. Standing next to her brother, the resemblance is undeniable. They both have pale complexions, curled lashes, stormy emerald eyes, and a light flush to their cheeks.

"Sam," she breathes, blinking back a fresh wave of tears. "Did you—was this—" She clutches her brother's hand tighter. "How?"

Malachi has been denied leave from school—or more accurately, the asylum he's been imprisoned in—for years. If I'd been paying attention sooner, I would have noticed and got him out a long time ago. It was yet another one of my father's schemes; keep the boy under lock and key in case he needs leverage.

Bringing him home now is meant to prove Vinicius's incompetence with his own family and how superior my father is, since he's taking credit for my idea. I don't give a damn so long as we ensure that Malachi is here to stay.

Rather than answer Mercy's question, I brush a stray tear off her cheek. "Please don't cry," I murmur, breathing in her every exhale. God, I needed to see her. To be with her. A huge weight is lifted off my shoulders by simply standing in her presence.

"These are happy tears," she laughs, smiling easily. "I can't believe you're here." She hooks her arm through her brother's. "Either of you." With her other hand, she reaches for mine and squeezes my fingers. "Thank you, Sam. This is the best gift I've ever had."

Anything for you.

Zane appears by Mercy's side and steals her hand from mine, lacing their fingers together with an ease I never imagined I'd see between them. "Let's go find Granny. She'll have a heart attack." Although he's taller than Malachi, they match in appearance, wearing only black. But where Malachi is full grunge, Zane has opted for a softer approach, wearing a button-down with his skinny jeans and canvas shoes. Except—

"Are you wearing eyeliner?"

Mercy glances up at Zane fondly, and they share a subtle smile that makes my heart quiver. That's a look of endearment, and it's new, much like the hand-holding.

Lifting an eyebrow, Zane challenges me with that simple of a gesture. "You got a problem with it?"

Hooking my hands in my pockets, I hold his gaze. "No." I'm just wondering how much I've missed over the past few weeks. Apparently, a fucking lot. Even his injured arm hangs by his side, still wrapped in a soft cast, but a small heart has been drawn in permanent marker over his thumb. The break must not have been as bad as it looked when I saw him wearing a sling the other day. "Glad to see you're healing."

He nods. "Can't stay down forever." Tugging Mercy's hand, he leads their band of goths to the back to find Grandma Star, leaving Kane and me to stare at each other.

Nudging my arm, Kane walks with me to admire the tree. "You ready?"

I don't see how that's relevant. "Are you?"

He takes a sip of his drink, something clear and fizzy. Soda? Is he not drinking tonight?

Seeing the unspoken question in my eyes, he offers me the plastic cup. "Not good to drink on the job. Don't want to carve my own finger off." He tries to get me to take the drink. "You, though. You need to relax. Hold this while I get you something stronger."

"No, I'm okay." I want to be clear-headed for this. "I'll have water."

Kane clicks his tongue. "Your dad will be suspicious if you don't have a drink."

The bar is in the back, so we take a detour to mix a virgin cocktail. I hear Mercy's laugh from another room and turn in that direction.

"She's fine, Sam."

I can't help but frown. "That's not what Zane told me."

"Yeah, well, Zane's a bit pessimistic. Glass half empty, and all that." Kane swirls the ice in his cup. "She's been stressed, but we're helping her relax." The smirk he attempts to hide behind his cup is incriminating as hell.

"Helping her relax," I repeat, crushing my plastic cup. The liquid sloshes over the side and drips onto the floor. As long as Mercy is happy, that's what matters. I know this, *I accept this*, and yet my jealous heart twists in silent agony.

I want to be there with her, no matter what it is the three of them are up to together.

Kane hums in the back of his throat. "Mhm." Clapping me on the shoulder, he grins. "But don't worry, Wright. We're taking good care of her until you get back, but that's the thing. You *will* be back. You standing here is proof of that. She hasn't given up on you, so don't give up on her."

I would *never*.

Dumping my drink into the sink, I grab a new cup and fill it with ice water. "Once this shit with my dad is over, I'm not leaving again." I meet Kane's eyes. "If you're here to stay, you'll have to get used to having me around. I won't compromise my feelings for her to make you comfortable."

With a grin, Kane chuckles under his breath. "So long as you get used to sharing, Sam, I don't give a damn if you stick around or not."

"Whatever makes her happy." I drain my cup to drown out whatever lingering jealousy stirs inside my heart. If I'm going to survive sharing Mercy's bed with two other men, I need to remember the reason we're all here. "Do you love her?"

"Absolutely," Kane answers immediately.

Adrenaline pulses through my veins as my heart clenches tightly. "Are you going to kill her?"

Kane's face lights up as we hear another peal of Mercy's laughter echoing down the hallway. "Even if I snuck that past you, I'd regret it the moment my knife hits her heart."

I nod. A rush of relief makes my knees weak. That's one less problem to deal with. "You won't change your mind?"

He shakes his head. "Nah. You don't have to worry about Zane, either. He's smitten as fuck, just stubborn about it." With a warm smile, Kane bumps my shoulder with his. "Welcome back, Sam."

I take a deep, calming breath and feel myself relax for the first time in weeks.

It's good to be home.

# CHAPTER 32

# MERCY

MY GRANDMOTHER WON'T LET GO of Malachi's arm. As soon as we stepped into the sitting room, she took my place by his side and hasn't let go. Once they sat at the round table in the corner of the room, he was done for, unable to get up without invoking her immediate sorrow at his parting. But the two of them have always been close; he used to help my grandfather tend to the grounds before he passed, and he and Grandma speak to each other in hushed tones, like they always do.

It's a special dynamic that I've never had with either of them, but it's okay. Now, I have three other men to confide in.

Zane walks in a steady loop around the room, ensuring that we don't stay in one place or conversation for long. What few times I catch up with my older sister and the dashing gentleman on her arm or speak with some of our longest-standing clients, I'm able to relax and go with the flow. I keep hoping that Zane will take the hint and do the same, but there's a wrinkle of tension written across his face that I can't riddle out.

"You don't have to be so tense," I tell him after our third rotation through the building. "No one's going to bite if you say hello and introduce yourself." I've had a hard time figuring out how to introduce him to others, switching between calling him my friend and my roommate, although neither are exactly true.

"And you don't have to be perfect," Zane replies smoothly, "but it's fun to watch you try."

I purse my lips. "What's that supposed to mean?"

"You keep filtering yourself when you talk to people. Just tell them how it is. If you're sad or bored or lonely or overwhelmed—be honest, and people will either understand, or they won't. You don't need to put on a fake smile."

"These are my family's clients," I protest, pulling him to a stop near the door to the morgue.

Zane raises an eyebrow. "Your dad calls them family."

I wave away the semantics. "It's a blurred line."

He taps my forehead with a teasing smile. "Then unblur it, Mercy."

Grabbing his hand, I frown. "But I don't know what to say."

He laces our fingers together and leans close. "You can tell them that we're lovers." Chuckling in my ear, he presses a gentle kiss to my neck. "I'm sure they'll be happy for you."

I clear my throat as someone walks by and studiously

ignores me and Zane. "No one actually says that out loud."

"I just did." His throat clicks on a swallow. "How does it feel?"

My emotions are too hard to grasp. I can't possibly sift through them. "I don't know. I can't think with—" His lips find my pulse point. "—you doing that." I dig my fingertips into the back of his hand. "Zane, my family's here. Stop it."

"They'll get over it."

"It's not appropriate!"

He pulls away from me and licks his lips salaciously. "Seeing you happy isn't appropriate?"

"Seeing us makeout isn't appropriate," I hiss.

A silver spark ignites in his eyes. "I want to kiss you, Mercy." He grabs my waist and hauls me against his chest. "You look beautiful tonight, by the way."

"That—that's not going to work," I stammer, feeling my face warm. How often does someone call me beautiful?

*Not often enough.*

With a twist of his wrist, Zane unlocks the door to the morgue and pushes it open. "Then let me find something that does."

Normal girls wouldn't makeout in a morgue, but when have I ever been normal?

As soon as we step into the room and the door clicks shut, Zane sweeps me into his arms and kisses me hard. Grabbing my throat, he pushes me against the cadaver coolers and smirks. "Looks like The Dead Girl isn't very dead, after all. I can feel your heart racing."

My voice catches as he lifts my leg and hooks it around his hips. "Z-Zane, how—"

He cuts me off with his lips on mine. "I've always known who you are, Mercy." Grabbing my wrists, he pins them over my head. "The question is, do you?" He stares into my eyes as he thumbs my pulse on my wrist. "It doesn't matter what people call you. What matters is how you see yourself."

I bite my bottom lip, and his eyes track the movement. "What if I don't like what I see?"

"Then change it, as many times as it takes." A crooked smile makes him even more handsome. "Don't tell Kane I said that."

"Why not?"

Zane puffs out a breath. "I'll never hear the end of it." Without elaborating further, he slants his lips over mine and traps me beneath his body, interlocking our hands over our heads and pinning me to the wall. The icy chill contrasts the raging heat of his body as he rolls his hips, stealing my breath and setting my heart on fire.

"I want you, Mercy," he breathes, his eyelashes fluttering against my cheek. "I want you so damn bad that I —" A laugh catches in his throat. "I can't think straight." He mutters something that I can't catch.

"What?"

"That's a problem," he says loud enough for me to hear. "Sam's going to murder me if I fuck this up."

"Fuck what up?"

He kisses me again, sliding his tongue into my mouth and groaning as we collide. The hard line of his body crushes mine, creating an ache that I feel in the depths of my soul. I shiver as he rocks against my core, sending shockwaves of pleasure deep within. Biting his bottom lip, I draw it into my mouth and suck, moaning in sync with him.

His erection digs into my panties, nearly spearing me through our clothes. "I have a—" I inhale sharply as he latches onto my neck with his teeth. "Condom."

A shudder rolls through his body. "Don't tease me, Mercy."

"I'm serious." I tug on his hair until he pulls up. "In my boot. I have one for you and Kane. He gave them to me after I got dressed."

Zane's midnight eyes smolder like liquid gunmetal. He releases me and crouches at my feet. "If you're lying, I swear, I'll—" Slipping his fingers inside my boot, he caresses my ankle as he searches for the package. Once he snags a corner, he pulls it out. "No fucking way." He chuckles deep in his chest and kisses my knee. "Remind me to thank Kane for the foresi—"

I pull him to his feet and lunge into his arms, shocking him badly enough that he stumbles backwards into an embalming table. He recovers immediately and spins us around, bending me over the stainless steel and lifting my skirt over my ass.

"I'm going to make this quick, are you—"

"Yes, God, yes." I arch my hips. "Hurry up and fuck me, Zane."

He smacks my ass and the sound echoes in the empty room. "Careful, Kitten, or I'll have to slow down and enjoy it." Rubbing my stinging flesh, he chuckles darkly. "I'd hate for someone to walk in and see their darling girl in such a compromising position." He drags my panties down my thighs but keeps them snagged around my knees. Then I hear him unzip his pants. "This might hurt at first." The wrapper crinkles as he tears open the package and rolls the condom onto his cock.

The only warning I get is the smack of his dick against my pussy before he thrusts, burying himself inside my heat with a loud groan. "*Ohhh*, fuck." Grabbing my hips, he slams me onto his cock in time with his thrusts, not giving either of us a second to breathe before he sets a punishing pace.

My walls stretch to accommodate him, the drag of his cock making me delirious. Pleasure builds slowly, burning through my body like a fever. I struggle to catch my breath as Zane rocks into me, growing more frantic with each passing second.

"Knew you could take it," he growls, "so fucking wet for me, Kitten, so—" He snaps his hips. "Fucking—" Grabs my ass. "*Wet.*" The slap of his hips bumping my ass is loud as hell, filling the air with the unmistakable sound of sex.

I whine as embarrassment floods my system.

Zane catches on immediately, slowing the drag of his cock to punctuate with hard, deep thrusts. Although anyone listening at the door can probably hear us, the cadence has dropped so that it's not nearly as obvious.

He squeezes my butt and groans. "God, you feel amazing, even with the—" He grunts. "Condom."

Part of me wonders how different it feels without one, but then I remember the intoxicating pulse of Sam's dick as he came inside me, and my pussy clenches.

"*Ooooh*, Mercy, don't—*fuck.*"

Burying himself as deep as he can, Zane's voice catches as he comes, his cock twitching as he fills the condom. Heat bursts inside of me, and I bite my hand to keep from moaning aloud. As Zane pulls out, he curses under his breath. "You didn't come, did you? Give me a second."

Something *thunks* into the trash can and he's back in a flash, spreading my cheeks and slipping his thumb inside of me. With a groan, he slides his fingers through my folds and presses against my swollen clit. "You'd let me take your pussy raw, wouldn't you?"

I spasm as he fondles my clit. Pleasure shoots like sparks up my spine, hardening my nipples into hard points.

"I could do it right now." He rubs his thumb against something inside of me, and I cry out at how good it feels. My desire liquifies, slicking his hand as he caresses my pussy. "There wouldn't be anything between us. Just my hard cock filling you up, Kitten." Leaning over me, he presses a kiss to the back of my neck and adjusts the angle of his wrist, sliding his fingers inside my heat and pressing down on some kind of— My body shakes and I cry out, unable to stop myself as he bares down on that spot. Every brush of his fingers causes my body to convulse, and I moan over and over again.

"That's it," he rasps, nipping my shoulder. "You're so beautiful when you unravel, Mercy." Brushing his lips over my ear, he chuckles, his voice dripping with desire. "I can't wait to come inside you."

White-hot pressure explodes deep inside of me, every nerve in my body sparking at once. I cry out so loudly that Zane bites my shoulder, making me gasp from the flash of pain and silencing the sound of my pleasure. He rumbles deep in his chest as he works me through the orgasm, sliding off of me only to bury his face in my cunt. He groans as he licks me clean, then rings my asshole with the tip of his tongue, unable to help himself.

"Zane!"

"Shhh," he coos, slipping his fingers back into my core. "Let me eat your ass, baby, please." My pussy flutters as he slides three fingers in and out of my soaking wet hole. Then his tongue pushes against my tight ring of muscle and I jump. Groaning, he teases my back door, the wet smack of his lips and glide of his fingers illicit.

But so is the way my body responds, burning from the inside.

This time, I come silently, praying to whichever gods can hear me that no one will know I just had my ass eaten. As Zane lovingly rubs my cheeks and steps away to grab a wipe, he hums happily. Only once he's done cleaning me up does he wash his face at the sink, a devilish smirk curving on his lips.

"Don't say a word," I hiss, my face flaming as I stand

on shaky legs. I adjust my panties so that I'm fully covered, but I can feel the slick heat of my pussy drenching the fabric.

I'm doomed for the rest of the night.

Zane kisses me hard before we rejoin the party. Cupping my face, his eyes soften as he smiles down at me. "You're beautiful, Mercy." Then he winks. "Beautiful *and* delicious."

I put on my best fake smile as he pulls open the door. "Breathe a word of this to anyone, Zane Hunter, and I'll fucking kill you."

He kisses my cheek where everyone can see. "Don't worry, I'm sure they already know." We turn towards the open hall and a few knowing smiles from old ladies without any shame greet us. My face turns bright crimson, and Zane laughs out loud.

At least there's no more ambiguity about who we are to each other now.

*Lovers* is as accurate as it gets.

# CHAPTER 33

## KANE

ACTING as a bouncer while Zane indulges in a private moment with Mercy is a rare delight. As much as I'd love to be involved, I'm more thrilled that they ran off together in the first place. A new tradition is being born right here and now—having sex in unconventional places while one of us keeps watch.

I love everything about this moment.

Sam avoids wandering too close as he mingles with both acquaintance and stranger alike, catching my eye across the hall multiple times as if to ask: *they're still going at it?*

I can't keep the grin off my face.

My boy is finally living with his own happiness in mind. I couldn't be more proud.

Mercy's younger brother Malachi Morningstar stares at me through the lobby archway, blindly shaking hands with people who recognize him and welcome him home. From what Sam told me before we split, he sprung

Malachi from his cage so we'd have an extra pair of hands when the time comes to fuck up Samuel.

I'm all for additional violence, but I'm not sure that Mercy will be on board with us turning her little brother into an accomplice for first degree murder. Her father Vinny, on the other hand…

I've seen the way he looks at Samuel, and there's not an innocent bone in that man's body. If his hands weren't tied, he'd slit Samuel's throat in a heartbeat, and I love him even more for it.

I'm grinning to myself when Samuel sneaks up on me—or tries to, looking about as subtle as a king cobra sizing up its prey. His outfit is gaudy as hell, with silver threads woven throughout his embroidered suit, the snowflake pattern lining the collar a gross display of fake winter cheer. And his hair—whoever dyes it tries their best to hide the grey streaks, but they peek through the chestnut strands all the same.

A splash of crimson on his chest will do the man a world of good.

I'm picturing all the places I can puncture as he slinks over to me.

"Kane," he greets, turning his nose up as his gaze travels down my body. "You never took a last name, did you? Despite everything your birth parents did for you, you chose to disrespect their memory and walk a wretched path."

I meet his disdain with my own. "My parents were dead to me long before they burned to death in that car crash." Abandoning their son because he became *an inconvenience* is unforgivable, but at least it introduced me to my real family: Zane, and now Mercy. "I hold no love for parents who abuse their children."

A cry of pleasure pierces the air, muffled by the door behind me but no less intelligible.

Samuel's eyes narrow at the dead air over my shoulder. "I see that your whore is keeping up her reputation. Who is she with this time: that man you string along like a puppet or the highest bidder for the evening?" He sips champagne from a gold-rimmed flute. "I bet it's her brother, now that the two are reunited. The way they cling to each other—"

My fist smashes the champagne flute into his teeth, cracking the glass and splintering shards into his mouth. I clamp his jaw shut as the flute crashes to the floor. "Chew and swallow," I order, vibrating from the sheer force of my anger, "or I'll shove the stem down your fucking throat."

Eyes wide, Samuel tries to pry his mouth open, but my hands are stronger than his weak mandible. He reaches into his pocket and flings a baby pistol into the air, but it clatters to the ground when he fumbles.

"Oops." Kicking the gun out of his reach, I grin at the panic in his eyes. "Tick-tock, old man. You gonna swallow or do you need something to wash that down first?"

Malachi appears a few paces away and blocks us from view of the rest of the party. He picks up the gun and slips it into his pocket. "This is a weapon-free event." Glaring at Samuel, he stomps on the champagne flute and picks up the largest shard of glass, a teardrop shape with a razor-sharp tip. "Good thing I don't see any, or I'd have to do something about it."

Samuel whimpers as Malachi takes a step forward.

"You know, Kai—can I call you Kai? I think Mr. Wright needs some encouragement. He bit off more than he can chew, and he's struggling to swallow. If I open his mouth, can you help him take a sip?"

"Of course." Bloodlust shines in Malachi's eyes. "It's the least I can do for my biggest sponsor. Haven't seen you around the institute in a while, Mr. Wright. Until your son rang my room, I thought you'd forgotten about me." He grabs an empty plastic cup from a nearby waste basket and spits in it, then he holds the cup up for me to do the same.

Sick bastard.

Once there's enough for Wright to swallow, I pinch his cheeks and pry his jaw open. His tongue flails as he tries to spit out the glass, but I tilt his head back. Blood drips down the corner of his mouth as Malachi pours the drink into Samuel's mouth. He chokes, gagging, until finally his throat bobs on a swallow.

"Was that so hard?" I release his mouth and smack his back as he doubles over and dry heaves into the trash can. "Hey, you don't look so good. I think we need a doctor." Snapping my fingers, I grab him by the nape of the neck. "But you know what? I've been studying under Vinny for a few days. That's almost the same thing, right?"

"Dad's got a degree," Malachi grunts, nodding. "He's a whiz with anatomy."

"There you go!" Hauling Samuel upright, I grin at my new friend. "Let's get him in for an emergency exam." Leaning back against the morgue door, I click my tongue against my teeth. Mercy and Zane are in the middle of *fun* right now, and I don't dare interrupt. "This room's occupied."

"I know a place." Malachi tilts his head back and widens his eyes, looking creepy as hell with his hair falling in his eyes like that. Guy's a freak, I bet.

I wonder what that institute he mentioned is about and how Samuel's involved.

As he leads us through the dwindling throng of guests, not that there were many to begin with, we catch Sam's attention and beckon him over. Then we slip into the storage room. "Not to be the bearer of bad news, but this is a little public for my tastes." There isn't even a door to the hall; it's a heavy black curtain that hardly makes the place soundproof.

Sam crosses his arms over his chest. "What the hell are you two doing?"

I grab Samuel's cheeks and push his lips up into a smile. "Bonding with your dad. I think he likes me."

"You will bleed for this," the old man garbles, spitting blood onto my hand.

"Funny, I was gonna tell you the same thing."

A cardboard box *thuds* onto the floor. Malachi starts deconstructing a huge tower of them in the corner of the room. "There's a room," he mutters, "where no one will find us."

I can feel Sam's blood pressure rise as he glances back at the curtain. "That's not the plan," he hisses, grabbing my arm. "Let him go, Kane."

"I'd rather not. He said some pretty mean shit about our girl."

Sam's hand clenches around my forearm. "What did he say?"

Another box hits the ground and spills open, throwing bleach white tablecloths onto the floor.

"Oh, you know, the usual bullshit that comes out of his mouth." I pat Samuel's cheek and enjoy the way he winces. "He called Mercy an incestuous whore and insinuated that she's sleeping with her brother."

Malachi grabs a candle holder and throws it at Samuel's head. He misses. "Gross."

"Exactly."

With a grunt, he pulls the final box out of the way, creating a makeshift path that leads to a cobweb-encrusted nightmare door whose wood looks like it came from the hull of the Mayflower. When he pushes it open —because the handle's fucking missing—it spits dusts. "Anyone got a flashlight?"

Sam pulls his cell phone from his pocket and turns on the flashlight. Inside the doorway is a narrow set of stone steps leading down into the dark.

Malachi grabs a handful of taper candles and shoves them into his jacket pockets, followed by two lighters, a hidden pack of cigarettes from a desk drawer, and a box of matches. Then he chucks one of the white tablecloths down the stairs. "Let's go." He steps into the darkness and disappears after the first few steps.

Must not be afraid of the dark or whatever bugs have infested the creepy ass cellar.

"I'll go first." Sam ignores his father as he steps in front of us and descends the first few stairs, lighting his own way but not ours. Great.

"You wouldn't kick your own son down the stairs, would you, Samuel?" After pushing Sam's dad onto the first dusty step, I shove a folded cloth napkin into my pocket and nab one of those heavy metal candleholders, wishing I had the knife clipped to Zane's belt. Hopefully when he comes looking for me, it isn't lying on the morgue floor, lost and forgotten after his impromptu romp with Mercy. I'm a little relieved that Malachi picked up Samuel's gun, but shooting in a dark, cramped space is risky even for me. I'd rather handle this quietly beneath everyone's noses—or in this case, their feet.

By the time I come up for air, Samuel Wright better have taken his last.

# CHAPTER 34

# ZANE

GLASS CRUNCHES UNDER MY FEET, and I look down to find blood on the floor. Smearing the shards the sole of my shoe, I stare at them as though they can speak and tell me what happened, or when.

Mercy's gaze drops to my shoe. "Is that... blood?"

I scan the hallway for Kane and listen for his booming laugh, but neither are present.

It makes me nervous.

"Let's find Kane." Leading Mercy around the building, we check every room. Party guests have dwindled since the night began, few of them equipped for late nights drinking and playing games, but Grandma Star sits at her table with her tarot cards out, idly pulling a five-card spread and staring intently at the card faces.

Slipping from my arm, Mercy approaches her grandmother. "Have you seen Kane, Grandma? Or, well, anyone? We can't find Sam or Malachi—"

Granny clasps Mercy's hands in her own and peers

up at her for a long moment. "You've blossomed into a beautiful young woman, Mercy, just beautiful." Her smile is as soft as her gaze. "I remember when your mother first came here. She was just as taken with the business as that young man of yours is." Patting the back of Mercy's hands, she turns her head towards the cards on the table. "I've been telling that other boy, the sour one, that he needs to take deep breaths and drink more tea. It's good for the soul, you know."

I crinkle my nose. She's been telling me that same shit for weeks now.

As though she can hear my thoughts, Granny tuts. "Don't be like that. The others are waiting for you downstairs. But be a dear and bring a drink with you; I think someone's parched." She makes a pained sound and touches her fingertips to her throat. "I don't know why he's so angry. It's bitter. So very bitter." Taking a shallow breath, she stands from her seat and hobbles towards the fireplace. "I think I'll have your father start a fire. It's cold tonight."

Mercy's panic ignites my own. She glances back at me with wide eyes before helping her grandmother sit in the rocking chair beside the brick fireplace. "I'll start the fire, Grandma. Do you want a blanket?"

"Downstairs," she murmurs, holding her hand out and pointing at a spot on the wall. "Your brother is downstairs. Didn't I tell you? He's thirsty. Bring him some tea with a nice splash of whiskey and lemon. It'll clear him right up."

Mercy tucks a knit blanket around her grandmother's legs. "You shouldn't be alone, Grandma. Where did everyone go?"

"I'm not alone, darling. I'm never alone."

Frowning, I pinch the bridge of my nose and take a deep breath. She's always been eccentric, but this is senile. "I'll keep looking for Kane."

"Wait!" Spinning around, Mercy grabs my wrist. "There *is* a basement, but it's been closed off for years. They can't have gone down there." She glances back at Grandma Star. "No one knows about it but us."

"Who?"

She gives me an annoyed look. "My family."

I glance at Granny and blow out a breath. She's falling asleep. "I think your grandma had too much to drink."

"I'll get my dad to watch her."

"Stay," I insist. "I'll find out what the guys are up to." I have a feeling that they're trying to get away with murder—something we didn't exactly tell Mercy was in the plans for tonight.

I suddenly regret keeping the truth from her.

Rather than spill our secret, I pull her in for a kiss and indulge in the feel of her body against mine. I can hardly catch my breath when I pull away, my racing heart making it impossible to keep my hands from shaking. "Mercy," I whisper, pressing our foreheads together. "We're going to keep your family safe."

Her eyebrows pinch together. "Is there something you're not telling me, Zane?"

Fuck, I shouldn't have said anything at all.

"I just wanted you to know that."

In case one of us dies.

It's not likely, but if Sam doesn't uphold his end of the deal or if Samuel has a trump card, we could easily get screwed over tonight.

I squeeze Mercy's hand. "Promise me that you won't do anything reckless tonight. I want you in bed by midnight."

Pursing her lips, she tugs her hands free. "I'm not going to turn into a pumpkin, Zane. You're acting strange." Her face pales a moment later. "Is it because... we..." She bites her lip. "Is this because we had sex?"

The air rushes from my lungs. I'm making everything so much worse. "No, Mercy, that's not it at all. I just want you to stay safe while I—" Murder a horrible human being— "Look around. Okay? I'll check the basement for the others."

"It's blocked off." Mercy crosses her arms over her chest as the color returns to her face. "Plus the door only opens with a key that my father has. It's an old, iron lock that won't budge without that key, Zane. You can't pick it. I've tried."

A smile tugs at my lips. "Since when are you into lock picking?"

She rolls her eyes. "Since I was ten with a mischievous younger brother to torment." Pushing me backwards, she huffs. "C'mon, let's check the damn door, if you're so curious."

"That's not necessary—"

Mercy doesn't take no for an answer. She marches

down the hall to a side room separated by a thick curtain. Pulling it back, she steps inside and doesn't wait for me to follow. "See, it's not even—"

Boxes litter the floor, with more than one sagging open and their contents spilling out. Mercy steps over them and shoves them aside as she cuts a direct path to the far corner of the room where an ominous wooden door sits half open.

"That's not possible. It should be locked." She bends down and picks up a worn door handle before dropping it into an open box. "No one should be down there, Zane, it's not safe—"

Voices float up from the stairwell. Male voices.

"What do you mean, it's not safe? Why isn't it safe?"

"It's *really* old. Like, one of the rooms from when this building was first built in the eighteen hundreds. I think it used to be a furnace, or something, before my family turned it into cold storage." She shuts her eyes and presses her palm to her forehead. "But my dad closed it off because the electrical never worked, and it showed signs of structural damage. He and my mom reinforced the main floor and installed steel beams to keep it from sinking, but the cellar isn't made from steel. It's original brick like most of the rooms up here."

"It's not safe." My chest contracts until my ribs pinch together. Kane wandered into some dank basement and is going to get himself killed for the sake of revenge—or love, I tell myself, although the two are closely related. The only reason he wants to take revenge on Samuel is because of how badly he hurt me and could hurt Mercy.

Taking a breath, Mercy opens her eyes. "No, it's not safe."

We both stare into the shadows, neither of us taking the first step into the darkness. I don't want her to go down there, but honestly, I don't want to go myself, either. Why the fuck would Kane go down there? Does he have a death wish?

"Malachi is down there," Mercy gasps, rushing towards the steps. "He's the only one who would have known it was here—"

Grabbing her by the waist, I pull her away from the ledge. "Hold on, Mercy, you can't just run down there!"

"Like hell, I can't! He's my brother, Zane. You don't understand."

"I'm not letting you get yourself killed!"

She sputters. "I'm not dying, Zane, I'm saving him!"

"We are *not* going down there without a plan." This is exactly why I didn't want to rush into anything with Samuel. When we go half-cocked, we get horrible outcomes. The only reason Kane and I almost got pinged for a double homicide a few years ago is because I hadn't analyzed all the variables yet. Tonight feels a lot like that exact situation; if we're not careful, we're all going down.

"Fuck the plan," Mercy snaps, tearing herself free from my grasp. "I'm not leaving my brother ever again. I can't let anything happen to him."

I want to ask what she means—what could possibly have possessed her to care this much about a brother she hasn't seen in years—but that must be the reason.

They've been separated for God knows how long, and she blames herself for that distance.

"It's not your fault, Mercy."

She doesn't hear me. By the time I say anything, she's already slipped into the darkness, leaving me behind to come up with a plan on my own. I scan the room for a weapon before I remember that I have one clipped to my belt. Brandishing my knife, I pull my phone out of my pocket and turn on its flashlight.

It's not a plan that propels me through the shadows after Mercy.

It's the hammer of my heartbeat in my ears and the way Kane's voice echoes in my head.

*You freak out when things don't go as planned. But that's life. You've just gotta have faith.*

I take a deep breath and taste stale air on my tongue. The voices at the bottom of the stairs grow louder, and I catch a glimpse of Mercy's red laces as she scurries down the stairwell in front of me.

Faith got me into this mess, and I hope that faith is what's going to get me out of it.

# CHAPTER 35

## MERCY

A FLICKERING LIGHT at the bottom of the stairs sends shivers down my spine. When we were children, Malachi and I used to lock each other in dark rooms and closets, cackling as the other would get scared and cry. It was mainly me doing the crying; Malachi never minded the dark, and he'd often sit in silence with the shed door unlocked while I picked dandelions among the graves. This feels different. We're not picking on each other, and he didn't tell me he was going to the cellar, he just... Left.

On his own.

I haven't seen him in at least a year—maybe two, even—and spoken to him very little since. I don't know what's rumbling inside his head: his own voice, or the ones that tell him to fight demons no one else can see?

Cobwebs stick to my arms as I descend, and it's like I'm stepping into the past, my buckled shoes and frilled socks pitter-pattering down the stone steps as I catch my brother playing where he shouldn't.

But then I hear Zane's footfalls behind me, and my nerves settle as I feel the length of my limbs, the brush of my hair against my elbows, and the heavy beat of my heart pounding inside my ribcage. I'm not a child anymore, and I'm not afraid of the dark.

Nor am I alone. Zane is right behind me, trudging down the stairs at a slower pace, and a twinge of guilt nearly makes me stop and beg him to turn around. He doesn't have to follow me into a dark, dank cellar to save my brother; he can wait at the top of the stairs where it's safe.

"Zane—"

"Keep moving, Mercy." He places a gentle hand on my lower back. "I won't let anything happen to you." He keeps his touch light as we descend together, popping out at the bottom to find ourselves at the only exit for a crowded, musky room.

It's smaller than I remember.

That could be the four grown men standing around glaring at each other, or it could be that the ceiling nearly touches the top of Sam's head, dusty cobwebs sticking to his hair like lint.

Our eyes meet, and he takes a shallow breath. "What are you doing here, Mercy?" Stepping over to me, he places his hand on my elbow and leads me to the corner of the room, away from the makeshift gentleman's club. Touching my face, he scans my body like he's checking for injuries. "Are you hurt?"

I roll my eyes despite the way my heart trembles

beneath his touch. "I'm fine, but you guys can't be in here. It's not safe."

His jaw clenches. "That's why *you* shouldn't be here."

"Why are you the exception?" I poke his chest. "What are you even doing down here? Where's—" I glance over his shoulder to find my brother holding a lit taper candle, the wax dripping onto his hand. "What's going on?" I listen close as Zane and Kane talk in hushed whispers, the two of them quickly glancing back at me.

Oh, please.

Pushing Sam away from me, I walk over to them. "What the hell are you two plotting—" I step in something wet and slide on the damp floor, gasping as I bump into Kane. He grabs me and holds me steady. "Shit, guys, there's gotta be mold down here—"

"Shhh," Kane murmurs, pressing a finger to my lips. "You'll interrupt the show."

"What show?"

While Zane turns my head, Kane bands an arm around my waist and holds me in place. "Let your brother work in silence, Siren. He's thinking."

"Too much," Sam scoffs, stepping up beside me. "I don't want to be down here forever."

"No final words for your dad, Sam?" Kane shakes his head. "What a pity. He loves you so much."

"Shut up."

Malachi tilts the candle towards the oldest man in the room, and the flame flickers as Samuel exhales harshly through his nose, his mouth stuffed with what looks like a white rag. His hands are bound behind his back, but his feet are free. Rather than run, because I assume he's outnumbered and he knows it, he stares down the bridge of his nose as the flame brushes his cheek.

An agitated garble of sounds catches on the gag in his mouth. He flinches back and slams his head into the brick wall, but the smell of burnt flesh fills the air.

My brother is torturing a man, and everyone is letting it happen.

"Are you—" I hold my tongue as the word *crazy* threatens to slip past. "Malachi, look at me. What are you doing?" In the past, he's had trouble controlling his anger, but that's why he was sent to a strict boarding school; he was supposed to learn coping mechanisms so that these kind of incidents didn't keep happening. "Stop!"

He ignores me and relights the candle as it goes out. "During the witch trials, people often died of smoke inhalation before the fire burned them alive." Waving the candle in front of Samuel's face, he hums to himself. "But those fires often started at their feet and worked their way up. If we start here—" He holds the flame beneath Samuel's chin. "How long do you think it will take for someone to die? An hour? Ten?"

Tears pool in the corner of Samuel's eyes, but he finally fights back. Kicking Malachi in the shin, he makes a run for the stairwell.

Sam punches him in the face before he even gets close and knocks Samuel to the ground. "You don't get to run," he hisses, hauling him up by his shirt collar.

The expensive suit jacket I'd spotted earlier has disappeared, along with the top few buttons of Samuel's shirt. Jagged cuts, mostly shallow, line his chest like tally marks, including the diagonal slash for counting fives. Blood pools along the deepest ones, staining his dress shirt.

"I thought Samuel was crazy, but your brother?" Kane whistles. "He's on a whole nother level."

"Don't call him that." I stare at my brother's back as he fiddles with something in his dominant hand. Something catches the light and shines in my eyes. A coin? A compact mirror? Only when he lifts his hand to wipe blood from his wrist do I recognize what I'm looking at.

It's a shard of glass, like the ones we found on the floor upstairs.

"I thought you were going to make this quick," Zane sighs, rubbing the back of his neck. "Someone will notice he's gone."

Kane grunts noncommittally. "So is Sam. It's fine. They came together, they left together."

"You've been planning this?" I stare at Zane in disbelief. "And you didn't bother to tell me?"

Zane keeps his face neutral but can't hide the twitch of his brow.

"We didn't want you to worry," Kane says, "like you're doing now." He nuzzles my cheek. "Everything's under control."

"Anyone could come down those stairs. Someone could have seen you. My *grandmother* knew you were down here! Seriously, guys? This is your big plan?" A laugh bubbles up inside my chest. Unbelievable. Three brains, and they couldn't come up with a better plan.

"Well, this part is a *little* unplanned."

"No shit," Sam snaps, dragging his dad deeper into the room. He tosses him against the far wall and crosses his arms. "I told you guys that I'd handle it so that no one was any wiser, but you just *had* to start shit, didn't you?"

"He started it," Kane grumbles.

"You're not supposed to take the bait, dumbass."

A growl rumbles through the air. "Shut up!" Malachi drops to his knees in front of Samuel, the *thud* of bone on stone making me flinch. "He's going to rot here." Dropping the candle, my brother strokes the shard of glass against Samuel's burnt flesh, dangerously close to the man's eye. "In this prison cell. Where he'll choke on mold and smell his own rotting flesh for eternity. All alone, where no one will ever come looking for him." He laughs darkly and punches forward, piercing Samuel's flesh.

I look away before I gag.

"How does it feel, Samuel? To know that your family has abandoned you? Isn't that what you told me, hm, all those times you came to visit? I wasn't—*fucking*—listening."

Taking a shaky breath, I focus on Sam's pinched expression. "Did you know?" I flinch at a wet, fleshy sound. "That your dad was visiting my brother?" The school told us that he wasn't allowed visitors as a disciplinary measure, but the ban never lifted, and every appeal we had was denied. Trips home for the holidays became less and less frequent as time passed. Phone calls, even, were scarce. I'd gotten a letter in the mail once, but it didn't sound like my brother, and it was typed. I'd doubted it was him when I first received it, and I still doubt it to this day.

Sam's lips press together in a fine line. "No. I had no idea."

"Must have been bad," Kane muses softly. "For him to be this aggravated."

"He's upset." I sniff and instantly regret it. A copper tang in the air makes my stomach churn. "I would be, too."

"It's not your fault, Siren."

I shrug and feign indifference. "What's done is done. We can only move forward."

Kane suddenly slides me beneath Zane's good arm and steps in front of us, grasping my hands in his as he stares into my eyes. "I am more than ready for that future, Mercy, but there's a promise I've got to keep first, and you might want to leave for this part."

A wave of anxiety makes my body shake. "What, um, what promise is that?"

Zane slips a long, heavy switchblade into our joined hands and wraps Kane's fingers around it. "Make the fucker bleed."

I inhale sharply. "*Here?* But it's—it's Christmas!"

"A lot of accidents happen during the holidays." Zane takes careful steps backwards and pulls me along with him. "Do you want to stay or go for this, Mercy?"

My heart hammers as I look between all three of my

men, each one as determined as the last. None of them are leaving, not even Sam, so I won't, either. "I'm staying." I hold Zane's arm tightly around my middle. "But please don't let go. I might—" I swallow hard. "Pass out?"

"I'll catch you," Sam vows, following us to the other side of the room. "I promise."

Samuel finally speaks, his breaths rattling and wet and grotesque. "You can't kill me. I *own* you, Samson, you and your whore and this whole goddamn cesspool. Even you, Malachi. You'll never escape my purview. I am everywhere and everything in this fucking city. Do you hear me? I am—"

"*Dead*," Malachi snarls, slamming Samuel's head against the ground. "Dead, dead, dead, and no one will mourn you, Samuel, not even your fucking son."

Mr. Wright's eyes latch onto mine, and the hatred burning in their depths makes me nauseous. Bile rises to the back of my throat as he chokes on his fury, blood pouring from his mouth and staining the floor. He says something that I can't hear, but my brother flinches hard enough that he slams his fist into Samuel's skull.

Sam must hear it, because he flinches, too.

I tug on his arm. "What did he say?"

"I don't want to repeat it." Hooking his fingers through mine, he takes a deep breath. "But I think he hates your family more than I realized, Mercy."

If my body weren't running so cold, I'm sure that I would flush with embarrassment. "I don't know why," I murmur, squeezing Sam's fingers. "We've never done anything to him."

Zane sighs in my ear. "Yeah, you did, baby. You stole his son from him."

Silence falls over us as Kane takes slow, steady steps towards his target. The cadence of his footfalls is like a metronome counting the final seconds of Samuel's life. The closer he gets, the louder Samuel's screeching becomes, filling the room with a panic greater than any I've ever felt before. My entire body is on edge, the hairs on my arms and neck standing up as shivers course through me over and over again. Zane holds on tight and rests his chin on my shoulder.

"You can close your eyes," he murmurs, staring straight ahead as Kane kneels beside Malachi. "I won't tell him."

"He'll know," I whisper, as sure of it as I am of death. The scent of it is familiar, and I'll recognize it when it arrives, but for now, Kane is taking his time. Cutting away Samuel's clothes, leaving him naked and afraid as the dull edge of the knife drags down his body like a lover's caress.

The funny thing is that Samuel suddenly goes eerily quiet. For all his barking, he doesn't put up much of a fight. I think he's waiting for Sam to jump in and save him, but Sam isn't watching his father's final moments, he's carefully studying my face. Trailing his fingertips up and down my arms, stepping closer as Kane makes the first cut, exhaling into the curve of my neck as he hovers, not impeding my view but shielding my body from the violence. He draws a shaky breath and leans into me, pressing my body firmly against both his and Zane's.

Tilting my head, I press a gentle kiss to his cheek, and he collapses, forcing Zane to hold both of us up as my knees buckle.

"Shhh, shh, shh, it's okay. I've got you."

A sob wracks his chest, and he buries his face in my hair. We don't speak. We don't kiss. We hold onto each other as part of his world collapses, seeping through the cracks and soaking into the earth, where it will be forsaken and forgotten.

# CHAPTER 36

## SAM

IN THE AFTERMATH of my father's death, not much changes. The businesses continue to prosper and his staff keeps me in the loop, but I'm not obligated to run around for him anymore, so I don't.

I spend time at Mercy's house.

All of my time, actually. Sitting at the kitchen table with Grandma Star as Zane attempts to make her famous chocolate-chip cookies, mixing cement with Malachi as we patch up old holes in the walls of the mortuary, and, yes, even having round table discussions with Kane and Mr. Morningstar as we consider the future of his business. With my father gone, the invisible ban on contracting the Morningstars' services lifts, and calls are slowly rolling in.

Not just for funerary services, either.

Everyone who comes by the mortuary sees the mural that Mercy's working on. We post progress photos online of both her artwork and the cemetery itself as we sweep it clean of decay and plant perennials for the spring and summer. It's attracted enough attention that people are asking us to "color the city," but I don't think Mercy's interested in that. She'd rather brighten her family's graves, both the ones on the property itself and in the city's sprawling cemetery.

It takes a while for me to find my mother's grave. It's unmarked, so while I'm researching equipment to survey the land, Kane digs until he hits her bones. She wasn't even buried in a coffin but laid to rest in the dirt. Grandma Star assures me that it's holy ground and that my mother is better off to have joined the earth than be kept from it.

I just wish that she hadn't been kept from me.

Mercy and I sit in front of my mom's grave for a long while, the snow melting beneath our butts and soaking into the blanket. "I think I want to move her," she murmurs, nodding towards an empty space beside my mother. "Right here. I think our moms could be friends."

I hold her hand and play with her ring finger. "I'm sure they already are. Star tells me that she can see them dancing sometimes. At sunset, usually."

"My mom used to love the sunset." Mercy holds up her hand to grasp the setting sun. "Do you think she knew, Sam? That she was selling us to your dad."

I lean into Mercy's side. "I doubt it. My dad was conniving. I'm sure he would have found a way even without the contract."

Mercy thinks about this for a moment. "What happens to her contract now that he's gone?"

I've avoided this topic so not to overwhelm her, but she deserves to know. "It passes down to his heir."

She tilts her head back and stares into my eyes. "So you own me now."

A gust of wind kicks up, knocking powdered snow from bare tree limbs and dusting Mercy's hair. I watch her eyelashes sparkle as she blinks. "I can tear it up." That won't break the agreement, but the physical evidence will be gone. With no one to enforce it, it'll fade like the rest of my father's toxic past, slowly forgotten over time.

"Do you want to?"

Closing my eyes, I allow the winter chill to seep into my bones. I should want to throw that contract as far away as I can and stomp it into the ground, but... "No," I answer honestly, curling my arm around Mercy's waist. "No, I don't."

Marriages can be dissolved, but a document like this lies deeper, settling into flesh and blood. Ingrid signed the contract in blood, too—a trick of my father's or whoever came before him, pricking her finger with the pen tip before having her sign. It's an archaic, somewhat occult practice that somehow still exists in certain circles.

"What are you going to do with it?" Mercy asks, handling this information much calmer than I anticipated her to. I haven't told her father or anyone else, really, other than Zane and Kane. It's a secret I'd rather not make public knowledge.

"Nothing," I answer honestly. "But it makes me

feel…" I struggle to find the right word. "At ease, I guess. Knowing that you're mine in a way that no one else can have." I bring her knuckles to my lips and kiss each one. "Plus, it makes me feel closer to her." I nod towards my mother's grave. "I can keep you both safe."

Mercy brushes her fingertips across my thigh. "You don't have to keep protecting her, Sam, or me."

A wry smile touches my lips. I'll never stop protecting her as long as I live. I've even considered digging into my father's contracts to ensure that no one can *ever* touch her in the off chance that I die sooner than expected. I could hire a full-time shadow ops team to monitor her and her family's safety at all times. Even *that* idea helps put me more at ease, and I relax into Mercy's touch.

I'll definitely look into it soon.

"I'm okay with it," she says resolutely, offering a small smile. "So long as you keep me forever, Sam."

Lowering my head, I ghost my lips over hers. "I wouldn't dream of anything else." She tastes like starlight. The subtle warmth of her body pours into mine, and I lean into the kiss. "I've missed you," I admit softly, stroking her cheek with the pad of my thumb. The last few weeks apart have been hell, and I never want to experience that again. "Zane told me that you haven't been sleeping. I'm so sorry, baby; I should have been here."

"You're here now," she whispers, nudging the tip of my nose with hers. "So kiss me, Sam." Clutching the lapels of my coat, she sighs against my lips. "And don't stop."

We lie down together and she steals my heart for the thousandth time, with a thousand and one tender kisses, wrapping her body around mine and breathing life into my soul. It glows brighter with the heat of her skin on mine and her breath in my lungs, the taste of her as addicting as it was the first time I ever kissed her. I shouldn't have ever let her go then, and I won't ever make that mistake again.

Sliding my hand beneath her shirt, I palm her breast and love the way she whines, her back arching into my touch. "Sam," she breathes, her face flushing, "don't stop; *please* don't stop."

I can't deny her anything, and I would never want to.

Kissing the curve of her jaw, I nip the delicate skin along her throat and draw blood to the surface, sucking hard enough to leave a bruise. She gasps, her eyes fluttering shut, and weaves her fingers through my hair.

Fuck, I've missed this.

Lifting her shirt, I catch the goosebumps prickling her skin and kiss each and every one, smiling as she pulls my hair to move my mouth where she wants it. Flicking my tongue over her tight nipple, I hum in delight as she moans, making my dick twitch in anticipation. I've been too strung out to jerk off. My balls are heavy and full, my cock aching to slip inside of her.

I take my time and lavish her tits with open-mouthed kisses before grinding my palm against her clit, enjoying the way she gasps and grinds right back, just as eager as I am.

"I want you," she breathes, opening her eyes to stare into my soul. "Right now, Sam, hurry."

I pop up to undo my belt and glance around the cemetery to make sure we don't have an audience. From this angle, no one should be able to see us unless I'm on my knees, so I quickly tug down my pants and free my cock. The cold bite of winter does nothing to dampen my desire; if anything, I burn hotter because of it. I pull Mercy's leggings and panties below her hips and notch myself at her entrance, gently rocking against her clit to build friction—or remove it.

She tosses her head back and moans, palming her tits as she rubs against my length. "Put it in," she pants, her pupils blown wide when she meets my eyes. "I need you inside me, Sam."

With a gentle thrust, I push the tip past her clit and slip the first inch inside, grabbing the top of her shoulder to anchor her as I thrust deeper, bottoming out in seconds. Her pussy's got a vice grip on my soul, choking my dick in euphoria that's beyond description. She squeezes around me as soon as I'm inside, rocking her hips to get momentum going.

"H-hold on," I gasp as a full-bodied shudder rattles my bones and makes it difficult to breathe.

She feels like heaven. Molten warmth caresses my dick as she wraps her legs around my waist and grinds her hips. Blood roars in my ears as my orgasm mounts, barreling through me at record speed.

Oh, *fuck.*

I come with a pathetic whimper clenched between my teeth. My dick pulses, spilling my seed into Mercy's tight channel until it overflows, gushing around my shaft as I pull back and thrust back inside, burying my cum as deeply as it can go. A bone-deep moan settles inside my chest. I know I shouldn't indulge like this, but she *is* mine, now more than ever.

Her fingertips skate across the back of my neck as she gazes up at me, cheeks flushed, heart pounding, lips parted. "That was fast," she murmurs, licking her lips. I can tell that she's unsure what to do, and I struggle to hold back a laugh.

Her face burns deep crimson as she smacks my arm. "Sam!"

"I'm not laughing at you!" Smiling brightly, I hug her body and press a flurry of kisses across her face. "I'm just so *happy*, Mercy. I'm so happy that you're mine." Drawing a breath, I kiss the frown on her lips. "Don't worry, we're not done." I rock my hips to keep my blood flowing. My cum slips out as I push inside, the semen dripping down her thighs and dirtying the blanket beneath us. With a huff, I rear back onto my knees and grab her hips, punching into her with deep, hard thrusts. "You just feel too good, baby" I rasp, feeling my desire build. "I can't help but come when I'm inside of you."

She bites her lip as her eyelashes flutter. A dark halo surrounds her head as her hair catches in the wind and carries her voice across the graveyard. I clamp my hand over her mouth as she moans, digging her heels into my ass to pull me deeper. It's risky for us to be in this position to begin with, but if she starts moaning like that, someone's going to find us—

"Ooooh, you should have told me we were having a little outdoor playtime."

I groan as Kane grabs my shoulders and squeezes, hovering way too close while I'm balls deep inside my girl. "Go away, Kane," I hiss, pressing my palm over Mercy's abdomen. She squirms, panting as I arch my back and hit a sensitive spot inside her. Mewling, she grabs my wrist and digs her nails into my skin.

This is *way* too intimate for an audience.

"No, no, keep going," he rumbles, his voice lowering an octave as he wraps his arms around my waist and grabs Mercy's hips. "I'll hold her. You take her to pound town."

Mercy whines, the sound muffled as her eyes latch onto the two of us. She tries to speak, so I relent and release her mouth. What's the fucking point, anyway; Kane's already here to ruin the moment.

"You're—here." Her words are punctuated by a hot exhale in between, her breath billowing out like smoke. "I thought you were—" A shudder courses through her body. "With Zane."

"Oh, *we* are." Kane winks, and I roll my eyes as Zane appears from behind one of the taller tombstones, a bright red lollipop in his mouth. He smacks his lips as he pulls it free. "Doc says I can start regular sessions in March."

"That's—" Mercy squirms as I apply pressure to her

abdomen, wishing to feel my cock pushing into her body. I'm not big enough or it's simply not possible, but I imagine it all the same, her body molding to the shape of my dick. "Far."

Zane hums as he dangles his sucker in the air. "Best they could do, Kitten. Sorry if it's not good enough for you."

I could get him an earlier appointment, but the absolute last fucking thing I want to do right now is help the guy interrupting my moment with Mercy. I clench my jaw as Kane rubs Mercy's clit, making her moan louder. "Could you not?"

Kane laughs in my ear. "You want her to come, don't you? This is how you do it, Sam. Take notes."

Closing my eyes would help block him out, but then I'd miss the way Mercy's lose focus. Her lips open and close silently as she clutches the blanket so tightly that it rips.

The three of us watch as she comes, a crimson flush trailing down her neck and disappearing beneath her shirt before reappearing across the pillowy tops of her tits. Her rosy nipples bud into tight peaks, and she squeezes my cock so hard that I groan aloud.

A sound catches in Zane's throat. "Damn." Reaching over Mercy, he holds out his fist for me to bump, and, you know what?

I'm in a good enough mood that I think I'll help him with that appointment after all.

# CHAPTER 37

## KANE

SAM PULLS some strings so that Malachi is released from whatever bullshit his father had him wrapped up in. Mercy's family couldn't be more thrilled, and we're all reaping the benefits. Vinny's spending more time with his family, Granny's more energetic than I've ever seen, Lilith is actually swinging by to have family dinners ever Friday night, and Mercy is...

Well, she's fucking perfect.

She slides the tip of my cock between her lips, barely able to suck on the first two inches before she has to come up for air. I scratch her scalp as she gazes up at me, unshed tears catching on her long lashes.

"You don't have to keep trying," I rumble, caressing her cheek with my free hand. "We can make it fit some-where else."

The insinuation makes her flush, but she doubles down on her efforts, rising on her knees to suck my swollen head. A burst of precum slicks her tongue, and she laps it up eagerly.

Zane and Sam have been sneaking behind my back to fuck her when they think I'm not around, but with Zane's camera system and my sensitive ears, I'm able to catch every session in high-definition. Screwing her behind the garden shed, on every fucking pew in this church, hitting it from behind in the shower, on and on the list goes, making me simultaneously jealous as hell and proud as fuck.

Our dirty girl can't get enough of our cocks.

I lean back on the bench seat, my ass sore and my balls heavy. She cups them in her petite hands and squeezes, drawing a groan from deep inside my chest. That pleases her, and she glows like the brightest star in the sky.

"You know," I start slowly, edging up to a topic I've been eager to discuss, "I don't have a last name."

She hums in response.

"I've been thinking of taking yours."

Her hand hovers in midair over my shaft. Eyebrows lifting, she pulls off of my dick and takes a gasping breath. I wipe the saliva off her chin as she catches her breath. "You, uh, want my last name?"

"Yeah." God, she looks so pretty when the light catches in her eyes. "I do."

Idly grasping my shaft, she gives it a half-hearted tug. I spread my thighs wide so that she can scoot in closer. "Why?"

Mmm. Why wouldn't I? Zane's asked me to come up

with a list of reasons why it's a bad idea, and I haven't been able to come up with a single one. Even his insistence about Sam pissing himself over it hasn't deterred me.

I want what I want, and that's every part of Mercy that she'll give me. Including her family.

"Have I ever told you about my parents?"

She shakes her head.

I take a deep breath. Here we go.

"When I was a kid, they'd forget to feed me. Or, what I think actually happened is that they chose not to. They'd hold my meals if I didn't say my prayers correctly, or if I got a low grade in school. Honestly, it's a miracle I survived past six." I scratch the back of Mercy's head as a distraction from the discomfort building in my chest. "So when they left me on a church's doorstep—not their own, of course, but one across state lines—I was older than I should have been. Not good enough for their precious church image, or whatever." I shrug. "They came back for me a few years later, and I'd already been in and out of half a dozen foster homes. Maybe more. I lost count after a while, and they stopped placing me with families." He pauses for that to sink in. "No one wanted me after that, not even my parents."

Mercy's lips twitch into a frown. "Kane, I'm so sorry."

Eh. I lean down and press a kiss to her worried brow. "I'm not," I murmur, closing my eyes. "Because when they left me behind a second time, I met Zane."

I take a deep breath and sit up, opening my eyes to

stare into hers. One of the things I've realized over the past few months is that Mercy holds constellations inside her heart. They bleed out onto her skin in all the freckles she insists don't exist as she smothers them in makeup, or in the depths of her honey brown eyes, sparkling like golden stardust every time she smiles. But the most profound moments are when I see their stories in action. As the new year came around, she started hosting her family's group therapy sessions so that her father could take a break, and every single one of those stories she's held inside her heart for years spilled free, capturing every single audience member in the room.

Myself included.

My heart stutters beneath her touch as she thumbs the pulse point on my wrist, a habit that she's picked up from Zane. "My parents' rejection taught me that you choose your family based upon the people you care about most. I wasn't important enough to be a part of their family, but I was already claimed by another, anyway."

"Zane," Mercy breathes, her eyes shining.

I nod. "Yeah. He'll tell you that I'm the one who dragged him into my circle, but I think it was mutual. Two lonely kids longing for a connection. For a family." My dick softens into a half-chub, and I nearly laugh. Damn, I thought it was impossible for anything to distract my cock, but I guess this is it. Sad, emotional bullshit. I clear my throat and take Mercy's hand to keep her from grabbing it. Sliding my fingers through hers, I lay our joined hands on my bare thigh. She stares up at me with the kindest eyes I've ever seen.

I don't deserve a woman like her.

"For a long time, my circle included Zane, and only Zane. I think... when I was seducing people, and when I finally got them to open up and let me in, I was trying to find another connection like that. Like the one I have with Zane." But none of them could break through their sorrow and pain, not even for me. Especially not when I wasn't even showing them who I really was. I doctored an image that made them fall in love, and then when I was disappointed with the outcome, I let them go, sending them to their graves with their loved ones.

They already had a family, and I wasn't able to fill the void that was left after they lost it.

"But you, Mercy..." I press the pad of my thumb against the bow of her lips. "You're different than most people." For the first time in my life, a lump forms in my throat, and it's hard to get words out. I stare at her pouty lips, wondering what it would take for her to read my thoughts so I don't have to say anything out loud. She could just *know* my feelings for her, and we'd be blissful as fucking kittens for the rest of our lives. Or rabbits, since they fuck all the time.

Zane really needs to change his nickname for her.

"I love that about you, Mercy. I love—" My cheeks flush bright red. *Goddammit.* Cupping her face, I lift her off her knees and pull her into my lap, needing to be closer. My breath shudders as my lungs threaten to collapse. "I love—"

She presses her fingertips to my lips, a glowing smile matching the warmth of her eyes. "I love you, too, Kane."

I crack a smile and tackle her mouth, knocking our teeth together in my rush to get to her. Fuck. "Shit, Siren, I'm sorry."

Her laughter lights up my heart. "No, it's fine, don't worry about—"

Her lips taste like my dick, and it kicks my desire into overdrive. I grab her ass and rock into the cradle of her thighs, suddenly desperate to be inside of her. She pulls her top over her head and flings it into the distance, baring her tits for me to suck. I greedily lap one with the flat of my tongue, groaning as I pull it into my mouth. She gasps, a beautiful fucking sound, and rolls her hips.

Fire licks at the base of my spine, pulling inward as delicious heat coils deep inside my body. Fuck, yes. I rub her pussy over my cock, drenching her panties in her desire, in my own, the two of us panting as I dry hump the fuck out of her.

God, I love this woman.

"Kane," she whimpers, biting her plump bottom lip. "Can we try?"

I snap the waistband of her panties to hear her squeal. "You wanna ride me, sweetheart?"

It takes her a moment to decide, but then she shakes her head. "I want you to be on top."

Picking her up, I carry her to the double-mattress—a recent upgrade with how often Mercy spends the night with us—and lay her down on her back. "Like this?" I run my hands up her warm thighs as she nods and lifts her hips.

"Undress me, please."

Gladly.

I take my time pulling her leggings down her thighs, carefully kissing every new inch of exposed skin. She giggles like she's nervous, but I can't blame her. My cock swings heavily between my thighs, and I squeeze the tip to rub another burst or precum along my shaft. I need to be lubricated as fuck if I'm going to fit inside of her.

"Condom?" I ask, stroking in time with my heartbeat.

She shakes her head. "I want to feel you."

A chuckle rumbles through my chest. Sam got her addicted to creampies, and it's become a bad habit for all of us, filling up her sweet pussy any chance we can get.

Well, *they* can get. But this is my time. My turn.

"Are you ovulating?" I should keep track of her cycle, but Sam's the anal one about it, not me. I couldn't care less if she gets knocked up, but that man is obsessed with ensuring it doesn't happen. It's like he thinks kids carry the plague or something.

Then again, I caught him looking at bassinets on his phone the other day, so it could be the other way around. He could be trying to knock her up.

Sneaky fucking bastard.

Mercy shakes her head again. "Nope, I should be safe this week."

Unless Sam's been lying to her about when she's fertile. But I don't have proof, so I take Mercy's word for it.

Leaning over her, I rest my forearm beside her head and run my cock through her slick heat, stealing a kiss as I rub my shaft against her lips *and* her clit, the only man between the three of us that can confidently say that I hit both at once. I exhale against her jaw as I stroke again and again, arching my back to get in deeper. Her breaths puff out against my chest, her body so goddamn hot that it's scalding to the touch.

"You okay, Siren?"

She answers with a searing kiss, sucking my bottom lip into her mouth and raking her nails down my back. I hiss as pain radiates from her touch, but then I slide the first half inch inside, and *fuck,* is it tight.

Zane and I worked up to fitting me inside of him for at least a week, training his ass to stretch to accommodate my girth, but he had already had a dick up his ass before. Grayson, or whatshisname. I forget. So it wasn't completely new territory.

With Mercy, I guess it isn't either, but the way she grits her teeth makes me feel like it's her first time.

"Breathe," I coach her, reaching between us to rub her clit. "You need to relax, or you'll only get tighter."

"I *am* relaxed," she chokes out, laughing once she realizes how much of a lie that is. "Okay, I'm not. Can you eat me out?"

I lick my lips as I pull out and slide down her hot little body. "Yes fucking ma'am." Zane would berate me for not doing it in the first place, but I'm itching to get inside of her. He doesn't get it; he's *been* to the promised land. I've glimpsed the golden fields from the tree line. It's not the fucking same.

Lifting Mercy's thigh and smelling her wet fucking pussy is a dream that I never want to wake from. Licking into her molten core and feeling her body tense up, the sharp intake of breath, the gentle quiver of her thighs, the smooth glide of my fingers stretching her out, it's the only Heaven I'll ever experience. Right here, in this body, with this woman, dry humping the mattress because I can't fucking help it.

I groan against her clit, holding my breath as I press my tongue flat and roll over it again and again, obsessed with the way she cries out and grabs my hair, pushing me harder against her. I curl my fingers and she gushes, dripping down my wrist as I lick and suck every delicious inch of pussy, top to bottom, tempted to move even lower. I bet she'd come her brains out if I played with her ass. I've watched Zane do it as he hits from behind, lubing up his fingers and sliding them in and out of her ass as he works her pussy with his dick.

Hell, I've *come* to the thought of him fucking her ass while I fuck his, the three of us a sweaty, delirious mess as we come our brains out. Sometimes, Sam will be in my fantasies, lying beneath her and rocking his hips up into her cunt while we plow her from behind.

An illicit shiver rolls down my spine.

I am *definitely* bringing that idea up at our next dinner date.

Mercy rocks onto my face and whimpers, getting close enough to coming that I can taste the difference in her pussy, her desire getting wetter and wetter until finally, she screams. Her voice catches partway through, but that's a good thing. She'll need the vocal rest, because once I'm finally inside of her, she won't be able to stop.

My dick throbs in anticipation as I grab the bottle of lube and coat it from root to tip, then pour a generous amount onto Mercy's pussy. I work it into her tight hole with my fingers before climbing up her body and claiming her mouth in a sloppy kiss, smearing her lips and tongue with her release. She's wet and wild, matching my passion with her own and eagerly rubbing her slick pussy against my shaft. The tip slips in first, and I push the head past the threshold, groaning as her walls finally give. Another inch. Another deep breath. I bite her neck and suck a bruise on her skin, hoping that it'll distract her from the absolute carnage I'm sure I'm wrecking on her pussy.

I've had a lot of sex. Hundreds of people have come and gone, each one different from the last, not all of them able to handle my dick size despite promises that they could. I haven't held it against them; I know that I'm above-average, and I know that sometimes, that can hurt.

But Mercy's pussy sucks me in and doesn't let go, and slowly, *very slowly*, I bottom out inside of her without having to pull out once.

Her grin matches mine as I kiss her hard and rock my hips, groaning into her sweet mouth as she trembles beneath me.

"Oh, Mercy. *Oh, baby.* You are fucking gorgeous." I

kiss a silent tear falling down her cheek and lick the salt from my lips. "I love you so fucking much." My heart bursts as she smiles, laughing and pulling me in for a kiss that rocks my world.

I get it now, the family thing.

Because here in this moment, that's what she is.

A big part of my precious, little world.

# Chapter 38

## Mercy

I always imagined that sex with Kane would be a wild, untamed thing. Heart racing, hair pulling, grabbing and pushing and pulling, until either my mascara is running down my eyes from the pain or the pleasure.

The reality is that it's a little bit of both.

His kisses turn tender as he whispers praise in my ear, muttering more for himself than for me, I think, to keep from ramming his cock too deep or stretching me so far that I tear at the seams. Every press of his hips against mine is a slow, careful pressure, the drag of his cock along my inner walls sending spasms through my body. I hold onto him as he carves space inside of me for himself, charting a path that neither Zane or Sam can touch.

There are parts of me that only Kane can experience, and I think he understands that.

The brush of his hand over my hair or down my waist, our mingled breaths turning into one, my hand holding his heart until our rhythm syncs. Sweat slicks his golden skin, glistening like summer rain on the horizon. He touches me gently, coaxing kisses from my lips, until all of a sudden, something changes.

The pressure builds into a crescendo as he pumps faster and his hand on my hip digs deeper. His teeth scrape against the curve of my neck, the sharp points of his canines stinging my flesh. And the *push* knocks my body higher up the mattress. Pain blossoms where our bodies meet as his hips slam into mine and his breathing turns ragged, the warmth of his body reaching a fever pitch. I dig my fingertips into his shoulders and break the skin, feeling the way his body shudders as he pumps harder, slamming home with enough force that the air in my lungs isn't enough.

I'm drowning in Kane's love.

It washes over me like a tidal wave, crashing into my ribs, filling up my lungs, burning through my bloodstream. His cock hits the end of my pussy and continues pushing, ramming hard into my cervix.

I gasp for air.

My world spins with Kane as its axis, the pleasure quickly turning to pain, the radiance of his light too bright, the hard planes of his body cutting like glass.

"Kane," I breathe, cradling his face in my hands. "Baby, it hurts. Stop. Please." A tear slides down my cheek. I should have never taken Kane to bed on my own. There's a reason why I wanted Sam here. Zane. *Anyone.* Someone to pull Kane back from the brink, because it's becoming clear that my strength isn't enough. He's overpowering me in every possible way, and I'm going to break.

"Kane!" I growl, clawing his face. "Fucking stop!"

His eyes instantly clear and his body freezes in place, his cock twitching halfway inside my body. "Siren? What's wrong?" Leaning into my touch, he blows out a breath across my neck. "Am I hurting you?"

I swallow hard. "Yes, but—"

He immediately pulls out, and the sudden *lack* stings. I hiss as he rolls off of me and pulls my thighs apart to check me out down there, frowning with concern as he scans my pussy. "You look okay. I don't see any bleeding."

I cover my face with my hands. "I don't know, I just hurt. Deep. Like, like you were hitting my—" I bite my lip. "Cervix," I whisper, my face flaming with embarrassment. "I don't think I've ever, um, felt that before."

Kane slides his gaze up my body, the hunger in his eyes lingering like a fire that won't go out despite a downpour. "You're bruised." He bends at the waist and kisses my hip, then the bottom rung of my ribs, the very top of my breast, until finally, he licks a stripe along the curve of my neck. With a groan, he slides his fingers into my hair. "I didn't mean to hurt you."

Tears pool in my eyes. "I know."

That isn't an apology.

Still hiding, I clear my throat. "I want to keep going, but..." My body trembles as he teases the underside of my breast. "I don't know if I can. I—" I bite my lip. "I think I'm not made for this?"

A smile curves on Kane's handsome face. "Oh, baby, you are. I promise. I'm impressed that we made it this far, honestly." He kisses my forehead and trails his fingertips along the curve of my cheek. "I'm really glad that you spoke up, or I could have hurt you more than I did. A lot of people grit their teeth and bear it without telling me, so I don't always realize that their screams are from pain." He nips my jaw. "Rather than pleasure."

I blow out a breath. "You have to be kidding. There's no way anyone can withstand that." A thread of insecurity wraps around my heart. "But, um, if they did, I'm sure you enjoyed it."

"Actually, no." Tilting my chin up, Kane meets my eyes. "I might come, Mercy, but that isn't the goal. Sex is supposed to be fun. *Free.* It clears the mind until all that's left is the weight of your body and the beat of your heart." He presses his open palm to my chest and taps his fingertips to my heartbeat.

It's like everything I've learned about sex in school is wrong.

Frowning, I purse my lips as he smiles down at me with the patience of a saint—more than I thought he could ever have, honestly. "But Zane and Sam always come. It's like they chase it." I reach out and grasp the air beside Kane's head. "Don't you do the same thing?"

He shakes his head. "I'm built differently. The same rules don't apply." He presses a gentle kiss to my lips before sitting up. "Let me clean you up, and we can cuddle all you want." He kisses my knee and pushes himself to his feet, his hard cock bouncing with each step he takes, its shaft shiny, the tip leaking.

If he was close to coming, he stopped because I asked him to.

My heart skips a beat as I watch him grab a pack of sanitary wipes and two bottles of water. "Kane," I call out, smiling as he looks over at me. "I love you."

The warmth in his eyes rivals that of the sun. He drops everything on the floor beside me and falls to his knees, quickly sweeping me into a searing kiss. "Keep saying that, and I might have to eat you out again."

"Please, no," I beg, already feeling my pussy twinge at the thought. "I can't take it."

"Mmm," he muses, teasing the seam of my lips with his tongue. "You think too little of yourself—and your pussy. She's a fighter." He curls his arm around my waist and smiles. "Someday, I'll prove it to you."

My final semester of college passes by in the blink of an eye. Kane doesn't drop out despite failing our fall painting class for not submitting a final project, and he walks behind me across the stage despite not receiving a diploma. I think he just wanted to check out my ass in high heels, a gift from my older sister that I don't think I'll ever wear again.

Still, she's right.

I look damn good when I dress up.

The curls in my hair have flattened into waves by the

time the ceremony is over. A moth flutters nearby, and I hold out my hand to give it a place to land. My classmates either smile politely at me or completely ignore me, the few of them who know about the party from last semester being in the latter category. Sam hasn't returned to campus despite being reenrolled once he petitioned his father's meddling in his affairs. I think he was only enrolled as a distraction from his home life, and now that he lives with me, he has no reason to continue.

My father is all too happy to hand him and Kane the keys to the family business, degree or not.

I walk arm-in-arm with my brother Malachi as the boys bicker about what to eat for dinner behind us. "You know, you could enroll. It's not *that* bad of a school."

He's quiet as he contemplates. Actually, he's been quiet ever since the new year, like he's stuck in his head about something. "I might apply," he says after a moment. "But I don't think my grades are good enough to get in."

"Anyone can get in." I nudge his ribs with my elbow and glance back at Kane. "Case in point..."

My blonde boyfriend catches my eye and winks, a slow grin spreading across his face as he lifts an eyebrow and looks me up and down. "Hot," he mouths, the corner of his lips curving into a smirk.

Zane catches him in the act and rolls his eyes. "I can't believe you walked across the stage." Still, he smiles when Kane presses a kiss to his cheek and laughs when Kane grabs his chin and smushes their faces together.

"You're just jealous that I got to flick off the Dean."

My father's waiting for us at the gate with a bouquet of white lilies in his hands. When he sees us, his shoulders droop as he relaxes, the smile on his face becoming genuine. I think he worries about Malachi adjusting to life with the family plus three, the knuckleheads I love breathing new life into our home. It's a little chaotic when someone eats Zane's leftovers—usually Kane—or Sam decides to join us in the chapel for a sleepover, but it's a good kind of chaos.

It's what we've been missing over the past few years.

The six of us pass through the gate to the city cemetery, and my father hands each of us a flower from the bouquet. Walking the stone path reminds me of a night not too long ago when someone glimpsed a grim reaper stalking his prey, and a girl stumbled into a grave and fell into his arms.

I slip free from my brother's arm and leave him to walk with my father to our family crypt. We moved my mother onto our property as soon as the ice melted, but our ancestors are laid to rest here. It's good to pay our respects to the dead.

Matching my pace to my men, I hook one of my arms in Zane's and another in Sam's. They both slide their hands into mine, but Sam's the one who kisses my knuckles. "Congrats, baby."

"Wait until you see your present," Kane murmurs, wrapping his arm around Zane's shoulders. "You're going to love it."

"Don't tell her." Zane glares at our boyfriend. "You'll ruin the surprise."

I pull our foursome down a separate path. "Before we celebrate our future, I wanted to honor our past." Sam quirks an eyebrow but doesn't comment, while Kane and Zane quickly pick up on our destination. We round the bend and walk a ways before we come across the Carrera family plot. I lay my flower against a familiar tombstone. "Rest in peace, Alejandro."

Sam squeezes my hand before laying his flower over mine.

But it's Kane that surprises me, dropping to one knee in front of the grave and laying his palm flat to the earth. "Alejandro, I know you don't need to hear this, but look after Maria. Treasure your time together, wherever the fuck you are. You deserve happiness." He digs a hole with his fingers and sticks the stem of his lily upright so that, with a little effort, it stands straight. "I'm sorry if I took any from you."

Zane helps Kane to his feet and kisses him softly. "You're both happy now, and that's what matters." He tears off the long stem and tucks his flower into Kane's shirt pocket. "He's with the people he loves, and so are you."

They share a moment that brings tears to my eyes, and Sam cups my cheek as he wipes them away. "What's wrong, Mercy?"

I shake my head. "No, it's... nothing's wrong." I laugh a little, feeling foolish for getting so emotional about people I never met. "I just wish that everyone here could be happy, too."

"Who says they're not?" Lacing our fingers together,

Sam presses a kiss to the corner of my lips. "If what Grandma Star says is true, people hang around after they're gone."

"When the veil is thinnest," I clarify. "I didn't realize you've been taking notes."

He puffs out a breath as he fights a smile. "Well, if I want the honor of your hand in marriage, Mercy, I should pay attention to the things your grandmother says. She could curse our union, after all. I'm still convinced that she's part witch."

"You—" My eyes widen. Nervous tingles trickle down my arms. "What did you say?"

"Your grandma. She's a witch."

"No, not that part. The other part." A blush dusts my cheeks as warmth fills my heart. "What you said first."

The corner of his lip twitches. "Oh, you mean the part about marrying you?" His emerald eyes sparkle in the flickering lamplight. "I already got your dad's permission, so all I need now is your grandmother's blessing. Do you think she'll say yes? I didn't get her anything for her birthday last year, so I don't know if she still likes me—"

I leap into Sam's arms and squeal as he spins me around. "You can't be serious! *Sam!*"

Kane's voice rumbles nearby. "What did he say?"

"He said that he's going to marry her."

"Oh, *hell no.* Not without fighting me for it."

Zane scoffs and grabs Kane by the nape of his neck. "You know the only person putting a ring on your finger is me."

"Look at what you've done," I gasp, smiling against Sam's lips. "You've started a trend."

"A bad one," Zane grumbles, fighting to hold Kane back. He's glaring daggers into the back of Sam's head. "He's gonna wanna marry both of us."

"You're damn right, I am!"

I double over with laughter, unable to stop the flow of tears. My heart soars as the three of them crack smiles, with Zane breaking first. He laughs as much as me, grabbing my wrist and stealing me away from Sam. "Mercy." Once he catches his breath, he tucks a strand of hair behind my ear and pulls me in for a hug. "Congratulations. Although, I'm not sure what to congratulate you on anymore: a degree or a wedding."

I bury my face in Zane's chest and let him hold me. The steady beat of his heart quiets mine down. "I haven't said yes yet." I haven't even *thought* about marriage before. I was never one of those girls who made finding love a priority.

Zane hums softly. "I guess we'll see who the winner is. My money's on Sam."

Sputtering, Kane throws his arms over both of our shoulders. "Hey! Whose side are you on?"

"Mine," Zane chuffs, rolling his eyes. "You can't marry two people, Kane, and I call dibs if you're serious about it."

Shaking my head, I meet Sam's eyes as he walks over to us, a confident smile playing on his lips. He doesn't have to say anything, because it's written all over his face.

No matter who marries who, we're stuck with each other in this life and every life after.

EPILOGUE

With a heavy sigh, I drop onto our new sofa, melting into the cushions as easily as sand settling into the bottom of a water glass. "I'm so glad that's over," I groan, unpinning my cap from my hair and tossing it into the air.

Sam catches it and flips it over to read the back. I painted my favorite quote, and Kane embellished it with a snow white raven.

"Momento mori," he reads. "Meaning?"

Kane calls out across the room. "Remember to die!" He pours a dozen glasses of champagne and carries them over in a clutch, sloshing liquid all over the hardwood. He sets them on the coffee table I thrifted from the secondhand shop down the road. "You know, YOLO."

I scratch my aching scalp where the pins dug in. "It means that death is inevitable, so don't waste your life having regrets." Lifting my foot, I plant my heel on Sam's thigh, dirtying his fresh-pressed suit. His eye twitches, but he wraps his palm around my ankle and tickles the side of my foot.

"Take it off, pleaaaase," I whine, wiggling my foot. "They're killing me."

Zane tears off his tie one-handed and tosses it onto an empty pew. His jacket is next, sliding off his shoulders and onto the floor. "Try wearing a suit for a few hours, Kitten, and we'll see how badly you want to take it off."

My eyes track his movements as he untucks and unbuttons his shirt, the thin wire frames on his face sliding down his nose. "It doesn't look so bad from over here."

With my heel unbuckled, Sam taps my knee until I lift the other for him to remove.

"I agree," Kane rumbles, his voice dropping as he stares at our lover. "But a closer look would make sure I'm not seeing things."

"Zane." I snap my fingers. "Come here, handsome."

He pauses with his hands on his belt. "Are you giving orders now?"

"As the only person in the room who completed her tenure in higher education, I think I have the right to call the shots." I tip back my champagne flute and nearly choke as Sam digs his thumb into the arch of my foot. "*Oh, God,* that's good." I roll my neck to relieve more aches and pains. "Someone rub my shoulders, please."

Kane pulls me into his chest and gets to work on my back, carefully unzipping my dress for better access to my muscles. His hands are warm as he kneads my skin.

"Alright, Siren. We'll take care of you tonight since you *did* graduate today."

"Unlike the rest of us," Sam mutters, kneeling on the ottoman and spreading my legs. Massaging my calf, he busies himself with his work and tries to hide the divot between his eyebrows.

"You can always go back, Sam," I remind him. Since he inherited everything from his father, he's loaded but hasn't spent a dime on himself. "Momento mori, remember? We're living without regrets."

He meets my eyes. "I don't have any regrets." He finds a knot in my muscle and rubs it with his thumbs. "Do you?"

"Nope. I am regret-free." A heated shiver rolls down my spine as Sam's gaze wanders up my bare thighs, snagging on the sliver of my panties on display. They're black lace—my new signature.

After choosing his path to the couch, Zane finally arrives, standing next to Sam as he slowly tugs his belt loose. A blush colors the tips of his ears. "Is this close enough?"

I can't contain my smirk. "No. Come closer."

"*Much* closer," Kane rasps in my ear.

I couldn't agree more.

Zane glances at Sam for a split second before he obeys, walking up to the edge of the couch. "Like this?"

"Closer."

With a huff, Zane plants his foot between my thighs and lifts his crotch to my eye-level. "Happy now?"

I bite my lip and drag my gaze up his body. The eagle

tattoo on his chest has been joined by a skull on the side of his ribs, its inscription in latin. *Amor vincit omnia.*

Love conquers all.

I skate my palms up his thighs, noticing the way his breath catches. "Strip for me."

He swallows. "Excuse me?"

"You heard the woman." Kane chuckles darkly. "Strip, babe. Shake that ass."

Zane's pinched frown is adorable. "I'm not shaking my ass." He undoes the button on his pants and slowly tugs down the zipper. The tip of his cock pokes out, tenting his boxers as he slides his pants down his long legs. He kicks them away and stands uncomfortably, hunching his shoulders as he looks at the wall over my head.

"Hey." I grab his hand and tug him closer. "I'm not trying to make you uncomfortable."

"It's not... you." A muscle in his jaw tics. "Sam's just really close to me."

"He won't bite." Seeing that Zane is still unsure, I pull my dress down so that my tits are out. "Here, I'll undress with you." Standing on the couch with Kane's help, I shimmy my dress down my body until it pools at my feet. All that's left are my panties, and they're cheeky. My ass is practically out.

Kane grabs a cheek and groans. "Fuck, Mercy. You're killing me with that ass."

Ignoring him, I step off the couch and up to Zane. I ghost my fingertips across the ink on his ribs. "Zane," I whisper, lifting onto my tiptoes. "Kiss me."

"Mercy..." Zane's chest expands as he takes the tiniest breath. Cupping my chin, he brushes his thumb across my lips. "You ask too much."

My knees shake until Sam grabs my hips to hold me steady. He slides in behind me and wraps his arm around my waist, sliding his hand over my navel and up my chest. "If you won't kiss her—" He grabs my jaw and turns my head to the side. "I will." Capturing my lips, he pours every ounce of his desire into a single kiss. Heat burns from his body into mine, the scratch of his clothes rough on my skin.

I whimper into his mouth as he cups my breast and pinches my nipple.

Then someone wraps their lips around the other, and I cry out in shock.

Opening my eyes, I blush as Zane latches on and sucks, pulling my tit into his mouth with a groan. He flicks his stormy eyes up to mine and bites down, sending sparks down my spine. He hums deep in his throat and plays his hands over my waist, drawing me closer.

Sam takes a step up with me, giving me no room to breathe between them. His tongue slips into my mouth, and my clit pulses in time with my heartbeat.

I've kissed all three men before, but not like this— not altogether.

"She's trembling," Zane muses, plucking my nipple between his lips.

"And forgetting to give orders," Sam grunts, squeezing my tit. "Tell us what to do, Mercy. We're here to celebrate you."

My mind races through half a dozen possibilities, but there's one specific thing I've been curious about for months. "I want to try..." My face flames. "Anal!"

Zane and Sam share a look as a silent agreement passes between them. "Get on the couch," Sam instructs while Zane rearranges the furniture. The coffee table disappears, the champagne flutes tipping over and spilling onto the floor. No one moves to clean the mess, focusing on getting me into position instead. The ottoman moves to the center of the couch, and Sam starts stripping.

"On your knees, Kitten, facing Kane."

"Come to Daddy," Kane chuckles, sliding to the edge of his seat and helping me onto my hands and knees. The moment that I'm situated, he grabs my throat and pulls me in for a heated kiss, our lips smacking as he sprints to catch up with the others. "You look so good on your knees, sweetheart. I'm jealous of whoever gets to cum in that tight little hole of yours."

Another wave of pleasure pulses through my body. Heat pools between my thighs, and I press them together as I wait for whatever comes next.

A sigh hits my shoulder. "Do you have to sit there?"

"Yes," Kane answers immediately, smirking at Sam. "Enjoy the view, Samson." He lifts me up so that Sam can crawl beneath me, lying on his back so that his cock juts out towards my pelvis.

"You're going to fuck me from there?" Is that how it works? "I thought you'd be behind me."

"*I'm* behind you, Kitten." Zane lovingly rubs my

cheeks before pulling my panties down my thighs. "Sam's going to fill your pussy while I'm inside your ass." Something cold and wet slides down my crack before it heats up against my skin. Zane rubs it in, starting with each of my cheeks before teasing my butthole. "This is medicated," he explains softly. "So you'll still feel me inside of you, but it won't hurt as much."

I didn't think it would hurt at all. Biting my lip, I nod. "Okay. I trust you."

There's a pause, then a soft whisper. "Thank you."

Kane's smirk curves into a smile. "Tell her how you really feel, babe."

Zane's hands shake as he pushes my hips over Sam's, but he doesn't reply. Instead, he brushes his lips over my spine, peppering kisses along each of my vertebrae. "Rub your clit on his cock until you're ready." He nips my skin as he lowers my hips, and with Sam's guidance, they align my slit with Sam's hot length.

With all three of their eyes and hands on my body, I give a tentative roll of my hips. Sam's cock wedges between my lips and glides without any friction, the tip bumping my clit and making me see stars. I clench my eyes shut as they rock my body for me, working me over Sam's dick so that I don't have to move a muscle. I cling to Kane's neck and pant in his ear, unable to help it as electric shocks ping through my nervous system.

"Fuck, that's beautiful." Kane groans, his breath hot on my neck. "You're coating his cock, Siren. How does he feel?"

"Really good." The words are a rush that my brain

barely registers. Someone's hands are on my tits as they pluck my nipples—*Sam*—while Zane pushes me down onto Sam's cock. The tip slips inside, and I moan at the stretch, my thighs quivering as he sinks deeper.

"Lean forward. That's it. Take him all the way. Good girl."

The praise makes my heart sing. I meet Kane's eyes and he kisses me sweetly, framing my face in his hands. "You're doing so good, sweetheart, I promise."

"Kane," Zane calls out, "keep her distracted while I work the lube in." A cap snaps behind me. "I'm going to touch you, Mercy, and finger your ass. Like we've done before."

I repeat what I said earlier. "I trust you."

He puffs out a breath, and I can picture the little smile on his face. "Stop saying that."

"But it's true." I curve my neck to glance at him over my shoulder. "I trust you."

A blush colors his face from the tip of his forehead down the length of his nose, and he pushes up his glasses with his forearm to hide his smile. "Alright, I hear you." Taking a breath, he nods towards Kane. "Your turn."

While Sam rocks into my pussy with shallow thrusts, Kane works his tongue into my mouth and dominates, exploring every inch. The contrast between the careful concentration below and the frenzy above is met with a third sensation as Zane keeps his word and rims my asshole with his fingertips. Pressing through the resistance, he drips lube into my hole and spreads it with his finger, pulsing in and out slowly.

I moan, the sound lost inside Kane's kiss. Liquid heat courses hot and fast through my veins, overflowing from my heart and spilling into my extremities. My heart beats frantically, unable to pick a rhythm with so many pulsing inside of me at once.

Zane pushes a second finger inside while Kane sucks a hickey onto my neck and twists my nipples, determined to overwhelm my senses. But I want to feel all of them, all at once, everywhere. I bite Kane's throat and he moans, dropping his hands to my waist and squeezing.

"If you want something in your mouth," he growls, "you know where to look."

Flicking my gaze to his crotch, I stare at the hard length trailing down his pant leg. Carefully, I place my hand on him and stroke, enjoying the way he hisses in pain.

"Take it out," he growls, snagging his fingers in my tangled hair.

Sam sits still as I struggle to free Kane's dick, but the moment I wrap my hand around the base, he's moving again, punching his hips harder, faster, gritting his teeth as he stares up at my bouncing tits. Zane doubles his efforts, too, stretching me with a third and final finger before pressing his dick against my hole. They both wait for me to lick Kane's slit and sink down over the tip before they move, both of them sliding a few inches inside.

I clench my eyes shut and cry out, my heart leaping to my throat. Zane tests our connection, breathing deep as he slides the tip in and out. "You're doing great," he mutters, grabbing my hip to pull me back onto his cock. Another inch slides in while Sam slips out, his dick slapping his stomach. With a growl, he presses it against my entrance and thrusts, punching his hips up and slamming home.

"*Ah!*"

Pleasure hits like a gunshot, radiating heat from my pussy. Back and forth, Zane and Sam fight for my body, creating a frantic rhythm that makes sucking Kane's cock impossible.

"Let me help you," Kane rasps, cupping the back of my head. Then, he pushes me down, quickly hitting the back of my throat and making me gag. "Relax, sweetheart, just like you're doing for the others. You can take it."

I know that I've held Sam's dick in my throat before, but he's half the size of Kane and not nearly as brutal. But Sam isn't coming to my rescue; he's snarling like a beast as he slams me onto his cock. My pussy flutters and he groans, holding me down.

Zane takes advantage and thrusts, his hips hitting my ass as he bottoms out. "Goddamn, Mercy, you're cutting off my circulation." He drags in a breath and rocks his hips, staying deep as he enjoys the warmth and grip of my ass. "That's a good thing," he clarifies, nipping my shoulder. "You feel fucking amazing."

Tears spill free and finally, Kane pulls me up by my hair. I choke on my saliva as I gasp for air, my eyes stinging as my mascara runs.

"God, that's sexy. *You're* sexy." Smearing my makeup

with his thumbs, Kane kisses my mouth. I tremble in his arms as hot liquid shoots inside my pussy, making me clench around Sam's pulsing cock.

Muttering nonsensically, Sam grips my hips with punishing strength, no doubt bruising both sides as he holds me in place. He grinds up into my heat as he comes a second time, tossing his head back with a hiss.

Chuckling darkly, Kane lines my mouth up with his cock. "You're gonna get knocked up," he says matter-of-factly, pushing me onto his cock the same way that Sam holds me over his. They both bury as much of themselves as they can in my body, Sam actually being successful while Kane shoves half his dick between my teeth. I feel the scrape more than I hear the growl, but that doesn't stop him.

It makes him swell on my tongue.

Thick ropes of cum spill into my mouth and hit the back of my throat. I can't breathe—*too much*—until finally, Kane lifts my head. Spots dance in my vision as his cum slips past my lips and drips onto his lap, but I don't care so long as the burn in my chest disappears. I gasp for air and choke on saliva and semen, crying out when Zane snaps his hips forward and pushes me onto my forearms. Sam's cock slips from my pussy and his cum leaks down my thighs, but Zane lifts my ass higher and pounds harder, panting and moaning as his body starts to shake.

Then he finally erupts, his dick twitching hard as he comes. Liquid heat pumps deep inside of me, and my body breaks. I come *hard* as Zane does, spilling his seed as my pussy clenches and more of Sam's cum slides down my thighs.

With a gasp, Zane slides his dick free and palms my cheeks, spreading them so that he can see the mess we've made together. "Kitten, you're fucking filthy." He pushes his finger back inside and groans as he plays with my gaping asshole.

I whimper and collapse, unable to hold myself up anymore. All three men take turns stroking my hair, cleaning my body with a warm, damp cloth, and kissing me all over. Once I'm drifting to sleep, they finally tuck me into bed and wish me goodnight, each of them curling around a different part of my body.

My muscles ache and my brain's fuzzy, but my heart is so full that it might burst.

"I love you," I whisper, knowing that one of them will hear me and say it back.

Someone caresses my spine and rubs my lower back. I open my eyes to find Zane's glittering like diamonds in the dark. He doesn't say I love you back, but he kisses me like he means it, and even though I don't hear the words, my soul does, and that's enough.

Thank you so much for reading *The Price of Mercy!*

I am in love with these characters, and one epilogue isn't enough. For another peek at their happily ever after, join my newsletter. I hope to see you on Discord for all the sexy previews of my angsty, hot mess men. 🩶

# Acknowledgments

This book has been wild, y'all.

Actually, this *duet* has been wild.

*Begging for Mercy* was meant to be a one-off standalone that I wrote on my journey to becoming a full time author. What happened instead is that these characters became so much more than I intended, and what started as a MFM serial killer romance turned into a slow burn that I never could have predicted.

I've never written slow burn before. I didn't even realize that I *liked* slow burn romance until I watched Season 2 of *Bridgerton*. Kate and Antony's romance lit a fire inside my heart for the push-and-pull of wanting someone you can't have, all while you watch them potentially fall for someone else. But rather than write a love triangle, I stuck to what I know and love and wrote more than one love interest.

Originally, Sam wasn't meant to be a part of the harem. He popped into my head as a supportive friend (because everyone needs a support system), but then I couldn't get the idea out of my head that there was something more between him and Mercy... and my earliest readers confirmed that, yes, we need Sam to pine after his best friend. Gemma, I can't thank you enough for being an anchor when I felt adrift in my thoughts. And Kelly, you busted ass to proof book one for me, girl, and gave perspective on the Sam dilemma as well. I am so grateful to you both. 🩶

Another huge, rousing *thank you* goes to two very important people: my darling husband, for enduring my endless monologues when I was stuck on a chapter and unable to find my way through, and to my best friend and coconspirator Angel, for keeping me sane (or trying) when I spiral into self-doubt.

Both of you instill me with confidence that I will someday believe in for myself.

To my readers, you are an absolute delight. I love seeing you light up over the same scenes, chapters, and conversations that make me squeal and kick my feet in the middle of the night. Every heartfelt message and comment brings me to tears in moments when I need them most, so thank you, from the bottom of my heart.

We can all be someone's light in the darkness.

🩶

*Misti Wilds*

# About the Author

*Just a smut-lover listening to angsty love songs on repeat.*

Misti Wilds is a lover of all things romance, especially when the spice is habanero hot and the men are morally gray and dangerous. She devours angst like her favorite M&M cookies--all at once with no regrets. When she isn't writing romance, she can be found floating in the lake with her favorite sun hat or playing video games while surrounded by Squishmallows. She lives in Southern USA with her number one fans (an adoring husband and two precious pups).

# ALSO BY MISTI WILDS

***Baranova Bratva:***

Rule of Three

Reign of Four

***Brutal Beauty:***

Brutal Beauty (prequel)

Claimed by Rage

Tempted to Rebel

Bound by Ruin

Born to Riot

***Dying for Love:***

Begging for Mercy

The Price of Mercy